W9-BEV-318

STAY WITH ME

MISTY RIVER ROMANCE

Stay with Me

Becky Wade

THORNDIKE PRESS
A part of Gale, a Cengage Company

GALE
A Cengage Company

Copyright © 2020 by Rebecca C. Wade.
Scripture quotations are from The Holy Bible, New International Version®, NIV® Copyright © 1973, 1978, 1984, 2011 by Biblica, Inc.® Used by permission. All rights reserved worldwide.
Thorndike Press, a part of Gale, a Cengage Company

Thorndike Press® Large Print Christian Romance.
The text of this Large Print edition is unabridged.
Other aspects of the book may vary from the original edition.
Set in 16 pt. Plantin.

LIBRARY OF CONGRESS CIP DATA ON FILE.
CATALOGUING IN PUBLICATION FOR THIS BOOK
IS AVAILABLE FROM THE LIBRARY OF CONGRESS

ISBN-13: 978-1-4328-8061-3 (hardcover alk. paper)

Published in 2020 by arrangement with Bethany House Publishers, a division of Baker Publishing Group

Printed in Mexico
Print Number: 01   Print Year: 2020

For Rel Mollet, Crissy Loughridge,
Amy Watson, and Joy Tiff.
Thank you so much for your
generous help with this novel.

Genevieve

JULY 12, EIGHTEEN YEARS AGO
SAN SALVADOR, EL SALVADOR
JUNIOR HIGH MISSION TRIP

The hallway floor jolts downward beneath my feet, throwing me off balance. The mesh bags full of soccer balls I'm holding bump against the concrete walls of the basement hallway. "Wh-what?" I gasp *What's happening?*

The building lurches from side to side more violently.

It's not me that's unstable. It's the earth Through my tennis shoes and the concret floor, I can feel movement coming up fror deep, deep below.

"Earthquake!" a boy ahead of me shou' as terror clamps my heart.

The ground begins to roll and the ligh bulb hanging from the ceiling blinks out.

CHAPTER ONE

Like Papa Bear in the Goldilocks story, Sam Turner had discovered a strange woman sleeping in the bed of a house he owned.

He stood inside Sugar Maple Farm's small guesthouse, hands on his hips, staring down at her as mid-August sunlight flooded the space through the uncovered windows. Neither the sunlight nor the sound of his entrance just now had woken her.

Was she dead?

A bolt of worry pierced him hard, so he leaned over to make sure he could see the rise and fall of her breathing. He could.

Good. Interruptions to his routine and his solitude weren't part of his plans any day of the week. Discovering a dead woman definitely hadn't been part of this particular Monday morning's plans.

What he had here was a trespasser, very much alive, who'd decided to help herself to his guesthouse.

She'd stretched out on the only piece of furniture in the place: a bed. Back when he'd moved onto this property four years ago, he'd taken this metal headboard and frame out of the main house and stored it here. More recently, he'd added the mattress and box spring set he'd received as a hand-me-down from his dad.

This stranger didn't seem to mind that the mattress was bare. Or that the guesthouse offered nothing but old pine floors and a cold fireplace.

She'd made do by cracking open her suitcase and tossing every item of clothing onto the bed to function as her sheet. She'd covered her bottom half with a black jacket and slipped her top half into a pink robe. Except she'd turned the robe the wrong way, so that the robe's back covered her front.

Her head rested on a light blue pillow, chin tipped to the side in a way that revealed a pretty profile. The smoothness of her expression communicated deep, worriless dreams. Due to his responsibilities and regrets, Sam couldn't remember sleeping that soundly since he was a kid.

She had prominent cheekbones, a delicate nose, a perfectly shaped mouth. Her hair started out a medium brown color near her scalp then magically, through some kind of dye job he couldn't imagine, started to turn different, lighter blond colors toward the ends. Her hair was big, but she was small. When she stood, he'd bet that hair would fall almost to her waist.

She wore makeup on her flawless skin. Large silver earrings. A ring with three interlocking silver bands, each band set with diamonds.

Had she come straight from a photo shoot to break and enter his guesthouse?

"Hello," he said.

No response.

One of his eyebrows twitched with irritation. "Excuse me," he tried, slightly louder. He didn't want to terrify her by raising his voice or by shaking her shoulder. "Hello?"

Nothing.

"Good morning. Miss?"

Not even an eyelid flickered. Most likely, she'd taken too much of some kind of substance. Sleeping pills, alcohol, drugs?

Sam picked up the huge purse that slumped on the floor beside a pair of tall leather boots. As far as he was concerned, she'd forfeited her right to privacy as soon as she'd become a squatter on his property. Grimly, he squashed a flash of conscience and rummaged past car keys, sunnies, a zippered case, feminine products, and a cell phone before pulling free her wallet. Within it, he found the usual credit and debit cards, then the thing he'd been looking for — her driver's license.

It read *Genevieve Woodward* next to a picture of her smiling brightly. She'd been born three years after him, which made her thirty. Her height was listed as 5'4" and her weight as 125. Eye color: hazel. Address: Nashville. Which meant, here in the north Georgia mountains, that she was more than a four-hour drive from home.

The last name *Woodward* stirred his recognition. Judson Woodward served as their county's district attorney. Sam had talked with him and his wife, Caroline, a couple of times. They had two adult daughters. Was *this* one of their daughters? If so, why would she have slept at his farm when her parents' house in town was only fifteen minutes away?

He carried her car keys into the cool morning and unlocked her Volvo XC-40. The compact SUV's interior smelled like the beach, crisp and fresh. He lifted items — a pink sweater, a laptop — as he searched for the substance she'd likely taken last night. A Starbucks travel mug filled one cup holder, hair bands and a lip gloss the other.

In the back seat, a bag full of books and notebooks rested on the floor.

No liquor bottles. No drug paraphernalia.

Even so, his instincts were telling him that something was off.

He made a scoffing sound. He didn't need Sherlock's instincts to know something was off. Any ten-year-old kid would know that sleeping on a bare mattress in a stranger's empty house wasn't what sober women did.

He strode back inside. Genevieve hadn't moved.

As he returned her keys to her purse, his attention landed on a metallic silver tin tucked in a side pocket. He pulled it free. Around the size of a box of Altoids, a cursive *G* engraved its top. He flicked the case open. Inside rested at least forty pills.

The pills were round and brown. Some marked with *OP,* others with *20.*

OxyContin.

He frowned as old memories slithered into his mind. Terrible memories that made his body brace and his stomach tighten with grief.

Grief and regret were never far from him.

They walked beside him every day. Laid down with him at night. Waited for chances to punch him in the gut and remind him of his failures.

For seven years, they'd been his two clos-est companions.

Oxy required a prescription. Either Gene-vieve had gotten these legally and was tak-ing them for justified medical reasons. Or . . . not. Given where he'd found her, he was leaning toward the latter.

He returned the metal tin to her purse and moved to stand at her bedside.

Oxy. A fashionable suitcase. Successful father. New car. China doll face. A pillow that traveled with her so that she didn't have to lay her precious head on anyone else's pillow.

Genevieve Woodward was messy in ways that had nothing to do with organization, and Sam didn't do mess.

He wanted *nothing* to do with her. In fact, he wanted her far away from him as fast as possible.

"Genevieve," he said.

She didn't stir.

"Genevieve."

Genevieve jerked awake on a yelp that sent her lunging into a seated position. Her heart whacked against her chest wall. Confused and startled, she squinted against the sun-shine.

A man — an unfamiliar man — stood

14

nearby, staring at her.

Panic vanquished every shred of sleep from her brain.

Where am I? She was . . . sitting on a bed in an unfamiliar room. Automatically, she scrambled away from him until her back clunked against the metal headboard.

The man took two steps back, holding up his palms. "No need to be afraid. My name's Sam Turner, and you're inside my guesthouse at Sugar Maple Farm."

Did he slip me a roofie and kidnap me? Her thoughts careened against the inside of her skull like horrified marbles. He didn't look like a kidnapper! But how was she supposed to know what kidnappers looked like?

"As far as I can tell, you broke in, then decided to spend the night." He spoke with what sounded like a British accent. Moving slowly, he slid his hands into the front pockets of his jeans. "When I saw your car this morning, I came to investigate. You're not hurt as far as I can tell."

Perish! *What!* No. She hadn't broken into this person's guesthouse, then . . . slept here.

Had she?

She'd been driving to her parents' house last night. She'd been stressed and anxious about the magnitude of her workload. She hadn't been able to face the prospect of

15

confronting her parents about the letter on top of all that. So she'd pulled over to the side of the road out in the country.

With a pang, she remembered reaching for her tin of pills. She'd reclined the driver's seat and turned up her car's sound system, letting hip-hop wash over her. She'd only intended to take a little break and get her head straight before continuing on.

Except . . . She vaguely recalled admiring the way the bronze sunset illuminated a quaint little white cottage set far back from the road. The cottage nestled into a meadow above a pond, hills forming its backdrop. Postcard perfect.

After that, she could only latch on to hazy recollections. Parking before the cottage. Brushing a fingertip over a morning glory vine. Opening a door that squeaked. Oh no . . .

Despite its outward cuteness, she could now see that the cottage's interior — just one large room and a bathroom — was not at all her style. She valued security and comfort. This structure was unprotected except by a doorknob lock, and empty, minus the bed.

Genevieve glanced down. Was the bed covered with . . . a jumble of her own clothing? A particularly colorful bra was on

16

embarrassing display. Her familiar pillow bore her head's indention. She had her robe on backward.

No one but her would know she couldn't sleep unless she slept on her own pillow, so no one but her would have bothered to bring it inside. Also, the fact that she had her robe on backward had her fingerprints all over it. She often slipped this robe on just this way when chilly.

How very, very far she'd fallen.

While not in her right mind, she'd spent the night in a stranger's cottage. She had no one in the world to blame for her stupidity but herself.

In a bid to inject a sense of normalcy into the situation, Genevieve scooted to the edge of the bed and swung her feet to the floor. She still wore yesterday's clothing, including gray socks decorated with the words *I'm complicated, thank you very much.*

As she stood and wrestled out of her wrong-way robe, it occurred to her that normalcy and this situation were mutually exclusive. Nonetheless, her pride commanded her to save face.

"I'm Genevieve Woodward." She extended her hand.

Guardedly, he shook it. He did not reply.

"Well then." Her mouth felt like cotton

17

and dizziness sloshed inside her, but she drew herself tall. Smoothing the turquoise print blouse she'd paired with skinny jeans, she angled her head up because Sam was so much taller than she was. "Just so you know, I don't usually sleep in homes that don't belong to me." She glued a smile to her lips.

Instead of smiling back, he considered her with frank seriousness. He had a fantastic body. Army green T-shirt, jeans, weather-beaten lace-up work boots. He kept his short brown hair shaved on the sides. His nose was a fraction too long, his eyes creased in a way that made them look melancholy. His teeth were straight, but not orthodontically straight. His faintly imper-fect masculine features added up to an undeniably appealing face.

People usually responded well to her. But Sam's pale green eyes, which struck a contrast against his slightly olive skin tone, transmitted no warmth whatsoever.

"Care to tell me why you slept here?" he asked.

"I . . ." She worked to invent a fairy tale he'd believe. "I was on my way to my parents' house in Misty River last night. I'd been on the road for hours and was tired. Scary tired. So tired I couldn't keep my head up."

He said nothing.

"So I pulled over. Near here, I guess." She gestured toward the road.

"And?"

"I didn't want to fall asleep at the wheel and injure anyone, so I decided to grab a quick rest."

"In a vacant building?"

"Yes." She tucked her hair behind her ears. "I'm very sorry. Obviously, I was so sleepy that I wasn't thinking clearly."

"The box of pills I found in your purse didn't have anything to do with it?"

Shock immobilized her. "You . . . looked through my purse?"

"Yes. I couldn't wake you and wanted to know what I was dealing with."

Her purse was private. She couldn't say that to him, however. For one thing, she was too polite to do so. For another, he'd simply respond by saying that his cottage was private, too. "My doctor prescribed those pills for pain."

"What kind of pain?"

She knelt and pulled up the hem of her jeans to reveal the scar marking her outer right ankle. "Ankle surgery pain."

"How long ago did you bust up your ankle?"

A blush bloomed on her cheeks. "A while."

19

"How long is a while?"

She straightened. "A year."

"And you're still taking OxyContin for pain?"

"I am, yes." Only one other person knew about her pills. And now, him. He knew.

He regarded her the way a teacher would a student who'd just told him she'd been too busy riding unicorns to finish her homework.

This was mortifying! How could this purse-snooping man with the alluring face and zero sympathy have uncovered her secret so suddenly and so thoroughly?

"Is your father the DA?" he asked.

"Yes."

"Do he and your mom know?"

She flinched. *My parents.* Heaven help her, they'd been expecting her to arrive last night and were probably frantic with worry. She was a terrible, *terrible* human being. She yanked her phone from her purse and saw that she had twelve missed calls and twenty-three text messages.

Thrusting her phone into her back pocket, she began tossing armloads of clothing into her suitcase. "Are you asking if my parents know that I slept here last night? Because unfortunately, the answer's no."

"I'm asking if they know about your

prescription drug habit."

She stilled momentarily, then resumed packing with even more gusto. "I don't have a prescription drug habit." She zipped the suitcase and wedged her feet into her boots.

"What kind of work do you do, Genevieve?"

"I'm an author and speaker."

"An author of what?"

She stuck her pillow under her arm and faced him. "Bible studies."

His brows lifted.

"I apologize for sleeping in your cottage last night," she said. "I'm more than happy to pay you to cover any expenses."

"Don't bother."

"Alrighty, then! Um. Thank you."

He simply glared.

She rushed toward her Volvo carrying her belongings. His footfalls followed as far as the cottage's porch. She heaved everything into her trunk, then hurried around to the driver's seat, desperate to escape Sam Turner's knowing stare.

Luke

The sudden darkness steals my view of the shaking basement. My heart thunders almost as loud as the building rumbles. *Earthquake.* A few minutes ago, our youth pastor asked some of us to put away the sports equipment we used today at camp. I know where it's stored, so I'm in front. I'm leading them — responsible for them. And now I have to find my brother, Ethan, and get him and the rest of the kids out of this hallway into the room ahead, where it's safer.

I reach back into nothingness. I reach farther and connect with someone's arm. I drag the person forward into the central room where the basement's two hallways meet. There are pillars here. Arches. Two thin windows set high at sidewalk level. Their light reveals Ben's face.

"What do we do?" he screams, his eyes round.

"You wait here. I'll get the others." I plunge back into the hallway.

CHAPTER TWO

She'd made herself — high-achieving, rule-following Genevieve Woodward — into a house crasher.

The peaceful hum of her Volvo's engine juxtaposed with her frightened pulse and spiked adrenaline. She'd just ended a phone call with her parents, during which she'd apologized profusely and informed them that she was on her way to their house.

Unfortunately, neither the phone call nor the miles she was putting between herself and Sam allowed Genevieve to outrun the truth of what had just happened.

She'd known for a long time that she couldn't continue as she had been. This morning's events had simply added a flashing neon exclamation point to the knowledge that she now *must quit* taking painkillers.

Like a windmill converting wind into energy, she'd converted the hardships she'd

24

endured in the past into success. There was no reason to think the same couldn't become true of this current hardship.

At the age of twelve, she'd survived a natural disaster. She'd come through it certain that she was destined to do big things for God, and sure enough, that event had launched her onto an international platform she'd used to lift high the name of Jesus.

At the age of twenty, she'd faced a devastating breakup. The sorrow of that had motivated her to dive into Scripture, which had inspired her to write her first Bible study, which had eventually led to her writing and speaking ministry.

A year ago she'd fallen while walking down a flight of stairs in high heels and severely fractured her ankle.

So, see? She was simply still in the *midst* of her current challenge. God hadn't redeemed it yet, but He would. He'd give her the strength she needed to quit Oxy, and then He'd turn this struggle into something amazing, exactly like He'd done before.

That sentiment would be easier to believe if God didn't feel so very, very distant.

Her pep talk fizzled like a faulty Fourth of July firecracker.

Not for the first time, she attempted to

pinpoint the moment when her relationship with God had begun to drift.

He'd been with her during surgery. She clearly recalled feeling His power and peace the day of her ankle operation and for weeks afterward.

Which meant the drift had started well after she'd returned to work. Between writing, traveling, speaking, and social media, her job had demanded a lot before she'd fallen on the stairs. After the fall, she'd continued to do everything she'd done before.

Her orthopedic doctor prescribed Oxy post-op, then weaned her off of it as soon as he deemed she could function without it. Full of resolve, she'd followed his directions and stopped taking it.

Ten days later, hobbling around a convention center in the UK, the pain had become too intense to bear. Overwhelmed, agitated, and unable to sleep, she'd taken the pills languishing at the bottom of her prescription bottle.

They'd helped her so much that she'd found a pain specialist back home in Nashville willing to prescribe more. Not only did the pills ease her ankle pain, they relaxed her and boosted her confidence. Oxy enabled her to give her best during her physical therapy sessions and — even better — to manage her career responsibilities.

She'd told herself that her orthopedic doctor had simply attempted to take her off Oxy too soon. Pain was such a personal thing, after all! Some people experienced more pain in the wake of surgeries than others. She'd taper off the Oxy as soon as her pain specialist told her that her ankle had grown strong enough for her to do so.

She continued to pray and study the Bible devotedly. She preached and ministered. But around that time, God had begun to feel far away.

Genevieve turned the steering wheel, pulling into a gas station on the outskirts of Misty River. A headache gripped her skull like a vise. Her hands were shaky, and anxiety was busily tying her digestive system into a knot. Before she could face her mom and dad, she needed to pull herself together.

Inside the bedlam of her suitcase, she located her cosmetic bag, a fresh shirt, and her cute new poncho. After purchasing a bottle of water, she retreated to the restroom and stared at her reflection.

Eight months ago she'd started breaking promises to herself.

When the pain specialist had instructed her to gradually whittle down her Oxy us-

27

age, she'd rationalized his advice away and found another physician. *This is the last pain specialist I'll have,* she'd promised herself. But a few months after that, she'd gone doctor shopping yet again. *This is the last Bible study I'll write while taking Oxy. This is the last speaking gig I'll do with Oxy in my system.*

She brushed her teeth, then worked to tame her hair.

Six weeks ago, after an especially challenging day, she'd taken one more pill than usual before driving to a dinner meeting with her publisher's publicist, Anabelle. At the restaurant, she'd plowed her car into one of the rectangular stone flower planters lining the parking lot's edge. The container had cracked, and its largest segment had rocketed forward, missing an elderly couple by inches.

When the police arrived, they gave Genevieve a breathalyzer test. Once that failed to condemn her, they asked about her medications. Anabelle had listened grimly as Genevieve told them about her Oxy prescription. The police had been sympathetic and let her off with a warning, but the moment she'd climbed into the passenger seat of Anabelle's car, Anabelle had confronted her.

Genevieve had told herself and Anabelle, "The pill I took before coming here is the last pill I'll take."

"It has to be," Anabelle had answered. "If it's not, I need to inform the rest of your publishing team. For our sake. But much more than that, for yours."

Later, holed up in her loft apartment alone, Genevieve had tried to carry through on her promise to Anabelle.

The first time she'd given Oxy up after surgery, her body had protested with little more than a murmur. This time, her body threw a full-blown tantrum.

Anabelle communicated with her frequently, offering encouragement, resources, information, hotline numbers. But Anabelle's support couldn't save Genevieve from the undiluted physical misery of withdrawal. Until that moment, Genevieve had imagined that she could stop Oxy at any point. She was appalled to discover just how dependent she'd become.

She'd *begged* the Lord for mercy. But like a set of keys you can't find right when its most urgent that you locate them, she'd misplaced God somehow. She'd lost the most important, crucial aspect of her life.

In the end, her detox symptoms had been so horrendous that no amount of willpower had been equal to them. Sickness had brought her to her knees, and to a new bottle of Oxy that she'd kept secret from Anabelle.

Every day since she'd driven into that parking lot planter, she'd held a pill in her hand and promised herself, *This is the last pill I'll ever take.*

Now Genevieve changed into her top, donned her poncho, and retouched her makeup. The mirror told her that she looked presentable on the outside, even though she felt guilty and corroded and ugly on the inside.

God had entrusted her with the task of providing spiritual guidance and instruction to thousands of women — a giant responsibility. Over the last year, a gulf had opened between who she pretended to be publicly and who she actually was. The shame of that had been growing through her like a poisonous, spiky weed. At this point, the weed had expanded its awful tendrils all the way to her fingertips and toes.

She flicked open her metal pill case, selected a pill, then balanced it in the center of her palm, as she'd done so many times before.

If she was capable of nearly maiming elderly people and sleeping in cottages that didn't belong to her, it was chilling to think of all the other things she might be capable of when under the influence of Oxy.

Had she given anyone a chance last night to take photos or record videos of her doing scandalous things, she'd have fatally damaged her reputation and her ministry. Anabelle would have seen, and Anabelle would have told.

Had she stopped near a bar last night, she could have gotten drunk, then climbed behind the wheel of her car. She could have wandered into the path of a kidnapper or an abuser or a killer or an oncoming train. She could have overdosed and died.

Even so . . .

Even so, she knew she'd need a few more pills in order to make it through this final day. She had to handle her parents. Then she had to put plans in place to prepare for detox. She couldn't accomplish those necessities feeling physically miserable and emotionally shaky.

This is the last day, though. Tomorrow I go cold turkey.

At the thought of the torment detox would bring, dread settled over her like a blanket drenched in ice water.

No point worrying. Worrying wouldn't make it better. God would show up for her. She was still destined to do big things for Him.

She double-checked the date on her phone, just to be sure. August 19. *This is the last day I take pills. The last, the very last . . .*

From August 20 on, she'd be drug free.

She popped the pill into her mouth and washed it down with a long drink of water. Then, hating herself for her weakness, she climbed back into her Volvo and continued toward her parents' house.

Soon, waves of gentle, warm light began to massage away her headache. Her nerves calmed. Her assurance steadied.

The familiar Swallowtail Lane sign, topped by its "Historical District" designation, slid past. The stately homes in this neighborhood just north of Misty River's downtown square had been built in the late 1800s by people who enjoyed both wealth and good taste.

Genevieve parked on the curb of her parents' tree-lined street. They'd moved into their Colonial Revival–style home when she was seven. Its flat front housed a central door, eight windows flanked with black shutters, and six columns that soared the full two stories to support the roof. Just like every other thing her mom touched, the house projected graciousness.

With her five hundred thousand Instagram followers, Genevieve was no slouch at good staging. However, her mom's artful arrangement of red, white, and blue bunting, lanterns, and potted white hydrangeas on the porch rivaled and perhaps even surpassed Genevieve's skills.

She'd tugged her suitcase two-thirds of the way up the brick walkway when the front door burst open, framing the form of her mom.

Genevieve noted her mom's lavender top and eyes red from crying in the millisecond before her mother's arms encircled her.

"I'm really sorry, Mom," Genevieve said, hugging her back. "So sorry. I know I cost you a sleepless night of worry. What I did was completely unforgivable." She was preempting what her mom would say in order to deflate the force of it.

They stepped apart. "Really," Genevieve said. "I'm very sorry. I deserve an F at being a daughter these past twenty-four hours."

Her mom's blond side bangs melded into a crisp bob that nearly brushed her shoulders. "Genevieve —" she started but was interrupted by the arrival of Genevieve's dad.

Judson Woodward's hug smelled like Irish Spring soap, just like always. All his life, thanks to his thin, six-foot-five frame, people had asked him if he played basketball. All his life he'd replied that he'd have loved to, had he the slightest amount of coordination or speed.

As it was, he'd been a glasses-wearing brainiac who played the trombone in the high school band. His ears too prominent to allow him to be considered conventionally handsome, her dad was a self-described nerd — good-natured, thoughtful, intelligent — who'd ended up winning the heart of a literal homecoming queen. After thirty-four years of marriage, Dad still believed himself to be the luckiest husband in the world.

And, indeed, if a stranger were to see them together, Mom's startling beauty might seem like a mismatch to Dad's lanky bookishness. But Genevieve knew just how challenging Mom could be. In her opinion, Mom was the luckiest wife in the world to have landed Dad.

Dad tilted his face down to assess her shrewdly through his spotlessly clean glasses. Silver streaked his close-trimmed brown hair and beard. "You all right?" he asked.

"Yes. Completely all right." She repeated her apologies to him as Mom led the way

34

into the house, Dad toting the suitcase.

They made their way to the modern kitchen at the back of the floor plan, the scent of cinnamon sticks hovering in the air.

"You haven't eaten breakfast yet, have you?" Caroline asked.

"No." Every minute since she'd been yanked to consciousness had been punishing, so it seemed like it should be later than it was. Genevieve's smartwatch read 8:30 a.m.

"I whipped this up after I received your call." Mom indicated the food waiting on the marble countertop. Scrambled eggs. Grits. Bacon. Fruit. Toast arranged next to ramekins containing butter and jelly. A pitcher of orange juice.

"Wow, thank you."

Mom moved toward the coffeemaker while Genevieve and her dad ferried the breakfast platters to the round kitchen table. The numerous panes of the bow window highlighted the backyard garden, which dripped late-summer color beneath a hazy morning sky. Mom had set out the periwinkle and white Limoges china, which meant that she was feeling especially emotional this morning. A daunting prospect, considering that Mom was very emotional at the best of times.

Joy, grief, wonder, hurt, love. Caroline Woodward, the belle of Athens, experienced them all with a wholeheartedness that frequently exhausted Genevieve.

If Mom were a line on a graph swooping upward and downward, her dad was the line through the middle. He liked to say that his wife's moods passed him on their way up, then passed him again on their way down.

"What happened last night?" Mom asked once they'd taken their seats. "Where were you?" If displeasure were visible, it would've been shooting from her in orange spikes.

Genevieve repeated the story she'd given Sam, about how tired she'd been behind the wheel. This time, she said she'd stopped for the night at a B&B in the town of Chatsworth. She explained that she'd stretched out to rest her eyes for a second, then accidentally slept clean through till morning.

"We tried calling and texting," Mom said. "Natasha tried calling and texting."

"I saw that this morning when I woke up. I had my phone on Do Not Disturb. Every once in a while I put it on that setting and then forget to take it off."

"Genevieve." Mom's lips thinned. "We called the police. They were out searching for your crumpled car."

36

She winced. "I truly did not mean to cause you worry. I absolutely should've called you before I lay down."

Mom's elegant face softened a degree, and Genevieve wondered, *When did I become such an expert liar?* The vine of shame unfurled even farther.

After today, no more pills.

Genevieve doctored her coffee, then took a long sip. She filled her plate, ate, and made the appropriate murmurs of pleasure because this situation required her to go through the motions.

"You were mysterious about your reason for coming to visit," Mom said. "I worried that your disappearance might have had something to do with that."

"I came for a few different reasons. One, I've blocked off the next several months to complete my study, and I really needed a change of scenery. Two, it's been a while since I've seen you, Natasha, and the kids."

"Far too long," Caroline agreed.

"Three, I wanted to discuss this with you." She unzipped the outer pocket of her purse and produced an envelope. "I received this letter two weeks ago." She passed it over.

Mom extracted the single sheet of white printer paper, then pulled on fashionable reading glasses. Her bright, almond-shaped hazel eyes were rimmed in thick eyelashes.

Her spine stiffened as she read. Wordlessly, she handed the letter to Dad.

" 'I know what your parents did,' " he read aloud, frowning. " 'And after all we've suffered, it's hard to watch you bask in your fame and money. Your parents aren't going to get away with it.' "

"Who sent this?" Mom asked.

"I have no idea. It's unsigned and the return address listed doesn't exist."

Mom flipped the envelope over to study the return address.

"What's the writer talking about?" Genevieve asked. "What does he or she mean when they say they know what you did?"

Mom met her eyes. "They can't mean anything by it, because we haven't done anything."

"Nothing?"

"No, of course not," Mom said. "Nothing."

"The letter writer made it all up?" Genevieve asked.

"Yes," Mom answered.

"But why would someone do that?"

Mom rotated her coffee cup. "Now that you're as well-known and prominent as you are, you get all kinds of mail, don't you? The good, the bad, and the ugly?"

38

"Yes."

"Then I'd say this one belongs in either the bad or the ugly category. I suppose they sent it to worry you or throw you off your game."

Genevieve looked to her father. "Dad?"

"Maybe this is their idea of humor," he suggested. "They could view this as a prank."

"It's just that I don't ever get letters about you two. This is a first."

"You receive mail via your publisher, right?" Dad crumbled bacon on top of his eggs, as if he'd forgotten that's not how he ate his eggs and bacon. He always took bites of eggs, then bites of bacon, then bites of eggs.

"Right."

"And do they screen the letters for you?" he asked.

"Yes." She received so much correspondence that she hadn't been able to keep up with it personally in years. "The publicity team typically passes along the funniest, most heartwarming, and most encouraging of the letters. They file the critical and complaining letters."

"Then why didn't they simply file this one?" Mom asked.

"Because it's unusual. It's not garden-variety praise or criticism. It's creepy and vaguely threatening." When Genevieve had first read it, while standing inside her publisher's suite of offices, a stone of foreboding had lodged in her chest.

"It's fiction," Mom said firmly.

"Are you sure?" Genevieve asked.

"Of course," she answered. "Judson? Is there anything you think we should do? In response to the letter?"

Her father was famous for his reasonable disposition and cool head. In every circle he was a part of, and certainly within the circle of this family, the members looked to him for advice.

"No," Dad said. "I don't think we should do anything in response to this other than ignore it."

It takes one skilled faker to recognize another, and Genevieve's instincts were telling her that the letter had the thrust of truth behind it. The stone of foreboding doubled in size.

As soon as Dad finished his meal, he carried his plate and glass to the sink. "I wish I could stay longer, but duty calls." He gave Mom a kiss, then squeezed Genevieve's shoulder. "I'm glad you're home, honey girl." His nickname for Natasha was cup-

40

cake. Hers, honey girl. "I'll see you later today."

"Bye, Dad."

He let himself out the back door, and Mom rose to refill their coffee mugs.

Genevieve watched her dad's silver BMW back down the driveway. Growing up in the Woodward house, when female tempers had flared, offenses had been nursed, or tears had been shed, Dad had retreated to his home office to read about Mercer University football, watch replays of football games, or listen to sports talk shows about the southern football conference.

As a boy, he'd hated playing the sports that his own father had encouraged him to try. But from his seat within the ranks of the band, he'd discovered that he loved *watching* the sport of football. His voracious brain reveled in the numbers, stats, and strategy of the game.

"Isn't this a moment to treasure?" Mom scooted her chair next to Genevieve's and clasped her hand. "The two of us having a beautiful breakfast together?" She smiled with heavy sentimentality. Moisture gathered in her eyes.

"A moment to treasure," Genevieve said.

"God is good."

"Very."

"Last night was so scary, not knowing where you were. Terrifying. I cried all night."

"Why don't you head to bed? I can run errands for you today."

"Not just yet. I want the two of us to have a long talk first." Mom patted her hand.

By "long talk," she meant a long, long, long, *long* talk dotted with laughter, tears, worry, and probing questions. Psychoanalysis. Reflection.

Mentally, Genevieve prepared herself the way she'd prepare herself for a yearlong voyage.

Mom released her hand to take a bite of strawberry. "Talk to me about how things are going with your publisher, the women's conferences you've headlined recently, your friends, your dating life."

Oy.

"Also, have you been eating enough?" Mom pushed the egg platter closer to her. "Sleeping enough?"

"Mmm-hmm."

"Are you managing your loneliness?"

Because Genevieve was single, Mom constantly projected loneliness onto her. "Singleness doesn't equal loneliness," she said lightly.

Mom took a sip of coffee. "I want to know *everything.*"

■ ■ ■ ■

Had any of Sam's employees ever had the nerve to arrive at his restaurant before he did, he'd have taken it personally.

So far, none had.

The morning after Genevieve Woodward had interrupted his life like an unwelcome news bulletin in the middle of regularly scheduled programming, Sam approached Sugar Maple Kitchen's front door, keys in hand.

At five in the morning, downtown Misty River was still mostly asleep beneath a comforter of darkness. Only Merrie at the Doughnut Hut down the street clocked in before he did.

In the light of a streetlamp, Sam scanned the sidewalk in front of his restaurant for rubbish. None. With the help of a designer, he'd chosen dark gray paint for Sugar Maple Kitchen's historic wooden exterior. The gray words stenciled across the two large windows on either side of the front door read *Coffee — Baked Goods — Breakfast.*

He neared the yellow mums and pale green potato vines he'd planted in tall pots. "How you doing there, lovely?" He tapped a flower, then rubbed one of the vine's leaves between two fingers. "Good on ya, then." He moved to the next pot. "Looking beautiful," he murmured. "Excellent. Everything's fine. It's going to be a hot one today, but nothing to worry about. I'll be back with water later. You're doing well, all of you. Very well indeed. You've made me proud."

He let himself inside, disabled the security system, and switched on lights.

The Kitchen had once been a pub called The Crow's Nest, built in 1868. The eighteen foot long bar was the only original item that remained. The wall behind it that had once housed liquor bottles now housed coffee mugs, teacups, small plates, glasses of all sizes, a coffee grinder, and an espresso machine.

He slid behind the bar and began making himself a cup of espresso. The familiar movements of grinding the coffee beans into the portafilter, applying pressure with the tamper, and locking the portafilter into the espresso machine centered him.

He began every workday this way. For that matter, he executed every day of every week by following the same routine. The Kitchen opened for breakfast at seven o'clock and closed at one o'clock, six days out of seven.

Yesterday, Monday, had been his day off.

Genevieve had gotten it off to such a bad start that he'd been on edge for the rest of the day. It had been difficult to relax and even more difficult to get Genevieve out of his head. In part because she stirred up painful memories of Kayden; in part because Genevieve herself wasn't an easy person to forget. Like a frustrating itch, thoughts of her wouldn't go away.

He intended to follow his usual schedule to a *T* today in an effort to recover his balance. Wake at 4:10. Put in his hours at The Kitchen. Hit the gym. Arrive home around two-thirty to work on the farm. Stay so busy that sorrow wouldn't have a chance to swallow him. Avoid questioning what the point of his life was. Convince himself that he could stand to pass all the rest of his days this exact same way.

The first sip of coffee was always the best sip. He took his time tasting his espresso, smelling its rich scent, observing the quiet interior of his restaurant. The espresso was excellent. Everything inside The Kitchen was in order. And still, sadness swept up from the floor and curled around his legs, trying to drag him down. Angrily, he pushed it away and carried his cup to the small office in the back of house. As was his custom, he checked email while he slowly finished

45

his coffee.

A knock sounded on the restaurant's back door right on time, and he admitted his three sous chefs so they could begin the complicated dance of baking pastries and prepping components for the dishes customers ordered off the menu.

Sam was both The Kitchen's owner and head chef. He'd painstakingly created the menu himself and still worked beside his sous chefs in the hours before the restaurant opened for business. After they opened, he'd spend most of his time either expediting orders or working in his office.

Thirty minutes later, he kneaded paleo cinnamon roll dough, the feel of it smooth beneath his hands.

Thirty minutes after that, he answered Mrs. Samuelson's knock on the restaurant's front door. She insisted on buying a coffee from him every morning at six-thirty, prior to opening. She always thanked him before placing $1.75 on the bar. Coffee cost $2.50. A fact he never mentioned to her.

Fifteen minutes after that, the waitstaff and baristas arrived.

Star, with the dyed black hair and tattoos on her neck, stopped before him, waiting until she gained his attention. "How was your day off?" she asked.

46

I had to deal with a long-haired addict who was sleeping in my guesthouse on a pile of her own clothes. "Pretty good, thanks. Yours?"

As she answered, she regarded him with the sort of frank admiration that communicated romantic interest.

He didn't reciprocate.

He helped behind the bar with the coffee rush. The espresso, the emails he'd answered, the food prep, Mrs. Samuelson, even Star's infatuation. The morning went exactly as expected.

His world had narrowed to include only two things. Sugar Maple Kitchen and his farm.

It was considerably less traumatic to wake to her alarm clock than to a stranger who riffled through women's purses.

Regardless, anxiety jumped on Genevieve like a sharp-clawed cat the morning after her homecoming. She'd taken the last Oxy she'd ever take last night. Today she'd start to get clean. Which was absolutely the right thing to do.

Anxiety over what was to come wouldn't help a thing. Anxiety was a wasted emotion!

Yet, stubbornly, dismay pooled in her stomach.

She sat up, hair falling heavily over her shoulders. Her attention fixed on the charming painting opposite her equally charming bed in the room her mom had decorated and redecorated for her over the years.

After the soul-purging with Mom yesterday morning, she'd spent the rest of the day trying to make penance by cleaning the already spotless house, running to the grocery store to secretly stock up on the fluids and foods that would help her survive detox, bringing her mom flowers, and making dinner for the three of them.

The prospect of staying here during withdrawal was appealing because this house was the lap of luxury and because her mom would make an extremely attentive nurse. The downside: Mom would be so attentive that she'd insist on taking Genevieve to the doctor or ER when Genevieve claimed flu, at which time a doctor would tell her mother that her beloved younger daughter was suffering from opioid withdrawal.

Her only other option was to race back to Nashville and fight through withdrawal in her apartment — just like she'd done the last time when her attempt at detox had crashed and burned.

She made her way to the adjoining bathroom (charming), piled her hair on top of her head, and stepped into the shower once it grew agreeably steamy. She scrubbed juniper body wash against her limbs. Perhaps she'd find God in the physical misery that was coming for her —

A knock sounded on the bathroom door.

Genevieve stuck her head around the shower curtain's edge. "Yes?"

"I brought you breakfast in bed, sweetie," Mom called.

"I'll be right out." She turned off the water and toweled dry.

Before the earthquake, her relationship with Mom had been simpler. Nowadays? Complex.

Their interactions tended to follow a well-worn path. Mom smothered her, which frustrated Genevieve, which led to guilt, which eventually concluded in irritability, despite the fact that Genevieve knew she didn't have the right to feel irritated.

She and Natasha had been blessed with a mom who loved them and fed them and cared for them and picked them up from school and bought them new clothes and said prayers with them and cheered for them at every event and served on the PTA and sent them to private Christian school.

Genevieve cinched the belt of her pink robe around her waist and exited the humid bathroom for the cooler air-conditioned bedroom.

"I was hoping to catch you before you got up." Mom held a breakfast tray.

"No worries. I can slip back under the covers just as quickly. See? Ready."

Caroline settled the tray over Genevieve's legs as if Genevieve were the recent victim of a spinal cord injury. "I made your favorite. French toast with cinnamon-spiced apples and pecans."

"Amazing."

"Butter. Maple syrup."

"Really amazing!" She'd have to eat the majority of this or she'd hurt her mom's feelings. "Thanks so much." A plate inscribed with *You Are Special Today* held the French toast. A cloth napkin cushioned sterling silverware.

Caroline held out a hand. Genevieve proffered her own so her mom could give it a heartfelt squeeze.

"Isn't this a moment to treasure?" Mom asked.

"Yep!" Squeeze. Meaningful eye contact. Squeeze. Tender smile. Squeeze. Honestly, Genevieve didn't need any more mother-daughter moments to treasure. What she dearly wanted were plain old ordinary moments. The pressure to make every moment

50

extraordinary was sapping her life force.

"Here you are." Mom shook out Genevieve's cloth napkin, then stretched toward her as if to tuck it into her robe.

"Got it." Genevieve intercepted the napkin and laid it across her lap. She was thirty years old. She didn't require her mom to tuck napkins beneath her chin. And just like that, with absolute clarity, she saw that she could not stay here while detoxing. What had she been thinking? Of course she couldn't. Mom made her want to swallow pills like Kool-Aid.

Back to Nashville, then. Which was such a lonely prospect that she wanted to cry —

A third option slipped into her mind in the form of an image. A white cottage near a pond. Hills rippling with leaves.

If Genevieve went through withdrawal inside Sam's cottage, she could continue to hide her secret from her family. Yet she wouldn't be entirely, horribly alone. She'd have someone nearby who knew the truth about the Oxy but wouldn't smother her.

Yes . . . But was she prepared for the "someone nearby" to be *Sam Turner*? After the introduction they'd had, it would be more than a little mortifying to see him again. Was she willing to endure mortification in order to gain access to his cottage?

51

The sweetness of French toast filled her mouth as she chewed.

She would make Sam's cottage very, very cute. Once she finished with it, the cottage would be worth a little mortification.

Also — other than riffling through her purse — Sam hadn't been rude. He'd seemed decent. He'd seemed like the type of person who'd treat her like a grown-up and give her space but who'd also respond if, in the case of an emergency, she called him. He wouldn't let her shrivel up and die.

At least she didn't think he'd let her shrivel up and die. Would he?

No doubt, Sam wouldn't consider her to be an ideal renter after their previous interaction.

But Genevieve could be persuasive.

She returned her focus to her mom, who had launched into a verbal list of all the treasured moments she had planned for the two of them today. "After lunch with Belle and Margaret, we can head to Gloria's, and you can get your roots done."

"I have dark roots on purpose, Mom. I like it like this."

Mom's brows elevated. "It's so pretty, sweetie. Very flattering. But I . . . are you sure?"

"Very sure."

"I suppose I can call and cancel the appointment I made for you and hope Gloria hasn't turned anyone else away. Maybe I'll just pay her because I hate to cancel. . . ."

"Mom, have you met Sam Turner? He lives out at Sugar Maple Farm."

She appeared perplexed by the swift change in topic. "I've chatted with him a few times. He's the Australian man who owns Sugar Maple Kitchen."

Ah. So Sam was Australian, not British as she'd first guessed. "I'm not familiar with Sugar Maple Kitchen."

"It's a breakfast restaurant downtown."

Genevieve moved the tray to the middle of the bed and crossed her legs. "He mentioned to me that he has a cottage on his property."

"Hmm? When did he mention this?"

"Yesterday when I stopped to get gas near his farm." More lies. Her conscience flinched. "I think I'm going to rent the cottage from him during my stay here in Misty River."

"Why would you want to stay on a farm when you can stay here?"

"Because I have a tremendous amount of work to do, and I feel like I'm ignoring you and Dad when I close myself into my room in order to get everything done that I need

53

to get done."

"No, no, it's fine."

"I'm going to talk to Sam about renting the cottage."

"Your father and I completely understand that you're busy, sweetie. You're always very, very busy." Chiding crept into her voice. "But you're working for the Kingdom, and so when you're here, we don't take it personally. Even though you're not here often."

"I love and appreciate the fact that I'm always welcome here. You and Dad and Natasha and this house are precious to me." She looked Mom straight in the face. The situation she'd gotten herself into was so serious that she simply could not afford to cave to mom guilt. "Even so, I'm going to stay in Sam's cottage this time around."

Natasha

The building is wailing and shaking. It's going to come down around us. On us.

I'm going to die. My sister's going to die.

"Yell so I know where you are," a boy — Luke — shouts.

"H—" My mouth has gone dry and no sound will come out. I swallow and try again. "Here!"

Hands roughly yank me forward into a dim room. Dust is falling like rain. I meet Luke's eyes and dig my fingers into his arm. "My sister!"

Genevieve and I were close when we were little, but I'm in eighth grade and Gen's in sixth, and she's been annoying me the last few years by borrowing my stuff and coming into my room and talking too much. I haven't been nice to her lately, and now I can't stand that thought. Because we're both going to die.

CHAPTER THREE

His trespasser was back.

Sam recognized the white Volvo parked in front of his house and groaned. What did Genevieve want with him? He was just beginning to regain his equilibrium after their last meeting.

His old truck bumped along the familiar gravel-covered dirt road that led from the farm's entrance gate, past the guesthouse, and eventually to his white two-story farmhouse. He parked and exited the cab. His gaze latched on to her as he approached.

Genevieve was sitting on one of his rocking chairs, once again looking like she'd come from a fashion shoot. She closed her laptop and set it on the side table next to a disposable coffee cup. "Good afternoon," she said cheerfully, remaining on her — *his* — rocker.

He stopped with one foot on the porch and one on the step below. "Am I going to have to call the cops?"

She smiled as if there'd been no serious-ness in the question at all. "Why in the world would you do that?"

"Because this is the second time in two days I've found you squatting on my land."

"As you can see," she waved toward herself, "I'm not squatting. I'm sitting on your land. Land that, by the way, I abso-lutely love."

"Is there something I can help you with?"

"Yes." Unlike a normal person, she didn't say anything else.

He'd created a predictable, quiet life for himself. Genevieve Woodward wasn't pre-dictable. And even when she wasn't talking, many things about her were loud. Her pres-ence. The energy captured inside her small frame.

She wore an ivory short-sleeve shirt. The scarf that looped around her throat — oddly — had no ends. Her leather earrings, in the shape of feathers, reached almost to her shoulders. She must have purchased her jeans with holes in them, because there's no way she'd ever worked enough manual labor to create those holes naturally.

"I've been doing research," she told him. "You were one of a select group chosen to lease a historic farm on Chattahoochee

57

National Forest land."

"That's right."

"How long ago?"

"Four years. I don't see what this has to do with —"

"How were you chosen?"

"I submitted an application."

"From what I read, it was quite a coup to score one of the sixty-year leases. Why do you think they picked you?"

"Did you come here to ask me questions about leases on national park land?"

"In part, yes. I'm interested."

He sized her up, trying to understand her motivation for being here. She sized him up in return, pleasantly and patiently. She wasn't just a stranger to him. She was also just plain strange. A weird blend of charming, confident, and confusing.

"I think . . ." His forehead furrowed.

"Go on."

"I think the park service picked me because they were looking for people who were into sustainable farming. They were looking for people who were young, because the farmers in this country are aging. And they were also looking for people willing to open their farms to the public in order to educate them about resource preservation."

"And you checked all the boxes?"

"Yes."

"What business plan did you pitch?"

He scowled, wishing she'd go and leave him alone.

She laughed. "Be nice! Didn't you just say that part of your job is to open your farm and educate the public?"

She had a point. "I told them I was planning a farm-to-table breakfast restaurant. That I'd grow much of the restaurant's food here and sell the rest to visitors."

Gracefully, she rose and moved to stand at the porch rail, looking out. A breeze rustled her hair.

He walked a few paces onto the porch, turning just enough to take in the scene she was studying. Behind the house at their backs, a wooded hill rose steeply toward the sky. In front of the house, the earth rolled gently down to a wide valley that held the farm road Genevieve had been driving the other night when she'd made the bad decision to stop.

Shade from the porch roof protected them from the sun pouring onto the meadow. The long rows of the garden he'd worked so hard to develop marked the earth a good distance away, on the lower side of the meadow. Near the garden, which butted up against the tree line separating his house from the guest-

59

house in the next meadow over, a simple farm stand waited to open for weekend business.

"If that's all, I have some things to do around here this afternoon," he stated.

"Do you love it here?" she asked.

He paused. "Usually, yes."

"By that, do you mean that you love it here when uninvited women aren't pestering you?"

"That's exactly what I mean."

"Are you the only person who lives on the property?"

"I am."

"Ever get lonely?"

Yep. I'm lonely every hour of every day. "No." That single syllable was easier than trying to explain to this high-maintenance person he was lonely in a way that was deep, complete, and undisturbed. She'd find fault with that. But that's how he wanted it.

"Why are you here?" he asked.

She faced him. He'd forgotten how bright her hazel eyes were against her perfect milky skin. "I'm here because I'd like to rent your cottage."

His brows crushed down. "It's not available for rent."

"I realize that. But I went and had another look at the cottage when I arrived at the farm a few hours ago. You'd locked the door —"

"I locked it the second you left."

"— but I was able to peek in the windows and inspect the outside. It's adorable. And, as I recall, it has electricity."

"It's not for rent."

"Does the plumbing work?"

"Yes."

"A/C and heat?"

"Yes."

"Dishwasher?"

"No. Not even a sink, except the one in the bathroom."

"In that case, I guess it's too much to hope that it has a washer and dryer."

"Way too much to hope."

"But you'd allow me to wash my clothes at your house from time to time, right?"

"That doesn't matter since it's not available —"

"It's small and simple and old, but you've also kept it very clean. Why is it in such good shape if you're not planning to rent it?"

He worked his back molars together. "At some point, I'm going to put furniture in it and rent it out to people wanting a holiday. I've been busy with everything else and haven't had time."

"You'll be able to make a mint off that thing," she said with assurance. "It's full of charm. It has excellent potential, in fact. All you need is someone with good design sensibilities to come in and decorate the cottage —"

"Guesthouse."

"— *cottage* with a sofa, chairs, rugs, art, a mini kitchen." She tilted her head. "Someone like me."

"No."

"Aren't you interested in hearing my offer?"

"No."

"If you'll let me live in it, I'll make it farmhouse chic. No one will be able to resist it when I'm through with it, and when I go, you'll keep everything in the cottage, which will be worth well over a few thousand dollars."

He didn't understand her. "Don't you live in Nashville?"

"I do, but I'm going to be researching and writing for the next few months. I want to spend an extended amount of time with my family, but I don't want to be *on top* of my family, if that makes sense." She gestured toward his land. "Your cottage is peaceful, but it's also close enough to town to be convenient. This setting is inspirational."

"You seem like a city girl to me."

"Who wants a country getaway. The cottage is just what I need."

"My answer's no." He moved toward his front door.

She stepped into his path. "Did you hear me say that I'm going to leave the cottage move-in ready for your guests? I'll also work in your garden and at the farm stand. I'll pick apples. If you need someone to update your website or strengthen your social media presence, I'm your girl."

"No thanks."

She didn't back down. "I saw online that you and the other leaseholders will be organizing a series of National Park Fall Fun Days. I can help with that. I'm good at event planning, and I'm good with people. You can delegate a lot of that responsibility to me so that you won't have to worry about a thing."

"If you're staying in my guesthouse, I'll have to worry about you. You're an addict."

Her expression cracked a little.

"I know exhaustion wasn't to blame for the night you spent in my guesthouse." He had at least seven inches of height on her, so he had to incline his head down to look her in the face.

He sensed what it cost her to maintain

eye contact with him, but she managed it. "You're right," she said. "Exhaustion didn't play a role in what happened the other night. If I'm sleeping in houses that don't belong to me, which I am, then obviously the pills I've been taking have become a huge problem. I took my last pill yesterday."

Did she expect him to be impressed? He wasn't. She should have figured out that the pills were a problem right after her surgery and quit then. He regarded her cynically. "Withdrawal is tough."

"I know."

"And quitting cold turkey isn't the best way to go. You'd be better off checking yourself into a rehab center."

"If I did, I'd have to confess my issue to multiple people."

"Good."

"Not good. I don't want this to become public knowledge."

"Who else knows?" he asked.

"A co-worker. And you."

A very bad word filled his mind.

"Anyway," she said, "I think a rehab center is too drastic an overcorrection for my situation."

"It's not." He didn't want her near him, disrupting everything, stirring up bad memories, bringing her drama and her

64

perfume that smelled like the beach and her to-go coffee cups and her scarves with no ends.

She studied him. "You seem to know something about this. Have you gone through withdrawal?"

"No."

"But someone you care about has. Right?"

He remained silent.

"Ah," she said. "Well."

He could sense that she wanted to ask follow-up questions. He let her know by his expression that follow-up questions weren't welcome.

"For better or worse," she said, "I've decided not to go the rehab center route. At this point, my choices are to rent your cottage or drive back to Nashville and detox by myself."

"You can't detox by yourself. You'll sabotage yourself doing it that way, so it's not even worth the effort."

"I've already failed once doing it that way. Look, I realize — fully — that you're under no obligation to rent your cottage to me. But if you do, I'll pay you back by doing a fantastic job decorating it for you." She formed prayer hands. "I won't be a burden. You won't see me or hear my wails of anguish or anything."

65

The words to turn her down formed in his mouth, but guilt over Kayden slid into him like a blade, preventing him from speaking them.

"I'd really, really love to stay here," she said. "I promise you that I'll make my time here worth your while."

If Kayden had found herself in the same circumstance as Genevieve, asking to rent a guesthouse so that she could get clean, he'd have wanted the property owner to provide her with a safe place.

Was he really considering letting her stay? He couldn't deal with having her and her addiction on his farm —

That wasn't true. It would have been true if he'd only had himself to consider. If that had been the case, he'd already have told Genevieve good-bye and shut himself inside his farmhouse.

For Kayden, he *could* find a way to deal with having Genevieve and her addiction on his property.

He hadn't done nearly enough for Kayden when he'd had the chance. Because of that, there was nothing he wouldn't do for Kayden now. Including helping Genevieve, who shared Kayden's struggle.

He took a few steps back, putting square footage between them. "You'll have to agree

66

to my conditions."

"Which are?"

"I can't have Oxy in that guesthouse, so I reserve the right to search it at any time. If I find Oxy or any other opioid or any illegal drug, then you're out." Ultimatums often didn't work with addicts, but he couldn't bring himself to do this any other way.

"Agreed."

"We'll need to exchange numbers, and you'll need to check in with me once every twenty-four hours over the next week while you're going through withdrawal to let me know that you're okay."

"Agreed."

"You have to confide in a family member or a friend."

"Sam."

"If you're going to kick this habit, you're going to have to tell the people closest to you about this."

"I can't."

"You can."

"I *sincerely* don't want to."

"It's not negotiable. Who are you closest to?"

"My sister, Natasha." She scratched behind her ear, then dropped her hand. "I'm embarrassed to tell her. She's . . . proud of me. She thinks I have it all together. Also, if

I tell her she'll be mad because this has been going on for months and I haven't said a thing."

He waited.

Her lips pursed.

"It's not negotiable," he repeated.

"I'll tell Natasha," she finally said. "But I'll do so after I get through the first week. Maybe then it won't be so upsetting for her, because I'll be over the worst of it."

He didn't like it. On the other hand, given the hole she'd dug for herself, he understood her need to hold her head up as high as she could.

"Any other conditions?" she asked.

"You'll have to go see a psychologist."

Her eyes widened.

"You're going to need one," he told her truthfully.

She blew out a breath. "Okay. Is that it? I hope? Any other conditions?"

"No taking a fancy to me. Okay?"

She paused, released a shocked bark of laughter, then gaped at him with disbelief.

Like most of his Australian countrymen, he was allergic to arrogance. Because of that, he'd made the statement in a joking tone even though he'd meant every word. He needed to make his position clear to her from the start.

"I will not fall for you," she said. "Do we have a deal?"

He regretted the words even as he spoke them. "We have a deal."

Women possessed mind-blowing magic.

Sam stood inside the guesthouse near nine o'clock that night. Genevieve's Volvo had been coming and going all day since they'd struck their deal. At one point, he'd driven past and seen people unloading a love seat from a U-Haul truck. Ten minutes ago he'd glanced out his second-story window and noticed Genevieve's taillights disappearing toward the road yet again.

He'd come to do what he'd told her he'd do: search his property for drugs. He'd found the place completely changed.

The bed had sheets, blankets, at least ten throw pillows, and one of those ruffles hanging off the bottom of it.

T-shirts lay neatly folded inside the top dresser drawer. He opened the armoire. Hanging clothes filled it. She'd pinned a firefighter calendar to the inside door. August's photo showed a shirtless guy on a ladder, smiling, and supporting a kitten with one arm. As if anyone with a brain would climb into a fire shirtless. Or smiling. Or holding a kitten.

The desk facing one of the front windows supported a flower arrangement, a container filled with pastel-colored pens, a candle, and a small sign with a cross on it that read, *With faith all things are possible.*

On the fireplace side of the structure, she'd placed a big gray-and-white patterned rug between a love seat stuffed with more throw pillows and an armchair and ottoman. He didn't have a single rug in his house, and he'd been living there four years.

She'd set out lamps, hung curtains, and displayed a set of gray, white, and pale blue pottery on the fireplace mantel.

Against the back wall, an open shelving unit straddled a mini fridge. Genevieve had imported a microwave, a two-burner hot plate, an electric teakettle, a toaster, and a tiny free-standing butcher block. She'd stocked plates, cups, utensils, and food, if you could call Jelly Belly jelly beans, a loaf of sliced white bread, and instant porridge food. He did not.

He set his hands on his hips. Without intending to, he'd acquired a tenant.

He'd found no Oxy, so he let himself out of the guesthouse. An Adirondack chair, footstool, and side table sat on the small porch. A throw pillow decorated the chair. He rolled his eyes. Another throw pillow.

He walked down to the pond and stood at its edge.

As a kid, his desire to belong had made him soft. When he was eight, he'd given his lunch to Nico Mallory five days in a row in hopes that doing so would buy Nico's friendship. He hadn't realized that Nico kept eating his lunch because Nico and his buddies thought it was funny.

When he was ten, he'd given Aaron Schuman his school supplies.

When he was sixteen, he'd given Elijah Moore his jacket.

When he was twenty-three, he'd given Kayden Westcott his heart.

He'd stupidly placed his trust in too many lost causes over the years.

He was now honor bound to do what he could to make sure Genevieve survived the coming week.

But he could never again place his trust in a lost cause.

Sebastian

The dark-haired kid pulls me into a room with a Black kid and a blond girl. I wrench my arm from his hold. Just as I do, the floor tilts.

The dark-haired kid disappears into the hallway.

The ground shakes and shakes. Metal bends. Glass shatters. Chunks of ceiling crash to the floor.

I'm desperate for it to stop. *Stop!*

The terrified boy and girl are staring at me. Why? They don't know me, and I definitely don't know them.

I never wanted to come on this idiot mission trip with these stupid people. My foster parents made me. When I die here with these strangers, they'll be sorry.

CHAPTER FOUR

Genevieve considered death an imminent likelihood.

With every passing hour of withdrawal, that likelihood became more and more welcome.

A day had passed since she'd finished moving into the cottage, and she was lying in bed, shaking and sweating. She didn't know whether to throw the blankets off or pull them tighter, but she was convinced neither would help.

Nausea and vomiting had overtaken her body. Terrible stomach pain. A fast, thumping heart rate.

Even harder to bear? The panic. When it gripped her, it gripped hard. More than once, she'd cried because she'd had no other outlet for her sorrow and terrified anxiety.

Squeezing shut her eyes, she pleaded with God to heal her body and remove her misery. But trying to find Him in the midst of this was like stretching her fingertips into darkness — straining to touch the thing she knew was there — and having her fingers rake nothing but empty air. The empty air had never been more harrowing than it was now, when she needed Him so desperately.

Maybe it was too much, to try to correct all her bad decisions with one mammoth step back in the right direction.

Yesterday she'd dumped all her pills into the trash along with the remains of the salad she'd eaten for lunch before driving to Sugar Maple Farm to talk with Sam.

How could she have been so foolishly confident? If she still had access to her pills, she'd have already taken some in order to minimize these symptoms.

Her doctor's office in Nashville had closed for the day. At this point, she had no choice other than to endure the night until they reopened in the morning —

Loud knocking jolted a gasp from her.

"I'm leaving supplies outside the door," Sam's Australian voice called from her front porch.

She couldn't muster a response. She'd texted him earlier, like she'd told him she would, but she hadn't expected a delivery.

After her next trip to the bathroom, she

dragged herself to the door, which seemed a mile away. He'd left a reusable grocery sack outside for her. She pulled it indoors, crumpled into a seated position next to it, and looked inside. It contained a six-pack of cucumber electrolyte water and a six-pack of organic protein shakes. Also, envelopes containing supplements, ibuprofen, and instructions on when and how often to take each.

Fabulous. She was at the mercy of a health nut.

The rest of her world — her family, her work, her friends, her loft in Nashville, her plans — had vanished.

The only things that remained: sickness, fear, the inside of this cottage, and her desperation to escape all three.

Later that night, Sam stood at his bedroom window.

His bed waited behind him, covers a mess because he'd just been lying in it, trying to sleep. He couldn't see the guesthouse from the first story. But from here, on the second story, he had a distant, downward view of the guesthouse's roofline and front wall.

Genevieve had left the porch light on.

Somehow, she'd changed the feel of his farm. She was only one petite person. But it

75

was as if she were transmitting invisible air waves that altered the whole place.

Tonight, those air waves carried suffering.

Before she'd come, Sugar Maple Farm had been full of solitude, his grim thoughts, and work. But at least he'd been able to concentrate enough to read before bed, to sleep.

Now all those things had become difficult for him.

She was sick, and no one but him knew why.

All his brain and body could do was worry.

Genevieve called her current pain specialist. His office agreed to log an Oxy prescription at the Riverside Pharmacy in Misty River.

As soon as she disconnected the call, she curled into the fetal position. It helped to know that, should she reach a point when she could no longer stand this, she could get access to pills.

So far, she'd been able to stand it. *Barely.* But she'd done it by forcing herself to remember hitting that stone planter with her car. Then waking up in Sam's cottage, ignorant of how she'd gotten there. Over and over, she confronted those memories.

Also, practically, she didn't feel close to human enough to drive to the pharmacy.

Also, she'd let a lot of people down. God, most of all. Her family, her friends, and the thousands of women who looked to her for inspiration. She didn't want to put herself through the pain and disgrace she'd face if she was caught doing something stupid while taking Oxy. But even more than that, she absolutely couldn't stomach the thought of subjecting her family and friends to pain and disgrace. She refused to hurt them like that.

Three brisk knocks sounded on her door. "I'm leaving supplies," Sam called.

She'd come this far.

She could make it just a little bit longer. She'd broken chunks of survival into small amounts. Another fifteen minutes. Another hour.

Just a little bit longer.

"Sweetie," Mom crooned, smoothing a wet washcloth against Genevieve's forehead. The coolness of it seeped into her heated skin. "I'm *so* sorry that you're sick."

Genevieve had kept her mother at bay as long as possible by telling her she didn't want her to come by because she didn't want her to catch the flu. Sadly, that type of logical reasoning only worked against her overactive maternal instincts so long.

"Where do you think you caught this?" Mom asked.

"I don't know." Pride and guilt formed a powerful muzzle.

"I'm going to bundle you into my car and take you to see Dr. Honeycutt."

"No," Genevieve gritted out. "I don't have the strength to move from this bed. Plus, I don't need a doctor. I just need to ride this out."

Mom's face pinched. "Dr. Honeycutt is excellent —"

"No."

Caroline sighed and mounded her hands on top of her crossed legs. "I hate that you're both lonely *and* feeling poorly out here on this remote piece of land. A husband would be such a comfort to you at a time like this."

Genevieve grunted. Morphine would be a comfort to her at a time like this.

"Come home with me, and I'll take care of you."

"No, thank you."

"Then I'll pack a bag and stay here with you until you're well. It'll be just like that time when you were three and I nursed you through pneumonia. That's such a sweet memory. You slept in my arms."

"No."

"But —"

"I'm staying here, Mom." Her uneven inhale ached. Having to hold up half of a conversation was taking more out of her than she had to give.

God! Please give me the strength to make it through this.

Please, please, please.

She felt nothing in response but distress and heard nothing in response but her mother's voice.

On the fifth day of detox, Genevieve transitioned from intense anguish to moderate anguish.

For the first time, she moved from the bed to the love seat. She sat, curled up on its end, sipping cucumber water and nibbling saltines. Desperate for something to distract her from her discomfort, she binge-watched one cheerful romantic movie after another on her computer. Ever again achieving the health and happiness of the smiling people onscreen seemed as possible as jumping to the moon.

Knock, knock, knock. "Supplies."

The next day she crafted social media updates. Her followers expected her to post several times a week, and sickness only granted a person a small amount of leeway. When walking through a difficult time, one simply micro-blogged in vague terms about hardship, then concluded with deep and meaningful thoughts.

For a while now, she'd suspected that she'd run out of deep and meaningful things to say. But her people awaited content, so she shared pictures of the cottage that made it look like an idyllic escape instead of the dungeon it had actually been for the past six days.

The next evening, when Genevieve spotted Sam's truck bouncing toward the cottage, she rose and gingerly crossed the space. As soon as she heard the newest delivery land on her porch, she swung open the door. "Supplies, I presume?"

He regarded her with surprise as he slowly straightened. He wore a black baseball cap with overlapping letters on the front, a gray T-shirt, jeans. His no-nonsense, hard-wearing clothes assured her he was a man who *worked*. Hard. And not behind a desk.

"Supplies," he confirmed.

"I wanted to let you know that I'm finally feeling a little bit better."

"Glad to hear it."

"Thanks for the text correspondence and

for the daily deliveries."

"You're welcome." He took a step back. "G'night."

She darted out a hand. "Actually. Sam. I was hoping you'd stay for a while and . . . visit?"

He looked like she'd proposed he eat dirt.

He was so taciturn! And his social skills were questionable. But he'd also been kind enough to check on her via text messages and spend his money buying her food. "I haven't conversed with a non-family member in a week. I'm an extrovert, and the isolation is starting to make me a little crazy. So . . . hang out with me for a bit?"

He hesitated. "All right."

"I'll try not to take your lack of enthusiasm personally." She chuckled ruefully.

He followed her inside to the mini-kitchen. His tall, powerful body gave her the sensation that her cottage was shrinking. "I'm in the process of making tea and toast. Would you like either?"

"Tea."

"Anything to eat?" She indicated the food selection on her shelves.

He chose one of the organic protein bars he'd given her a few days before and stuck it in his back pocket. "You shouldn't have this many electrolyte waters left," he told her. "You need to work harder at hydrating."

"Mmm-hmm."

"Is that what you say when you're not interested in taking advice?"

"Mmm-hmm." She glanced over at him in time to see a sudden grin transform his face. Grooves fanned out from his eyes and down the sides of his cheeks to bracket his matched set of deep dimples. She'd bet those grooves had indented his face this exact same way when he was eight.

"What?" he asked. "Why are you looking at me like that?"

"Because you . . . smiled."

"I smile."

"You *do*?"

"Yes."

"I'm astonished."

Her toast popped up and a rumbling jet of steam shot from her kettle. She prepared two mugs of tea.

"I don't suppose you have any Vegemite?" he asked.

"No, indeed."

"It's good on toast when you're trying to recover from something. I can nip up to my house and get some for you if you'd like."

"The only thing I know about Vegemite is that it's brown. Oh, and isn't there a song lyric about a Vegemite sandwich?"

"From the song 'Down Under' by Men at Work."

"What's in Vegemite?'

"Yeast."

She managed not to wince at the prospect of brown yeast on toast. "Thanks for the offer, but I think I'll stick with butter and jelly."

He spread butter on her toast. "You don't know what you're missing."

"Ignorance is sometimes bliss."

A week had passed since she'd begun detox. Instead of pajamas, she had on clothes for the first time. Yoga pants and her softest T-shirt. Still, it felt like a victory. Earlier, she'd even blown her hair dry and put on a small amount of makeup.

At long last, her stomach had calmed. Her body temperature had returned to its proper setting. Recovery was beginning. Very gradually. Yet it *was* beginning. A slight sense of normalcy had climbed out of its burrow like a rabbit today, looking around with wide eyes, skittish, poised to vanish at any moment.

What she'd been through had been *so* awful that she mostly felt dazed and bruised and sad. Her link to God remained severed, and Genevieve wanted Oxy desperately, even now. She *really* needed another human being to talk to. "How about we sit outside?" she suggested. "The weather's nice."

"Sure."

She only had one patio chair, so he carried the ottoman outdoors.

Genevieve followed with the tea. "I'll sit on the ottoman."

"No. The chair's yours." He brushed off the chair for her, then went back inside and emerged with her toast.

He wasn't a warm or open personality type, so she didn't quite know what to do with this evidence of his gallantry. Should she file it under quirks: occasional gallantry? Or under character: hidden gallantry?

He sat on the ottoman, leaned his shoulder blades against the house, and crossed an ankle over the opposite knee.

The days were long in August, and the sun would linger for another hour yet. Genevieve let the warmth soak into her skin and savored the scent of distant woodsmoke and summer grass.

Short, hardy shrubs with pale green leaves lined the base of the cottage, interrupted only by one ambitious vine of morning glory. The vine framed the window in front of her desk, then followed the building's roofline up toward its central point. Early tomorrow, its sky-blue petals would open to celebrate another morning.

One minute drifted into the next as she drank tea and listened to the buzz of a bee, whispering leaves, a car coasting along the road.

Usually she felt compelled to fill silence with words. But not this time. Selfishly, she wanted to trap this moment in a mason jar.

"You've made it a whole week without Oxy," he said.

"Yes."

He rolled his head toward her. His base-ball cap's brim slanted shadow over a section of his face. Darker green ringed the pale, mellow green of his irises. "You've done well so far."

She gave him a look of mock amazement. "Did you just compliment me?"

"No."

"Because it kind of sounded like a compliment."

"If so, it came out of my mouth wrong."

"You did well taking care of me," she told him.

"Did you just compliment me?"

"No."

"Because it kind of sounded like a compliment."

"If so, it came out of my mouth wrong."

She smiled and took a bite of toast. Delicious. The crisp bread, butter, and tangy raspberry jam had all come from him in yesterday's delivery, wrapped in containers labeled *The Kitchen.*

Her stomach didn't revolt. Her taste buds approved.

"Time to schedule an appointment with a psychologist," he commented.

Man, he really knew how to squish the levity out of a conversation.

"Do you have one in mind?" he asked.

"Yes. Dr. Quinley counseled me for a few years back when I was in middle school. I trust her."

"How soon do you think she can fit you in?"

"She likes me. So I'm guessing she'll be able to squeeze me in before the end of the week."

"Is she certified in addiction treatment?"

"I don't know."

He pulled out his phone and appeared to run a search on Dr. Quinley.

"Back when we hashed out our agreement," she pointed out in a friendly tone, "you didn't specify that the psychologist had to be certified in addiction treatment."

"Well," he said as he scrolled down, "she is certified in it, so we're good."

"You might be good," she said wryly. "I'm a mess."

He pushed his phone into his pocket. "Once you have the appointment scheduled, let me know. I'll drive you there."

"That's okay. I have a car. And a license, even."

"And I have a suspicious nature. I want to be sure that you meet with her."

"Oh." Genevieve was accustomed to people liking her, admiring her, and believing her to be better than she was. Blunt Sam, in contrast, knew the worst thing about her. She didn't have to pretend with him, which was both humbling and incredibly freeing. "In that case, I'll reach out to you when I have the appointment scheduled."

He resettled his baseball cap and tilted the back of his skull against the house.

She considered him, this man who owed her *nothing* and who'd been there for her nonetheless. She couldn't help but like him a little. He was very easy on the eyes, for one thing. For another, it was difficult to dislike a man who baked bread this yummy.

"Are you familiar with the Bible?" she asked.

"Why'd you shift to that topic?"

"I followed my thoughts there. Are you? Familiar with it?"

"Somewhat familiar, yes."

"You're a Christian." It wasn't a question.

"Yeah."

She could often tell a believer from a non-believer. Even when the believer was a virile, straight-talking man who didn't seem like the type to raise his hands when worship music played.

"Do you remember when Joseph's brothers threw him into the pit with the intent to kill him?" she asked.

"I do." He hesitated. "Are you about to compare Joseph's time in the pit with your time in the pit this last week?"

"Yes, lucky you." She might not be scheduled to preach on a stage for the next few months, but that didn't mean it was possible for her to stop preaching. "God knew how everything would play out, so His rescue plan was already underway long before Joseph was thrown in the pit. Joseph's brothers wanted to kill him, but then, lo and behold, a caravan bound for Egypt arrived on the scene. The caravan had been on its way for days. Think about that. The brothers decided to sell Joseph as a slave to the people in the caravan instead."

Sam nodded.

"This cottage and you, Sam, were my caravan."

Sam didn't roll his eyes or shake his head. He simply met and held her gaze.

She'd lost hold of her connection to God, but Genevieve could recognize His hand at work.

"That's the first time anyone's called me a caravan," he said, deadpan.

"You were on the way before I stopped in front of your farm the other night," she said. "You're the vehicle of escape He provided." Goose bumps skittered down her arms.

"You're giving me too much credit. I didn't even want to let you stay here, remember?"

"Thank you for everything."

"Wait to thank me until after you receive my bill."

He was joking. . . . She was pretty sure he was joking. "I'd love to reimburse you," she told him sincerely, even though half the groceries he'd brought were so wildly healthy that she might not be able to lecture herself into eating them.

"I'm expensive," he said.

"That's fine, because I'm rich."

Another one of his rare smiles flashed across his mouth, devastating in its power. He'd been joking.

"What's an Australian doing in the north Georgia mountains?" she asked.

"It's a long, boring story."

"Then give me the short, not-boring version."

He peeled the wrapper from his protein bar and took a bite. "I'm half Australian. My dad's American. After my mum graduated from uni, she got a work visa, moved to Atlanta, and met my dad there. Two months later they got married, and nine months later they had me."

"And?"

"Their relationship was a battlefield. It didn't help that my mother was from one continent, my dad from another." He chewed another bite of his bar. "Mum had only planned to stay in the States for a few years. Dad never planned to leave Georgia. When she wanted to return to Australia, there was no way he was going with her. They divorced when I was two, and apparently, that was the easiest and most civil thing they ever did. I think they were both relieved. Mum and I moved to Australia."

"Did your dad remain in Atlanta?"

"Yes. He's still there."

"Where did you and your mom live?"

"At first when we moved back, we lived in her home city of Melbourne. When I was six, she married a cattle grazier who'd inherited a big piece of property in Victoria.

90

Mum and I moved to the country. Over the next few years, my sister and then brother were born."

"Are your mom and stepdad still married?"

"They are. Happily."

"What became of your dad?"

Sam rubbed the tip of his pointer finger against the pad of his thumb. "He stayed single for a long time. Ten years ago, he married a nice woman who never wants to leave Georgia, either. They're well suited."

"Are you his only child?"

"I am."

"How often did you see him after you moved Down Under?"

"At first, once a year when he'd travel to Australia to spend time with me. As soon as I was old enough to fly alone, I started seeing him twice a year, because one of those times I'd travel here to see him."

She and Natasha were the beloved daughters of a long marriage. At times, Genevieve felt that her mom might love her a little *too* much. Had there been times when Sam hadn't felt loved enough? It had to be hard to live halfway around the globe from your father, to grow up as the only child of an unhappy marriage in a home that included your stepdad and the products of your

91

mom's happy second marriage — your half-sister and half-brother. "How come you didn't stay on the cattle ranch?"

"Because it wasn't *my* cattle station. When I was eighteen, I went to uni."

"Where and what did you study?"

"I studied business at Victoria University in Melbourne."

"Did you always want to own a restaurant?"

"Not at first. During the last two years of uni, I worked part time in a kitchen. It was then that I decided what I wanted to do. I went to cooking school, then worked as a sous chef."

"Why did you move to America?"

He crossed his arms. No reply.

"C'mon." She bumped his knee with her foot. "You know about my fondness for Oxy. I'd really like to know one personal thing about you."

"I don't like talking about personal things."

"Yes, I realize. I didn't like going through withdrawal. But I did it."

He looked across his shoulder at her. "You're comparing talking about personal things to going through withdrawal?"

"Yes, because both are ultimately good for you."

Long pause.

"Why did you move to America?" she repeated.

"I moved because I lost someone I loved."

"I'm sorry. What happened?"

"I'd rather not say." The muscles at the hinge of his jaw tensed. "I . . . I needed a change. So I moved to the States. To Atlanta."

"Did you work in another restaurant?"

"I did. I continued to save money for a place of my own. Then moved here."

She contemplated Sam and his globe-trotting past. Misty River had been her home base since birth. It sounded like for Sam, belonging had been harder to find.

She watched his throat work as he drained the last of his tea. He disappeared inside and returned without the mug, then stood on the grass facing her. "No need to keep texting me. Think you're strong enough to get your own groceries?"

She didn't want their communication or his deliveries to end. But of course, he'd already done more than enough for her. "Yes. I'll be fine now on my own. Thank you."

Tomorrow, she and Natasha were planning to meet at their parents' house so that they could begin hunting for secrets in their mom and dad's past. She'd texted her sister a photo of the mysterious letter the day it had arrived, then briefed her on the breakfast discussion she'd had with their parents about it.

On top of that, she was committed to telling Natasha about the Oxy.

Unfortunately, the thought of the threatening letter — and of having to confess her addiction — had ignited a flickering flame of apprehension within her.

Sam's presence, his air of competence, his firm, endearing face — were calming. While he'd been here, he'd blocked depressing thoughts from devouring her mind. It was tempting to think that so long as he was close, she'd be all right.

Which was ridiculous!

Sam wasn't the remedy for her problems. He was simply her caravan. A *temporary* rescue.

" 'Night, Gen."

"You know," she pointed out, "no one calls me Gen except for my sister." Usually when people tried to shorten her name, she politely asked them to call her Genevieve. She couldn't quite bring herself to say that to him, though, because Gen sounded adorable when he said it.

"Well, now it's your sister and me who

94

call you Gen."

"I realize Genevieve is hard to spell, but it's only three syllables." She smiled, playing devil's advocate.

"Which is two syllables too long. Can I call you Gen?"

"You may."

" 'Night, Gen."

"Good night, Sam."

Tears tightened her throat as she watched him walk toward his truck.

Don't go.

But he did go, plunging her back into solitude.

If she was going to be okay, truly okay again, then that outcome could not depend on anyone except herself and God.

Ultimately, she was the one who had to manage her recovery from pills, the Bible study she'd committed to write, and the secrets her mom and dad might be hiding.

I know what your parents did. The words of the mystery letter carried a menacing echo. *And after all we've suffered, it's hard to watch you bask in your fame and money. Your parents aren't going to get away with it.*

Ben

The earthquake goes on and on. I'm panting and my teeth are chattering and I'm sweating even though I'm freezing.

I need to try to get us out of this building, fast, to safe, open grass.

But I can't see any doors or any stairs. Only rattling walls.

Luke hauls Genevieve into the room. Natasha releases a sob and wraps her younger sister in a hug.

A loud *boom* splits the air. The hallways in every direction begin to cave in. Even so, Luke turns to run down the one they'd come from.

Sebastian lunges and grabs Luke's arm, stopping him.

"Let me go!" Luke's eyes flash. "I have to get my brother."

"You'll be crushed," Sebastian yells. He's just as tall and just as strong as Luke.

Luke twists himself free. But as he does, concrete crashes into the hallway, filling it. A cloud of dirt rolls over us.

"No!" Luke screams.

CHAPTER FIVE

Natasha Woodward MacKenzie sailed through the door of their dad's home office the next morning wearing exercise clothing and carrying a travel mug in one hand and a lump of yellow knitting in the other. "I've arrived!"

Genevieve walked into her sister's hug, which smelled like a mixture of oranges and vanilla and communicated the same brisk reassurance it always had.

" 'You must allow me to tell you . . .' " Natasha began.

" 'How ardently I admire and love you.' " Genevieve finished the quote from *Pride and Prejudice.* Her practical sister had discovered a passion for Regency-set romances. This past January she'd embarked on a self-proclaimed "Year of Living Austenly" and had been integrating elements of Jane Austen's world into her own.

They pulled apart. "How are you?" Genevieve asked.

"Ovulating." Natasha delighted in announcing bodily news bulletins.

"Ah."

Natasha passed over the lump of knitting. "For you."

Natasha had attempted many of the crafts practiced by ladies of Jane Austen's day. Embroidery had been a disaster. Wooden dolls dressed in shells, worse. Early this summer, she'd settled on knitting and had been clothing her family members in mediocre-to-bad knitted accessories ever since.

"Yay!" Genevieve unfolded it and was relieved to recognize what it was. "A winter hat." Not only did it look like it might fit a ten-year-old, it was too short on one side. "Thank you."

"Try it on!"

She squeezed it onto her head and smiled. The hat gripped the crown of her head like a toddler grips its mother's legs.

"You know how bank robbers pull panty hose over their heads?" Natasha asked.

Genevieve nodded.

"You look like a bank robber who only managed to get the panty hose part way down."

"Just the fashion statement I was hoping

to make!"

"Then wear it with pride." Natasha lowered into the desk chair.

"Thanks for agreeing to help me snoop through Mom and Dad's stuff this morning."

"Mom took Millie and Owen to the children's museum, and there's nothing I'd rather do with my two kid-free hours than assist you, sister of mine."

"May you receive a crown in heaven for your tremendous generosity." Genevieve gestured expansively.

Natasha saluted with her mug, which no doubt contained Jane Austen's drink of choice: hot tea. "Are you feeling better? The flu can be brutal."

Genevieve faltered. Nothing within her wanted to vomit her Oxy issue onto Natasha. Yet she'd promised Sam she'd tell Natasha as soon as she made it through withdrawal, and she didn't want him to kick her out of his cottage. "About the flu . . ."

"Yes?"

Genevieve dragged a straight-backed chair from the wall close to Natasha's position. "I was sick, but not with the flu." She sat.

Her sister's expression melted from teasing into confusion. "You told us you had the flu."

"I lied." Remorse gathered like heartburn in the center of her chest.

"Why? What did you have?"

"I was going through prescription drug withdrawal," Genevieve forced herself to say.

For a second, terrible silence held sway. *"What?"* Natasha said.

"I've been taking OxyContin since my ankle surgery."

Natasha regarded her with astonished concern. "Wait. Wait, wait, wait. Back up." She began asking questions.

Genevieve answered each one. She put as rosy a spin as possible on her predicament.

When her questions ran dry, Natasha knotted her hands together on the desktop and regarded Genevieve squarely.

Genevieve waited, throat tight. This was the older sister she'd looked up to since birth. Wise, funny, dependable Natasha. She'd always wanted Natasha to think well of her, and that hadn't changed.

"This is really scary," Natasha said. "People die because of opioids every day."

"I know."

"I love you. We *all* love you. We'll do whatever we can to help you get well."

Genevieve hadn't felt like herself since she'd stopped taking the pills. All her emotions were much too close to the surface, and it took effort not to burst into tears. "I love you, too."

"What can I do to support you?" her sister asked.

"Just . . . be there for me, I guess."

"Are you getting professional help?"

Genevieve told her about the appointment she'd made with Dr. Quinley. "I'll know more about how you can support me after I meet with her."

"Do you want me to go with you? To the appointment?"

"I think I'd like to go alone."

"Who else knows about this?"

"My publicist, Sam Turner, and now you."

Natasha didn't condemn her, but Genevieve could hear the unsaid words reverberating in the space between them: *"Why didn't you tell me?"* Not only could Genevieve understand that question, she could empathize with the hurt behind it. She'd have been hurt, too, if Natasha had hidden a hardship like this from her. In keeping silent, Genevieve had betrayed the closeness of their relationship, and they both knew it.

"I'm really sorry I didn't tell you," Genevieve said. "At first, it didn't seem like a big deal because I thought I could quit the pills at any time. It wasn't until recently that I realized I was in trouble."

Natasha nodded. "When are you going to tell Mom and Dad?"

"I don't know. Right now, it's hard enough to resist popping pills to make myself feel better. I can't think about coming clean to them at this point." Her mom already worried about her constantly. If Genevieve gave her this — very real — thing to worry about, Mom would likely become unbearable.

"They should know about this," Natasha said.

"I just . . . can't."

A long, fraught gap of quiet opened. The other thing Genevieve couldn't do right now? Continue talking about this. This topic made her feel like she'd been pinned naked to a clothesline near a busy street. She was willing to do just about anything to shift Natasha's attention, so she returned her chair to its place. "I say we start snooping around."

"Gen?"

"We can talk more about my recovery later, okay? That's sort of all I can manage at the moment."

Natasha considered her.

"Can we talk about the search we're about to undertake? Please?" Genevieve asked.

"If you insist."

"I do."

"In that case, what's our plan of attack for this morning?"

"I say we go through Dad's files and Mom's albums and memory boxes."

"Looking for?"

Genevieve shrugged. "Clues to their hidden past."

"I don't think we're going to find anything. I still think someone sent you that letter to mess with you."

"Possibly. It's just that when I talked to Mom and Dad about it over breakfast, I'm telling you, something was off. If the letter writer knows facts about them that we don't, I'd like to find out what we're dealing with before a stranger goes public."

"Are you sure this is the best time to be launching an investigation into our mother and father?" Natasha looked doubtful. "You're dealing with plenty right now."

"I'll feel better once I know what's going on. I really don't want to be blindsided." As soon as she said the words, conviction boomeranged into her. She'd just blindsided Natasha.

"All right, then." Natasha opened one of Dad's files. "I'm assuming that we're searching for something that occurred before they moved to Misty River?"

"Yes."

104

"Because it's hard to imagine them pulling off something secretive here."

"Agreed." Their parents had settled in Misty River shortly after their wedding. It strained believability to think that they'd covered up a secret that had occurred in their small Georgia hometown.

"I say we start as far back in time as possible," Natasha said, "and move forward. I'll handle the filing cabinet."

"I'll handle the albums." Genevieve retrieved as many as she could carry and settled on the office floor with them so she could be near her sister while they worked.

These albums, with their black paper pages and black-and-white photos held in place with photo corners, were the oldest of the lot. Nanny, their dad's mother, had carefully filled them with pictures of Dad when he was small.

The first album contained baby and toddler photos. The second album began around the time he'd gone to kindergarten. There were pictures of Judson on his first day of school wearing a buzz cut and a collared shirt. Pictures of him standing proudly in his tidy bedroom, with its precisely made bed, meticulous bookshelves, methodically organized action figures, and cowboy lampshade. Pictures of him with missing front

105

teeth and his birthday cake.

She saw nothing that would indicate her dad had experienced anything less than the stable, all-American childhood she'd known him to have.

Every once in a while, Natasha would murmur under her breath or drink from her travel mug. Genevieve would hum or catch Natasha's attention to show her an old artifact she'd uncovered.

After the things she'd just divulged to her sister, the companionship that usually came very naturally to the two of them felt fragile. Genevieve was having to work for it, and "fake it till you make it" required effort that sapped her energy.

She glanced at her sister's bent head. The line of her neck and profile were sweetly familiar.

Ever since Genevieve had caught up to Natasha's height, people had asked them if they were twins. The question should have been insulting to Genevieve, the younger sister. Instead, she took it as a compliment. Though the family resemblance was very strong between them, Genevieve had always thought Natasha to be the prettier sister.

They both had hazel eyes, ivory skin, and their mother's cheekbones. When they were young, they'd had matching golden blond hair, but their hair had darkened during their college years. Nowadays, Natasha highlighted hers to keep it light. She either wore it in a ponytail or parted down the middle, tucked behind her ears, the ends breezing against the base of her throat.

Genevieve's features sloped to a pointy chin, giving her a narrower but still heart-shaped face. Natasha's face was more square, her jawline pronounced.

Genevieve's body introduced her as someone who had thin genes but very little muscle. Natasha's body introduced her as someone who began every day by walking, a la Elizabeth Bennet.

There were differences between them in temperament and personality, too.

Genevieve was an extrovert. Natasha, an introvert.

Genevieve was passionate. Natasha, steady.

Genevieve felt things deeply. Natasha reacted to things with practicality.

Genevieve second-guessed and worried. Natasha cut a path through life with certainty.

Both were driven, high-achievers. Natasha metabolized stress well. Genevieve did not.

Both of them knew that their sister had their back.

After the earthquake, when Mom had become overprotective, their family's dynamic shifted. It was no longer one sister competing with the other for the attention of their parents but both sisters commiserating as a team against their mom.

"Nada," Natasha announced almost two hours after they'd started searching. "I can't find anything amiss."

"Me neither."

No clues.

No suspicious items or documents.

Since their mother's powers of observation could have been a great asset to Scotland Yard, Genevieve and Natasha put everything back *exactly* as they'd found it.

"Do you now believe that Mom and Dad are as normal as they seem?" Natasha asked as they walked downstairs.

"No." After sitting on the floor, Genevieve's bad ankle had stiffened. She paused to shake it out and continued down carefully.

"What's our next step?" Natasha asked.

"I think I'll see if I can find records on them. I went online and hunted around a little after the letter arrived. I couldn't find anything then, but I'm willing to give it a more thorough try."

"A lot of counties haven't made their

records available online. Rabun County records are stored in a building in downtown Clayton. You may have to stop at a few different offices inside. One for vital records. Another for court records." Natasha had been a practicing family law attorney until three years ago, when her oldest was born and she chose to stay home with her.

"In that case, I'll head to Clayton." Clayton was less than twenty minutes from Misty River.

Natasha held the front door open, and they made themselves comfortable on the porch's wicker chairs as they waited for their mom to return with Natasha's kids.

"I want to come see your cottage," Natasha said.

"Come by after this."

" 'Kay. We won't be able to stay long because the all-important nap time beckons, and I'd rather swallow glass than miss nap time."

"Yes. I know this about you."

Natasha poured the last of the liquid from her mug into a potted plant. "You know, Mom can't decide whether to be thrilled that you're spending the next few months in Misty River or despondent over the fact that you're staying at the cottage and not with her."

"I do know."

"What do you think of your landlord?"

The mention of Sam triggered a picture of him from last night, standing in front of her. Those grave features spoke of caution. His body, of easy strength. Mentally, she clasped the image to herself, dwelling on it because it filled her with warm pleasure. "I think he's very . . . direct. But he seems to have a good heart."

"He's hunky."

"You think so?"

"Of course I do. I haven't officially met him yet, but I've seen him at his restaurant. I think he's hunky, and you think he's hunky, too. As you should."

"But you shouldn't because you're married."

"I'm a married person with twenty-twenty vision and there's just *something* about Sam Turner."

"We struck a bargain when he agreed to rent the cottage to me, and his final condition was that I not fall for him."

Natasha's mouth sagged open. "You're kidding."

"No."

Natasha snorted. "That's preposterous!

Objectively speaking, you're a nine out of ten."

"May you receive a crown in heaven for your tremendous generosity —"

"Yeah, yeah," Natasha interrupted good-naturedly. "You're a nine, so it seems narcissistic of him to assume you'd want to fall for him."

"I think it was past experience more than narcissism that motivated that condition. Maybe women throw themselves at his feet all the time and it's becoming a distraction?"

"Possibly," Natasha allowed. "Single, good-looking men are as rare around here as Captain Ahab's white whale."

"Well, this white whale isn't interested in me. Which is for the best, because I'm clearly not in a good enough place to embark on a romance at the moment."

Mom's five-year-old Lexus sedan pulled into the driveway. Genevieve and Natasha crossed the lawn to her.

"Make way for Aunt Genevieve." Playfully, she elbowed Natasha behind her so that she could open the rear door and unbuckle her beautiful little niece and nephew from their car seats. She scooped them up, one in each arm, and gave them loud smacking kisses on their necks until they laughed. She exclaimed over the cuteness of their pink-cheeked cherub faces.

Natasha had attended Belmont University ahead of Genevieve. From there, she'd gone on to law school, where she'd met Wyatt MacKenzie. Red-haired and genuinely friendly, Wyatt had provided Natasha with a winning ticket in the dating lottery. He was a fan of all things Star Wars, but he was an even bigger fan of Natasha.

No slouch in the decision-making department, Natasha had married Wyatt at the age of twenty-six. At twenty-nine, she'd had their first baby. Three-year-old Millie was imaginative and social. Like her father, she'd taken to Star Wars. She also, more inexplicably, had taken to cows. When Millie wasn't wearing Han Solo garb or toting a lightsaber, she dressed in cow-themed items. Today's cow offering: a pair of boots covered in faux cowhide.

Owen, who'd recently celebrated his first birthday, tended toward quiet and serious. He typically had either a ball or a package of crackers clasped in his tiny dimpled hand.

When Owen had been born blond just like his sister, Natasha had whispered to Genevieve that she was probably going to have to go for a third because she could hardly marry a red-haired man and accept zero ginger-haired babies in return. Genevieve had no doubt that, before all was said and done, her determined sister would receive her ginger-haired offspring.

There were times — at Natasha's wedding, on the days Natasha had announced her pregnancies — when Genevieve had struggled to quash her envy toward her sister. Ultimately, though, Genevieve liked Natasha too much to stew in that emotion for long.

"I missed you!" Genevieve exclaimed to her niece and nephew. It struck her that she'd been taking Oxy about as long as Owen had been alive. Looking into his face, she wondered if she'd missed any crucial details of his or Millie's lives because of her painkiller haze.

"We missed you, too!" Millie answered, placing her hands on Genevieve's cheeks.

"Ball," Owen told her, cautiously opening his fingers to reveal a small hacky sack.

"*I* missed you," Mom said. "It's been so long."

"You came by the cottage to check on me yesterday morning," Genevieve replied.

"Surely it's been longer than that. Come inside so we can visit."

"Actually, Natasha and the kids are going to stop by the cottage so they can take a look. Would you like to join us?"

"I'll join you if you're sure that I won't be a third wheel." The look in Mom's eyes reminded Genevieve of a malnourished kitten.

Natasha was more matter-of-fact and bolder with their mother. She didn't cater to Mom's neediness nor hesitate to articulate clear limits. Life would be simpler for Genevieve if she could be more like Natasha.

"Of course you won't be the third wheel," Genevieve assured her. "Let's all go."

Natasha loaded her kids into her own car.

Mom climbed into the passenger seat of Genevieve's Volvo.

"Did you have fun at the museum?" Genevieve asked when they were on their way.

"It was a precious time. Millie, bless her, was so sweet to Owen, bless him. I'll treasure this day every minute of my life."

"Great."

"The role of grandmother is such a sacred gift. I know of no other heart-to-heart relationship as tender, other than that of mother and daughter."

"Mmm."

"Now that Owen is walking, though, it's challenging to keep up with both of them at once. I don't dare take my attention off of

114

them for even half a millisecond."

Lest an earthquake swallow them. Genevieve's brain inserted the rest of the sentence.

"I want to know everything you've been up to yesterday afternoon and this morning, sweetie," Mom said. "Don't leave anything out."

Sam had spent a fair amount of time at psychologists' offices, back when he'd been trying to deal with everything that had gone down with Kayden. Now here he was, once again inside a psychologist's office, remembering just how dark his days had been during the year he'd been paralyzed by grief.

He stood near the waiting room's door, hands in his pockets.

Gen sat on the sofa, looking at a magazine. She'd invited him to sit, but he'd declined. He'd driven her here, and his goal was simply to wait until her name was called and he'd watched her walk into the psychologist's office. Then he'd head to The Kitchen, just a mile from here, and catch up on office work until he needed to drive her home.

This practice was small. One secretary for one counselor. At the moment, the secretary's attention was centered on her computer as she tapped her keyboard.

The door to the doctor's office abruptly swung open, emitting an older man and woman. The man said his good-byes and left. Sam assumed the remaining woman was Dr. Kai Quinley. "Genevieve," she said affectionately.

The two hugged, then tried to outdo each other with their *It's so good to see you*s.

The doctor's blond-gray hair curled outward and upward in every direction. Her square face was tanned, lined, and without makeup. She looked to Sam like someone who'd probably been at Woodstock back in the day.

He edged toward the commercial building's hallway.

"Come in, come in," Dr. Quinley said to Gen. Then her vision snagged on him. "Are you here with Genevieve?" she asked warmly.

"Sort of."

"Lovely. Sir, please," she called, beckoning him forward with a deep, easy smile. "Join us."

Something like horror bolted down his chest. He motioned toward the parking lot and his escape. "I'm just her ride."

"Come." She continued waving him forward. "Just for a few minutes. Please. I insist."

What in the world?

"I insist. Nothing to be concerned about. C'mon."

Reluctantly, he passed the secretary — still tapping her keyboard — and followed Gen into Dr. Quinley's office.

The room was decorated in furniture that would have been modern in the 1950s. Several plants hung from holders made from what looked like twisted white rope. Stacks of books and papers cluttered the desk. The second-story windows framed a view of an outdoor atrium at the center of the complex.

Instead of sitting behind her desk, Dr. Quinley selected one of the four leather and wood chairs positioned around a circular brass coffee table, like camp chairs around a bonfire. The doctor wore a loose shirt and pants. She tucked one of her moccasins underneath herself and began chewing on seeds she scooped from a small bowl. "What's your relationship?" Her brown eyes twinkled with interest.

He sat there stiffly, with no idea what to say.

"Um." Genevieve shot him a humorous glance. "One notch above strangers?"

"Oh?"

"Yes. You see, I broke into his cottage while under the influence of OxyContin. And . . . he found me there, sleeping in a pile of my own clothes wearing my robe backward." She started to giggle at the absurdity of it. "He searched my purse and found my Oxy, and it was mortifying. And then I realized I needed to get clean and asked him if I could rent his cottage, and he said no. So then I sort of stubbornly charmed him into it, and one of his conditions was that I get psychological counseling. Which, clearly, I *do* need. And he's —" her giggles increased — "a health nut so he very kindly brought me all kinds of organic GM whatever —"

"Non-GMO," he supplied. "I hate GMOs."

"Of course you do."

"And pesticides."

"Yes. Anyway, because of him, I survived on organic, non-GMO foods for a week while going through withdrawal." Tears of amusement fell over her eyelashes. "He drove me here because he doesn't trust me to follow through on our bargain. And that" — she swept out both arms like a conductor — "is our relationship."

Dr. Quinley placed her seed bowl in her

lap and threw back her head to laugh along with Gen.

Dr. Quinley might need psychological counseling.

"He's not very fond of me at all." Gen bent forward, a forearm across her stomach, shoulders shaking. "I think Sam views me as an enormous" — more giggles — "pain in the booty."

She wasn't wrong. Yet, he found he couldn't look away from her.

Gen was so . . . vivid. He'd been living in a black-and-white world. She was Technicolor. Her shirt was bright pink against the fall of all that hair. Light sparkled against her big gold earrings. Her pretty face creased with uncontrollable laughter.

Humor tugged at his own lips in response. He gave in to a small smile.

Dr. Quinley continued to laugh. "In all my years of counseling, this is a first."

"We've managed to shock my counselor, Sam." More crazy giggles. "Congratulations!"

"Congratulations, Gen," he replied.

"I told my sister about the Oxy yesterday," she said to Dr. Quinley. "But why in the world would I want to bring her here, when I can have my disgruntled landlord here with me instead?" Gen wiped her eyes.

119

"Whew!"

"Laughter is good medicine," the doctor stated.

"My emotions are taking me on such a ride! Every minute of the day, I feel like I'm on the verge of crying or laughing."

"That's normal at this stage."

Sam wasn't convinced that *normal* and *Genevieve* belonged in the same sentence. Still, he was having trouble focusing on the doctor and not on Gen.

"How do you feel about everything Genevieve just said, Sam?"

He snapped his attention to Dr. Quinley. "I feel it was pretty accurate. Can I go?"

The doctor regarded him as if he'd said something delightful. "Not just yet. We're having too much fun."

He looked from side to side, wondering if he was being filmed secretly for a show that pranked people. Was this a setup?

"Tell me about your Oxy usage," the doctor said.

Gen gave her a recap of the past year.

"And you took your last pill on which day?" Dr. Quinley asked.

"August nineteenth."

"Well done, Genevieve. And you, Sam! I have to compliment you on the support you've given Genevieve, and, of course, on the non-GMO foods. Excellent call." Dr. Quinley drew her other foot under herself so that she now looked to be doing a yoga pose on the chair. She wore an irregularly shaped piece of sea glass on the hard silver circle of her necklace. "What we're working toward now, as a team, is assisting Genevieve as she strives to reach the ninety-day mark."

Why was the doctor including him in Genevieve's "team"? He couldn't afford to get any more involved with her recovery than he already was.

"You've been free of opioids for ten days now," Dr. Quinley continued. "Eighty days free of opioids to go. If we can make it to that important mark, your chance of relapse will decrease sharply, and your brain chemistry will have likely found its balance." She crunched some seeds. Hunger twanged inside Sam's stomach. How come he and Genevieve didn't get snack bowls?

"Opioids turn off dopamine," the doctor informed them. "Dopamine's a neurotransmitter. It regulates emotional responses, among other things. Thirty days into your recovery, some of your dopamine will get back to work. At sixty days, even more. At ninety days, it should all be back at work and clicking right along." She snapped the fingers of both upraised hands. When he expected her to drop her hands, she didn't. The snapping formed a pattern. " 'Like a bridge over troubled water,' " she sang, smiling, in time to the beat.

The psychologists who'd treated Kayden and him back in the day had been very serious people. They hadn't sung Simon and Garfunkel.

"You're awesome," Genevieve announced.

"*You're* awesome." The doctor seemed to mean every syllable. Unlike him, Kai Quinley was comfortable voicing affection. She set aside her bowl, planted her moccasins on the carpet, and leaned forward. "Every day will get a little bit easier than the last. But we can't ever underestimate the power that these narcotic medicines have to draw us back in. Tremendous power. Are you tracking with me?"

"I'm tracking," Genevieve told her.

"We'll need to be very careful today, tomorrow, the next day, and every day after that."

"What do you recommend I do?"

The older woman began counting things off on her fingers. "If I'm going to help you, I'll need you to be totally honest with me."

"All right."

"You'll have to take exceptionally good

care of yourself, mentally and physically. Healthy food, exercise, water, sleep. Those things will quicken your body's ability to rid itself of the drugs."

"Without Oxy, I'm not sleeping well. At all."

"Then we need to address that immediately. We'll collaborate with your primary care doctor to make sure you're able to rest."

She counted off the next point. "You'll need support from friends and family. The more the better, which is why it's so, so good that Sam's here for you."

"I'm the guy who's one notch above a stranger," he felt duty-bound to point out.

"What's my favorite phrase, Genevieve?"

"It takes a village."

"That's right. It takes a village, Sam. You're *here*, and that says a lot."

He was only in this room because she'd forced him.

"Next, we don't want you spending too much time alone right now. It's harder to resist cravings when alone because you might begin to feel miserable and lonely and obsess over worries."

"Check, check, and check," Genevieve said.

"We'll carve out a daily schedule for you

to follow," the doctor said.

"I'm sure Sam will volunteer to keep me company," Genevieve joked.

"Uh . . ."

"Yes! We all need to remember that this process isn't about quitting Oxy. It's about getting to the heart of the things that triggered you to rely on Oxy in the first place. And it's about recreating your life. Oxy will leave a void. We'll work to fill that void with other and better things. And last but not least, we'll be conscientious about celebrating the good." She started the snapping again. " 'Like a bridge over troubled water,' " she sang. "Join me!"

Genevieve joined her.

It was more likely for Sam to swim the freestyle at the next Olympics than join in this sing-along.

"We're going to celebrate every single accomplishment," the doctor said, still swaying and snapping. "Every choice you make that helps you avoid relapse is worth valuing and acknowledging." The doctor turned a broad grin on Sam. "You may go now."

Within half a second, he was out the door.

Three days later, Genevieve rapped on the door leading from Sam's laundry room to the rest of his farmhouse.

124

While she'd been sick, her mom had carted her dirty clothing to the house on Swallowtail Lane and brought it back in carefully folded stacks that smelled like Tide. That service had ended, so Genevieve had reached out to Sam and he'd granted her laundry privileges at his house.

As prearranged, she'd found the key to the back door under a rock near the side porch steps. She'd let herself through the exterior door that ushered directly into the laundry room. The door at the room's far end — the one she knocked on again now — was locked.

She hadn't intended to disturb Sam.

Well . . . she may have intended to bang the appliance lids a little, to see if he was interested in coming by for a chat. But she hadn't planned on knocking. He'd given her no other option, however, because something was very wrong with his laundry room.

Surely he'd recovered enough from the trauma of her initial meeting with Dr. Quinley to answer the door —

She heard footsteps approaching and stepped back.

The knob lock gave a *shnick,* and then Sam stood before her. He looked more bemused than annoyed, which she took as an excellent sign.

"May I help you?" he asked.

"I hope so. I'm confused."

"Because?"

"Because . . ." She extended a hand toward the gaping empty space next to the washing machine. "You have no dryer."

"An excellent observation."

"How do you dry your clothes?"

"The Australian way. In other words, the best way." He sailed past her onto the porch. "Come."

She followed him down the side porch steps and around to the back of his house, where an umbrella-style clothesline sprouted from the ground. She stared at it, openmouthed. "I . . . thought these went extinct in the 1950s." Not once in her life had she dried clothes on a line. It was becoming rare even to spot an outdoor clothesline. Whenever she did so, the sight struck her as quaintly old-fashioned.

"My dryer broke a year ago, and I didn't replace it. I like the way clothes smell when they dry outside. This is better for the environment and less expensive. I've never understood why Americans love dryers."

It would be one thing if he'd been unable to afford a new dryer. But he actually . . . preferred this route? "We love them because they're so convenient. When you pull clothes

126

out of the dryer, they're all warm and toasty."

"Clothes aren't supposed to get that warm." He looked at her, his chin set.

"I can see that your anti-dryer stance is as ironclad as my pro-dryer stance."

"It is."

"I don't know if we can be friends, after this," she said wryly.

"We're friends?"

She laughed. "I was hoping so."

He headed back to the house, her trailing behind. "North Korea and South Korea marched together a few years ago at the Olympics," he pointed out. "So there might still be hope for us."

"I'm not so sure. Our difference seems even more fundamental than theirs."

Inside the laundry room, he handed her the basket of clothespins. "Here you go, North Korea."

"Why don't I get to be South Korea?" she asked.

"Because you're the one in the wrong."

"I . . ." But he was already gone, stealing her chance at a zingy comeback. The door to his house shut behind him.

Later, she discovered that she did not enjoy wrestling wet fabric onto clotheslines. When she saw people in movies pinning and unpinning clothing, it looked meditative, at the very least.

The breeze slapped her in the face with a sleeve.

This was not meditative.

Also, did he expect her to hang her underwear out here in full view of him? No thank you. Yet, if he didn't spot any underwear, would he deduce that she didn't wear any?

After a good deal of internal debate, she decided that hanging her underwear in full view was the greater of two evils.

She drove her damp lingerie back to the cottage and draped it over every available surface. Her panties hung from the mantel like depressed Christmas stockings. A bra sagged from her armoire's doorknob.

She might be detoxing, but she'd recovered her mind enough to ascertain that Mr. Australia was wrong about this.

Clotheslines stunk. Clothes dryers were the bomb.

"Genevieve Woodward is renting my guesthouse," Sam told his friend Eli Price the next day.

Eli's chin swung in his direction. His eyebrows rose. "She is?"

"Yeah."

Sugar Maple Kitchen's usual rush hour

128

noises surrounded them. Conversation, cutlery tapping against plates, ice water pouring into glasses. They sat side by side on two of the stools that lined a portion of the bar.

"You know who she is, right?" Eli asked. "Genevieve?"

Trouble waiting to happen. "Judson and Caroline Woodward's daughter. A Bible study author."

"And?" Eli prompted with an expression that told Sam he expected more.

"That's all I know."

Eli was a fighter pilot stationed at Ricker Air Force Base. They'd met at the gym soon after they'd both moved to town. Eli had been raised in Montana, Sam hadn't. Eli had dark blond hair, Sam didn't. Otherwise, they were close in age, size, and athleticism. They'd become friends over weekly games of pick-up basketball. They'd often gone to Cubby's to play pool or to The Junction for fried chicken or Pablo's for their Taco Tuesday special. Eli had invited Sam over to watch the NFL a few times. Sam had invited Eli and Eli's girlfriend, Penelope, over to watch his footy team, Hawthorn, play the greatest game on earth — Aussie Rules football. Eli drove to The Kitchen once or twice a week to eat breakfast.

"Genevieve is one of the Miracle Five," Eli said. "There's Genevieve and her sister, Natasha. Sebastian Grant, Ben Coleman, and Luke Dempsey. Genevieve's the youngest. Sebastian and Ben are a year older. Natasha and Luke are a year older than them."

Sam's brain spun. He'd thought he'd been doing well to pair Gen with the correct parents.

He'd moved to Misty River after the town's successful rebranding as a tourist destination for city residents interested in a mountain getaway. He often struggled to grasp connections between people that everyone else had no trouble grasping. Likely because he spent so much time alone on his farm.

He'd been a teenager living on his stepdad's station when the earthquake in El Salvador had become worldwide news. Shortly after arriving in Misty River, he'd learned that the Miracle Five were hometown kids. Amazingly, the five of them had survived a catastrophe that a tremendous number of people hadn't, and their story was a point of pride for everyone who lived around here. The Miracle Five were a part of Misty River's heritage, just like mining for gold and land lotteries.

At the smoothie shop down the road, a framed newspaper article about the Miracle Five hung on the wall next to the cash register. One of the floats in Misty River's Fourth of July parade always commemorated the Miracle Five. Miracle Five Childcare's logo depicted cartoon kids walking hand-in-hand toward the sun.

Sam knew the basics of the Miracle Five story, but he'd never had a reason to research its details. The whole thing seemed more removed from him than from those who'd lived through it here in Misty River.

It wasn't removed from him now.

He stared at Eli, thinking about an adolescent version of Gen, trapped underground by an earthquake.

The woman was taking up way too much space in his head. He drove by the guesthouse several times a day. He saw her car coming and going. He felt her presence. He caught himself gnawing on concerns about her. "I didn't know that Gen was one of the kids."

"Yeah." Eli chewed a bite of bacon. He'd ordered the farmhouse scramble. The second — and final — espresso Sam would allow himself today sat before him on the bar.

"They were there on a mission trip, right?" Sam asked.

"Right. Their church organized a junior high mission trip. About twenty kids, plus a few pastors and chaperones, flew to El Salvador. They were scheduled to help run a week-long sports camp for kids there. At the end of the second day of the camp, one of the pastors asked some of the kids to return sports equipment to the basement of a nearby building."

"What building?"

"It belonged to the charity the church was partnering with. It was tall and old. Built of concrete. The kids were in the basement when a 7.8 earthquake hit."

In high school, Sam had been too irresponsible to fold his laundry and too lazy to do anything except play video games once he finished his homework and his long list of chores. He couldn't imagine how he would've responded, at that age, to a natural disaster.

Eli loaded his fork with veggies and eggs. "Around here, the Miracle Five are still considered different and special. Whenever one of them walks into a room, you can bet that the first thing anyone's thinking is that they're one of the Miracle Five, even though none of them have spoken about it publicly in years."

"Why?"

Eli shrugged. "I don't know. You'll have to ask Genevieve."

Sam took a sip of coffee.

"Those Bible studies Genevieve writes are popular," Eli commented.

"How popular?" Sam found it hard to believe that women were racing out to buy books written by someone who wore her robe backward.

"They're bestsellers. She films teaching videos that go along with her studies, and she speaks at women's events. She can easily fill a megachurch every time she gives a talk."

Sam eyed Eli with surprise.

"Take it from me," Eli said. "She's extremely successful."

Genevieve

Suddenly, terribly, the walls in the room begin to lean inward.

We rush to the middle as the walls on opposite sides tip toward each other. All five of us crouch on the wrecked floor, which continues to jerk back and forth, back and forth, back and forth.

I lace one arm through Natasha's and cover my head with my other.

A grinding *crash* sounds, and I look up to see that the walls have hit each other, forming a triangle above our heads.

I can't get enough air into my chest.

How long will the walls stay like that? Propped against each other? Seconds?

And then, suddenly, the earthquake ends.

The ground is stable again, but the building isn't. It's still collapsing around us in slow motion.

CHAPTER SIX

If a girl was going to spend time farming, it was best to begin with a thick layer of good-quality, non-pore-clogging sunscreen and a ponytail. That pretty much summed up Genevieve's knowledge of farming.

Even so, she was walking from her cottage to Sam's house on this blustery afternoon because she was determined to help Sam with his garden. For two reasons.

One, she'd told him she'd assist around the farm back when they'd negotiated their rental agreement. Until today, she'd been feeling too lethargic to follow through. But a deal was a deal.

Two, she needed conversation. Two weeks had passed since her first appointment with Dr. Quinley. At that appointment, they'd crafted a daily schedule that Genevieve had been carefully following ever since. Wake. Eat. Go for a thirty-minute power walk around the farm. Shower. Work. Leave the cottage to eat lunch at a public place. Finish workday at public place. Hang out with others. Pursue life-giving hobbies. Take sleep medicine so she could rest. Meet with Dr. Quinley weekly.

The "work" part of the schedule had been limping along. Eight months ago she'd committed to submit a new Bible study, due to her publisher four months from now. She'd organized and added to her notes, fine-tuned her outline for the chapters she still had to write, conducted research, and crafted a writing timeline. She was making progress, but sans Oxy, the progress was like walking through waist-high snow.

The "hang out with others" part of the schedule had been the most helpful piece. She'd been spending time with one or both of her parents, Natasha, Natasha's kids, or her Misty River friends. When laughing, shopping, playing with her niece and nephew, or talking over a meal, she felt closest to normal.

But then, back at the cottage afterward, she'd crash. She was spending every bit of energy she had resisting her intense cravings for Oxy and hauling her body through the daily schedule. By the time she completed it, she had nothing left. Certainly no enthusiasm for "life-giving hobbies." Each night she collapsed into her love seat and attempted to concentrate on a romantic movie and not on her deep feelings of sorrow (and how effectively Oxy could wipe them away).

Some nights she did a better job of coexisting with the sorrow than other nights. On her good nights, she'd dance and sing along to her favorite rap and hip-hop songs as she dressed for bed. Nicki Minaj and Iggy Azalea could be trusted to lift her mood.

On her bad nights, like last night, she'd weep in the shower and wonder, *Is depression the reward I get for sobriety?*

Every day she prayed. And prayed. And continued to seek a peace she could not find.

She'd made it to day twenty-four and was committed to making it to day ninety. Then onward, through the rest of her life, without ever reverting to Oxy. She understood that Oxy was like an island that she must *never* revisit.

Yet she didn't exactly love the island she was currently living on, either. She longed to feel like herself again. She longed for the Oxy high that had softened the edges of everything.

As August dissolved toward mid-September, she'd begun texting Sam with questions about the upcoming Fall Fun Days. She'd been using his washing machine as loudly as possible, in hopes that he'd hear and respond by coming by to talk.

He hadn't. Which meant that she hadn't spoken to him face to face in a week and a half.

She couldn't quite explain it, but she . . . missed him. And it wasn't that she just missed general human interaction — her daily schedule mandated that happened.

There was just something about him. About Sam.

Approaching his house, she noted that his truck was nowhere in sight. Which meant he wasn't at home. The realization demoralized her far more than it should have.

That's just the lack of dopamine talking, Genevieve. Focus on the good.

This farm. This farm was *good*.

She paused between the farmhouse and the barn, which was set to the side and well back from the house.

The clapboard farmhouse wore a fresh coat of white paint. Its prominent covered porch ran along the front and sides of the first floor. Enormous pots of flowers stood between the downstairs windows, windows that were almost as large as the door. Dormer windows marked the upper floor.

Sam had painted the barn the same slate gray as the farmhouse shutters. As Genevieve made her way into the barn in search of gardening supplies, the scent of apples enveloped her. Her eyes adjusted to take in the hulking shapes of a tractor, a riding lawn mower, two ATVs, and numerous wooden bins. Every item within the barn appeared scrupulously clean. The gardening tools were all tidily arranged near the front of the space.

She supposed the term *happy chaos* would be lost on Sam. He didn't seem the type to leave a dish towel on the floor or fling dirty clothes over chairs.

She selected gloves, a handheld spade, and a long shovel. Might these do the trick? Did she even want to attempt the kind of gardening that required more than this?

She walked down the sweep of land from the barn to the garden, eyes squinting toward the drive in search of Sam's almond-colored Dodge Ram.

When sick, she'd been unaware of the galaxy beyond the walls of the cottage. Over the past week, she'd become a very nosy neighbor. Each time his truck rumbled by her cottage, she wondered where he was going, where he'd been, how he was doing. During the long stretches when no one drove that road she wondered why. Where were his friends? Business associates? Employees?

As far as she was aware, no one had used that road in the last week but her and Sam.

The evidence suggested that Sam was more alone, *much more alone,* than she'd realized. She'd asked him once if he got lonely, and he'd said no. However, she'd been living and working in the cottage for just a short time and already she comprehended the profound quiet of these acres.

Pushing up the sleeves on her baseball-style shirt, she knelt in an area of the garden that looked suitably weedy. Within ten seconds, she wished for some sort of pad to cushion her knees and protect her jeans. She had on her oldest, most casual pair. But even these couldn't be considered work pants.

She weeded. Moved down the row. Weeded some more.

When she heard the rumble of a car's engine, foolish hope jumped into her throat. She raised her head in time to see Sam's truck through the tree line.

When he drew even with her, she waved with her whole arm. She probably looked like a stranded person flagging down a plane. But honestly, that's kind of how she felt. If he kept on driving and didn't stop, she'd chase him down, intercept him before he entered his house, and wring as much conversation from him as he'd allow.

He brought the truck to a stop, thank you, Jesus. Then made his way toward her position.

He'd donned his baseball cap and an extremely soft-looking navy shirt. The shirt wasn't tight at all. Loose, even. However, the very thin fabric accentuated the easy strength of his torso. No doubt he'd pulled the shirt on without giving it a thought. He wasn't *trying* to look sexy, which was part of his appeal.

Sam wore his clothes — and his personality, for that matter — with understated confidence. She frequently wondered what others thought of her, but she'd bet Sam almost never did.

"Are your pants made out of twill?" she asked.

He regarded her with confusion tinged with amusement as he neared. "What kind of question is that?"

"An honest one?"

"I have no idea what my pants are made of."

"Well, I think they're made of twill. That makes three things I know about farming."

141

He didn't bother to ask what the first two things were, robbing her of the opportunity to tell him about sunscreen and ponytails.

He peered down, obviously assessing her efforts.

"I've simply been pulling weeds," she told him. "I figured I couldn't go wrong pulling weeds."

"Right. Except these" — his work boot nudged a pile of shoots she'd uprooted — "are chives."

"Oh!" She looked from the chives to him and started to laugh. "I'm sorry."

"Apparently, you can go wrong pulling weeds."

"Yes. It seems that way. My apologies. Perhaps we can replant the poor chives?"

"Doubtful."

"I'll do it —"

"Allow me," he responded firmly, dropping to his knees. The disapproving grimace he sent her incited a giggle. She knew he already thought her unbalanced. Another fit of the giggles like she'd had at Dr. Quinley's wasn't going to improve her standing in his eyes.

"Are you sure you're feeling up to gardening?" he asked.

"Yes. I told you that I'd help in your garden, and I'm a woman of my word."

"Your use of the word *help* is debatable."

"Touché."

"I didn't expect you to start volunteering for me this soon." His attention settled on the soil he was working. "I don't want your health suffering because you're pushing yourself too hard."

"If either of us is in danger of pushing themselves too hard physically, I don't think that person's me. Before Dr. Quinley's plan, the most strenuous exercise I got some days came from lifting Jelly Bellies to my mouth."

"So you're feeling good?" he asked after a time, seeming to need double confirmation.

"As good as can be expected."

"How about mentally? Emotionally?"

She ripped a small weed from the earth, minuscule clods of dirt clinging to its roots, then tossed it aside and met his eyes.

The sight of his masculine body against the backdrop of trees caused her to swallow. His neck ended in defined collarbones. His olive complexion turned his green eyes luminous. The breeze rustling through the plants carried snatches of the scent of his soap to her. He smelled like eucalyptus and sun.

She resumed pulling weeds the way she imagined a good farmer woman might in order to compose herself and buy time before answering his question.

Sam could clearly see that Gen didn't know what she was doing. She was yanking out weeds so violently that half the time, she was breaking them off and leaving the roots. The other half of the time, she was "weeding" actual produce.

"Hey," he said. "Steady on. Like this." He demonstrated, his movements careful, patient.

She imitated him.

They finished weeding the area before them and scooted down to work on the next section.

As usual, she was stealing all his peace. This garden should be his therapy. Only, not today. She'd overtaken every inch of it. And because she hadn't answered his question about her mental and emotional health, worry was now needling him.

Despite himself, he'd begun to hope that Gen would remain clean. He didn't want to hope in that, *couldn't* let himself hope in that, after what he'd gone through with Kayden. Each time, his hope had been demolished.

He took stock of her as they worked. Her skin was still pale, but no longer dull. Pink now brightened her cheeks. The dark shad-

144

ows under her eyes hadn't gone away, but they'd lessened. Her glossy hair swung down her back. She wore another pair of large earrings, which made no sense. Why would anyone garden in big earrings?

"So?" he asked. The word came out more demanding than he'd intended. "How are you feeling mentally and emotionally?"

A hesitation. "Decent."

"Just decent?"

"Isn't decent sufficient?"

"Yeah. I mean, I think it's normal not to feel okay right now." He continued his work, arguing with himself over whether or not to drop the subject. "Is something in particular bothering you?"

Taking a break from weeding, she plopped cross-legged onto the grass, facing him.

He sat, resting his forearms on his up-raised knees. He didn't want anything to do with her crazy. Why, then, was his heart thudding as he waited to hear what she was about to say?

"I could answer your question in numerous ways. In order to protect the last remaining shred of my pride, I'll tell you the one thing that's bothering me that's not actually *about* me."

"Okay."

"Something . . . weird is going on with

my family. It's sort of troubling."

Don't ask about it. Just go back to weeding and ignore it at all costs. "Tell me."

"I received a strange letter about my parents before I left Nashville."

"What did it say?"

"It said, 'I know what your parents did. And after all we've suffered, it's hard to watch you bask in your fame and money. Your parents aren't going to get away with it.' " Her lips pursed. "That's it."

"What did your parents say?"

"That the letter has no basis. But I believe that it does. So Natasha and I searched their house."

"Looking for?"

"Secrets."

"And?"

"We didn't find any."

Genevieve Woodward had a talent for jumping from the frying pan into the fire. No doubt, she'd spend her whole life like this. Rebounding from one drama into the next.

"But you're not going to give up," he guessed.

"No." She adjusted the gardening gloves she wore. They were his gloves, and seeing her wearing them distracted him so much that he lost his train of thought.

146

"I'm going to drive to Clayton tomorrow to see if I can find records on my parents," she said.

He didn't want her crisscrossing north Georgia on a wild-goose chase that was likely to upset her. If she got upset enough, she'd take Oxy, and he couldn't watch the progress she'd fought for ruined by a ridiculous letter. "I'll go with you," he heard himself say.

"To Clayton?"

"Yep."

"You will?"

"Yes," he said curtly, warning her with a glare not to ask follow-up questions.

"I'd like that." Her attention traced down his cheek to his lips.

Heat dove all the way through him, as hot as a comet. "Stop checking me out, Gen."

"Hmm?" Her hazel gaze jerked guiltily to his eyes.

"You can't fancy me, remember?"

"No, no. I wouldn't dream of it."

Sam's truck was no luxury vehicle, that was for sure. It had to be at least fifteen years old. A tree-shaped air freshener that read *Royal Pine* dangled from the rearview mirror and emitted a scent that might be piney but didn't strike Genevieve as royal. He kept his truck clean, just like all his other belongings, yet the vehicle gave off the impression of utility over comfort and age over beauty.

Earlier, when they'd met to embark on their trip to Clayton, she'd suggested that she drive, since she was the one on a mission to dig up her parents' past. Also, secretly, because she had a newer car. He'd insisted they take his truck. At which time, she'd offered to drive his truck. At which time, he'd told her she was insane if she thought he was going to let her drive his truck. They'd climbed into his Dodge, and he'd given the dashboard two fast, affectionate pats before turning the key in the ignition.

A cloudy afternoon sky watched over them as they zipped along the ribbon of highway past meadows, occasional roadside shops, and orchards. As it turned out, the passenger seat was the best seat in the house because it allowed her to study him as he drove.

His hat was gone, revealing thick, short-cut brown hair. Muscles, ligaments, and veins corded his forearms and wrists —

"I heard the other day that you're one of the Miracle Five," he said.

Regret burst the bubble of her musings.

She supposed she should feel grateful that

148

it had taken him this long to learn of her status as a Miracle Fiver . . . but she couldn't quite manage gratitude. Sam hadn't viewed her as an oddity, at least any more so than her very odd actions had demanded. Now he likely would.

He sliced a brief look at her. "Why aren't you saying anything?"

"I suppose because I liked being just Genevieve with you."

"You're still just Genevieve with me. Why didn't you tell me that you were one of the Miracle Five?"

"When? In between my bouts of fever and vomiting?"

"Anytime would have been fine."

"I worried I wouldn't seem very miraculous to you while recovering from prescription drug withdrawal."

He didn't respond for several beats. "I was under the impression that God was the only miraculous one involved in the Miracle Five rescue," he finally said.

She flourished a hand in his direction. "Yes! Exactly. If you start expecting me to be miraculous, you'll be sorely disappointed."

"I don't plan to set myself up for disappointment."

"Good!" She consulted her phone's GPS.

149

"Take the next exit and turn left."

"I have questions."

"About the directions?"

"About the Miracle Five."

"I . . ." She straightened her posture. "I don't tend to answer questions about the earthquake."

"Why not?"

"Because two thousand people died. Thousands more were injured. Thousands more lost their homes. Police and firefighters risked their safety to save others. But somehow, even though we deserved the spotlight the least, we were the ones everybody wanted to talk to the most."

"And did you talk about it?"

"For two years straight."

"To?"

"At first, the news media. Then churches, so many I can't count them all. We talked to the author assigned to write the book about us. Documentary film producers. Movie producers. We spent two summers and all our school vacations traveling. When the movie about us came out, the four of us went to Los Angeles for interviews —"

"Hang on. What happened to the fifth?"

"Luke's always refused to be involved. With the media and with us. We tried to include him over and over, without success."

"Where is he now?"

"Prison." That hard word . . . that hard fate . . . sat between them like a landmine. As always when she thought of Luke, sorrow, love, and guilt knotted her stomach.

After a long moment, Sam spoke. "You were saying that the four of you went to LA."

"Right. We were together in a hotel room in LA one night and had a long discussion. We were only fourteen, fifteen, and sixteen, but we were mature enough — and maybe weary enough at that point — to agree that we'd spoken about the earthquake enough."

"How come?" He took the off-ramp, then eased to a stop at a red light, adjusting to assess her.

"Back when we started talking about the earthquake, it was obvious that God was giving us a chance to tell everyone what He'd done. Over time, though, we no longer felt a sense of peace about what we were doing. It seemed like the big corporations behind the book and the movie were only interested in making money. The travel and the attention put a strain on us and our families. Basically, God was telling us as a group to step back from it."

"Do people still ask you about it?"

"All the time. New acquaintances ask me

151

about it. Reporters and writers contact me about it. A producer reached out to me about it a week ago." She consulted her GPS.

"I know where we're going, Gen."

Should she trust him? Or was he the type of man who had a wretched sense of direction but always imagined he knew the way?

He delivered groceries and made bread. A grocery-delivering, bread-making man deserved the benefit of the doubt. She clicked off her phone.

The light turned green and the car slid forward. "You turned the producer down?" he asked.

"We all did. God hasn't let any of us know He wants us to start talking about it again. If He does let me know that, then I'll talk about it." She was holding on to her faith the way she'd hold on to a branch protruding from the sheer side of a canyon. She had to wonder, sometimes, if God was still holding on to her. Had He dropped her because she was too much bother?

Sam parked and set his wrist on top of the steering wheel.

He had the *most* endearing face. There was something mournful about his eyes. The rest of his features were serious and pensive. On those rare occasions when she'd seen him smile, solemnity and joy had collided into an explosive result.

She'd been talking about her natural disaster, but irrationally, she had an urge to comfort *him.*

The weight of his gaze warmed her skin like the heat from a fire. Her pulse ticked up. Her mouth went dry.

You're not stable enough to develop a crush at this particular catastrophic moment, Genevieve! She had a long way to go before she could even contemplate —

Abruptly, Sam exited the truck. He opened the passenger side door for her before she'd gathered her wits.

They walked side by side into the building that housed the records for their slice of northern Georgia. First stop, vital records.

An employee helped Genevieve access documents concerning her mom and dad. It didn't take long to confirm that everything was completely in order, just as it had been at her parents' house. No surprises. Nothing out of the ordinary.

They moved on to the probate office. This time, a middle-aged, red-haired clerk assisted them as they ran searches for court proceedings involving either Caroline or Judson Woodward.

"I don't see anything at all," the woman

153

told them with a smile. No doubt she imagined the lack of court proceedings against DA Judson Woodward must be good news.

In a way, it was. So far, the evidence proved her parents to be upstanding people without skeletons in their closet.

Genevieve thanked the woman, who left her and Sam alone at a utilitarian office table. Genevieve contemplated the textured ivory wall opposite her, trying to think.

Her judgment had been clouded by Oxy back when she'd received the threatening letter. Had it struck her as ominous because of the drugs in her system?

No. The drugs had helped her view everything in her life as less ominous, not more.

The letter hadn't upset Natasha the way it had upset Genevieve. So why had it had such a jarring effect on her?

Intuition.

It was the only explanation she had. Even now, in the face of today's dead end, she wasn't ready to call off the search.

"The two offices we've just visited," Sam said, "only have records for Rabun, Habersham, and Stephens Counties. Have your parents lived anywhere else?"

"Yes." She overlapped her hands on the table. "My mom grew up in Athens, and my dad grew up in Augusta. Then they both attended Mercer University in Macon. Their paths didn't cross there, though. My mom was a freshman when my dad was a senior."

"And then?"

"After he graduated, Dad went into the navy. After she graduated, Mom taught second grade for a year or two. Then she moved to Savannah and taught first grade there. By that time, my dad was in law school in Savannah. They met at a church social. He asked her out that night, and they've been together ever since."

"Did they move straight from Savannah to Misty River?"

She nodded. "They got married in Augusta while my dad was still in law school and my mom was still working in Savannah. After he passed the bar exam, a job offer brought them to Misty River." She considered their history. "Maybe I'll look at records next in my mom's hometown of Athens. It's the closest of all the places they've lived."

Sam followed her to the clerk's desk. The redhead raised her face with pleasant inquiry.

"Do you happen to know where I can find records for the city of Athens like the ones

155

you keep here?"

"Athens is in Clarke County, and that county's records are kept in the courthouse in Athens." She consulted her computer, then jotted down a phone number.

Genevieve checked her watch. Too late to head to Athens today. It would take her an hour and a half to get there, and it was already three forty-five on a Friday. She'd have to wait and travel to Athens on Monday — no, Tuesday. She and Natasha had made plans for an early lunch on Monday with Wyatt's mother.

The clerk slipped the number for the Athens courthouse across the counter to her.

She accepted it, glanced at Sam, and caught him watching her.

Her blood rushed in response.

Oh my.

This really wasn't good.

They made their way out of the building in the direction of his truck.

She'd been in love just once, during her college years. With a funny, confident fraternity president and baseball player named Thad. They'd dated for two years, and she'd been dreaming of marrying him when she'd learned that he'd cheated on her. Their

156

relationship had ended in a blast of shrapnel.

Since Thad, it was unusual for her to experience a pang of attraction as powerful as the one she'd just experienced for Sam.

Since Thad, she'd gone on what felt like hundreds of first dates and had pretty much exhausted the supply of single men her friends knew, were related to, or worked with. She'd liked many of the guys she'd met. She'd dated a couple of them for a handful of months.

But that elusive, mystical thing — *love* — had never revisited her again. Dauntless, she'd continued to dress up and stride into coffeehouses to shake hands with yet another new man a friend had assured her would be perfect for her.

But what if God had only given her one allotment of love . . . that she'd squandered on Thad? Or maybe, since God had already granted her a successful career, He didn't intend to give her love, too.

God had a sense of humor, yes. But knowing her heart and her history on the subject of men, surely, *surely* He would not have allowed her to meet a highly eligible man after taking too many painkillers and house-crashing a cottage, right at the most inopportune low point of her life.

God wouldn't dare do that to her. Would He?

158

Luke

My brother.

My brother had been pestering me, back on the soccer field. Ethan's talkative, and he's always asking a million questions. Every time I turn around, questions. It drives me crazy.

When today's sports camp ended and our youth pastor asked us to put away the sports equipment, Ethan was right behind me at the top of the stairs, asking questions. I couldn't deal. So I took him by the shoulders and steered him to the back of the line behind the other kids. "You're last," I told him, glad to put some space between him and me.

Now I'm here, in this wrecked room. The windows that should be pointing out at the sidewalk are pointing straight up at a bright blue sky.

And my brother isn't with me. Because

he was bugging me, and so I put him at the end of the line.

Is Ethan dead?

I moan with terror and regret and clasp my head to keep my brain from exploding. He can't be dead. He can't have been crushed by this building.

He has to be fine.

CHAPTER SEVEN

Vault.

The term *vault* tempted a person to conclude that the items stored within were of great value. Genevieve wondered if that would prove true in her case as she carried the item she'd just found inside the vault — a file on her mother — toward the reading room of Clarke County's courthouse.

The temperature outside today: chilly for the middle of September. The temperature inside the courthouse: pleasant. She liked today's furry vest, long-sleeved top, and wide leather earrings. Even her burgundy skinny pants were comfy, though every woman knew that it defied physics to use *skinny pants* and *comfy* in the same sentence.

She'd lain in bed at the cottage last night battling loneliness and struggling to fall asleep. She'd concentrated on Sam instead of the dark voices that kept trying to command her attention. She'd thought about his shoulders, his rare smile, his voice, his scent, his truck, his solitude. She replayed everything he'd ever said to her. She imagined him looking at her with those grave eyes.

It had taken ages before she'd at last nodded off, but at least she'd passed that time dwelling on someone who stoked a comforting glow inside.

She'd woken early, eaten granola for breakfast, and downed one cup of coffee at the cottage, then stopped for a latte en route. The caffeine had helped her energy level, but she could still feel the underlying weight of her tiredness. She blinked dry, scratchy eyes and focused on the folder she placed before herself on the small table. Her chair faced a sunlit window and a view of a tree covered in leaves that hadn't quite yet decided to turn color.

After providing ID to prove her relationship to her mother and thus her right to access the documents, she'd been entrusted with the file without incident.

Her mom, Caroline Harmon Herrington Woodward, was the daughter of parents who'd despaired of having children before suddenly conceiving in their late thirties. They'd lavished love on Caroline, their only child. Her traditional childhood had included the Southern pillars of Christianity, manners, and class.

Mom had paid her parents back for their devotion by living a life of excellent decisions. She'd been a Brownie in elementary school, a class officer in middle school, a member of the local junior charity board, cheerleading squad, and homecoming court in high school.

Both Genevieve's maternal grandparents had lived to the age of ninety. Both were now gone.

Reverently, she opened her mother's file. Instead of the birth certificate she'd expected to see, she took in the details of an application for a marriage license.

She stared at it blankly. Mom and Dad had been married in Augusta. Clearly, they must have applied for their license here —

Her vision snagged on the groom's name.

Russell Michael Atwell.

The world around Genevieve turned to smoke. All she could see were the letters printed so clearly and neatly on the page.

She checked her mother's name. Correct. She checked her mother's birth date. Correct. Her mother's parents' names. Correct.

She checked the groom's name. Russell Michael Atwell.

Who? Her heart drummed.

She'd never heard of this person.

This was only an application. Perhaps Mom had been engaged to a previous boyfriend and called things off.

Genevieve slid the application to the side, revealing what lay beneath. A marriage license. And below that, a marriage certificate.

For her mother and Russell Atwell. They'd been married on July 18, 1982. Mom had not called the wedding off. She'd gone through with it.

Mom had never breathed a word of this to her.

This couldn't be!

. . . And yet it was. This document proved a wedding had occurred.

Mom would have been twenty-two in 1982. Fresh out of college.

Her mom? Married to a man named Russell?

Did Dad know about this? What if he didn't? What if he thought he was Mom's first and only husband?

Genevieve placed a hand over her heart and waited for her body's clamor to calm.

Down in her soul, she'd known since the moment she'd received the anonymous letter that there was something to be found in

164

her parents' past. She'd driven to Athens today to chase that very suspicion. Even so, now that she'd uncovered a secret, she didn't want it to be true. Accepting this meant accepting that her family wasn't as she'd believed all her life.

At her third-grade Halloween parade, Mom had stood with the other parents, clapping and snapping photos. As Genevieve had walked by in the Mulan costume that she and Mom had worked on for two weeks, her mother had called out, "Go, Mulan! Girl power!" The sleeve of Genevieve's robe had slipped down to her shoulder as she'd raised her fist in acknowledgment. That costume had been her favorite of all time.

Later, in El Salvador, the curtain around Genevieve's hospital bed had jerked back and Genevieve had laid eyes on the two people she'd been desperate to see for days. Her mom and dad. Mom had looked so familiar to her in that moment and simultaneously different, too. Smaller, older, thinner. But when Mom had released a sob and wrapped Genevieve in a hug, her arms had communicated fierce strength.

Caroline had spent hours moving things into Genevieve's freshman dorm room at Belmont and arranging the decorations for maximum beauty and charm. When there was nothing left to do and it was time for her to go, Mom had stood in the middle of the room as if suddenly and totally lost. Her arms had dropped to her sides. "Oh, sweetie," she'd whispered. Tears had tumbled over her eyelashes.

They had such a long history, she and her mom. Genevieve was as accustomed to her mother as she was to anyone on earth. She comprehended her mom's foibles and virtues. She'd lived with her for the majority of her life and had talked with her at least every other day since moving out. There'd been a million chances for her mom to say, *"Hey, by the way, Genevieve. I was married once before."*

How could her mother have been another man's wife?

A lightning bolt carved into her. What if her mom and Russell had had a child?

That possibility was almost too disturbing to consider.

What had happened to Mom's first marriage? Had she and Russell gotten a divorce? Had Russell died? Or was Mom a . . . polygamist? What if she was one of those people on the TV shows who had two families?

Genevieve pulled her phone from her

166

purse and snapped pictures of all the records. Then she walked on quivering legs to the gray-haired woman at the information desk. "Do you happen to have any documents on my mother's husband, Russell Michael Atwell?"

"I can check. Birth date?"

Genevieve consulted the file and supplied his birth date.

"One moment." The clerk ran a search. "Yes." She kindly directed Genevieve back into the vault.

They walked down the rows of long-undisturbed papers that chronicled the lives of thousands upon thousands of people, many of them gone from this earth.

She needed to call Natasha. She needed to tell Sam.

Sam? How strange that he'd sprung into her mind.

Yet, in this moment when her sense of security regarding her family was careening the way the walls had during the earthquake, he had. Because she knew Sam would be stationary.

He'd offered to travel with her today, but he didn't finish at The Kitchen until after lunch, right when she hoped to return to Misty River and buckle down on her own day's work. So she'd come alone.

167

The gray-haired woman slid Russell's file from its resting place. Genevieve thanked her and returned to her table. Inside Russell's file, she discovered the same marriage documents she'd found in her mother's file. She flicked past them and came to —

A will.

Russell had died. Russell Atwell had *died* in . . . 1983, when he'd been twenty-three, approximately a year after his wedding to Genevieve's mother.

Silence gathered in and around her. She could hear the ticking of a wall clock.

What? Why? What could have ended his life at such a young age? Nothing here specified his cause of death. A death certificate would, though. She checked behind the will and found nothing. This file didn't contain a death certificate.

As best she could understand, Russell had died intestate. That is, without a will. The probate court had been petitioned. His spouse, Caroline Atwell, had requested that his estate go to Russell's family. The judge had assented to that request.

Genevieve pressed the pad of her thumb against the file's edge.

Had Mom never mentioned Russell because their marriage had been so brief? Or maybe because it had been too painful to

168

talk about him? Mom must have been devastated by the loss of her young husband so early in their marriage.

Caroline and Judson had married in a small ceremony less than three years after Russell's death. Genevieve had looked through their photo album many times. Dad had worn a suit and tie. Mom had worn a fancy pale blue dress. There'd been no cadre of bridesmaids or groomsmen.

When Genevieve had commented on the simplicity of their wedding, Mom had said that they'd wanted to keep it intimate, that the love they shared had been more than enough for both of them.

That her mom would focus on the emotion of the event — definitely within character. That she'd choose a small wedding — out of character. That she'd choose to marry in her groom's hometown instead of her own hometown — out of character.

Now, looking at Mom and Dad's wedding through this new lens, those out-of-character decisions made sense. Mom and Dad had kept their wedding low-key because Mom had probably already done the big, white, hometown wedding once before, with her first husband.

Genevieve snapped more photos and revisited the information desk.

"Find what you were looking for?" the woman asked.

"To some extent, yes. I expected to find birth and death certificates in the files, but I didn't see any."

"In our county, the health department keeps all the birth and death records."

"Is the health department nearby?"

"It's just five minutes down the road."

Almost before the male health department clerk had finished handing her Russell's death certificate, Genevieve had already started reading it.

At the top it listed information she already knew: Russell's name, birth date, death date. Lower, it also listed his cause of death.

Blunt force trauma to the head.

Genevieve whispered prayers that had no beginnings or endings, only middles.

He'd died at an address in the town of Camden, Georgia. "I've never heard of Camden," she told the clerk.

"It's a small town located in the southeastern corner of Clarke County."

She read the certificate over and over again, trying to process each detail, then took a photo of it. Returning the document to the clerk, she asked, "Is Russell listed as the father on any of the birth certificates in the system?" While he ran a search, she held herself immobile, bracing for his answer.

"No," he replied. "He's not."

She released a quivering breath.

Back in her car, she sat in the driver's seat, mind rioting. A lot of things could cause blunt force trauma to the head. Right? Car accidents. Falling off a horse. It's just that the words *blunt force trauma* were so sinister that, when she'd read them, her mind had leapt straight to murder.

She typed *Russell Michael Atwell's death* into Google on her phone.

Numerous search results came up. The first one read, *Local Man Potential Fourth Victim of Shoal Creek Killer.*

"Perish," Genevieve breathed. She clicked the link.

Russell had been found dead at his home, apparently murdered by a serial killer. A grainy black-and-white image of Russell clad in a tux was embedded in the article. He wore his blond hair in a preppy, side-parted style. With his firm jawline, straight nose, and chiseled brow, he struck her as young, handsome, athletic.

Her mom's first husband, this youthful person named Russell, had been murdered by a serial killer.

A tidal wave of shock submerged her.

■ ■ ■

"Ready to check out?" the cashier at The Bookery asked Sam that afternoon.

"Yes, thanks." He did his best to quash his embarrassment as he set *Bearer of a Woman's Soul* by Genevieve Woodward on the counter near the cash register.

The book's cover was unnecessarily girly. Lots of pink flowers.

He forced himself to meet the cashier's eyes without flinching.

Real men could buy women's Bible studies. He'd like to see her try to tell him otherwise.

She scanned the book. "Did you know there's a DVD series that goes along with this study?" She had a friendly, plump face.

"No."

She arched back as if a strong wind had hit her. "Oh my goodness! The DVD lessons Genevieve recorded for this study aren't to be missed. They're excellent. Not to be missed! You need to tell the woman you're buying this for about them. I guarantee she'll get goose bumps watching them."

He sincerely doubted the person he was buying this for would get goose bumps. "Do you sell the, uh . . ."

172

"DVD series? We do. It's one hundred and twenty dollars for the set."

He blinked at her. *What on earth?* He could buy a top-of-the-line cordless drill for that price.

"Would you like for me to grab them for you?" she asked.

"No thanks. Just the book please." After his discussion with Eli about Gen, he'd decided to buy one of her books, read it, and see for himself what all the fuss was about. He wasn't willing to trade a new drill for a set of DVDs, however.

"That'll be seventeen dollars and ninety-five cents," she said.

He handed over a twenty.

"Just be sure to tell the woman you're buying this for that she can purchase and watch each teaching session individually online." Her forehead wrinkled. "What do they call that, when you can watch things automatically online?"

"Streaming?"

"Exactly! Streaming. Please tell her that she can stream each of the recordings online. She's going to want to watch those sessions!"

"I'll tell her."

Sam worked in the orchard until night fell,

then made a quick meat marinara over spaghetti squash. He ate it at his dining room table while reading the newspaper. After cleaning up, he settled at his desk in the front downstairs room he'd converted into a home office. In addition to the desk, the room held a chair, two bookcases, and one large piece of framed photography. An artist had given him the photograph after Sam had given him permission to take black-and-white photos of the farm.

He clicked on the desk light and opened *Bearer of a Woman's Soul.* The table of contents was impressive. Ten weeks of study — each with five assignments? Eleven recorded teaching sessions.

Sam scratched the back of his neck. He hadn't realized there was a demand among women for ten-week-long Bible studies. He flipped through the book. Lots of blank spaces and questions. Not only did this study last ten weeks, it came with home-work.

He wasn't afraid to rebel against the as-signed order and skip the first teaching ses-sion, which was supposed to come before the first assignment. Except his curiosity was stirring.

Gen . . . teaching a lesson?

He powered up his computer, went to the

site noted in the book, and paid for the first recording.

High-quality graphics. Music. Then Genevieve came into focus on screen, sitting on a dock at a lake.

She wore the same type of fashionable clothing she always wore. Her hair and makeup were even more done up for the recording than they were in real life. She communicated relaxed warmth as she made introductory remarks.

More graphics and music. Then the picture showed Genevieve walking onto the stage at a sleek, modern church. She set her Bible on the podium. Women packed pews that swept away from her in a semicircle. And she began to . . . preach. Teach? It seemed like a combination of the two.

He lifted his eyebrows. His desk chair gave a squeak as he leaned back and interlaced his hands behind his head, watching.

She'd clearly researched the material. Even so, she came across as genuine and humble, never condescending. She spoke to the large group in a way that guaranteed that every woman in every seat would not only like her but also feel as if they knew her.

She told stories that illustrated her points. She strode from one end of the stage to the other. Down the stairs to the first row of pews. Up again.

She used her hands to emphasize her speech. Sometimes she raised her voice. Sometimes she lifted both palms. Sometimes she whispered.

His respect for her climbed.

When he was growing up, his mom and stepdad had taken him to church twice a year, on Christmas Eve and Easter. The two of them were good-hearted, moral people who'd put a lot of effort and love into their family but very little effort into organized religion.

He'd followed their lead. He'd tried to be good and moral and loving toward his family. But that hadn't stopped him from testing every pleasure the world offered. Starting at sixteen, he'd tried heavy drinking. Partying. Drugs. Girlfriends. Sex. Money. Travel.

A year after he'd graduated from uni, he'd been working as a sous chef and partying hard on his days off.

His roommate, Benji, had taken a contract job for a couple of months in Europe. Benji had asked Sam if he could sublet his room while he was gone to the daughter of his parents' closest friends. Sam had told him he could.

176

Memories started to tow Sam beneath the surface, deeper and deeper, until he was no longer sitting in his office but entering his old Melbourne apartment one hot summer day to find a woman standing in the living room. Moving boxes, two suitcases, and a surfboard surrounded her. She wore tight shorts and a bikini beneath her tank top. Her hair was sandy blond and wavy. Her body, tan and athletic.

She leveled her pale blue cat's eyes on him. "G'day."

"G'day."

"I'm Kayden Westcott."

"Sam Turner."

"I was a year behind you and Benji at school."

"You just graduated, then?"

"Yeah. And now I'm wondering if I made a mistake when I told Benji I'd sublet his room. It's gross in there."

Benji had never said that his parents' friends' daughter looked like a poster of the classic Aussie beach girl. He wanted to kill Benji for not giving him a heads-up. He wanted to kiss Benji. He wanted to make sure Kayden never regretted her decision to stay in this apartment.

"Do you think I should fumigate it before

177

I move my stuff in?" Kayden asked, grinning.

A half second passed before he laughed in response to her question. But that half second had lasted long enough for him to fall in love with her. "I'll help you clean it. Once we finish, we can decide if fumigation is necessary."

He spent that whole summer with Kayden. Surfing, going to concerts, working out, sharing a bottle of wine over dinner, making love. Long before Benji returned from Europe, Kayden had become a permanent resident of Sam's room. A month after Benji moved back in, Sam and Kayden had gotten their own one-bedroom flat.

When a buddy at work offered to sell Sam weed and a Baggie of twelve Percocet pills, Sam had taken him up on it because the combination of weed and Percocet had sounded to him like a good weekend waiting to happen. He'd known, too, that Kayden would like the weed. She'd been no angel before they started dating. Like him, she'd sampled several different substances, and weed was her favorite.

The Percocet had simply come with the weed. Like when a grocery store gives you a free box of crackers for buying a certain brand of granola bars. Percocet hadn't been the main draw. Sam had taken painkillers before and hadn't been all that keen. He'd expected Kayden to feel the same.

However, when he'd introduced her to Percocet, she'd surprised him. She'd loved the way the pills made her feel.

And he'd loved her. Intently. Wholly.

Their first year together had been perfect. She talked about Freud and oceanography and feminism. She could go to a library or to a club and have fun either place for hours. She listened to The Doors albums on her record player. She rolled her eyes back into her head with joy every time she tasted a dish he made for her. She easily befriended all her co-workers at her graphic design firm. She laughed hard and sometimes cried hard. She went barefoot everywhere.

Sam was the son of two countries. He'd grown up spending time in both but never feeling like he fit in either. His mother had married the love of her life, a man who was not his father. His sister and brother were full-blood siblings of each other but only half-siblings to him. Since birth, he'd looked for belonging in friend groups, sports teams, activities, entertainments. All without success. Until Kayden.

With her, in their flat in Melbourne, he

belonged. At long last, he'd come home. He was appreciated and needed. He was integral to their circle of two. He was the happiest he'd ever been.

Kayden took Percocet more and more frequently, but still recreationally. It hadn't interfered with her ability to function.

Until, gradually . . . it had.

As intimate as they'd been, Sam didn't know when Percocet had changed from her diversion into her addiction. Kayden had successfully hidden that from him.

Little by little, the pills sucked the perfection from their relationship. Kayden began to lose things. At first little things, like her sunglasses. Then her memory of the appointments on her calendar. Then a few of her friendships. Then her entire existence came to revolve around pills — how to get them and the taking of them.

He asked her to quit. She said she would. She didn't.

He came home from work one night and called her name. No answer, even though he'd seen her Jeep in its parking spot. An episode of *Dance Academy* played on TV. He walked closer to the TV in search of the remote, so that he could turn it off, and the patch of rug in front of the sofa became visible. Kayden was there. She was having a seizure.

Blind fear consumed him. He knelt beside her. Helpless and panicking, he phoned for an ambulance.

Later, the doctor informed him that she'd mixed Percocet with alcohol and overdosed. Once they'd stabilized her health, she'd gone directly to a rehab center.

He'd slept alone in their flat. Ate alone. Moved through life alone while she was in treatment. Their circle of two had been broken, and he'd counted the hours until she returned to him.

But the day he'd arrived at the center to bring her home, she'd been a pale and withdrawn version of her former self.

A few weeks later, when searching for positive things to replace what the pills had been to her, she'd informed him that she wanted to go to church. Eager to support her, they'd attended a church service held in an old, renovated building. The band rocked. The pastors and members were welcoming and around their age.

He looked over at her during one of the songs. Her braided blond hair shone under the light. Her profile was wildly beautiful. Her hands, raised, palms up. Her smile peaceful.

His hope expanded. He wanted so badly for church, for *anything,* to keep her from a relapse.

Kayden grasped onto God immediately. He, the more cautious of them, needed time to consider the things the pastor taught.

They had long, deep conversations about death and souls and whether their existence on the planet could be accidental or had to have been purposed. They read books by scientists and theologians and philosophers and — at the end of all that — decided that the evidence against God was far harder to accept than the evidence for God.

A friend from church explained what faith required, and he and Kayden prayed for salvation. They attended church on Sundays and small group meetings weekly.

He'd gone to that original service because it's what Kayden had wanted. Yet slowly faith had changed Sam's heart. Many — but not all — of his behaviors shifted.

At one point their small group leader, who'd become a friend, expressed concern over the fact that he and Kayden were still living together, despite their unmarried state. It seemed to Sam that his friend had stepped way over the line, and Sam responded with defensiveness. He had no intention of changing their living situation, and he didn't want Christians judging him and Kayden or trying to take away their freedom. He loved Kayden too much to change. For the first time in his life, he had a place. He filled his head with proof that justified his own rightness. Kayden needed him in order to have a chance at recovery. Practically, it made no sense to pay for two separate apartments. Living together was convenient, comfortable. It's what kept their relationship strong. They weren't hurting anyone.

They parted from their small group but continued to attend church. Then, all of a sudden, Kayden's company was sold and the employees let go. Kayden couldn't find another job. The sorrow and stress of that, coupled with the difficulty of staying clean, covered her with depression. In order to bounce back, she reached for Percocet.

All the hard-won progress she'd made — destroyed.

Her ability to function again began to crumble.

She went through detox at home. He nursed her through it.

She reconnected with God. Found work. Found purpose and stability.

Then her grandmother wasted away from cancer. Kayden reached for Percocet to help her through her sadness.

Her ability to function again began to crumble.

He nursed her through detox.

She reconnected with God. Found work. Found purpose and stability.

Then she developed migraines and couldn't bear them without Percocet.

Sam begged her to return to the rehab facility.

She assured him that she had it under control. She promised that she'd limit herself to just enough Percocet to treat her migraines, so little that he wouldn't even notice.

Her ability to function began to crumble and — all at once — he couldn't face going through it again: The worry that came with his role as her caregiver. The belief that she'd stay clean, followed by heartbreak when she fell off the wagon. The fights. The pleading.

The futility.

The repetitiveness of it all.

The violent emotions.

He'd locked himself to Kayden when he'd fallen in love with her. Then she'd locked herself into a destructive cycle, which meant *he* was locked into that destructive cycle, even though he hadn't misused a single prescription or recreational drug since the day he'd found her having a seizure on their living room carpet.

He told her he'd leave unless she quit using.

She didn't quit, and so, after a particularly bad fight, he followed through on his promise.

He left.

By then, they'd been together for three years. One day, she'd been the closest person to him. The next day, she wasn't in his life at all. There, then gone.

He'd moved in with a co-worker and existed in misery. A misery that seemed like nothing compared to his feelings when Benji called him three months after his breakup with Kayden to tell him, through tears, that she'd overdosed again on Percocet and alcohol. This time, she'd killed herself.

He'd been the one who'd introduced her to Percocet.

He'd been the one who'd broken up with her, and so he hadn't been there when she'd needed him to call an ambulance for her.

At her funeral, he stared at the casket containing her young, beautiful body. He experienced physical pain in response to the desolation on the faces of her parents and siblings.

Grief tangled with guilt sent him down a dark tunnel in the seasons following her burial. He couldn't shake the conviction that, if he would have done something differently, if *God* would have done something differently, Kayden could have lived a long, healthy life. He was furious with himself and with God, but he didn't have the strength or the heart to turn from his faith. Desolation drove him to his knees. He *needed* God. And so he clung to Him.

It had taken a year of therapy before he'd finally reached the end of the tunnel.

His whole life he'd been flailing. Because he didn't want to be an outsider. Because he didn't want loneliness.

Enough.

He embraced the things he used to fear. He made them part of his identity. *I don't belong. I'm an outsider. I'm lonely. That's who I am.*

He'd managed to hold on to his relationship with God and, as long as he had that, he didn't need anything or anyone else. Very purposely, he turned his life upside-down by moving to America.

To this day, he still had his faith. It was steady. Simple.

Gen's faith seemed public, bold. Complicated.

186

Sam paused the video and hunched over the computer's keyboard to run a search for Gen. Her impressive website supplied links to social media accounts on Facebook, Twitter, and Instagram. He visited all three and saw that she had a huge following on each.

So. His tenant was a professional Christian with an image to maintain and hundreds of thousands of people looking to her for guidance on how to live their lives. The women who consumed her Bible studies and packed churches to hear her speak expected her to do the impossible — live a perfect life. The pressure of that had to be heavy.

Both he and Gen had made mistakes. They'd both fallen short.

He lifted his vision to the glowing moon hanging in the sky beyond the window.

He worked Sunday mornings, so he attended the contemporary worship service at The Vine Church on Saturday nights.

Back in Australia and here in America, he sometimes heard pastors speak about their past struggles in vague terms, but only in the context of having overcome them on the road to their current, better place. He'd never heard a pastor confess a present struggle. Nor had he heard a pastor confess an opioid addiction.

He and Eli talked about issues surrounding the Bible. Viewpoints, controversies, archaeology. But even though Eli was his closest friend in Misty River, Eli had never admitted an area of failure to Sam. Sam hadn't admitted an area of failure to Eli.

Why was it so hard for Christians to come clean to one another about the sins that had them by their throats? Because of pride? Because every Christian wanted every other Christian to think they were doing it right? That they were strong and good?

If so, that was idiotic.

His pastor liked to say that the church wasn't about helping sick people become well. It was about bringing dead people to life. Every single one of them was dead except for Christ. So what was keeping them from trusting other people with their deadness? Why so superficial? Everyone was messed up and hurting. It didn't help to pretend the opposite.

Kayden's smoke screen of silence and lies *had not helped her.* Kayden had gone to worship services and small group meetings before, during, and after her relapses and never once mentioned her issues with Percocet to their church friends.

He could see why it would be brutally hard for Genevieve to admit her own strug-

188

gle. Once she admitted she'd been relying on painkillers to get through her days, she couldn't continue to stand on her pedestal. If her addiction became public knowledge, some of her fans might turn on her. The media might view her secret as a scandal. Her career might take a very hard hit. So would her reputation and her reach.

Even so, he knew that silence and lies wouldn't help Genevieve, either.

He hit play and watched the rest of the video.

Troubled, he climbed the stairs, then came to stand at his bedroom window. He rubbed his arms in an effort to get rid of the cold inside.

What was he doing? It was dumb to stare at his guesthouse.

He went back downstairs. Swept the first floor. Walked back upstairs. Showered. Stared aimlessly at his closet for long minutes, as if he'd forgotten where he kept the drawstring pants he slept in. Pulled a pair on. Tried to read. Found himself at the window again.

Gen's invisible airwaves grew stronger every day.

Light glowed from the guesthouse windows this evening, telling him that Genevieve was still awake. Which royally frustrated him for two reasons. One, she was drinking down electricity the way a thirsty border collie drinks water. She was probably running the heater full-bore and taking an hour-long shower, too, in order to drain him of all his resources at once. Two, she didn't seem to have the sense to know that, in order to recover, her body needed sleep.

By some terrible twist of fate, *he* was one of very few people who knew that she was attempting to make it to ninety days sober. Unfortunately, he was also the least qualified to help her.

Genevieve could have crashed so many houses on so many farms. He didn't understand why God had brought her to his. He couldn't afford to get mixed up with another person going through treatment, relapse, addiction, treatment, relapse, addiction.

Yet he also couldn't afford to stand aside and watch Gen pile the rare abilities God had given her into the back of her car and then drive that car off a cliff. Gen was gifted. Very.

Kayden had been gifted, too. It still made him sick to his stomach when he thought about how Kayden's potential had been spilled like a box of puzzle pieces.

It felt as though God had given him a level of responsibility where Gen was concerned.

God was doing a lot through her — all of which was at risk. Was he supposed to fight to protect her gifts? If so, how would he know when he'd crossed the line from intervening because it's what God wanted into intervening because of his own sad history?

It wasn't his job to keep Gen alive or to save her ministry. But what *was* his job here?

He had no idea.

He couldn't get mixed up with Gen.

He'd couldn't stand back from Gen.

He was at war with himself, and he didn't know what to do.

Natasha

I can feel Genevieve trembling beside me, and she's making a whimpering sound. I bite my lip to keep from wailing because that will only scare her more, and I'm the older sister.

"Is everybody okay?" My voice is tiny and weak.

Harsh breathing answers.

"I'm okay," Ben finally says.

"I'm bleeding." Genevieve motions to her arm. Blood seeps from a cut that starts under the sleeve of her T-shirt and continues most of the way to her elbow.

I swallow.

"A piece of the ceiling hit my head," Sebastian says. "It hurts. Bad."

"You're both going to be all right," I say, because that's what they need to hear. I'm terrified, though, because I can't do anything for them. I'm not a doctor. I'm four-

192

teen years old.

I look to Luke. He's the cutest, most popular boy in the middle school youth group. My friends and I all have a crush on him.

He doesn't speak. His chin is shuddering.

I cup my hands around my mouth and yell, "Help!"

CHAPTER EIGHT

Genevieve parked in front of Sam's restaurant, Sugar Maple Kitchen, the next morning at nine fifteen.

After leaving Athens yesterday, she'd driven in utter silence for an hour while her mind scratched and strained down wild tangents. Then she'd called Natasha and poured out everything she'd learned in a torrent. She and her sister had decided to table their discussion and any and all research until they'd had a chance to sleep on the news.

Genevieve had suggested they meet at The Kitchen because she'd been wanting to see it and because eating here might afford her a glimpse of the elusive Sam.

She sailed past the storefront and into a restaurant that smelled of coffee, bacon, and cinnamon rolls. The combination immediately stirred a sensory memory of the times she'd woken in her grandmother's house when she was a girl to this same tapestry of smells.

One small blackboard sign pointed to the takeout line. The other pointed to the dine-in line. Several people waited in both, and almost all the tables across from the long bar were occupied. It appeared that Sam's place had become a local favorite. No surprise. He was so serious and determined that it was hard to imagine him failing at anything.

She planned to consume two strong lattes back-to-back and possibly eat something that had been grown on Sam's land. Grabbing a menu, she took her place in the dine-in line. Breakfast casserole with hash brown crust. Quiche. Egg scramblers. Pancakes. Waffles. Every item was marked paleo, gluten free, dairy free, or vegan.

Her expectations for her breakfast dimmed. It was asking a lot of a paleo waffle to expect it to be both healthy and tasty. She knew that Sam ate incredibly clean, but she hadn't realized that he'd applied his personal dietary habits to his restaurant, nor that there was such a high demand in Misty River for this type of food.

After texting Natasha to ask what she wanted for breakfast, Genevieve placed their order, then carried the number an employee gave her to an open table.

Sam had obviously hired a skilled designer to help him execute his vision. The restaurant had a great vibe. Cool, simple, sophisticated, and a little bit rustic all at the same time. Lots of natural wood and clean lines and a great mishmash of old and character-filled with new and modern. The ambiance here reflected the ambiance of his farm.

Once, she'd wanted to become an interior designer. She'd always loved homes and home decorating and art. She'd been on her way to an interior design degree at Belmont when her romance with Thad had imploded. Before their breakup, her only experience with women's ministry had been the years she'd spent in high school and college leading Bible study groups.

After their breakup, she'd clung to the Bible with desperation, believing it to be the antidote to her heartbreak. She'd dedicated every spare minute to reading it, scouring commentaries, and conversing with professors. Somewhere along the line, she'd decided to funnel everything she was learning into the writing of a study.

Amazingly, a Christian publisher had purchased *The Deepest Love You'll Ever Know* right before her senior year and released it just as she was graduating. The hugely positive response to that study had been a stunning gift, a mercy. Akin to finding a golden coin in the gray ashes at the bottom of a fireplace.

Seemingly overnight, she'd been catapulted into Christian celebrityhood, and she'd marveled at God's amazing ability to redeem sorrow.

Requests for speaking engagements followed. She spent the six months after the study's release traveling, always with the intention of returning to Nashville, putting her author persona on the shelf, and becoming a designer.

Over time she'd eventually recognized that her role as author and speaker wasn't a short-term calling. It was her long-term ministry. God had used the debacle with Thad to guide her to His will for her in a way that nothing else could have.

Every so often, like now, when she was surrounded by the visible skill of a talented designer, she remembered the road not taken with a fond, nostalgic tug.

Natasha strode toward the table wearing running gear, her hair in a ponytail, and sat in the chair across from Genevieve. "Morning."

"Morning."

"Recovery update?"

"Still clean."

"Not today, Satan." Natasha had come up with the phrase, which she used often when questioning Genevieve about her well-being.

"Not today, Satan," Genevieve agreed. "How are you?"

"I've got the worst headache."

"I'm sorry."

"Also, I'm a bad wife because Wyatt wanted me to watch a Star Wars documentary with him last night, but of course I'm not watching any TV during my Year of Living Austenly."

"Naturally. You read or knit of an evening."

"Naturally. But he kept after it, so we compromised. Since neither of us can play the pianoforte, I consented to watching someone else play the pianoforte on TV."

"Because Jane and her people do a lot of sitting around, watching people play pianoforte."

"Exactly. Turns out watching someone play pianoforte is dead boring, and now he's vexed with me, as Jane would say. I didn't think it was the time to mention that I bought tickets for Wyatt and me to attend a concert tonight."

"What kind of concert?"

"Glee singers accompanied by the harp.

Jane would be so proud."

"Mmm." Poor non-musically-inclined, non-Jane-Austen-inclined Wyatt.

"So Wyatt's vexed with me, and I'm vexed with Mom for having a first husband she never remembered to mention."

A black-haired girl with a tattoo on her neck brought Genevieve's latte and Natasha's tea.

They'd swirled a leaf design into the foam atop Genevieve's drink. She took a sip. It tasted hot and strong. Milky, too, with just the right amount of sweetness. Perfection in a cup. "This thing with Mom is crazy pants," Genevieve said.

"I mean, *what in the world?*" Their discovery was likely hitting Natasha extra hard because Natasha hadn't expected Genevieve to uncover anything. "How could she have married someone and then covered it up?"

"With the cooperation of others, I'm guessing."

"Like Dad. He must know about this. Right?"

"I think he must." Genevieve had turned this question over and over in her mind since yesterday. "The fact that they had a small wedding in his hometown points to that."

"Everyone on Mom's side of the family

must also know," Natasha said. "They almost certainly attended her first wedding."

"Right."

"But they never once said anything about it to us."

"I suppose that's because Mom asked them not to."

She and Natasha had been very close to their mom's parents. But because Caroline had no siblings, there'd been no Herrington first cousins to grow up with. Mom's larger family gathered yearly for a picnic reunion, and Mom occasionally hosted a relative of hers at their house for a meal or an overnight stay. But Genevieve wasn't connected with any of them the way she was with Nanny and Pop, and her cousins, aunts, and uncles on her dad's side.

Genevieve opened the photos app on her phone and handed it over so Natasha could survey the pictures she'd taken the day before.

Natasha scrolled through the images, forehead knit.

Genevieve cast a look around for Sam. She'd yet to catch a glimpse of him.

Natasha slid the phone back to Genevieve.

"What are we doing to do?" Genevieve asked.

"The way I see it, we have two options. We can take these findings to Mom and Dad as soon as possible, today even. Or we can do more digging."

"What's the advantage of more digging?"

"My experience as an attorney has taught me that it's unwise to wade into a situation without first learning everything there is to learn. We know Mom was widowed before she married Dad, but we don't know what that might have to do with the weird letter you received."

"I know. I don't get it. The letter indicated that Mom and Dad had done something shameful. But what's shameful about remarrying years after your first husband's death?"

"Nothing. So right now, I feel like our information is very incomplete. We've simply learned that Mom has been lying to us by omission —"

"And probably Dad, too," Genevieve added.

"If we confront them, I'm worried they'll only confess to the information we can substantiate. Nothing more."

"And if they actually did do something shameful, and we tell them what we've learned, they might even destroy any remaining evidence."

201

"And we still won't have a clue about what really went down back in the eighties."

Genevieve sat back in her chair. "It's surreal to be talking about Mom and Dad destroying evidence." Her mother had received a ticket for running a red light back when Genevieve was in tenth grade. To her knowledge, that was the worst thing either of her parents had ever done.

"It's surreal to think that Mom was married to another man," Natasha replied. "But she was. So here we are."

Genevieve licked a dab of foam from her lip. "I'm good with waiting to talk to them until we've learned everything we can." The more she and Natasha could uncover, the more honesty they could force out of their parents. Also, she wasn't exactly looking forward to tackling this topic with them. They'd expressly told her that the letter held no merit. Then she'd gone behind their backs anyway to research their past.

"It's not practical for me to drive all over Georgia chasing down leads," Natasha said. "I can only make it about forty-five minutes in the car with the kids before I want to kill myself."

"Well, I'm not on board with you killing yourself, so I'll drive places when necessary."

"I want to contribute my share, though, so I'll spend time online researching whatever I can."

"Because TV is a no-go when living Austenly, but computers and cell phones are permissible."

"Precisely. I started researching last night, after the pianoforte fiasco, by reading articles about Russell's death."

"What?" Genevieve squawked. She lobbed a crumpled napkin at her. "We agreed to postpone research until we could sleep on the news."

"And you stuck to our agreement because I raised you right."

"Natasha!"

"I know. I'm sorry. I couldn't help myself."

A young man with a name tag reading *Luis* delivered their breakfast plates to them.

"Wow," Natasha murmured admiringly.

Once they'd assured Luis they had everything they needed, Genevieve prayed over their food. Halfway through the prayer, sentiment swamped her, and her voice quavered. Shoot. Her state of mind during recovery: still so volatile! She brought the prayer to an end.

"Are you crying?" Natasha asked.

" 'Have you no consideration for my poor nerves?' " Genevieve asked, quoting *Pride and Prejudice.*

" 'I have the utmost respect for your nerves,' " Natasha quoted back without hesitation. " 'They've been my constant companion these twenty years.' "

That was unquestionably true.

Genevieve considered her waffle, bordered by a garnish of berries and topped with a dollop of coconut cream. She took her first bite, and her spine liquefied as she chewed.

Natasha swallowed. "This breakfast casserole is amazing."

"Mine's amazing, too."

"I love eating here because I don't have to leave wracked with shame."

Genevieve savored more coffee, then sectioned off another bite of waffle. "So what did you learn last night about Russell Atwell?"

"Russell graduated from Mercer the same year Mom did."

"It's pretty safe to assume that they met in college, then, since they got married just a few months after graduating."

"I agree. Russell's from Camden, which explains why he and Mom were living in Camden after they married."

"Ah."

"As far as I could tell, Russell himself wasn't all that remarkable. He was a clean-cut, all-American guy. His death, however, was very remarkable."

"Death by serial killer."

"Yes. How many people are you person- ally connected with who've been murdered by a serial killer?"

"Russell's the first."

"The Shoal Creek Killer was a man named Terry Paul Richards. He was active for about seven months before Russell's death and for about five months after. When he was caught, he confessed to six murders, including Russell's. He got his nickname because he terrorized a region of Georgia that more or less followed the path of Shoal Creek."

"Did he kill all his victims by hitting them in the head?"

Natasha set aside her fork. "He did. He always broke into the houses of his victims at night when his victims were alone. He'd attack and sometimes enter into a life-and- death struggle. He murdered his victims by striking them in the head, usually with something he found in the house. A small statue. A shovel. A curtain rod. He always clipped off a lock of his victim's hair and he always left the house dark. No exterior lights, nothing."

"Were all his victims men?"

"Yes."

"Did he steal anything from the houses? Or was murder his only objective?"

"Murder was his only objective."

"How did the police catch him?"

"Through his neighbor. Apparently, she thought he was strange and reclusive, and, because of that, she never trusted him. She kept a close eye on his comings and goings from her front porch, where she often spent the hot part of the day in order to catch the breeze. As soon as she realized that the occasional bruises on his face synced up with the timeline of some of the murders, she called the police."

Genevieve ran the tines of her fork through her puff of coconut cream, leaving tracks. Their poor mom. She'd been through something unimaginable, and her children hadn't even known.

Mom's motivation for keeping Russell a secret was becoming clearer. *"Sweetie, my first husband was murdered by a serial killer"* wasn't exactly the bedtime story you'd want to tell your four-year-old.

On the other hand, Natasha and Genevieve were adults. For a long time now, they'd been old enough to hear that kind of hard information. Keeping Russell's existence a secret wasn't very respectful to his memory. Shouldn't Mom have honored him by talking about him? "Did Terry Paul Richards receive capital punishment?"

"Yes. He was electrocuted in 1995. I'm sort of obsessed with the Shoal Creek Killer now. I say we continue to read whatever we can about him and about Russell. Then go from there."

"Boss, I think there's a celebrity eating at table six."

Sam's attention cut to Luis, who was leaning out The Kitchen's back door. Up until five minutes ago, Sam had been in the back of house, expediting. He'd let his sous chef take over while he'd stepped outside to slug back some water and stare at the drifts of clouds snagged on the mountain peaks behind town.

"Which celebrity?" Sam asked.

"I don't know. A woman. I've never seen her before in my life."

"Is her presence creating an issue?"

The younger, shorter man shrugged. "Sort of. Four women went up to her first. When the other diners saw them talking and taking pictures with her, then more people recognized her. Now there's a pretty big group. Diners who want to walk to the back of the space are having to squeeze past the crowd."

"Thanks. I'll look into it." He headed to the dining room, where he found at least ten women in their twenties and thirties standing around table six, listening, nodding, smiling.

A somewhat-famous country singer who owned a cabin nearby came in from time to time. Every month or two, their congresswoman brought her family to The Kitchen on a Saturday morning. However, neither of those had drawn a crowd this large.

Sam made his way to the front of the group as politely as possible. "Excuse me."

A tall woman glanced at him, then stepped to the side, revealing the person at the center of their attention.

Sam's progress came to a sudden stop. Gen. The celebrity in his restaurant was . . . Gen.

She hadn't seen him. Her attention was currently focused on a brunette who was talking passionately about Gen's Bible study on courage and how much it had meant to her.

As he took in the details of her profile, affection for her stole around his heart. He tried to block it, to stop it. But failed.

Gen was ruining the peace at his farm.

Now she was ruining the peace at his restaurant.

All the women were watching her with round-eyed adoration, hanging on every word. All of them, anyway, except a woman who looked so much like Gen that she had to be Gen's sister. She'd positioned herself on the outside of the gathering with her purse over her shoulder and a look of friendly patience on her features.

He'd learned that Gen's studies were successful, but how had she generated this kind of fandom in the middle of his restaurant? Weren't all but the most bestselling authors anonymous? It wasn't like he spent a lot of time looking at photos of his favorite author. He wouldn't recognize the guy if he passed him on the street.

"I wept," the brunette told Gen. "After the final day's homework, I got down on my knees and wept before the Lord. You've changed my life. Seriously! You have. Thank you so much for what you do."

"You're welcome," Gen said. "I'm really honored to hear how the study impacted you."

"May I hug you?" the brunette asked.

No, Sam almost said, but he caught himself. What was the matter with the brunette? Didn't she have any respect for Gen's

209

personal space?

"Of course," Gen replied. She and the woman hugged.

It had been years since he'd witnessed this much feminine emotion on display. "Good morning." Sam kept his focus on Gen but spoke with enough volume to be heard by all her fans.

Gen's hair tumbled over one shoulder as she quickly faced him. Her eyes met his and immediately warmed. "Good morning."

Everyone was waiting for him to say something further. "Nice to see you."

"Nice to see you, too."

"It seems your readers have found you."

"We're having a girlfriends getaway at a cabin nearby," the brunette explained, gesturing to many of the nearby women. "We couldn't believe our eyes when we spotted Genevieve Woodward two tables down. I mean . . ." She extended both hands palms-up toward Genevieve. "Genevieve Woodward." She and her friends grinned.

"Yes," Sam said dryly. "Genevieve Woodward."

"Genevieve Woodward!" the brunette repeated.

He gave Genevieve a small lift of his brows.

The humorous expression she gave him

said, *"It's bizarre that I have fans. There's no accounting for taste."*

"To celebrate *Genevieve Woodward,* I'd like to shout you all some of our scones," he said.

"What does shouting have to do with scones?" Gen asked, amused.

It took him a split second to understand the reason for her question. "In Australia, when we say we'll shout something, we mean we'll offer it for free."

"You're offering us free scones?"

"I am. Also, let me lead you to our side patio. The weather's warming up, and I think you'll be more comfortable there because it's quieter and there's more space." *Plus, you'll be out of everyone else's way.* "Follow me."

He stopped to ask Star to bring out scones, then led them through the side door.

"I admire your crowd-control skills," the one with the family resemblance to Genevieve said as she took up a position beside him on the patio. Everyone else closed around Genevieve. "I'm Natasha MacKenzie, Gen's sister, former attorney-at-law, wife, mother of two."

"Sam Turner, half brother to people you don't know, restaurant owner, farmer, father of none."

211

"Delighted to make your acquaintance."
She shook his hand with a confident grip.
He remembered that she, too, was one of
the Miracle Five. She'd been buried under
the rubble with Gen.

"The casserole I just ate was excellent,"
she said. "I respect you hugely."

"And I respect you hugely because you
have a good palate."

She laughed.

"Does this happen often?" Sam inclined
his chin toward the adoration session.

"Relatively often, yes. Among a certain
demographic, Gen is very popular."

"What demographic is that?"

"Christian women between the ages of
eighteen and thirty-eight."

"And these Christian women between the
ages of eighteen and thirty-eight found her
at my restaurant while she was eating breakfast?"

She gave a good-natured shrug. "Christian women between the ages of eighteen
and thirty-eight need breakfast, too."

"Does this bother Gen?"

She sized him up with a look of surprise.
"She lets you call her Gen?"

"Life's too short to call someone Genevieve."

"Hmm." She considered him for a long

212

moment, then moved her focus to her sister. "If the attention bothers Gen, she's never admitted it to me. She knows she's fortunate to do the work she does, and she genuinely loves the women who take part in her studies. She feels connected to them."

Sam eyed the strange scene before him.

"I don't typically abandon her when she's outnumbered," Natasha said. "But my daughter and son are at Mother's Day Out and the kid-free hours I have per week are more valuable than crude oil. If you think you've got this under control, I might split."

"I've got this under control."

"Great. *Thank you.* If this goes on for more than fifteen minutes, I suggest that you ask Genevieve if she has to work on one of her studies today. When she says that she does, insist that she get back to it because you wouldn't want to delay the writing of more amazing studies. That will give her a graceful and truthful way out."

"Thanks for the tip."

Natasha moved to go, then paused. "I'm glad Gen's staying in your cottage."

Guesthouse. Men did not have cottages. He couldn't bring himself to reply with the expected response, which was, *I'm glad, too.* So he said, "She seems to like it there."

"She absolutely does."

He and Natasha exchanged good-byes, and she left with long strides that communicated how pleased she was to be free.

"Would you mind taking a picture of me with Genevieve?" a round-faced woman asked him.

A line was forming for photos. Gen was posing with the first in line, and the round-faced woman was up next.

"Sure."

All of these people seemed fine. None threatening. Yet, as Natasha had said, Gen was outnumbered. Which made her seem in need of protecting.

As the round-faced woman moved forward for her turn, the toe of her shoe hit one of the brick pavers and she stumbled forward. Sam shot out a hand to steady her before she collided with Gen.

The woman laughed self-consciously. "I almost fell. Sorry about that."

"Got it?" Sam stared at her with seriousness as he began to release her.

"Yes."

Convinced that Gen wouldn't be crushed and that the woman wouldn't sue him over an injury caused by his brick paver, he raised the woman's phone and centered her and Gen in a camera shot.

He continued to function as volunteer

photographer, ready to intercede on Gen's behalf if she needed him to. Her public persona was more polished than her private persona. With these women, she was "on." She came across as kind, energetic, gracious. With him, she was funnier, more wry, more pushy, more casual.

The group ate the scones.

When no one had left after fifteen minutes, impatience began to grind at him. He needed to get back to work, and he was ready for these people to leave so he could have Gen to himself, just like he had her to himself at his farm —

He didn't want her to himself. It irritated him that he'd even thought that.

These women had probably done all of her studies. They had far more claim to her, far more in common with her, than he did.

He employed the exit strategy her sister had recommended, and Gen separated from her admirers with three times as many good-byes and hugs as necessary.

He walked her to her car.

"That was a sophisticated extraction maneuver you just pulled," she commented.

"Your sister's idea. I don't think I was as subtle about it as she would have been."

"You were even better at it because you buttered everyone up ahead of time with scones and picture taking. The scones, especially, were a very nice touch."

He thrust his hands into his jeans.

"Thanks for stepping in and helping out," she said.

"No worries."

They reached her car and he waited, then waited some more while she rooted around in her gigantic purse for her keys. He considered the top of her bent head. The part was perfect, her hair beautiful and thick. Her fans hadn't caught her in sweatpants because, as usual, she was dressed well. Shirt ironed, makeup done, nail polish shining.

Her beach-scented perfume drifted to him, and he tried to draw more of it into his lungs so that he could memorize it. Whenever she was this close to him, his grief and regret loosened their hold on his chest.

She glanced up, smiling, and her eyes informed him that she might be interested in him as more than a landlord. More than a friend.

He wasn't naïve. Women had given him that look — and continued to give him that look — often enough to recognize it.

But it had been a very long time since he'd experienced a physical response to a look like that.

Need — simple, instinctive — overtook his body.

He forced himself to step back. "Catch you around."

"Do you have a second?" she asked. "I wanted to talk with you about the Fall Fun —"

"I'm sorry. I can't right now. I've got to get back to the restaurant." He thrust a hand through his hair as he strode back to The Kitchen. Sitting at the desk in his office, he opened his email and stared sightlessly at it. He'd run from Gen to escape from this feeling. But it hadn't worked.

The need had followed him here. And it wouldn't let go.

Sebastian

My head is killing me. Even so, I've been letting the two blond girls and the African-American kid scream for help because we need help.

"Stop it," I finally rasp because I can't stand their screaming anymore.

They've been yelling so long their voices are getting hoarse. Not one time has anyone answered. Everyone else in this building and all the buildings around us is probably dead.

"Nobody can hear you," I say into the silence, furious at them for thinking that someone might be able to hear. Stupid, naïve, hopeful kids. They don't know anything. They're as dumb as babies. "Does anyone have a cell phone?"

The people in charge of this trip told us over and over that cell phones were against the rules, which wouldn't have stopped me from bringing one. But I'm not rich enough to have one.

There's a pause.

Then Luke, face hard and streaked with dirt, pulls a cell phone from his pocket.

CHAPTER NINE

"Let's talk about how you were feeling in the months leading up to breaking your ankle," Dr. Quinley suggested.

Three days had passed since Genevieve's eye-opening trip to Athens. In that amount of time, the weather had turned from sunny to gray and rumbly. Beyond the psychologist's large picture window, rain tumbled from the sky, light but steady.

Genevieve tilted her head to the side in confusion. "The months leading up to breaking my ankle?"

"Yes."

"I was doing great. Everything with work was . . . amazing."

The doctor pushed a curl behind one ear and observed Genevieve with kind perceptiveness. Genevieve watched the curl slowly spring free again.

"Do the months leading up to my ankle surgery have any bearing on my Oxy addic-

220

tion?" Genevieve asked. "I took Oxy to treat physical pain from the ankle surgery."

The older woman took a bite out of a ring of dried apple, nodding as her attention focused on one of her pots of hanging ivy. She chewed, swallowed. "Or," she proposed mildly, "you took Oxy to treat physical pain from the ankle surgery *and* to dull emotional pain." Her gaze meandered around the room before meeting Genevieve's eyes with such forthright knowledge that Genevieve felt the impact of it.

"I . . ." Her brain whirred. Instinctive denial rose at the idea that she'd used Oxy to treat her emotions.

"Is there a reason why you've been avoiding thinking about the possibility that emotional pain played a role in your Oxy dependence?" Dr. Quinley asked.

"I suppose I've avoided that possibility because it just . . . it feels ridiculous. Everything was going great prior to breaking my ankle."

"Was it?"

"Yes."

"Why was it great?"

"Because I'm so . . . wildly fortunate. I mean, dozens of things have gone *beautifully* for me. Beyond my highest expectations. Before I broke my ankle, I was the luckiest girl in the world."

"Were you, though? Let's think back." She gnawed on a bite of dried apple.

The diffuser on Dr. Quinley's desk hummed and blew a stream of scented mist into the air. At their weekly sessions, Genevieve had taken to sitting in the same chair she'd selected the first day she'd come here, with Sam.

The doctor liked to vary her location. Today, she'd brought out a brown velour beanbag. She was ensconced in it, legs crossed casually, like a white chocolate chip embedded in the center of a mound of chocolate frosting.

"As you know . . ." Genevieve started slowly, trying to order her thoughts so she could order her words. "Ever since the earthquake, I've believed that God had big plans for my life. Even so, to watch Him fulfill those plans the way that He did right after I graduated from college was mind-blowing. I mean, I was a design major. There's *no* way to explain the success of my first study except to say that God orchestrated it."

"You found yourself the recipient of a miraculous blessing for the second time in your life."

"Yes. For several years after that first study

everything was so very . . ." She hunted for the right word, then shrugged. "Rosy. I existed in this state of — of euphoria and amazement. I threw myself into my work, writing and speaking with everything I had."

"There must have been struggles."

"There were. But the satisfaction was far, far greater than the struggles."

"And then?"

Genevieve hesitated. "I can accept sympathy over the broken ankle, but I'll feel like a whiner if I complain about the few things in my life, before I broke my ankle, that weren't perfect."

"I'm a professional at listening to whining." The doctor grinned. "It's what you pay me for."

Genevieve laughed. How she loved this doctor's slightly irreverent sense of humor. It cracked icy chunks of awkwardness and pain more quickly than a blowtorch.

"I prefer to focus on the positive," Genevieve said.

"An admirable trait." Dr. Quinley rolled to her feet and extracted a small spray bottle from a drawer. "And yet, that trait can get us into trouble when we focus on the positive in lieu of dealing with the pain." She approached one of her plants. She sprayed it in time to a musical beat only she could hear, swaying her hips.

"You were on the verge of telling me about the pain," Dr. Quinley prompted. "Take a moment. Remember. Put yourself back in the place where you were when the work became less rosy." Dr. Quinley continued her task, moving from plant to plant.

"At some point along the line, I may have started overscheduling myself. As people became more familiar with my name and my books, I was invited to more and more conferences, webinars, worship events."

"To which you said yes and yes and yes."

"Not to all. But to as many as I could. I had a hard time turning down opportunities to glorify the Lord."

"I remember that flying on planes was scary for you when you were in middle school. Are you still a nervous flyer?"

"Yes. It's gotten worse over time, to be honest." She hated flying. While in the air, she hovered on the verge of inner panic the whole time. "Are you familiar with the verse 'Lo, I am with you always'?" Genevieve asked.

"I am."

"I take that literally." She ran her hand an inch above her arm rest. "*Low,* I am with you always."

"Ha!"

"Every time a plane takes off or hits turbulence, it makes me incredibly anxious. I spend most of the flight counting down the minutes until we land or solving the crossword puzzle in the airline magazine in an effort to distract myself from thoughts of fiery crashes."

"Yet you fly all the time."

"Sometimes as often as four times a week."

"The travel also deposits you in hotel rooms, which can be lonely places for some. Are they for you?"

Genevieve nodded.

"Tell me more about what was going on before the broken ankle."

Genevieve pulled her hair forward and combed her fingers through the last few inches of the strands. "The stress of the deadlines sometimes feels heavy. I'm contracted to write one study per year, which means I have to write and research at my maximum pace."

"Anything else?"

"I have a difficult time absorbing criticism. I've received lots of criticism from the secular market. Far worse, I've been criticized by fellow Christians who disagree with me."

"Mmm."

225

"I often feel like I'm caught in this weird place, feeling proud about the studies on one hand and feeling sheepish and undeserving about the studies on the other hand."

The older woman put away the spray bottle and hoisted herself so that she was sitting on the edge of her desk. Her Teva sandals swung back and forth beneath the hem of her long prairie skirt.

"When the audience applauds for me," Genevieve continued, "or when people ask to take a photo or when TV stations call me, it strokes my ego, which isn't good. It also makes me afraid that my prior studies were a fluke, that I don't know what I'm doing, and that no one will buy or like my next study. Which isn't good, either."

"How long were these pressures mounting before you broke your ankle?"

"Like I said, things were mostly great before I broke my ankle. I don't want to paint an inaccurate picture."

"Yes, but for how long were these pressures mounting?"

Genevieve toyed with the three bands of her rolling ring. "Two years. No. Three, maybe."

The doctor zipped a fingertip through the diffuser's mist stream. "At any point during the past four years did memories or nightmares about the earthquake begin to increase?"

The gentle, conversational question collided with Genevieve, unsettling her. "Yes, actually." A few years ago, nightmares about the earthquake began to sneak back into her life. Thoughts about the quake had followed. Which had fed more nightmares.

"Trauma never disappears, Genevieve. The things we've experienced are always a part of us. When we're stressed, old traumas like to rear their heads."

Genevieve sighed. "It sounds to me like we've got our work cut out for us."

"Take heart. It sounds to me like we're beginning to get to the root of the matter."

Almost a week later, Genevieve let herself into Sam's laundry room. She closed the exterior door loudly. She moved around noisily. She banged the washing machine's lid.

But alas. Sam did not appear.

Surreptitiously, she tried the door that led from the laundry room to the rest of his farmhouse. Locked, just as it had been the previous times.

A sense of disappointment descended over her like black confetti. Since she'd spoken with him at The Kitchen, she'd done laundry two other times and pulled weeds in his garden three more times. On every occasion, his truck had been parked at his house. On every occasion, she'd hoped to speak with him. On every occasion, he hadn't showed.

She'd now crawled and scraped her way to day thirty-seven of sobriety. She'd made it more than a third of the way toward the ninety-day mark. According to Dr. Quinley, some dopamine was supposed to have RSVP'd *yes* to her brain's invitation by this point.

It didn't feel like it tonight. After dinner, she'd tried and failed to watch a movie. She'd tried and failed to read a non-fiction tome on theology. When she'd caught herself fantasizing about how quickly and easily the Riverside Pharmacy could fill her remaining Oxy prescription, she'd bolted down to the pond.

Skipping rocks on the moonlit surface of the pond while whispering, "Not today, Satan" hadn't helped, so she'd decided to do something healthy both about her craving for human interaction and about the laundry in her dirty clothes hamper. She'd changed out of her sweatshirt and yoga pants into a sweater the color of a mocha, black jeans, and her cute new pair of leopard print flats. Then she'd come here.

Tonight, without the benefit of Oxy, she really needed Sam to answer the SOS she was sending him via washing machine.

She got the washing machine's cycle going, then closed the lid with another *clang*. *It's only 8:15 p.m., Sam!* The sun set less than an hour ago —

The door to the interior of the house sailed open. Sam stood in the doorway, looking tired and rumpled from a long day's work.

Sam!

"Is there something you don't understand about how to operate my washing machine?" he asked grumpily.

He came! "Hmm?" Genevieve tried to look inquiring and repentant, but she couldn't seem to hold the expression. The internal confetti turned pink and swirled happily upward. "No, no. I understand the operation of your washing machine perfectly."

His eyes narrowed. He wore yet another soft, casual T-shirt with jeans. His feet were bare. "No banging allowed."

"No, indeed. Certainly not." She smiled in a way she hoped would win him over. Then waited for him to soften.

And . . . *there.* The skin around his eyes crinkled with reluctant amusement.

Grasping his non-verbal invitation, she moved forward to peek around the edge of the door's casing into the mysterious confines of his house. "What are you up to tonight?"

"Nothing."

"Really? Me too!" She slid past him into a mudroom that ended in a short hallway. "Care to give me a tour of your house?"

"No."

"But you will anyway, right?" she asked over her shoulder as she slipped into the hallway. "Because I've already infiltrated past the drawbridge?" If she moved quickly, it would be harder for him to tug her back and quarantine her in the laundry room. The hallway led to a walk-in pantry, which emptied into his kitchen.

And what a kitchen.

The space had been renovated in a clean, unfussy style that suited the old bones of the house. Concrete countertops. Lower cabinets stained the same medium brown as the original wood floors. A white shiplap backsplash ran behind open shelves holding glasses, plates, bowls, pots. She didn't spot a single piece of clutter. Only spotless, empty spaces.

The kitchen opened in two directions. Toward the dining room at the front of the house and toward the living room that spanned the remaining width at the back of the house.

"You're not saying much," she mentioned.

"If you want someone to talk about furnishings, I'm not your bloke."

She slid the tip of her pointer finger along the dining room table as she passed it, then stopped for a moment to glance out one of the windows. Until now, she'd only been able to look in from the outside. This was her first, and maybe only, chance to look out from within.

She continued to the central foyer. On its far side, she found an office. Her senses feasted on the surroundings, savoring every detail the way she'd savor bites of chocolate cake. She backtracked to the foyer and ascended the stairs to the second floor —

Masculine fingers encircled her wrist.

Instantly, she stopped. Her inhale stilled partway as bands of awareness spread outward from the place his hand touched.

"No need to go upstairs," he said.

Heavens, he was private. "Okay," she said lightly. Truly, it had been a miracle that he'd allowed her to see the first floor.

His hand moved to support her elbow as

she backed down the stairs. "Careful. I wouldn't want you to break your other ankle." The deep, quiet timbre of his Australian accent curled into her ear and ran a delicious shiver down the side of her neck.

"There's a very real danger of that, I assure you."

He dropped her elbow as soon as she was stable, but the eye contact between them felt even more charged. The beauty of that darker ring of gray-green encircling the paler green of his irises . . .

Sam broke the moment by moving into the living area, which reflected the same spare, masculine design of his other rooms.

His desk and dining room table were both utilitarian farmhouse antiques without any frills. The chocolate brown leather sofa before her oozed smooth angles and quality. She liked both it and the mission style chairs that accompanied it, but she couldn't fathom how he existed without rugs, throw pillows, and all the other accent pieces — vases of flowers, pottery, photos, art — that she'd arrange on every surface if given a chance.

"This is a *great* farmhouse," she announced.

"Thanks."

She'd lived in Nashville since the age of

eighteen. She appreciated its restaurants, shopping, coffeehouses, museums, and theaters.

This was the first and only time that she'd passed weeks of her life on a large tract of land. While she hadn't decided yet whether she was suited to life on a farm, she knew *for sure* that it suited Sam. The life he'd carved for himself here was plain and straightforward. A man who lived and worked on his land was a self-sufficient, competent, independent man.

She motioned to a portable laundry rack, around the size of a small wall piano, standing in the room's corner. Clearly, he'd set it above a heating vent, because the upward air flow ruffled the clothing he'd arranged there. "I see that you have an indoor clothesline."

"Yep. For when it's cold or dark or rainy."

"You failed to mention this revelation when you introduced me to your outdoor clothesline. I've . . ." Her concentration slipped because it appeared that the man preferred boxer briefs, which was infinitely more interesting than talking about clotheslines.

See, she wanted to crow, *clotheslines can rob you of privacy, Sam!* But how could she? Then she'd have to call attention to his briefs. She dragged her focus up to him. "I've been waiting for nice weather to wash my clothes. You've forced me to become a laundry meteorologist!"

"You may want to invest in an indoor rack, North Korea."

"Winter's coming. You may want to invest in a dryer."

"Not going to happen," he stated. "Hungry?"

"A little."

"What did you have for dinner and when?"

"Ramen. Two and a half hours ago."

He shook his head in a way that communicated contempt for ramen. "Fancy a banana muffin?"

"Maybe even more than one."

He padded into the kitchen and went immediately to work, every move efficient. He did not consult a recipe.

"Oh. You're going to make them from scratch?"

"I make almost everything I eat from scratch."

"And I'm the opposite. I'm very pro-processed foods."

He ignored her.

"Do you ever splurge and eat something that's bad for you?" she asked.

"Almost never."

234

"Which means you occasionally *do* splurge. What is it that you eat on those occasions?"

"Tim Tams."

"Never heard of them."

"They're chocolate cookies."

Since her weaknesses had been on such ample display, it comforted her a little to know that his willpower wasn't infallible. "Can I help?" she asked.

"In a sec."

She washed her hands at the sink. It turned out that her help amounted to whisking the dry ingredients and then placing muffin cups in the muffin pan, which was probably what her level of baking expertise deserved.

He added strange, super healthy ingredients to the mix. Almond flour. Cashew butter.

Little wonder he had such a fantastic body.

"No sugar?" she asked.

"The natural sugar in the bananas is enough."

Enough for you, maybe, she wanted to say, but didn't. That would have sounded ungrateful when she wasn't. On the contrary. A melting thankfulness was overtaking her by degrees. So much so, she felt a little on the wobbly and tearful side. He'd invited her in. His company was comforting, and he was making muffins in a kitchen bathed with bright, cheery light.

It would have taken Genevieve ages to make muffins. Within a matter of just a few minutes, Sam was sliding the muffin tray into the oven.

She hurried to the sink before he could beat her to the post and began rinsing the mixing bowl and utensils he'd used to make the batter.

He opened the dishwasher and propped one narrow hip against the counter. She handed him items. He inserted them in the machine.

"Every time I see you," he said, "you look like you're feeling better."

It wasn't exactly an effusive compliment. In fact, it would've been hard *not* to look better than she had after withdrawal, when she'd resembled a cadaver. Yet, his statement delighted her. "Thanks. I'm feeling a little bit" — *a very little bit* — "better all the time."

"Yeah?" he said, utterly serious. With that one word, he asked a whole essay full of things.

Genevieve didn't know whether Sam liked her true self. At least, though, she felt free to *be* her true self with him. He didn't need

236

anything from her, except for her to abide by the rental agreement they'd struck. He had no ulterior motives. Her career, what she could do for him — none of that mattered here.

"I'm still adjusting to living alone in the country," she confessed. "The isolation's tricky. I . . . miss the benefits of Oxy. Every physical pain hurts worse than before and my job feels more stressful."

Grave lines etched into his face. "If you're tempted to take Oxy, you can call me."

"I can?"

"Yep."

"And you'll pick up?" she teased.

"For sure."

"The truth is that I didn't come here tonight to do laundry." She handed him the final spoon. He inserted it and closed the dishwasher door. "At least," she continued, "laundry wasn't my first priority. I came because I was hoping for someone to talk to. The solitude wasn't exactly helping matters tonight."

"In that case, I'm glad I was here."

"Me too." The moment stretched. She really shouldn't and couldn't fall for anyone until she had herself back in order. And yet . . . she didn't know if it could be helped. She could feel herself falling for Sam slowly and unavoidably. And, disastrously, it felt *good.* In fact, the delicious chemistry tugging her to him was one of the few bright spots in her life at the moment.

"Any news on your search into your parents' past?" he asked.

"Quite a bit, actually."

"What have you found out?"

"That they've been keeping something that happened before their marriage a secret from my sister and me."

"What's the secret?"

Oh, perish. This was awkward. She straightened her leather earring, which had twisted. "I'd rather not say. Which sounds very rude, especially considering that you're making me banana muffins. It's just that I feel honor-bound to protect my parents' privacy. For the moment, anyway. Do you understand?"

"Gotcha," he said simply.

Her posture relaxed. "I have about twenty things I'd like to ask you about the upcoming Fall Fun Day. Can we talk about that?"

"Sure."

They stayed in their spots, her at the sink, him at the oven, as the muffins baked and they discussed their plans for the Fall Fun Day they'd be hosting the first Saturday in October, a mere week and a half away.

After taking the muffins from the oven, he placed one on each of their plates. He split them with a knife so that steam danced out, then applied a pat of butter to the center and propped the two halves back against each other. He made for the dining table.

"How about we take our muffins to the sofa?" she asked.

"I don't eat in the living room."

"Of course you don't. But I'm a terrible influence, so c'mon. Bow to my peer pressure." She curled onto his sofa, balancing her plate on its arm rest. She tapped the top of her muffin to see if it was cool enough to eat. It wasn't.

He took the sofa's far end, putting as much space as possible between them.

"You're a very structured person, aren't you, Sam?"

"That's how I've hit my goals for myself."

"What goals? Give me an example."

"I wanted to own a restaurant," he answered. "I wanted to lease one of the national park farms. I wanted peace."

"And now that you have those things, do you think you can afford to be a little less structured?"

"Nope."

"Why?"

"Because if you're not careful, people will

sleep in your guesthouse and eat your banana muffins."

She grinned so widely her cheeks stretched.

He smiled back, his face creasing in that way that stole her breath.

To save herself from a swoon, she took a morsel of muffin, held it like a diamond to light, then ate it. It wasn't as sweet as she was used to, but it was rich, dense, and bursting with flavors of cinnamon and nutmeg. "Admit it. It's fun to have me here, sleeping in your guesthouse and eating your banana muffins."

"Hmm," he replied noncommittally.

"I'm outgoing and unpredictable, and I provide conversation." Regardless of what Sam believed, he needed people. He also needed a little spontaneity in his life. It would do him a world of good if he could give himself the freedom to occasionally fudge one of his own rules.

She had problems. But so did he. It seemed to her that he had the steadiness to help her with her problems. And she had the exuberance to help him with his.

"Go on," he said dryly.

"And I'm not terribly structured, which provides a . . . lively complement to your, uh, regimented ways."

"If you say so." His sentence communicated ambivalence, but his eyes communicated a very different thing. Heat. Fondness. Desire.

It was as if he were standing on one side of a lake and she on the other, and he longed to cross the lake but would never allow himself to do so.

He'd chosen his very separate life and had no intention of changing.

Ben

While Luke brushes the grit off his cell phone, I pat my arms to reassure myself that I'm not dead.

I'm alive.

For now.

I look around at the four kids with me — all of them white except for me. I wish my mom and dad were here. Or any of my brothers and sisters. Or Jordan and Derrick, my closest friends in the youth group and the only two other Black kids on the trip. They're still on the soccer field above. It's dumb to want them here. I shouldn't want that, because they're safer where they are.

I've grown up in the same town and church as the sisters and Luke. They're cool. But I don't know Sebastian. He's never come to anything at church before. He's quiet and angry, and when I tried to talk to him yesterday, he shut me down.

Luke dials the phone and all of us watch, desperate for him to make contact with anyone who can help.

CHAPTER TEN

Over the days of the following week, autumn began painting a collage of fall color across the north Georgia mountains. Genevieve continued to stick to the daily schedule Dr. Quinley had given her as if her life depended on it. Which, perhaps, it did.

She'd made two additions to the original schedule.

One, she'd taken up a hobby. Granted, the macabre pursuit of researching the Shoal Creek Killer and Russell Atwell's death may not have been what the doctor had had in mind.

Two, she'd been talking to and hanging out with Sam more often. He'd told her she could call him, and so she had been. Also, at long last, he was comprehending her "I'm desperate for human interaction" signals. If he was at home when she gardened or did laundry, he joined her.

She didn't know whether the Shoal Creek

Killer research was benefiting her. But she knew for certain that her time with Sam was. His presence was like body butter for her parched soul.

She'd gone on outings with her parents. Joined Natasha's family for dinner. Enjoyed her morning walks on the farm. Downed coffee and more coffee. Eaten convenience meals cooked in her mini-kitchen. Made time for lunch dates with old friends. Taken a visit to see Nanny, her dad's mom, who was suffering from dementia.

Whenever she was at the cottage, she'd taken to lighting her apple cider candle. It was burning even now, on this Friday night, twining its rich scent through the small space.

Had she been at home in Nashville this evening, she'd have plans with friends or she'd have a date. Not so, here in Misty River.

She tapped her big toe against the leg of her desk and leaned forward to try to catch a glimpse of Sam's farmhouse through the trees. She could make out a small glow through the darkness, nothing more. It was enough. Warm sparkles revolved within her chest.

She'd get to see him tomorrow at the Fall Fun Day.

She transferred her vision back to her computer and continued reading the article that filled its screen. No one knew how the Shoal Creek Killer, Terry Paul Richards, had chosen his victims. The experts speculated that he may have seen them on the street and followed them to their address. Or he may have simply parked in a random neighborhood and waited until a male entered one of the houses alone.

Great similarities linked his six murders, and only slight variances from his pattern made each of them distinct. He'd killed his first victim without any apparent struggle. He'd killed his second victim with his own hammer, instead of with an object belonging to the victim. He'd killed his third victim, then taken his shirt, in addition to a lock of hair, as a trophy. He'd killed Russell and arranged his body afterward, instead of leaving it where it fell. He'd killed his fifth victim with a single blow because the man had been elderly. He'd killed his sixth victim and taken the man's money from his wallet —

That did it. She couldn't take any more. She closed her web browser and turned on "Black Widow" by Iggy Azalea. She sang every lyric, dancing hip-hop from one corner of her cottage to another in order to lift her mood from serial killer gloomy to hip-hop hopeful.

Feeling slightly better and a little out of breath, she ate a package of jelly beans, then dialed her sister.

In lieu of a simple hello, Natasha answered with " 'In vain I have struggled. It will not do.' "

" 'You must allow me to tell you how ardently I admire and love you.' " Genevieve finished the quote from *Pride and Prejudice* with gusto.

"I love you, too," Natasha said. "Recovery update?"

"Still clean."

Natasha gave a *whoop.*

"I've finally finished reading everything about Terry Paul Richards and Russell that I could find online. You?"

"Same. I've also finished the two books I told you I checked out from the library." Children's shrieks came from Natasha's end. "Hang on," Natasha whispered. "I'm going to hide from my kids in the pantry, which might buy me one and a half minutes of privacy. There." The shrieks dimmed. "Oh, gosh. I'm so bloated! Maybe I'll down a shot of apple cider vinegar while I'm in here. Um . . . what were we saying?"

"I was about to say that I'm frustrated

because there's not a lot of reliable news from the time period about Russell specifically."

"I know, there's only those two articles from the *Camden Chronicle.* I've run search after search, and every time I get those same two articles."

"Then tons of speculation spouted by amateur investigators and conspiracy theorists in all the years since," Genevieve said.

"Which I don't put much stock in."

"Me neither. I tried to call the *Camden Chronicle* earlier today to see if I could get my hands on more back issues, but they closed down in 1990."

"What about the Camden library? Would they have back issues of the paper?"

"I'm way ahead of you, sister of mine." Genevieve had a perfectly good brain, but because she was older, Natasha often couldn't resist rushing in with suggestions before Genevieve finished talking. "The librarian I spoke with told me that they once had every issue of the *Chronicle* in their collection. However, they lost the issues in a fire in 2007."

"Bummer."

"The librarian went on to tell me, though, about a woman who lives in Camden. Her name's Mrs. Birdie Jean Campbell. She's ninety, and apparently she's kept a scrapbook-style diary for eighty years. Whenever people ask for old newspapers, the library sends them to Birdie Jean." Genevieve crossed to the fireplace and arranged logs inside. Since coming to stay at the cottage, she'd become a decent fire builder. A remote cottage with a fire in the fireplace was cozier than a remote cottage sans fire in the fireplace. "The librarian recommended that I call and schedule a visit with Birdie Jean. Evidently, Birdie Jean feeds visitors delicious but very sticky pecan pie, so she warned me about my dental work."

"That sounds promising."

"The visit or the pie?"

"Both."

"If I can reach Birdie Jean this weekend, I'm hoping to set up a meeting on Monday."

"Gen! I'm impressed."

"Thanks." She added kindling to the logs.

"I, too, have something new to report." A door rattled in the background. It seemed one of Natasha's kids was mounting a siege. "Everything I've read about Russell showed one of three photos of him. The college yearbook one, the grainy one from high school, and the one with his church baseball team. None were with Mom. But then it

249

occurred to me. A wedding picture of Mom and him must have run in the Athens newspaper along with their wedding announcement, since she was from Athens and they were married there. Right? So after two phone calls and some time online, I was able to locate their announcement."

"What? Why haven't you sent it to me?"

"Because I found it a little while ago, right when Owen was having an epic meltdown. Here. I'm sending it to you now."

"Mo-mmy!" came the muffled sound of a child's wail.

"Got to go," Natasha said. "Talk later?"

"Yep." They disconnected, and Genevieve opened her text messages. Natasha had sent two photos. One containing a picture. One containing text.

She inhaled sharply as she studied the photo. The close-up image captured her mom, the bride, with Russell, her groom.

In contrast to the dress her mother had chosen when she'd married Dad, here she wore the style of gown Genevieve would have expected of her. Formal and southern. Its sweetheart neckline lay beneath a sheer layer of tulle covering her chest and arms. Delicate needlework embellished the tulle at her throat and wrists, and along the contours of the bodice. She wore her hair swept up beneath a veil. Her bouquet burst with small roses.

Russell looked dashing and confident in his tux. His smile was broad and sure, his blond hair a gleaming match to Mom's blond hair.

The couple appeared just the way a couple should appear on their wedding day — happy and excited about their joyful future. They couldn't have known, in the millisecond when this photo was snapped, that Russell had very little future ahead of him. Which meant their marriage had very little future.

Genevieve rubbed her forehead. It bent her brain to see photos of her mother with this other man.

Dad was Mom's spouse. Dad, not this stranger. Mom and Dad had been a pair for as long as Genevieve could remember and for years prior to the start date of her memories.

Mom belonged with Dad.

Dad belonged with Mom.

Their identity as husband and wife was a foundational part of who Genevieve had known — *knew* them to be.

Yet she was holding in her hand evidence that proved Russell to be the one Mom had fallen in love with first. Picked out china with first. Exchanged vows with first.

Genevieve moved on to the second image Natasha had sent. The text of their wedding announcement.

> Caroline Herrington, daughter of Rosemary and Marcus Herrington of Athens, Georgia, married Russell Atwell, son of Helen and Gordon Atwell of Camden, Georgia, in a ceremony at St. George's United Methodist Church on July 18. A reception followed at Timmon's Restaurant.
> The bride is a graduate of Mercer University and is employed at Shady Grove Elementary as a second-grade teacher.
> The groom, also a graduate of Mercer University, serves as an associate at Colonial Savings and Loan.

She flicked back to the wedding photo. Russell had been more attractive than her father, which left her feeling protective of her dad. Which was ludicrous, since poor Russell had been the one in need of protection. She didn't want to feel bitter toward Russell at all. *Not at all.* He'd been murdered incredibly young, his life . . . and his wife . . . ripped from him. Russell deserved nothing but her compassion.

252

She returned to the announcement, poring over every detail of it for long minutes. Then she lit her fire and thought about Mom and Russell and Dad as she contemplated the flames.

"This event is precious," Genevieve's mom called to her as she walked toward Genevieve's position at the farm stand the next day.

Dad ambled a few steps behind Mom, hands in his pockets.

"Thanks!"

"Sweetie." Mom greeted her with a long, tight hug.

Dad gave her his customary one-armed side hug and kiss on the temple.

"I love what you've organized for this Fall Fun Day," Mom said, squeezing Genevieve's hand. "It's so good of you to volunteer your time this way. So giving."

"I'm happy to do it. Things are going really well so far." They'd opened for business at ten, two hours ago.

"Tell us what you have going on here," Dad said.

She explained the complimentary hot apple cider, the pick-your-own produce in the garden, the farm stand, and the hayrides Sam was giving that included a stop to harvest fruit at the apple orchard. People had been arriving in a steady stream and leaving happy.

With the exception of the couple who'd come to pick their own beets and had needed to be rescued from a discourse given by a volunteer named Oliver, their Fall Fun Day was clicking along very successfully.

"Aren't you too warm?" Mom asked.

"No, I'm okay." Genevieve had dressed in a lightweight sage green and white plaid shirt and artfully holey skinny jeans for the forecasted high of seventy-four. She'd weaved her hair into a messy side braid.

"Sure you're not too hot, sweetie?" Mom asked. "I have a travel cup of iced tea in the car."

"I'm sure."

"It's been *so long* since we've seen you."

It had been three days. "I'm glad you could come by."

"We wouldn't have missed it. I didn't want you to be lonely out here today all by yourself." Mom was still holding her hand.

"A girl named Anna will be taking over for me here at the farm stand any moment now. As soon as she arrives, I'll give you a tour."

"More satisfied customers," declared a deep voice.

Genevieve turned to see Oliver returning from the garden with a group of four visitors holding baskets brimming with the vegetables they'd harvested.

Genevieve extracted herself from her mom to ring up the guests' purchases.

Oliver addressed her parents with an air of importance. "Oliver Kingsley." Earlier, Oliver had informed Genevieve that he'd recently retired from his work at a local museum.

"Judson and Caroline Woodward," Dad said.

"We're Genevieve's proud parents," Mom added.

"And well you should be proud. Genevieve's a writer and speaker, which is work for the thinking person! I've done a fair bit of writing and speaking myself."

"Oh?" Mom asked.

"My PhD thesis, of course, is on the pre-Columbian peoples of South America. After that, I wrote a great many articles for those of us who roam the hallowed halls of academia. I've been asked to speak on numerous historical topics, history being my professional area of expertise. But I've also taken it upon myself to educate on topics in which I've invested personal study. For example, wine, art, literature, horticulture, and symphonic music."

"How fascinating!" Mom said.

"Mmm." Dad gave Oliver his polite attention.

Genevieve bagged the guests' produce and handed them receipts. Once done, she poured cups of steaming cider for her parents.

Oliver was of medium height and, likely thanks to his personal study of wine, husky around the middle. He kept what was left of his sandy gray hair short and tidy. He'd clocked in for work this morning dressed in the most dapper gardening clothes Genevieve had ever witnessed on someone who wasn't an online model. A field shirt from L.L. Bean, zip-off pants he (mercifully) hadn't zipped off, a bush hat, and gardening boots.

"During my years in Bogota, after receiving my PhD, I was pressed into service as a writer and speaker. The people practically broke down the doors, insisting to hear what I had to say."

"Mmm," Dad murmured again kindly, sipping his cider.

"Do you have a family, Oliver?" Mom asked, making a naked bid to steer the conversation toward the topic she cared about most — the God-ordained fabulousness of mothering and grandmothering.

"I do not." Oliver gave his belly two satis-fied taps. "Many the lady has tried to turn my head from the delights of the scholarly world, but my heart has stayed true to its first love." A gusty laugh. "Learning."

"Well, we have two daughters," Mom told Oliver, undaunted by Oliver's lack of either interest in or experience with families. "And two grandchildren whom we're crazy about — just crazy. When they say that the role of grandparent is the best in the world, they're right. What a joy. What a joy."

"I happen to believe that sommelier is the best role in the world. And I won't be dis-suaded." More gusty laughter.

Just then, a bright blue Chevy Cruze roared up the farm's drive and skidded to a stop in the makeshift parking area. A slim blonde stepped out almost before the tires had stopped spitting gravel. She walked toward them, her attention glued to her phone.

This must be Anna. Sam had told her that Oliver gave his time because he enjoyed talking to a fresh audience. Anna gave her time because she was attending community college and looking to accumulate service hours before applying to universities.

"A sommelier in Madrid," Oliver blustered, "introduced me to a divine Tempranillo one humid night at a sidewalk restaurant on one of the plazas. Let me think how many years ago that was. . . ."

Anna lifted her head once she was upon them. "Oliver!" She gave him a wide smile and a hug.

Oliver stiffened. "Anna," he said, the way someone might say *Ebola.*

Anna exchanged introductions with Genevieve and her parents. The girl projected sweet and wholesome prettiness. Her long hair appeared to have dried of its own accord, but had nonetheless dried in a mussed way that looked great.

"It's so cool that your parents came by," Anna said to Genevieve. Before Genevieve could reply, she continued. "I just finished brunch with my parents. My mom's a nurse and my dad's an accountant. You'd think accountants wouldn't have any personality — because . . . *numbers.* But he has lots of personality." Her phone beeped, and she looked down at it for a few seconds. Her focus lifted again. "He took me golfing with him the other day, and he had the guys laughing and laughing. They were all drinking way too much on the course, by the way. I was all, *'How are you expecting to drive the ball straight after flagging down the cart girl for beer every time she comes by'* — and they called me a rookie. The day was so warm. Perfect for golf! Anyway . . . numbers."

Anna's conversation made as much sense as a preschooler's scribble.

"Mmm," Dad said, nodding.

Oliver cleared his throat. "About that night in Madrid," he ventured, just as Mom said, "Do you have siblings, Anna?"

"Yep!" She tucked her phone into the back pocket of the tight jean shorts she'd paired with a voluminous T-shirt. "I have two older brothers. One's still in college, and one's working in Atlanta. I'm definitely going to stay with him for a few days over Christmas break, which can't get here soon enough, you know?"

Mom's face pinched with consternation as she waited for the tiniest of opportunities to talk about herself.

"I'm taking twelve hours this semester," Anna continued, "and chemistry is kicking my booty. I need about five cups of apple cider to make me feel better after all that chem. Is the apple cider hot?"

"It is," Genevieve supplied.

"Yay!"

Just then Genevieve spotted Sam's John Deere tractor and her heart hitched with delight. The tractor topped a rise and continued toward them, slowly towing guests back to the farm stand.

Anna checked her phone, turned the mobile receipt printer a different direction, started to jot a note to herself, got distracted, then unstacked the baskets guests used to pick their own produce and displayed them in a different way.

Frowning, Oliver stacked them back the way they'd been while Mom provided Oliver and Anna with dossiers on her two grandchildren that Oliver and Anna obviously cared nothing about.

The visitors who'd taken Sam's tour moved toward the farm stand with their apples. Anna snapped to attention when they were just feet away, as if she hadn't seen them coming, as if they'd materialized out of thin air.

Sam strode toward Genevieve and her parents wearing a white T-shirt, his black baseball cap, and black jeans.

"Everything running smoothly?" he asked her.

"Very smoothly."

Sam greeted her parents courteously.

In Sam, her mother at last found an audience willing to give her undivided attention while she spoke about her children and grandchildren.

It wooed Genevieve, watching Sam listen so carefully to her mom.

As soon as Oliver finished unfixing every fix Anna had made to the farm stand, Oliver clapped Sam on the shoulder. "Samuel. Never fear, I've been guiding your guests through your garden with the utmost respect. One couple so appreciated the recipe for tamales I rattled off and the tidbits I shared regarding sustainable farming practices that they asked to take a photo with me. I consented, of course."

"Thanks, Oliver."

"Can *I* have a picture with you?" Anna asked Oliver. "You look so cute today — like an ad for fly fishing."

"I beg your pardon. I'm clearly attired for gardening —"

"Fly fishing is super boring," Anna said, apparently forgetting her fleeting plan to snap a picture. "Also, the river is really cold. I went with my family once, and we couldn't figure out why our feet were freezing because our guide was fine. We found out later that our waders were leaking. Our feet were standing in puddles of water! No wonder our toes were freezing. Which reminds me, I need a pedicure."

Oliver regarded Anna with deep disdain.

"Genevieve has such a wonderful way of communicating her thoughts," Mom was saying to Sam. "So relatable. That the Lord has called one of our children to serve Him in this way means so much to us. What a rich, rich blessing. He is so good."

Genevieve intervened before Mom could bathe Sam in the full spectrum of her emotions. "So far, my parents have only seen the farm stand," she said to him. "I'm about to show them around."

"If you'd like to see the apple orchard, we can get there quickly on my ATVs," Sam told her dad.

Instantly, Dad perked up. "I'd like that. How many ATVs do you have?"

"Two. Each one can carry two of us."

They made their way to the barn. Mom sat behind Dad, which meant Genevieve was paired with Sam. He slung a leg over the four-wheeler first. Oh my. This was going to throw the two of them into very close proximity. She positioned herself as respectfully far behind him on the seat as she could without jeopardizing her life.

"Hang on," he murmured.

Tentatively, she set her hands on his lean sides. Sensation rolled up her arms, stealing her breath.

They shot through the open mouth of his

262

barn going what felt like sixty miles an hour.

Their vehicles ate up the ground as the earth rose, fell, and turned. Whiffs of Sam's delicious soap kept snapping back to her on the breeze. Through the fabric of his shirt, the contact of her palms against his ribs radiated heat.

They were going faster than she would've chosen to go on her own. The exhilaration of that, plus the air singing against her face and the beautiful landscape, made her feel as though she was one hundred percent alive.

This is what life is, Genevieve.

She needed more living in her life. Now that she was adjusting to the slower and quieter rhythm of the farm, she'd realized that she'd made constant activity into an idol worth pursuing. She'd spent more time crafting social media posts to make it look like she was flourishing than she'd invested in *actual* flourishing. She'd let her work consume too much. . . . But then, she'd always found it hard to know where to draw the line. How could anything she did for Jesus be considered too much?

When they reached the orchard, Sam stepped from the ATV, then helped her off, his touch sure.

As their group walked along the rows

between the lines of apple trees, he answered her parents' questions and explained the varieties he grew. The oldest section of the orchard had been planted in the 1800s and contained historic strains like the Yellow Transparent, Red Detroit, Early Rus, and the Esopus Spitzenburg apple. "Which was Thomas Jefferson's favorite," Sam said. "He ordered twelve apple trees for Monticello."

He indicated the far portion of the orchard, populated by smaller trees. "When I moved in, I planted newer varieties. Honeycrisp, Rome Beauty, Red Delicious, and Granny Smith."

"Can we taste an apple?" Mom asked.

"More than that, you're welcome to pick as many apples as you can carry back on the ATV. My treat."

Mom clasped her hands together. "Thank you! This is a moment to treasure, Sam. What a sweet memory this will be."

Sam took her mom's syrupy words in stride. "I'm glad you stopped by."

Her parents drifted toward the old section of trees. Genevieve ambled toward the new, Sam following.

"Thanks for being great with my mom and dad."

"Anytime." He bent and moved a large stick out of her way. "Does your dad have a

264

problem with his eyes? I noticed that something seemed different about his left eye."

"Very perceptive, Sam. Most people don't pick up on that." She hadn't known her dad any other way, so she herself didn't tend to see anything out of the ordinary when she looked at him. She settled her braid forward over her shoulder. "He was in a car accident before he met my mom. A piece of glass punctured his left eye so badly that it couldn't be saved. He has an artificial eye."

"It looks a lot like the real thing."

"The doctors did a great job. They left all the muscles around the eyeball intact, which is why he still has some movement in the artificial eye. Just not as much as a real eye. Also, it can't dilate. Nor can it change color slightly, the way real eyes do in different light."

"It seems like he's adapted well."

"Apparently he had a hard time adapting immediately after it happened. But over time, he's learned to deal with it. He's less coordinated than he was, but he was never an athlete to begin with. He positions himself so that his artificial eye is the one next to a wall or sits at the end of rectangular tables so he can see everyone better. He's a very defensive driver and doesn't drive at all at night."

Sam made a thoughtful sound.

"He has to see a chiropractor fairly often because the way he holds his head, angled to the side, throws him out of alignment. And, of course, he and his eye doctor are very, very careful of his remaining eye."

They strolled together between healthy green branches.

"My mom has to tell him when his glasses are dirty on the side of the artificial eye. Otherwise, he'd never know." She rose to her tippy toes to reach for a Honeycrisp. Too high.

Sam adroitly snapped it from its branch. After shining it on his shirt, he handed it to her.

His eyes met hers. So much lived in his expressions.

She took a bite. The apple gave way with a satisfying crunch. Firm, tangy, juicy.

As they walked, they talked about the changes she'd advised him to make to his website and social media accounts.

His gorgeous accent flowed over her like poetry. His hard body moved with grace. His size and sturdiness reassured her.

Sam Turner was a man who knew his own mind. He was comfortable in his skin. He was also secretive and occasionally prickly. He had a grip on what was important and what wasn't. The more she dug past his closed-off exterior into his character, the more she found decency and goodness at his core.

The National Park Service had entrusted every growing thing and every structure on these acres to Sam's care. She shouldn't be surprised that a man who had a way with growing things also had a way with women. Like these trees, and partly because of Sam, she was starting to thrive in this soil.

It had been a long, long time since she'd felt for anyone the way she was starting to feel for Sam. The rush of emotions. The glittering hormones. The awareness.

She needed to be careful. Super careful. Dr. Quinley had told her that the absence of Oxy would leave a void that needed filling. It had. Intellectually, she knew the hole needed to be filled by God and God alone. So why was she instinctively tempted to fill that void with Sam? If she let herself go there, then she'd be exchanging one crutch — painkillers — for another crutch — a man. A man who had, let her not forget, informed her from the first that there would be no romance between them.

What if she told him about her interest, and he shut her down? (Highly likely.) What if, by some miracle, he eventually reciprocated her feelings (unlikely) and then ended up shattering her heart (likely)? Where would she be then? Devastated. And what effect might that have on her recovery? Detrimental.

She'd be wise to do what Dr. Quinley advised: focus all her energy on confronting and dealing with her issues so that she could hope to stay clean in the future.

The sound of her mom's laughter traveled to her, and Genevieve angled a look at her parents. Dad had made a basket out of the hem of his polo shirt, and Mom was giggling as she added apples to it.

What exactly had her mom and dad done all those years ago?

Genevieve

"Nobody's answering," Luke says. Then he whispers a curse word I've only heard at school a couple of times in my life and dials his cell phone a second time.

I swallow hard. My arm is cut, and I don't want to look at the blood. It's stinging, and there's dirt in it. Sebastian's head is hurt. And where's Ethan? He was behind us in the hallway.

Tears are burning my eyes, but I'm not going to cry in front of handsome Luke and mean Sebastian. I press my teeth into my bottom lip.

Faintly, I can hear the phone ringing that Luke's pressed to his ear. *Answer. Answer, someone. Please.*

"Mom?" Luke says.

I blink and blink to fight back tears.

"Mom, there was an earthquake, and we're in the basement of the building where we —" he pushes a trembling hand to his forehead — "where we were storing the sports equipment. We need help."

A very short pause.

"I'm okay."

Another pause.

"I don't know. Ethan was with us. But now . . ." His voice breaks and, angrily, he turns away from us and walks as far as he can toward a ruined wall. "But now he's not."

CHAPTER ELEVEN

Genevieve had been imagining Mrs. Birdie Jean Campbell as small and frail. Thus, she was slightly taken aback when a tall, buxom African-American woman answered her knock. Birdie Jean did not radiate frailty. She moved slowly and spoke slowly but accomplished both with dignified assurance.

The older woman ushered Genevieve into the parlor of her two-story Victorian near the heart of the town of Camden, Georgia. The tidy, antique-filled interior smelled like pastry crust and had the ambiance of a museum.

The first several days Genevieve had tried to reach Birdie Jean, the phone had rung and rung. When Birdie Jean had finally picked up, she'd told Genevieve this Monday morning time slot was her earliest opening.

More than a week had now passed since the Fall Fun Day, so Genevieve and Natasha had been given a chance to exercise the virtue of patience.

Genevieve and Birdie Jean settled at a round table and shared pecan pie, lukewarm tea, and conversation. Birdie Jean asked Genevieve questions in a way that reminded Genevieve of an employer interviewing a job applicant. Perhaps she only gave diary access to those who passed her pecan pie test?

Each time Genevieve finished speaking, the elderly woman paused before replying, as if mulling over what Genevieve had just said.

Birdie Jean's gray-black hair was coiled into a low bun. She wore an elegant pewter-colored sweater set and slacks. No jewelry, save for a simple wedding band. No makeup, save for a neutral shade of peach lipstick with just a hint of shimmer.

Horn-rimmed glasses perched on her large face. Either Birdie Jean was attuned to current eyeglass styles or she'd been wearing that style since the first time it had been popular in the 1950s.

Unobtrusively, Genevieve worked to free a stubborn bit of pecan pie from her molars. The woman at the library had been right to warn her. If Genevieve had tried to eat this pie with a loose crown, she'd have been a goner.

Birdie Jean rested her hands in her lap and studied Genevieve owlishly. Though Genevieve had been working to win the older lady's approval since entering her home, she didn't think she'd succeeded. It seemed likely that Birdie Jean might deem her unworthy of the diaries and send her away empty-handed except for the sliver of pie wedged against her tooth.

"Tell me what brought you here today," Birdie Jean said.

"My mom has been married to my dad for thirty-four years. But she was married once before that, briefly, to a man from Camden who was killed. My sister and I would like to read all the articles about her first husband's death. We can only find two of them online."

"What's your mother's name?"

"When she lived here in Camden, her name was Caroline Atwell."

At once, clarity came into Birdie Jean's time-worn eyes. "I remember."

A thrill glided down Genevieve's arms, raising goose bumps.

"She was married to Russell Atwell, yes?" Birdie Jean asked.

"Yes, ma'am."

273

It took Birdie Jean quite some time to rise. "Right this way."

They passed a bedroom containing a bed covered in a jewel-toned quilt. "Just here." Birdie Jean motioned for Genevieve to enter a small rectangular room with a single window and armchair situated at its end. Shelves ran the length of the two long walls and housed volume after volume of twelve-inch-tall scrapbooks. "I believe Russell was killed in 1983. Is that correct?"

Birdie Jean had a card catalog for a brain. "Yes, that's correct."

The older woman located the scrapbook from that year. Genevieve helped her slide it from its place, and they set it on the narrow standing table occupying the center of the room.

The book's spine gave a protesting creak as Birdie Jean opened it and carefully turned the pages. It was somewhat insulting to call this tome a diary. It included handwritten entries, yes. But much more than that, too. She'd adhered newspaper pages to it. A candy wrapper. A movie ticket. Photos.

When she found the page she sought, Birdie Jean positioned the scrapbook before Genevieve, then unfolded the front page of that day's newspaper so that it expanded beyond the confines of the book. She held her silence, seeming to want Genevieve to learn the details through the sources she'd saved instead of through her own memories.

Man Found Dead in His Home, the headline read. Below, a photo depicted crime scene tape in the foreground and a modest ranch-style home in the background.

Genevieve leaned over the small print and read silently.

Russell Atwell, 23, died at his home on Farm Road 481 on Saturday evening. "Mr. Atwell was struck in the head amid signs of a struggle," Police Chief Stanton said at a press conference in the early hours of Sunday morning. "The exact time of his death is unknown at this point."

The similarities to the three murders perpetrated by the Shoal Creek Killer are unmistakable. Like the others, Mr. Atwell died of blunt force trauma. Like the others, he was a white male who was at home alone when the intruder entered his home. Like the others, he was subdued via hand-to-hand combat.

At the press conference, Chief Stanton was quick to address the concern of local citizens. "It's too soon to say whether Mr.

Atwell was a victim of the Shoal Creek Killer. You can be certain that we will gather every piece of evidence and investigate this crime to the fullest extent of the law in hopes of bringing the offender to justice."

The deceased's wife, Mrs. Caroline Atwell, was attending Bible study with her sister-in-law Sandra Atwell when the attack occurred. Upon returning home, the women discovered Mr. Atwell's body and notified authorities.

Mom, Genevieve thought, her heart heavy. What an unbearably traumatic thing to have found upon returning home.

"This is a tragic event," Chief Stanton stated. "We can't allow mass fear to run rampant and overshadow the fact that our community has lost one of its longstanding members. Our deepest condolences go to Mr. Atwell's family and friends."

Russell Atwell is survived by his wife, his parents, Alice and Gordon Atwell, and his younger sisters, Sandra and Dawn.

Genevieve stepped back from the table and considered Birdie Jean, who returned her regard evenly.

"I'm guessing that the *Camden Chronicle* continued to follow this story closely," Genevieve said.

"Oh yes. The residents of this town were shaken from the time of the first murder, which happened in Winterville." She released a mournful clicking sound of regret. "Winterville is close. Just a handful of miles up the road. Then the murders continued. It was all people could talk about and think about in those days. People were sleeping with handguns and arming their teenage children if they had to leave those children home alone to go to work. Everyone suspected everyone else. A very scary time."

"It must have been a relief when Terry Paul Richards was arrested and put behind bars."

"It truly was."

"I don't want to take up too much of your time, but I'd love to read all the articles you have about Russell's murder."

"Make yourself comfortable there in the chair and take as much time as you need." She paused in the doorway to look back. "You can find me in the front of the house when you're ready to leave."

"Yes, ma'am. Thank you."

Genevieve toted the scrapbook to the

armchair and adjusted the pages to catch the sunlight. The brightness almost seemed to enliven the words and images and mementos preserved there, making them buzz with life once again.

She refolded the front page along its crease marks, turned the diary's page, and unfolded the newspaper on the next page. Again and again. The articles, as well as Birdie Jean's handwritten entries and all the other artifacts saved, gave her a feel for the town at that particular point in history.

She took copious pictures of each article so that she and Natasha could go over them later in greater detail. Articles that brought to life the crime scene, the autopsy, the investigation. She read all the way until the Shoal Creek Killer was found, then glanced through the two weeks of entries following for good measure before slotting the scrapbook back into its place.

Birdie Jean sat on her fancy sofa, legs primly crossed, spine straight, reading. Graciously, she gestured for Genevieve to assume the spot at the sofa's other end.

Genevieve perched on the cushion, purse strap over her shoulder, very aware of how long she'd already been in Birdie Jean's home. She didn't want to overstay her welcome.

"What is it that you'd like to ask me, Genevieve? I can see a question in your face."

"Since you were living here in Camden during those years, I'm wondering if you have anything to add that wasn't reported in the articles. About Russell's death or the Shoal Creek Killer?"

Birdie Jean's glasses seemed to magnify her astute eyes. "Right when we first heard about Russell's death, I recall that some people around here suspected Angus Morehouse. That was before Terry Paul Richards was arrested, of course."

"Angus Morehouse hasn't been mentioned in any of the reading I've done."

"He was Russell and your mother's nearest neighbor. A difficult man. Quick to anger. He and Russell had some disagreements about the property line between them, and they came to blows one night at a party over your mother."

"My mother?"

"Russell accused Angus of making advances on Caroline."

"Had he been making advances?"

"No one knows."

"How long before Russell's murder did this fight occur?"

"Several months before."

"Did the police question Angus after Russell's death?"

"I believe that they did. As far as I know, though, not a single piece of evidence tied Angus to the scene. It's a far leap to assume someone who's willing to fight with another would be willing to kill another. There are plenty of men around here who are willing to fight."

From what she could tell, Russell had been one of them. He'd broken lamps and a mirror when defending himself from the Shoal Creek Killer.

"Some years after Russell's death," Birdie Jean said, "Angus had an altercation with a co-worker and injured the man so badly that Angus was sent to jail. When he was released, he moved back to town and worked as a welder. He's been in a fight or two since then, but for the most part, he's settled down and kept to himself. He's retired now."

"Is he still living in the house near the one my mother lived in?"

"Yes."

Genevieve nodded. "Do you have any memories of my mother, either before or after Russell died?"

"I have no recollection of her before Russell's death. She'd only been in Camden a short time, and she and Russell lived a good ways outside of town. I did see her a few times after Russell's death, though. At his funeral. And once, walking into the grocery store."

"What were your impressions of her?"

"She looked very sad, certainly. Lovely woman. After Russell's death, she didn't mix with the community much. As soon as she could, she moved away, and we understood why, of course. Caroline was young and her people didn't live in these parts."

"Do you know what became of Russell's family?"

Her forehead creased. "I'm close in age to Russell's mother, Alice. We didn't go to school together because, in those days, schools were segregated. I was on a committee with her once, though. We were both women of faith, and we talked about that a few times. She and the rest of her family were active in this town up until Russell's death. After that, like your mother, they moved away. To Atlanta, I believe."

The Atwells' oldest child had been stolen from them with swift finality. Years later, her mother would come within inches of having her own children taken from her as irrevocably as her first husband had been. "Thank you," Genevieve said.

"You're welcome. Call again, should you like to come back."

They said their good-byes, and Genevieve returned to her Volvo. Sitting in the driver's seat, she pulled out her phone and scrolled to the photo she'd taken of the very first newspaper article about the killing. The house where Russell and Mom had lived looked small, well kept, rural.

She hunted through her photos and located the picture she'd taken of Russell's death certificate. She enlarged it until she could make out the address given for the location of his death.

47130 Farm Road 481, Camden, Georgia.

An inaudible voice was calling her toward her mom's old house.

A pall settled over her when she pulled to a stop in front of the home her mother and Russell had lived in as newlyweds.

For a protracted moment she sat, peering through her side window, before turning off her ignition and exiting the car. The orderly brick house immortalized in the newspaper picture had fallen into disrepair. The roof sagged. Weeds choked the foundation. Today's moody gray sky highlighted the somber temperament of the place. The windows bore cracks that reminded her of spider webs and holes that reminded her of open mouths.

Clearly, the structure had been abandoned long ago. Immediately after Russell's death?

Had Russell not been killed, Genevieve would not be alive. Her mother would have given birth to different children, Russell's children. Genevieve was distinctly aware that she, the daughter who lived only because Russell had died, was not necessarily welcome here, in the epicenter of her mother's secret past.

The house was set a good distance back from the road, nothing but desolate acres around it. She walked halfway to it, then stopped. Any farther, and she'd feel like an intruder.

Her phone dinged, startling her so deeply that she yelped. Sam had sent her a text. *Your car hasn't been at the guesthouse for hours. Everything okay?* The Kitchen was closed on Mondays, so he wouldn't have gone to the restaurant this morning. She knew him well enough to know he'd spend his day working on the farm instead.

Yes! she replied.

Where are you?

Genevieve paused. She wasn't ready to divulge the long path that had brought her to Russell's home. Plus, things were going so well between her and Sam lately. At the moment, she was technically trespassing, and if he found out she was pursuing the investigation to this degree, it might throw a wrench into things. And that, she did not want.

I'm shopping, she typed.

From this vantage point, she could see only one other structure. A simple house about a half a mile or so down the road. Angus's house.

Genevieve lived alone, but here, her alone-ness made her feel vulnerable. She swallowed against the unease scratching its way up her esophagus.

Her mother's husband had died in this building, and the sorrow of that seeped up from the earth. The wind bemoaned the fact that Russell's future had been robbed from him.

Troubled, she studied the plywood blocking the door.

Where had the Atwell family gone? And what did the writer of the mysterious letter know that Genevieve did not?

After grabbing lunch in Camden, Genevieve arrived back at the cottage during the long, lazy hours of the afternoon best suited to napping. She'd need to resist the urge to nap, however, because she intended to spend the rest of the day and evening catching up on the work she'd sacrificed this morning.

She let herself inside, tossed her purse on her desk, then froze when Sam straightened from the love seat and turned to face her, wearing a simple gray shirt and jeans. Her pleasure at seeing him stuttered when she registered the uncompromising seriousness of his face. What was the matter?

"I didn't see your car," she said stupidly.

"I walked." He stared at her. "Where are your shopping bags?"

Shoot! "I . . . didn't end up buying anything."

His jaw firmed in a way that communicated his disbelief.

He was going to see through her lie about shopping, exactly like he'd seen through her lies the morning he'd found her sleeping in this cottage. Her mind moved too quickly — darting in many directions — and too slowly, struggling to adjust to his surprise appearance. "D-did you let yourself in to search for Oxy?"

"Yes."

"And you found none."

"I found none," he confirmed.

Back when they'd hashed out their rental

agreement, he'd reserved the right to search her cottage. Given that, why did the realization that he'd been here, searching for Oxy, hurt so badly? Why did it feel like a colossal betrayal?

. . . Because almost two months had passed since he'd agreed to let her stay on his farm. In that time, she'd come to trust him, and she'd hoped he'd come to trust her, too.

This proved that he hadn't. Which *stung.*

"I've had a bad feeling all day," he told her. "It got worse when you said you were shopping. If you'd wanted to go shopping, you'd have gone on Saturday or Sunday like usual."

"I wasn't shopping," she admitted. "Nor was I in some dark alleyway getting high on Oxy. I was in the town of Camden researching my parents."

"Then why didn't you tell me that?"

Agitated, she thrust her fingers into her hair, fanning the heavy mass around her shoulders. "I didn't want to explain, and I didn't want to risk upsetting you."

"Upsetting me? Did I react badly the other night when you said you couldn't tell me more about your parents?"

The quiet snapped with electricity, and her heartbeat began to accelerate. "No."

286

He held his powerful body still.

She couldn't tease her guilt apart from her anger. She'd been wrong to lie, of course. Very wrong. But *he'd* been snooping through her cottage!

"Is it your instinct to lie whenever you're faced with something uncomfortable?" he asked.

His words hit so close to home that defensiveness rose inside her like a flash flood. "Why is it that I have to answer to you, Sam? Why is it that you expect me to let you search the place where I live —"

"You know why I expect you to let me search this place."

"— and you expect me to tell you the truth, the whole truth, and nothing but the truth, when you haven't told me *anything* about yourself?"

He didn't move outwardly. Deep in his eyes, though, she sensed a fire igniting. "I want you to be honest with me," he said with stony control, "because I think honesty will help you. Your lack of transparency is strangling you."

"Your lack of transparency is strangling *you*!" she said vehemently, gesturing toward his farmhouse. "As far as I can tell, you've sequestered yourself up there so you don't have to see or speak to anyone."

"I've made peace with being alone."

"God didn't make any of us to be as alone as you are, Sam!"

"He did."

"*No.* He didn't." She glared, her hands fisting. "I suspect that someone close to you has gone through drug withdrawal. And you told me that you once lost someone you loved. That's it! We've had numerous conversations, and that's all you've ever told me."

"You want to know about me?" he demanded coldly.

"Yes!"

"I fell in love with a woman named Kayden once. She was beautiful and talented and young and full of life." He threw the words at her, his features expressionless. "I brought Percocet home for us to try. She got hooked, and it dragged her down. She spent two years trying to get free of it, and I spent two years trying to save her. We both failed. I walked out. She overdosed and died." A tendon in his neck tightened. "That's me, Genevieve."

All her organs seemed to slip downward as if on an escalator. What he'd been through was so shockingly awful that it rendered her instantly compassionate and instantly mortified that she'd found fault with him over his reluctance to share.

No wonder he'd been hesitant to open up. No wonder he hadn't wanted to rent this cottage to her. No wonder he'd demanded to search this place at will.

She was a painful reminder of the woman he'd lost.

He bent and picked up his hat from the love seat. Rolling it in the fingers of one hand, he moved toward the door. "You asked me earlier why you have to answer to me. Other than following through on the things we agreed on when I said that you could stay here, you don't have to answer to me. In fact, it's better if you don't. I don't want to get wrapped up in this."

"I . . ."

He hesitated on the threshold, holding the door half open. "So long as you do the things you said you'd do when you moved in, that's all I need from you."

"Sam —" She hurried to the doorway, but he didn't look back. Shivering with the force of her emotions, gnawing on her bottom lip, she watched him go. Recriminations formed a cyclone within.

Convincing Sam to befriend her had been like convincing a wolf to eat from her hand. In losing her temper, what had she done? Had she just ruined all the headway they'd made? Their relationship was more valuable to her than gold.

She closed the door, sat heavily on the edge of her bed, and burst into tears.

The north wind blew against Sam as his strides ate the distance between Gen's guesthouse and his farmhouse.

Fury roiled inside him.

Hadn't he shown Gen that she could count on him? Why, then, had she lied to him instead of simply telling him the truth? He couldn't stand it when people lied to him.

His memory swam back in time. He'd texted Kayden one day to ask what her lunch plans were, very similar to the way he'd checked on Gen today.

I'm planning to work through lunch at my desk. XO XO, she'd texted back.

Sam drove to her favorite sushi place and ordered a rainbow roll and a side salad to go.

When he arrived at her office carrying Kayden's surprise lunch, the receptionist greeted him with a smile. "Hi, Sam."

"Hi, Torrie. Is it all right if I head back and drop this off for Kayden?"

Her expression dipped. "Oh. That's thoughtful of you. And it would be all right, of course, to take it to her." She fidgeted. "Except that Kayden doesn't work here anymore. She was . . . let go. Her last day was Tuesday."

It was Monday. Almost a week had gone by, and Kayden hadn't told him that she'd lost her job. She'd been pretending that everything was normal. Getting up, getting ready, going to work.

They were so close — *he'd thought* they were so close. The realization that she'd been lying impacted him like a body blow.

"I see." He stood in the lobby of his girlfriend's former firm, humiliated, stunned, afraid down to his bones because Kayden was everything to him. "Thanks for letting me know," he'd said.

Even now, his relationship with Kayden was part of who he was. A large part that equaled years of his life. Her death had scarred him more than any other event. There was no way that Gen could interact with a version of him that hadn't been marked by Kayden. And because of Kayden, he had no tolerance for lies. Even small ones.

He pinched the bridge of his nose. He'd been lonely for a long time, which should have made him strong. But in some ways, it had made him weak.

The weakest part of him had come to care about Gen, despite his determination not to.

If he were a color, he'd be brown. But Gen was one hundred bright colors. She was feisty and outspoken and felt things deeply. He respected her gifts and her ministry. Her personality, her appearance, her profession — all were larger than life. When he was talking to her in his farmhouse or garden or restaurant, she drove every other person out of his head. Even Kayden.

He didn't want to forget Kayden, especially because he *could not* go through what he'd gone through with Kayden a second time. The way he'd left things between him and Gen just now was for the best. There was no reason for them to communicate as much as they had been. With any luck, she'd leave soon. In the meantime, he didn't want the stress she made him feel. He didn't want the desire, either. Or the doubt or the amusement or the pleasure.

Good riddance.

Why, then, did his gut twist like a sponge at the thought of her leaving?

Luke

I grip the phone hard. I've been talking for a long time now. First to my mom, then my dad. They're panicking and at the same time trying to stay calm. I know they're terrified for Ethan. I know because I'm terrified for Ethan.

Mom had Misty River's sheriff call me. The sheriff contacted someone who called and said he was a specialist in urban search and rescue. After that, I talked to someone with the United Nations. Then to someone in San Salvador, who was hard to understand.

Now I'm talking to my dad again, and I'm clinging to his voice because my phone is almost out of battery.

I can't lose this connection. I can't lose him.

"Son, Mom and I are going to fly down there. We'll arrive tonight, and we'll make

293

sure the authorities get you out of there as soon as possible."

"Okay."

"You and the other kids just need to stay safe and wait. Tell them to hang on —"

Silence.

No! Please, please, no.

The other kids stare at me.

I look at my phone. The screen has gone dark. No more battery. No more communication with the outside world.

CHAPTER TWELVE

The second Genevieve woke the next morning, a bad feeling expanded in her chest. The next second, she knew why. Her argument with Sam.

Dr. Quinley had been suggesting that she spend time daily on introspection. Genevieve preferred action to introspection. Especially in recent months, because introspection forced her to confront the wrong turns she'd taken, the fraudulent persona she'd built. Which, unfailingly, submerged her in guilt.

Yet, her Oxy dependency had to do with several complex things — pressures and fears and hurts. All of those had joined together to open the door of the cage where she'd trapped the childhood trauma of the earthquake, which had come snarling out, bringing with it flashbacks and nightmares.

She understood why she needed to work through all of that in order to identify her triggers and manage things in a healthier way in the future. It's just that the old saying "too much of a good thing" certainly applied to introspection.

Since Sam's departure from the cottage yesterday afternoon, she couldn't seem to *quit* assessing her motives, reactions, and bad habits.

Her dim, morning-lit surroundings spoke of charm and comfort. She'd filled this building with high-quality, tasteful items. Yet the air inside the cottage felt cold. The light leaking around the curtain's edge looked cold. The regret and self-loathing lodged in her stomach? Also cold.

She huddled more deeply under her luxurious duvet. Lying on her back, she contemplated the wooden beams supporting the ceiling.

Sam had asked her if she responded to uncomfortable situations by lying. He'd said that her lack of transparency was strangling her.

He'd been right on both counts. Even in the moment, she'd known he was right. She wished she'd simply taken responsibility for her lie and apologized. Instead, she'd attempted to protect herself by striking back. Her response had alienated Sam, leaving her wretched without his friendship.

Why was transparency so hard for her?

It hadn't been, back before she'd started Oxy. She'd been a truthful person once, fairly open about her mistakes in her writings and on the stage. Of course, in those days, she'd never made any mistake half as shameful as an addiction to prescription drugs. So the truth hadn't been quite so expensive as it later became.

How could she have come out and confessed Oxy publicly? Doing so would have jeopardized her entire ministry. Christian women didn't read books or line up to hear speeches by drug addicts.

As a consequence, and because she hadn't succeeded at kicking her Oxy habit in secret the first two times, she'd started lying. Just like anything, with practice she'd become more and more skilled at it. The lying, like her reliance on the pills, had become more and more automatic. White lies smoothed over awkwardness. They helped her avoid confrontation. They made her likable. They made her seem more perfectly Christian.

She knew the lies were wrong. Over time, though, the more she'd sidestepped the Holy Spirit's conviction, the quieter the Holy Spirit's voice had become. She'd told herself that the results of her Christ-honoring ministry justified the means. But deep down, her integrity wailed, and shame grew inside her. The lies increased. The shame increased. And her relationship with God unraveled.

She *hated* the lies she told. "I'm so sorry, God. Please forgive me," she whispered.

Genevieve rolled onto her side and tucked her hands beneath her pillow.

Over and over in the Bible, God's love was described as steadfast. In fact, she'd written an entire study on that facet of His character. So even though it felt — when longing for Him, when searching for Him — as if He'd drifted away, He hadn't. He was *steadfast.*

She's the one who'd drifted. When you'd walked with Him as she'd walked, her mortal life weaving with His immortal hand, His absence echoed.

The shame that had driven a wedge wasn't from Him. The lies weren't from Him.

She had to find a way to lay down the shame, and she absolutely must stop her knee-jerk reaction to lie. But that was easy to say and hard to execute when you'd done something that embarrassed you deeply.

After twenty-nine years of stellar choices, she'd spent the past year messing up in spectacular ways. The most recent of those with Sam. The only thing she could do about that at this point? Try to repair the damage. Which she would do, once she'd given him a bit of space and time.

The alternative — the two of them existing here at Sugar Maple Farm with animosity between them — absolutely would not do. Especially now that she knew about Kayden. Obviously, Sam had loved Kayden deeply. He'd loved her in a way that no man had ever loved Genevieve, and so Kayden's death had gutted Sam.

In light of this information, she understood why he was living in a self-imposed prison. He was grieving and probably condemning himself, wary of connections with people that could cause him pain.

Her phone alarm sounded. She plucked it from the bedside table and punched it off. Empathy had always come naturally to her. She earnestly wanted to lighten Sam's load. To make him smile more. To bring him joy. But today, she didn't even have the energy to walk to the coffeemaker and brew herself her morning cup. She certainly didn't have the heart to follow her schedule.

Forget breakfast. Forget walking the property.

Sam answered a knock on his farmhouse door Thursday evening to find Gen's sister standing on his front porch.

Her presence immediately put him on guard.

He hadn't spoken with Gen since their argument Monday afternoon. He'd hoped putting some distance between them would improve his state of mind. Instead, his state of mind had been a war zone for the past three days.

He'd liked Natasha when they'd talked the other morning at The Kitchen, but he didn't want reminders of Gen in the form of her sister.

"Good evening," she said cheerfully. The sky behind her blazed orange and pink with sunset.

"Good evening." He flicked on the porch light.

"Sorry to disturb you."

"No problem," he replied automatically. Even though the way that Gen and, in this case, her family member, disturbed his solitude had become a very big problem for him. "Would you like to come inside?"

"No, thank you. I can't stay." She lifted the bag she carried. "One of my husband's clients owns a butcher shop that specializes in grass-fed beef. He sent several steaks home with Wyatt today. More than we can eat. I'd like to give these last two to Gen, but, Sam. This is *filet mignon*. Gen can't cook, and even if she could, I doubt she could cook this properly on a hot plate. So I wondered if you'd like them."

"Sure."

"Great." She passed them over.

"Thank you."

"Thank you," she said sincerely, "for allowing Gen to rent your cottage. Living on your farm has been really good for her."

He inclined his chin.

"She told me that you know about the Oxy," she said.

"Yes."

"I've been worried about her, but she's now made it to day fifty-eight. She's almost two-thirds of the way to the ninety-day sober mark." He read acute hope in Natasha's face. He could tell that she loved her younger sister, that she desperately wanted Gen to succeed at recovery.

He understood. He'd experienced that same intensity of determination toward Kayden's recoveries once. He'd hate for Gen to let Natasha down. At the same time, no one — not him, not Natasha — could will another person to change.

"She's doing well, overall," Natasha continued. "But the past few days, she's had trouble sticking to her schedule."

301

Worry sliced him. "She has?"

"Yeah. I just wish that her recovery were the only thing on her plate right now. That would be more than enough to deal with. But, on top of that, she has to write a new study and handle this thing with our parents." Natasha hooked her thumbs through her belt loops. "I know you went with her to Clayton a while back."

"I did. But she hasn't told me any information about your parents since then."

"I'm not surprised. We haven't even told our parents what we've found yet. And what we've found is . . . heavy."

"Ah."

"I've been keeping tabs on her, but I can't do so all the time. It's reassuring to know that you're nearby and can keep an eye on her, too."

He wanted to insist that he had no plans to keep an eye on Gen. But that was only true in theory. In practice, he'd been keeping an eye on her since the day she'd moved in, and was apparently physically incapable of stopping. Since he'd walked away from her on Monday, he'd been every bit as aware of her movements around the farm. Maybe even more so. He knew when she was home, when she was away, how late she went to bed, how early she rose.

302

"I'll let you know if I notice anything concerning," she said. "Will you please let me know the same?"

"Yes."

"Gen's lucky to have you in her corner, Sam."

"No," he said quickly. "I wouldn't go that far."

"She has a ton of acquaintances and a ton of followers. But she needs more people like you in her life. People who actually know her, who care."

"I agree that she needs people in her life to know her and care about her, but it would be better for her if I wasn't one of them."

She pondered him.

"What?" he asked.

"I still think she's lucky to have you in her corner."

"She's lucky to have *you* in her corner," he told her, meaning it.

"Good night." She gave a small wave and made her way to her car.

He watched her pull away.

Had Gen told Natasha about their fight? Was Natasha trying to patch things up between them by bringing him two steaks? Did she expect him to cook one for himself and one for Gen?

Back inside his empty house, he picked up his cell phone and reread the text Gen had sent him more than an hour ago. *I'm sorry about the other day,* she'd written. *Will you allow me to buy back your friendship? At present, I can offer you three purple pens, a coupon for a free iced coffee at The Grind, or a jar of rosemary olive oil that I've never opened.*

He'd yet to respond.

For long minutes, he peered at her words, conflicted.

His logic demanded that he keep her at arm's length. Further involvement with Genevieve Woodward was guaranteed to injure him, because she made him hungry for things that weren't good for him.

On the other hand, Natasha's words ripped at his conscience. *"Thank you for allowing Gen to rent your cottage. Living on your farm has been really good for her. . . . It's reassuring to know that you're nearby and can keep an eye on her, too. . . . She needs more people like you in her life. People who actually know her, who care."*

In giving up her prescription drug habit, Gen had done something hard and brave. In deciding to distance himself from her, he'd done what was safest for him.

He wasn't a Bible expert like she was, but

304

he knew Scripture well enough to know that God hadn't called him to live the safest possible life.

Restless, he went to his front porch to water his pots. Usually, he told his plants about the forecast or complimented them on their growth. Tonight, he caught himself grumbling to them angrily about Gen.

"I've been worried about her," Natasha had said. *"The past few days, she's had trouble sticking to her schedule."*

With a growl, he set down the watering can and pulled out his phone.

Have you eaten dinner? he asked Gen via text, then hit send.

Almost instantly, she replied. *No.*

Of course she hadn't. Taking care of herself by eating early made far too much sense. *I'll sell you my friendship for the jar of olive oil if you'll sell me yours for a steak dinner tonight. I'm cooking.*

Sold! When should I arrive?

Thirty minutes.

Genevieve climbed Sam's front porch steps wearing an outfit she'd debated way too hard.

She'd finally settled on the fifth ensemble she'd tried on: a long, sheer navy shirt embellished with deep pink flowers that she wore over a navy cami, gray stretch pants, flats.

She came bearing olive oil. Her mom had given her the oil and several other items as part of a housewarming basket back when she'd visited Genevieve during the throes of withdrawal. She hadn't opened it since because she was far more inclined to use a toaster or microwave while preparing a meal than upscale olive oil.

The oil didn't seem the right gift for a hunky single man. But it made more sense than her other offerings. Purple pens, too feminine. Coffee coupon, unnecessary because he could drink the best coffee in town for free at The Kitchen.

She paused at his door, then rang the bell. Anxiously, she wiggled her toes inside her shoes. It frightened her a little, just how important it was to her that she get their friendship back on track.

Sam answered his front door wearing clean work pants and a plaid shirt, rolled up at the wrists and hanging open over a white T-shirt.

"Hello," she said, trying to ignore the attraction tingling at the backs of her knees.

"Hi." He stepped back. His neutral expression gave nothing away.

She walked into the foyer and handed over

the olive oil. "For you."

"Thanks. Dinner's almost ready." He moved in the direction of the kitchen. "Hungry?"

"Yes." She realized it was true. She wasn't always in tune with her own hunger or lack thereof. She tended to eat because it was time to eat and because she knew she'd get weak and shaky if she didn't. Or she ate because she was nervous. Or sometimes because she was bored. When she did eat because she was hungry, she was *really* hungry. At that point, if she opened a bag of chips to tide her over, she'd end up inhaling the whole thing.

She came to a stop beside him at the counter, then watched him drizzle her olive oil on top of a bowl of dip. He smelled fantastic, bracing and crisp. His damp hair looked finger combed. "This is my riff on hummus," he said.

"What do you mean by a riff?"

"There aren't any chickpeas in it." He gestured with his head toward the plate holding cut squash, zucchini, and carrots.

She dragged a circle of squash through the dip and sampled it. The subtle, rich, creamy flavors took her taste buds on a sensory roller coaster of delight.

"I love it." She helped herself to another

bite. "What's in it?"

"Squash, macadamia nuts, tahini, roasted garlic, lemon juice." He chewed a bite of carrot. "The olive oil's excellent."

"Excellent enough to establish a truce between us?"

Their eyes met.

"I'm sorry about Monday." She set her palm against the counter's lip as if doing so might steady her. "When I realized that you'd searched the cottage for Oxy, it made me feel, well, crummy. You're completely entitled to search, of course. But after hanging out with me and listening to me talk about everything I've been through to make it this far past withdrawal . . . I'd hoped that you believed in me."

"I do believe in you. I didn't want to find Oxy. But when I got your text and suspected that you weren't telling the truth about where you were, I felt like I needed to check."

"I get it." Thoughtfully, she ate a piece of zucchini and hummus. "You were right when you said that I respond to discomfort with lies. I'm going to work on that. In the heat of the moment, I got defensive and said things I didn't mean that I now regret. Can you forgive me?"

"Yes. I'm sorry that my search of your

guesthouse made you feel crummy."

"I forgive you. The truth is that I don't want you to write me off. I need people like you and Natasha to call me out when I mess up. Even if it doesn't feel great at first to be called out. Even if I don't respond well. All right?"

"All right."

She waited for him to say that he needed people, too, for the same reasons. But he said nothing more. Stubborn, complicated, *wonderful* Sam. "Are we okay?" she asked.

"We're okay." As if that settled it, he went to the cutting board and began slicing tomatoes with fast precision.

She'd made peace with Sam. Relief started to unknot the tension she'd been carrying since their argument. Quiet, slow bluegrass music hummed on the air.

"What can I do?" she belatedly remembered to ask.

"I'll put you to work in a minute."

On top of his very professional range, a pot boiled next to a sauté pan and a cast iron skillet that supported a melting square of butter. He arranged the tomatoes on a plate and began prepping asparagus. "I've been watching your videos," he said.

"My videos?"

"The video teaching sessions from *Bearer*

of a Woman's Soul."

"You *have?*" she exclaimed, astonished.

"You're a brilliant speaker."

"I *am?*"

"Yep," he answered patiently.

He was doing one of her studies? Sam thought she was a brilliant speaker?

She had women in mind when she researched and wrote her studies and when she shared from her own life in print and on stage. On the rare occasions when she discovered that a man had done one of the studies or watched her videos, it always felt a little like discovering that a boy had infiltrated a tree house meeting for girls only.

Sam was one of the most manly men she knew. Imagining him watching her videos was equal parts endearing and disconcerting. "Have you been doing the homework that goes along with the videos?"

"Not yet."

"You're not following the order?"

He lifted a brow. "Are you going to issue me a fine?"

"I'd like to!"

He placed two steaks into the cast iron skillet. They sizzled loudly. "What topic are you writing about in your current study?"

"Living a life transformed by grace."

"How's it coming?"

"Slowly and painfully. I'm behind schedule, and I'm uncertain about the quality of what I've written so far."

He drained the boiling pot into a colander, revealing handfuls of glossy fingerling potatoes. After moving them into a serving bowl, he dropped a few pats of butter over them.

"You eat so healthy that I would have expected butter to be your enemy."

"Empty carbs are my enemy. Not fats." He added fresh dill and seasonings to the potatoes. "When your sister dropped off these steaks earlier, she told me that you haven't been following your daily schedule."

Natasha had finagled this dinner by bringing him steaks?

Of course she had. Natasha could be crafty. Genevieve had confided in her about her fight with Sam, and this was her sister's way of helping repair things between them. "That's true. I've gotten off track with my schedule the past few days."

"How come?"

"After botching things up with you, I was feeling blue." He was an unlikely confidant. Yet, as usual, she found it liberating to tell him things. "Plus, I'm tired and overwhelmed in general. I haven't had the

311

energy for the schedule this week."

"That worries me because the schedule's been working for you."

"I know. It's helped."

"So? Are you going to return to it?"

"Someday soon."

"How about tomorrow?" he asked, insisting on pinning her down. Then he smiled a persuasive smile. Olive skin, green eyes, dimples, slightly imperfect white teeth.

Absorbing the sight was like trying to catch a fifty-pound ball of starlight. She'd have agreed to anything he asked in that moment. "Um, I'll return to the schedule tomorrow."

"Beaut." He moved aside to make room for her in front of the cast iron skillet, where he'd finished searing the steaks. "Is there anything else I can do to support your recovery, Gen? Because if there is, let me know."

"Cooking me dinner seems like enough at the moment."

He tilted the skillet and used a spoon to scoop up the butter floating in the corner along with fresh herbs. Then he ladled butter on top of the steaks over and over. "Just do like this."

"Got it." She did her best to imitate the action he'd demonstrated.

He sautéed asparagus. They were standing very close now, the outside of their arms brushing as they worked.

"Have you considered stepping away from the study you're working on?" he asked. "Would that help you feel less overwhelmed?"

"It would. But I can't step away."

"Why not?"

He clearly didn't understand the magnitude of her job. "I've signed a contract that requires me to submit the study to my publisher by its deadline. In all the years, I've never been late for a deadline, and I've never canceled a speaking engagement."

"Right, but this time's different. This time your health's at stake. You get well, you'll be able to write more studies in the future." He made a spooning motion. "Baste," he reminded her.

She resumed basting. Since the day when she'd crashed her car into a parking planter, she'd doubted whether she was qualified to continue serving as a Christian leader. But whenever she considered taking a break, she immediately thought of all the employees of her publisher, all the readers, all the conference directors who were counting on her. "I've been managing my deadline and my health so far. I can continue." And she could. Though the idea of facing weeks jammed full of work responsibilities made her feel as if someone was squeezing her throat. "I live off the income from my writing and speaking."

"I'm guessing you can afford to take a break. The lady at the bookstore told me that the DVD set for *Bearer of a Woman's Soul* cost one hundred and twenty dollars."

She dropped the spoon and set her hands on her hips. "The DVD sets are for groups! Also, I don't price the books and DVDs. My publisher does."

He eyed her with something that looked suspiciously like amusement.

"Sam!" Even though his feet were inches from hers, he was stepping all over her toes. She'd hoped to maintain their cease-fire longer than two and a half minutes.

"Baste," he said.

She huffed, picked up the spoon, and ladled butter. The cooking beef smelled mouth-watering. "The direction of my career is something I'm going to have to think through and pray through on my own . . . without intervention from my landlord."

"And mate."

By that, he meant friend. She softened slightly. "And thorn in my side."

314

"And grocery shopper when you were crook."

"Crook?"

"Sick." He transferred the steaks to plates. "Dinner's ready."

Together, they relocated the meal to the dining room. Gorgeous cutlery waited there on top of neatly folded linen napkins.

"Sit," he said. Then added, "Tenant."

"And person who is donating her considerable talents to better your farm."

"And thorn in my side."

"And woman you called a brilliant speaker." She took her seat with as much dignity as she could muster.

"House crasher."

"Local girl made good."

He bent his head to pray.

She peeked at him from beneath her lashes.

"Thank you, God, for this food, this place, and Gen. Amen."

Was that it? She'd have required ten sentences to say what he'd said plainly in one.

He skewered a potato with his fork.

"I forgive you for ambushing me about my career," Genevieve said.

His lips quirked. "I didn't ask for forgiveness."

315

"Nevertheless," she said primly, "I choose to extend grace. I'll expect grace in return should I ambush you about your career in the future."

"If you see that I'm screwing up my career in any way, then please ambush away. Bring it on."

He did not appear to be screwing up his career. This steak was not just the best thing she'd eaten this month but the best thing she'd eaten all year. It melted in her mouth, tender, with just the right amount of sear and salt. In response to the taste of it, her stomach begged her to marry him.

She noticed that he held his knife in his right hand, his fork in his left, and only rarely set either one down. Aussies seemed even more casual than Americans in most ways, but this — his style of eating — struck her as adorably proper.

They took their time over the meal, discussing the similarities and differences between her childhood in Georgia and his in Victoria, Australia.

When they'd finished eating, they angled their chairs farther from the table and continued to talk. The food and his company and the light from the fixture overhead spun a delectable spell. She didn't want to leave. Ever. And she definitely didn't want to break the spell, but it occurred to her that the spell might be strong enough to coax Sam to talk to her about Kayden.

"I'm interested to hear about your years in Melbourne after you graduated from the university," she said.

His face shuttered.

C'mon, spell. Hold.

"Sam," she said reasonably. "We're trying to be truthful with each other, remember? I'd like to know about those years."

Pressing his thumb against the table's corner, he took a slow breath. Just when she was sure he was going to refuse her, he asked, "What do you want to know?"

She started asking questions. In an even tone that likely disguised soul-deep feelings, he answered every one.

He'd loved Kayden. And she could clearly see that he'd done his very best for Kayden. Unfortunately for Sam, his love for Kayden had ended tragically.

Did he view her as Kayden's understudy, the one who had to get it right because the star of the show, the one he'd loved, had failed? Was he constantly measuring her against Kayden? Even if she did get it right and stayed clean, would she ever be able to compete with Kayden?

She didn't know.

What did she know? She wanted to try to make things better for him. After hearing his history with Kayden, she was more ferociously determined than ever to stay off Oxy for good. For herself. For him.

"Will you tell me what you've found out about your folks?" he asked.

He'd just placed his confidence in her by telling her the hardest and most private things about him. In return, she found that she couldn't shut him out. More than that, she *wanted* to tell him.

She explained about Russell, the Shoal Creek Killer, and her visit to Birdie Jean's house in Camden. He listened in a way that was exceedingly rare in the current culture. He wasn't distracted by technology; his attention didn't fracture. He leveled the weight of his focus on her as she talked.

When she finished, he leaned back slightly, interlacing his fingers over his lean abdomen. "What do you and your sister plan to do next? Are you going to look into Angus Morehouse?"

"Yes. I went to see the house where my mom and Russell lived, and it was creepy. The whole setting felt wrong, including Angus's house, which I could see in the distance. So, we'll look into Angus. We'll go back over all the photographs I took of

Birdie Jean's newspapers. We're still also planning to check if anything unusual happened during the years when my parents lived in Savannah."

"Because the person who sent you the mystery letter seems to be accusing both your parents of doing something. And they didn't even meet until Savannah, right?"

"That's right. Russell's death happened before my parents met, and there's little chance of my parents getting away with anything after moving to Misty River." She combed her fingertips through the last few inches of her hair. "If my parents did something, they probably did it in Savannah."

Dark eyelashes fringed Sam's watchful eyes. Genevieve saw within those depths his loyalty and loneliness, his humility and sorrow. Those qualities made him beautiful to her, and like a hot air balloon, her heart pulled so strongly toward him that it snapped the ropes she'd been using to anchor it down.

She hadn't yet been clean for ninety days. He was very likely still in love with a woman who'd died. In this moment, however, those concerns fell away like chaff in the face of how badly she wanted him to kiss her —

Abruptly, he rose to his feet. "It's getting late."

She stood, indecision swirling with disappointment. How was she supposed to get through to a man this disciplined? "Let me help you with the dishes —"

"No need."

"I'd like to lend a hand."

"No. I'll take care of the dishes."

She paused. "All right."

They made their way to the foyer. Politely, he opened the door for her. She passed through, then turned to face him. Every reflex she had screamed at her to kiss him.

She couldn't kiss him! She fidgeted, reluctant to leave.

" 'Night," he said.

Her desire and her self-control rammed into each other. The silence lengthened until it became fraught. "Good night," she finally said.

She walked down the steps toward her cottage.

The farther she went from the light of his porch, the more the darkness encroached, and the more certain she became that she'd chosen wrong when she'd chosen caution.

Sam retreated to his office.

He wrapped his fingers around the metal

container that held his pens. With odd detachment, he noticed that his hand was shaking. He observed the container, then very deliberately threw it against the wall. It made a satisfying *crash* and pens rained down.

He scowled at the mess, which somehow satisfied him more than neatness could have.

What was the matter with him? What fatal flaw was buried in him that made him want to be loved so badly?

He'd spent years depriving himself and deepening his faith and telling himself that he was strong.

He wasn't strong. He was a fool because his stupid heart that hadn't made one right decision was giving itself piece by piece to Genevieve. No amount of structure or routine or control was good enough to hold it back —

A knock sounded on his front door. His attention cut to the foyer as his pulse began to pound.

His footfalls loud in the quiet, he made his way to the door and opened it.

Gen looked beautiful, standing there with her delicate face and long, thick hair. She gave him a raw expression of apology. Then she launched herself into his arms and kissed him.

The shock of it barreled him back a few paces. He carried her with him, not wanting to drop her.

Like a landslide, his mighty defenses fell. His hands speared into her hair. Need roared, blotting out thought and light and sound and worries. He was kissing her hungrily. He'd waited his whole life for this, and his world was never going to be the same, and all he wanted was *more.*

She smelled better than any scent he'd ever known. She tasted better than anything he'd ever tasted. She felt like softness and femininity and strength.

It seemed like a century since he'd kissed anyone, and the sensory details of it rushed through his bloodstream, making him realize he was starving —

She pulled back, breaking the kiss with a gulp and a rueful laugh. Her chest expanded and contracted.

His unfocused eyes centered on her. Her lips. Her green-brown eyes.

"I just needed to catch my breath." She smiled.

But the fact that she'd pulled back, that she'd needed to catch her breath froze him. He'd forgotten his own power and size.

What was he doing?

At what point would he have stopped?

He'd lost his mind and his control, which rattled him as much as if he'd come to his senses in the middle of committing a crime he hadn't planned to commit. He didn't know or trust himself.

Gently, he reached up and unlocked her hands from behind his neck.

"Sam?" she whispered in confusion.

He paused, unable to resist pressing a kiss to her palm. Releasing her hands, he stepped back. "I'm sorry," he said hoarsely.

"For what?"

"For . . ." The hope and concern and bewilderment in her face scrambled his brain. She must think he was crazy.

"For what?" she repeated.

"For kissing you like that just now."

Her brows lifted. "I loved how you kissed me just now."

"I didn't plan to do that."

"I know you didn't. I'm the one who flung myself at you."

"But then I took over."

"I liked it!"

Not as much as he had. Which was part of the problem. He'd liked it too much. "I wasn't thinking."

She pressed her hands into the front pockets of her pants. She looked like a woman who'd just been kissed, and he

wanted to carry her away to a cave somewhere and keep her there forever.

"It's okay not to think every second of
every day, Sam. Sometimes it's nice to feel.
You know, to be present in the moment."

She had no idea what she was talking
about. He had to be able to think. Otherwise, he'd focus only on how good kissing
her felt. He'd want more. And then he'd fall
in love with her. And then life would hand
her something challenging, and he'd find
her hidden stash of pills. They'd start fighting, and he'd take her to rehab. And then
she'd be dead, lying in a coffin with her nice
sister and her nice parents looking at him
with devastation.

No. No, God. Not again.

His pain decided the matter for him. He
could assist her, the way he'd envisioned
when he'd invited her over for dinner
tonight. But he couldn't have her as his
girlfriend because she had the ability to
crush him. He'd spent too long recovering
from his year of depression to allow himself
to be crushed. "I overstepped," he said.

"No —"

"I overstepped my rules for myself," he
insisted. "We can't be more than friends."

She winced. "Why?"

"It's just not a good idea."

"You're going to have to do better than that," she said kindly.

"I'm not . . . meant for relationships."

"Of course you are."

"They're not good for me."

"Maybe they haven't been in the past, but they can be in the future. My past romances, one in particular, ended horribly. But I still have hope."

His expression tightened.

"We're both single, with no commitments to other people, right?" she asked.

"Right."

"Then I don't see the harm in kissing now and then."

He did see the harm. He wasn't built for superficial dating relationships. He was wired for serious love and commitment. Kissing Gen would be like playing with a stick of lit dynamite. "I can't. I'm sorry."

She didn't lash out. Slanting her head a little, she scrutinized him the way she would a chessboard. "Okay."

He had an irrational urge to jerk her to him and kiss her again and tell her that he'd already changed his mind.

"Friends?" she asked. "Don't forget that I purchased your friendship fair and square with olive oil earlier."

"Friends," he agreed.

"Good. Thanks for dinner." Then she disappeared into the night.

He'd done what he'd had to do.

He'd done the wrong thing.

No, he'd done the right thing.

He pressed his palms to the sides of his skull.

He'd told her not to take a fancy to him the day she'd moved in.

Then he'd gone and taken a fancy to her.

Natasha

Luke's cell phone just died, and this quiet is so much worse than the sound of him talking.

We're alone.

Genevieve and I are sitting criss-cross applesauce, like we used to at VBS or when watching *The Sound of Music* in our living room or when we'd play with dolls in our tree house.

"My dad said someone will come get us," Luke says, looking at the ground. "He said to be patient and wait."

"How long do you think it will take?" Ben asks. "A few hours?"

"Yeah," Genevieve says hopefully. "Probably a few hours."

"It'll take longer than that." Sebastian's eyes are slits, and I know his headache must be terrible.

I glance up at the fallen building on top

of us. The earthquake was so strong and this city is so large. There must be hundreds of crushed buildings just like this one. Crushed roads. Crushed cars.

"How long do you think it will take, Natasha?" Genevieve asks.

"A day?" I say. I try to sound normal even though the thought of being trapped here for a whole day makes me want to cry.

"A day!"

When Mom leaves us at the house to run errands, I'm always the one in charge. Just like I'm in charge of my sister now. "We might want to search for water and food."

"Where?" Sebastian demands. "Look around."

I see exposed pipes and hallways stuffed with concrete and piles of what used to be the ceiling. "I think we should look," I say. "Just in case we're down here for a while."

Sebastian snorts. "There's no water and there's no food. If we're down here for a while, we'll all die."

CHAPTER THIRTEEN

The next morning Genevieve stopped at the apex of Sugar Maple Farm's highest walking path. Breathing hard, she unscrewed the top of her stainless-steel water bottle and took a drink. The October breeze cooled her perspiration as she contemplated both the sweeping view of the valley below and the state of her feelings toward Sam.

For the first time in her life, she'd initiated a first kiss with a man. And what a kiss! It had been urgent and brain-spinning, and she viewed the fact that she'd had to come up for air as *a very good thing.*

But what she'd intended as a tiny intermission before more kissing had given Sam just enough time to think twice.

It was difficult to regret the fact that she'd kissed him when the kiss itself had been the very best kiss she'd ever experienced. She kept going back over it and over it in her memory, hugging the nuances of it to her like priceless keepsakes.

But each time, thoughts of what he'd said afterward intruded. *"I'm not meant for relationships."*

Any woman with a kindergarten diploma could see that he was made for relationships. But Sam himself couldn't. Until he could see what she could see, he couldn't move forward.

She soaked in the beauty of the scene before her — the slope of tree-covered land glinting orange and rust and yellow, the quaint buildings, the tranquil pond. Every day she cherished this farm more.

Her phone rang. Anabelle, the publicist at her publishing house.

Genevieve answered the call, and they exchanged greetings.

"I'm sorry to disturb you," Anabelle said. "But we received another strange letter about your parents, and I thought you'd want to know."

A sense of foreboding coiled around her like a snake. "Thank you. Yes, I do want to know. What does it say?"

"It says, 'Your parents have ignored what they've done too long. That's not going to work any longer. Either they face it, or I'll call a reporter.' It looks exactly like the first letter, Genevieve. Same envelope, paper,

330

return address."

"Please let me know if another one arrives."

"Will do. I'll take a picture of the letter and email that to you. I'll also mail you the hard copy."

"That would be great."

"Are you doing well?"

Genevieve knew what Anabelle was really asking, *"Are you still doing well post your dependence on prescription drugs?"* "I am, yes."

"So glad to hear it."

"You've been a true friend to me. I'm grateful."

"Sure! I'm here if you ever need to talk."

They chatted for another few minutes before disconnecting.

Genevieve then dialed Natasha. "Another mysterious letter arrived."

"What?"

Genevieve relayed the letter's contents. "I'll receive a photo of the letter by email soon. I'm having lunch with Mom and Dad today, so I think I'll show it to them."

"I'm fine with that. It'll give them another chance to come clean and explain what the letter writer's referring to."

"And if they don't?"

"I say, hold your tongue. Until we know

more, we don't want to show our hand."

"We need to press the gas on this investigation, Natasha. I really don't want the letter writer to call a reporter."

"I don't, either." Natasha made a frustrated noise that sounded like air blown through her lips.

"On another note, Sam told me that you delivered steaks to him last night."

"I did."

"In hopes that he'd cook for me, then fall wildly in love over medium-rare filet mignon?"

" 'It is a truth universally acknowledged . . .' "

" 'That a single man in possession of a good fortune, must be in want of a wife.' You do realize, right, that you've ruined my life?"

"How so?"

"Your steak dinner plan backfired. It only worked on me."

"Explain."

Genevieve told her about the wave of pent-up feelings that had propelled her into Sam's arms. And his reaction.

"But you're a nine out of ten!" Natasha contended.

"And he's a ten."

"No he isn't."

"I think he is," Genevieve said glumly.

"If he's a ten, then you're not going to let his misgivings scare you off, are you?"

"Shouldn't I?"

"Not if you really like him! You told him back before you moved in that you wouldn't fall for him, yes?"

"Yes."

"Then the solution's simple. You have to make *him* fall for *you.*"

"Why, yes," Genevieve said. "Very simple."

"There's no condition against him falling for you, correct?"

"Correct."

"Then take it from your sister, the lawyer, who knows all about contractual loopholes."

Natasha anointed her with a pep talk for a few more minutes before they hung up.

Lifting her chin, Genevieve drew crisp mountain air into her chest and resumed her walk. Her bad ankle protested, but she powered forward anyway.

Just once, she wanted to be the one that a guy set his heart on. She didn't have that elusive thing, the thing that brought men to their knees, the thing that Natasha and her mom and so many friends possessed.

Thad had dealt a blow to her romantic self-confidence that she still hadn't fully recovered from. She firmly believed that

333

God's approval was the only approval she needed. Yet Sam's rejection stirred up a multitude of hurts that tempted her to feel *less than.*

Last night and this morning, she'd repeatedly refused that feeling.

She wasn't less than.

Sam had liked the kiss, of that she was certain.

Her instincts told her that he cared about her and desired her, even. It's just that he had issues of his own that prevented him from giving in to something as human and wonderful as a kiss.

It might not be noble of her, but she was actually glad that she'd cracked some of his discipline, if even for a moment. She was gladder still that she'd kept her cool when he'd told her he couldn't date her.

She'd been disappointed in that moment. However, she'd seen that he was even more upset. Sam seemed set on punishing himself as some sort of weird tribute to Kayden. The fact that he'd dated no once since Kayden's death proved it.

Genevieve was no great beauty. She didn't possess the power to make a man forget his first love.

She was a Southern girl from a small town. She had self-respect and wrote Bible studies, used colorful pens and liked coffee. And once, she'd been Thad's second choice.

Because of that, she could not bear to become Sam's second choice, too. It would be best, for her mental health and her sobriety, if she resisted the impulse to throw herself at Sam the next time the impulse arose.

"Sweetie, whoever is writing these letters is playing a very cruel joke on you," Mom said to her at lunch, in response to the photo of the new letter. "I don't know what else to tell you. It's very perplexing and . . . and disturbing."

"It's disturbing, all right. Is there anything you'd like to tell me?" Genevieve asked her parents. "Anything at all?"

"No, nothing," Dad said.

"Because you can trust me with . . . whatever."

"We know that. If I had something to tell you, I would. Listen," Mom said earnestly, covering Genevieve's hand with hers. Her nails were painted a milky white. "You can't let this upset you."

Genevieve looked into her mother's face and detected underlying strain.

Someone here was upset. But it wasn't Genevieve.

■ ■ ■ ■

Because they were known far and wide as the Miracle Five, every single time the four of them — she, Natasha, Sebastian, and Ben — gathered, the incompleteness of their group wailed like a siren. Genevieve supposed it always would.

Luke had broken off from their group a long time ago. The rest of them respected the bond they shared, and so made time to meet several times a year. Old friends who'd known you since you were in middle school were comforting. Old friends who'd survived the same trauma that you had were essential.

Alone in her sister's kitchen for the moment, Genevieve chopped an onion in preparation for the dinner they were about to share with Sebastian and Ben on this Saturday night. The pot of chili Natasha had made bubbled sluggishly on the stove.

Natasha was the unofficial administrator of the Miracle Five (minus one), which meant she kept up with everyone's news, sent birthday cards, and coordinated their get-togethers. Because their hometown provided their only overlapping location of connection, they always met in Misty River.

Natasha and Ben lived here. Sebastian was based at a massive hospital in Atlanta but had a house in Misty River that he frequently commuted to via his private plane. Genevieve traveled here regularly to visit her family.

A knock sounded, and Genevieve checked her watch. Seven fifteen. Right on time. Since Natasha was still upstairs, helping Wyatt bathe the kids, she made her way to the front door.

When Genevieve had first arrived tonight, she and Natasha had shoved all the kid paraphernalia into the big chest of drawers and the ottoman with a lid. Thanks to their efforts, Natasha's living room, dining room, and kitchen now looked less like a day care and more like a Pottery Barn.

Genevieve swung open Natasha's front door, revealing Sebastian Grant and Ben Coleman. The two men stood side by side on the threshold bearing the dishes Natasha had asked them to bring.

They exchanged hugs filled with familiarity and fondness, then she ushered them inside.

Sebastian had clothed his imposing six-foot-two frame in suit pants and a white dress shirt opened at the neck. His stylishly cut thick black hair complemented his perceptive eyes and angular face.

Ben was the leaner of the two and shorter by three inches. His features were handsome and symmetrical, but not harsh. His long-lashed eyes and quick smile spoke of kindness. He wore his hair shaved close and sported a long-sleeved Atlanta Braves T-shirt.

Both men trailed her to the kitchen. "Natasha will be down shortly," she told them. "I'm responsible for the chili toppings since my sister only trusted me to chop onion and open bags of Fritos and sliced cheese."

"What about jalapeño?" Sebastian asked. "Chili is not the same without jalapeño."

Genevieve plucked a jalapeño from the grocery sack she'd brought with her. "I might have been given the humble assignment of chili toppings, but that doesn't mean that I'm not good at my job."

A crooked smile spread across his mouth. "Bravo."

She knew Sebastian well enough to know that he liked his food spicy.

Ben set a small chocolate cake on the counter, baked, no doubt, by his mother, who liked to spoil the four of them. Sebastian opened a box of cornbread from Tart Bakery in town. Sebastian could always be counted on to bring something wonderful

338

to their gatherings, because he never did *anything* halfway or poorly.

"How's your family?" Genevieve asked Ben, scooping the onion she'd cut into a serving bowl.

Sebastian snacked on Fritos while Ben brought her up to speed on the large, loud Coleman clan.

Ben was the third of four kids and one of what seemed like a thousand first cousins. His siblings were all married and adding babies to their families the way people added stocks to their portfolios.

"Hey." Natasha sailed into the room and gave out hugs, then used a wooden spoon to stir the chili. "What's happened with your career since we saw you last?" she asked Sebastian.

Inevitably, some new and awe-inspiring thing had occurred.

"I was promoted."

"What?" Natasha asked.

"Again?" Genevieve asked.

"Are my promotions boring you?" he asked dryly.

"I wouldn't say they're boring me," Genevieve answered. "I'd say they're frustrating me."

"My great success is frustrating you?"

"It really is," Genevieve replied with a

smile. She and Natasha could afford to tease Sebastian because they'd spent years proving to him how proud they were of him and how much they supported his accomplishments.

"Your great success is frustrating me, too," Natasha concurred. "My highest aspiration for each day is that my kids nap well."

Ben laughed.

"You're the one who asked me about my career," Sebastian pointed out to Natasha.

"That's because I'm trying to be a loyal friend," Natasha said. "Which is sometimes hard where you're concerned, Sebastian."

"Very hard," Genevieve echoed.

"In response to your latest promotion, I mostly want to pelt you with onion." Natasha flicked a square of onion at Sebastian.

He caught it adroitly and for a split second, Genevieve saw a shadow of the boy he'd once been in his face. Almost immediately, he threw it back at Natasha, who squealed and dodged. The bit of onion plunked harmlessly against the backsplash.

They filled their bowls with chili and took seats around Natasha's dining room table. Her sister had taken a page out of Mom's book and crafted a fall centerpiece complete with pumpkins, vines, and votive candles.

"Tell them about that surgical procedure

you did on that three-month-old baby," encouraged Ben, ever Sebastian's biggest fan.

Sebastian used words like *cardiopulmonary* and *aortic repair.* It sounded wildly impressive because it was. That said, Genevieve had no earthly idea what he was talking about. She could tell that Natasha had no idea, either.

Their close-knit foursome divided evenly into two more closely knit groups of two. She and Natasha, sisters, sat on one side of the table. Sebastian and Ben, brothers in all but name, on the other side.

When they'd returned home from their disastrous trip to El Salvador, the Colemans had pulled Sebastian into the solar system of their family. Sebastian had resisted, but Ben's outspoken, sassy, sweet, strict mother had overruled Sebastian's objections. So had Ben's sentimental rock of a father and noisy siblings. So had food. The Colemans loved to eat, and much of their family's life revolved around talking about their next meal, making the meal, eating the meal, and cleaning up the meal.

The Colemans, an African-American family living in mostly Caucasian Misty River, were in the minority. So was a foster kid surrounded by kids who had permanent parents. With the Colemans, Sebastian had found the first family he'd known since the age of eight, when his mom had died.

Before El Salvador, Sebastian's attitude toward school had been apathetic. He'd done the least amount possible to get by.

After El Salvador, Mrs. Coleman whipped him into shape. He'd tackled high school with unswerving ferocity, graduating in just two years.

Huh? the rest of them had often said to one another as they'd watched him climb toward what had seemed like impossible goals. *He's doing what?*

He'd gone on to graduate from college in two years and medical school in three. *Huh?*

He'd become a pediatric heart surgeon at age thirty, a feat most doctors couldn't hope to accomplish before thirty-five. *Huh?*

His focus was legendary. His ambition, boundless.

Whenever people tried to call Sebastian a child prodigy, he corrected them. He didn't think God had gifted him with an extraordinary amount of skill or knowledge when young. He'd had a good brain, an excellent brain. But then, a huge number of young people with excellent brains didn't become pediatric heart surgeons at the age of thirty. Sebastian believed he'd achieved what he had not because of any particular inborn gift but because of simple, old-fashioned hard work.

Privately, Genevieve *did* consider him to be a prodigy. A prodigy of determination.

If Sebastian was a windstorm, Ben was a ray of light. Optimistic, patient, calm. He was the one who'd set up the cot, sheets, blanket, and pillow every time Sebastian had spent the night in his room. He was the one who'd informed his parents that Sebastian needed to come with him to church on Sundays, church camp in the summer, and on family vacations.

During Sebastian's two years of high school, Ben had been his closest ally. Ben was a strong athlete who'd played college baseball. Even so, Ben had convinced Sebastian that his choice to focus solely on academics was the right one. He'd brought Sebastian's homework to him whenever Sebastian had been sick and made sure that Sebastian had a ride to and from school and study groups.

Genevieve dipped her spoon into her chili and scooped up a perfect bite that offered just the right amount of cheese, Fritos, onion, and jalapeño. The chili contained lots of deep, rich-flavored beef, but not a single bean, just the way Genevieve liked it. Since dinner two nights ago at Sam's, she'd been trying to eat slower and spend time tasting her food. This dish probably wouldn't be healthy enough for Sam. She'd have to ask him if he ever made Paleo chili —

For Pete's sake! Why was it so difficult to get him out of her mind and focus on something — *anything* — else? Forty-eight hours had passed since their kiss, and she couldn't stop thinking about him.

"What's been going on with you guys?" Ben asked.

This was her chance to tell them about her Oxy problem. But guilt kept the words stuck in her throat. "Nothing much. I'm living in the cottage out at Sugar Maple Farm, which I'm enjoying. I'm spending most of my time working on my next Bible study."

"Sam Turner runs that farm, right?" Ben asked.

"Right."

"And owns Sugar Maple Kitchen?"

"Yes."

"He cooked dinner for Gen the other night," Natasha told them.

"Did he?" A gleam came into Ben's eye. "Do you like him? In a non-platonic way?" he added for good measure.

"Yeah. I kind of do."

"I've heard Sam has that effect on every

woman in this town," Ben said.

"Ben here still likes Leah Montgomery in a non-platonic way," Sebastian stated.

"Oh! Of course." Genevieve couldn't believe she'd forgotten to ask for an update on Leah sooner.

Ben taught science at Misty River High School, where he was every eleventh grader's favorite teacher. More than a year ago, Leah had moved to town to teach the high school's advanced math students. Apparently Leah was very smart and very pretty. Ben had been interested in her from the start but wasn't sure whether she had feelings for him in return. Thus, he'd been building a friendship with her in hopes that it might, one day, lead to more.

"Correction." Ben took a sip of iced tea, then set down his glass. "I love Leah in a non-platonic way."

Natasha leaned forward, flattening both palms on the table. "Love!"

"Love?" Sebastian asked skeptically.

"Did you forget to mention to us that you and Leah started dating?" Genevieve asked.

"No," Ben answered. "We haven't started dating. Do you have to date someone to love them?"

"Usually." Sebastian spoke with the confidence of a doctor delivering a diagnosis.

"But not always." Genevieve hadn't gone on a single date with Sam, yet she could see how very easy it would be to tumble into love. "I think that love can come before dating in certain circumstances." Inwardly, however, her protectiveness of Ben stirred. It was precarious to fall in love with someone you *were* dating. Even more so to fall in love with someone you *weren't* dating. She could only hope that Leah would recognize Ben's awesomeness and love him back.

"Ask her out," Natasha urged.

"I'm going to. It's just that I don't want to make any mistakes. I'd rather take it slow and play my cards perfectly with Leah. You know?"

"What's your plan?" Sebastian asked.

"I'm going to run with this friendship thing a little longer while simultaneously upping my flirting game."

"What flirting game?" Sebastian asked, deadpan.

Ben socked Sebastian on the shoulder and bent at the waist laughing. "I have flirting game, man. And I'm hoping that Leah isn't immune to it."

"She isn't immune to it," Natasha said. "I'd bet a jumbo box of my kids' Goldfish on that."

346

"Good luck, Ben," Genevieve told him. "If she doesn't swoon over you, she's crazy." She moved her attention to Sebastian. "And you? Have you been swooning over anyone since we saw you last?"

"I have not."

Women adored Sebastian. Sebastian, however, didn't freely give his adoration in return. He'd had girlfriends from time to time, but he'd never appeared to invest himself in any of them. Which concerned her.

She didn't want him to become a lifelong bachelor. Singleness was certainly biblical and — hello — she herself was single, so she didn't have the right to thrust marriage aspirations on anyone else.

Nonetheless, she *did* want marriage for Sebastian. With his background and personality and scars, she'd always felt that he needed a family of his own just a little bit more than the rest of them.

He'd scoff at that if he knew that's how she felt. *Everyone* would scoff at that because it didn't take good eyesight to see that Sebastian was already earning an A-plus at life.

"Are you still dating that oncology doctor?" Natasha asked him.

Ben began shaking his head even before

Sebastian responded.

"No," Sebastian answered. "It didn't work out. Which is fine. You can count on me to make a good groomsman at your wedding to Leah, Ben." He saluted first Ben, then Genevieve. "And at your wedding to Sam, Genevieve."

"If I were a girl, I'd marry Sam," Ben told her, "for his buttermilk pancakes alone."

Ben had a point.

"By the way," Sebastian said to Natasha, "you're not going to make us play that old-fashioned card game —"

"Piquet," Genevieve supplied.

"You're not going to make us play piquet after dinner this time, are you?" Sebastian asked.

"Definitely not," Natasha answered.

"Whew."

"Tonight," Natasha proclaimed resolutely, "I'm going to make you play whist."

Sebastian

No one's come to rescue us.

I can see morning sunlight through our wrecked windows. I tried to sleep on my arm as a pillow, but I have a migraine, and the floor's hard and cold. Sirens woke me every time I dozed.

Even though it's still mostly dark in here, I can make out the shine of Luke's eyes, which are wide open. He's hardly said anything since his phone's battery ran out.

The other three — Ben and the girls — kept telling each other last night that someone will be coming for us soon. They're so spoiled that they can't imagine life without their parents to make every-thing easy for them.

I don't have to imagine that life. I've lived it.

I'm like a broken toy nobody wants.

CHAPTER FOURTEEN

Sam's life had gone down the toilet.

He'd worked so hard to build a life that meant something, that satisfied. He owned a restaurant, and he was the caretaker of Sugar Maple Farm, and he had God. That had almost been enough.

Then it had started to come apart.

And not just when Gen had kissed him four days ago. It had started to come apart the morning he'd found her sleeping in his guesthouse.

He'd continued to follow his daily work routine, yet he was forcing his body through the motions while chaos reigned in his brain. His muscles felt like they'd been beaten. His sleep and eating and purpose — all torn in some fundamental way. He didn't know how to sew them back together.

What was he doing? What was the point if he was going to spend the rest of his days alone, doing the same things every morning, afternoon, and night? Over and over and over again.

When Eli had asked him at their basketball game earlier if he wanted to grab dinner, his first instinct had been to say no, and then go home and hole up as usual.

In the end, he'd said yes to Eli because eating dinner with a friend had to be better than eating another meal of doubt and regret.

He was sitting across from Eli at a booth inside The Junction, a dive bar that served the best fried chicken in northern Georgia. Crowds filled the establishment just about every night of the week, and this Monday night was no exception. Locals came either for the inexpensive booze, the chicken, or the atmosphere, which wasn't fancy but was authentic.

Red vinyl booths surrounded a scuffed wooden dance floor. Hits from the 1970s and '80s stocked the jukebox. The curtains were red-and-white checked. The napkins, paper. The restaurant's smell, down-home cooking.

He'd ordered the only menu item that gave a nod to dietary restrictions — gluten-free, dairy-free fried chicken. Sam's chicken crackled as he took his first bite. In addition to the chicken, his large oval plate held mashed potatoes with brown gravy and a mound of shiny green beans.

He didn't drink anymore, and he almost never ate fried food. But tonight he didn't care. In fact, eating fried food suited his self-destructive mood. He might order two more helpings of chicken and consume it all in an effort to fill up his empty places.

A few yards from their table, an older couple slow-danced to the song "Wonderful Tonight."

"What's on your mind?" Eli asked. "I can tell something is."

More like . . . *someone* was. "I'd like to know more about the Miracle Five."

Eli wiped his fingers on his napkin. "What would you like to know?"

Sam speared green beans with his fork. "How long were they trapped underground?"

"Eight days."

Five middle school kids, one of whom had been Gen. *Eight days* underground. "It really is a miracle that they were able to survive down there for eight days."

Eli sat back. "It's impressive that they survived. But that's not what's miraculous about them."

Surprise caused Sam to still. "No?"

"They were in the basement when the

earthquake hit. Huge sections of a three-story building collapsed around them, trapping them in a space around the size of a living room." Eli took a few more bites. "Luke had his cell phone with him, so he called his parents and told them what happened."

Sam set his utensils down and rested his hands on his thighs.

"The kids' parents immediately contacted reporters," Eli continued. "They were smart enough to understand that media coverage would lead to public concern and that public concern might help their kids."

Sam waited.

"The best engineers and architects and emergency specialists in the world gathered in El Salvador and raced against time to save them. But the building was in terrible shape. Slabs of concrete were resting against each other like so." Eli demonstrated the supporting angles with his palms. "Some experts predicted that the structure would collapse at any moment. Others said that if they tried to move one of the slabs in order to get the kids out, the other slab would fall and crush the children."

"So how did they do it?"

"Well, remember." Eli's hands remained propped against each other. "When all of this was going on, global attention was focused on those five kids, trapped in one building in the middle of one devastated Central American city. The kids' parents told the media that they were trusting God to protect their children. And literally all over the world, people prayed for God to rescue them."

"And?"

"And miraculously, He did."

Sam searched Eli's face and found calm truth there.

"A team finally went in and began taking the building apart piece by piece because it was that or let the kids die from dehydration or starvation. Their initial plan was to reach the kids from the side and leave the two main slabs of concrete in place. But as they were digging, some of the building's support collapsed. A slab fell in." One of Eli's palms met the table. The other remained up at a diagonal. "As it happened, the kids were all sitting under this other slab at the time. By all accounts, this slab should have fallen as soon as the other one did. But it didn't. It remained at this angle, almost as if it were protecting the kids."

"Until they got the kids out?"

"*Just* until. Within minutes after they'd evacuated the kids by air, the last slab fell."

His remaining palm gave the table a soft slap.

"And that's why they're called the Miracle Five," Sam said.

"That's why. After the fact, architects could not explain why the concrete didn't come down on them. All the experts agreed. It should have killed them." Eli adjusted his drink on its coaster. "If you ask anyone in this town what happened, they'll tell you that God intervened and saved those kids."

A shiver tingled down the back of Sam's neck. "I'm assuming they took the kids to the hospital?"

"Yeah. A few had minor injuries. Once the government cleared them to leave, most of them spent the rest of the summer traveling with their families, telling their story. When it came time for school to start back up, their parents brought them home so they could return to their normal lives. But according to the locals who were here at that time, nobody considered them normal after that. How could they? The kids were international celebrities." Eli inclined his chin toward the front door. "Speaking of . . ."

Sam glanced in the direction he'd indicated to see Gen shrugging out of her coat. A woman with curly black hair slid into a booth and Genevieve took the seat across from her.

His throat tightened. Was there anywhere he could go in Misty River where she wasn't?

He feared there wasn't anywhere in America or Australia — or the entire planet — he could go to get away from her. She changed the air he breathed.

She picked up a menu and cast a relaxed look around the interior. Their eyes met with the force of metal striking metal.

Her face blanked for a full second. Then she put on a smile and lifted a hand in greeting. He lifted his hand in response.

She faced her menu.

He caught himself staring at the way the light glinted against the strands of her hair. He jerked his focus to his plate.

"Huh," Eli said knowingly.

"Don't say anything," Sam warned. Shortly after their server had taken away Sam's plate, two guys left the bar and made their way to Gen's table.

Sam's torso tensed.

Gen and her friend raised welcoming faces. The guys' body language communicated confidence as they chatted with the women. They were white-collar types around Gen's age. No doubt they had more in common with her than he did. They'd

356

probably never felt like outsiders in their life. They'd probably be better for her than he would.

After a time, Gen and her friend scooted over to make room for the men at their booth, and the food Sam had just eaten turned into a lump of sand in his stomach.

He was the one who'd told Gen they couldn't be more than friends. So it was beyond stupid for him to feel jealousy now.

Except he did.

He'd told her they couldn't be more than friends, but that didn't mean he didn't want more. He did. He wanted her to look at him with tenderness and keep him company and laugh with him and stay with him on his farm.

Their server returned with their check, startling him.

Gen and one of the men rose and moved to the jukebox.

Sam pulled his wallet from his back pocket and laid out bills to cover the cost of the meal and tip.

"Everything okay, man?" Eli asked with a note of concern.

"Sure. Everything okay with you?"

"I'm doing great." Eli appeared to want to say more.

"Don't say anything," Sam told him for

the second time.

"Fine." Eli shook his head wryly and stood. "I'm glad we did this."

"Me too." Sam pushed to his feet.

"I'll see you at the gym."

They shook hands, and Eli made his way out.

Sam hesitated, split between wanting to be *anywhere* else and wanting to talk to her.

Since they'd kissed, they'd texted each other about the next Fall Fun Day. He'd seen her gardening once and heard her doing laundry once. But they hadn't spoken face to face. They'd agreed on friendship the other night. So he'd speak with her and, after he did, maybe it would get easier to be near her.

He crossed to the jukebox.

"Good evening," he said and realized instantly that he sounded forty years older than he was.

"Hey," she said warmly.

The guy with her gave him a mask of friendliness that didn't cover the message of *"Back off, I was here first."*

"It looks like you had the same idea my friend Ellie and I had tonight," Gen said. "Were you craving fried chicken?"

"I was."

"Same."

358

Sam met the shorter man's eyes and gave him a look that said, *"Back off, I was here first"* far more strongly. "Can you excuse us for a moment?"

"Uh." The guy looked uncertainly to Gen.

She gave him a nod, and the guy moved back to their booth.

"That was a bit gruff," she whispered.

"I'm gruff."

"I thought I'd choose a song." The ends of her plaid scarf swung forward as she leaned over the selection. "I think I'm going to go with 'Walk This Way' by Aerosmith. A classic."

He was more of an INXS fan.

She pushed a coin into the machine. She'd repainted her nails since he'd seen her last. They were short, square, and burgundy.

The opening notes of "Walk This Way" played.

"You'll be pleased to know," she said, "that I gardened alone the other day and didn't murder a single chive. I don't think." She looked right into his eyes. One edge of her lips tipped up.

In response, desire cut through him. Clean, hot, unmistakable.

"Your garden is safe with me," she said.

But what about him? Was he safe with her? At this point, he'd gladly let her murder every vegetable he had if she'd just let him escape with his life. How was it possible that a temporary tenant who took too many painkillers but could preach like Billy Graham had turned his life upside-down to this degree? "Are you back to your schedule?"

"Yes."

"Good."

Here's the thing. He could tell himself that she was a temporary tenant who took too many painkillers all he wanted. However, she couldn't be explained that simply. Gen was much more to him than a tenant. Much more to him than Oxy. Much more to him than a preacher.

She was Genevieve, and he was terrified that he might love her.

It had given him no pleasure to react to their kiss the way he had. All he'd received out of it was the cold knowledge that he'd done the right thing. For seven years, that's what his life had been. An endless series of right choices.

Now she was acting like she was content never to kiss him again, and he didn't want her to be content with that, because he wasn't.

He'd thought talking to her would make things easier. So far, it felt harder.

"I'm glad everything's going well," he said

abruptly. "Catch you later."

"Oh. Okay." The lightheartedness in her tone informed him that she couldn't care less whether he stayed or went.

He went, stalking into the night in a temper blacker than Kayden's coffin.

Ben

I didn't sleep much last night.

I kept waking up in a panic. Then I'd pray and pray and pray until a sense of calm would finally come over me. Then I'd think about my family, my house, my bedroom, and my dog until I fell asleep again.

Once, I had to go to the bathroom really bad. I tried to hold it and go back to sleep, but couldn't. I felt my way to the corner of the space that we set up last night as a bathroom. We didn't want anyone else to see or hear when we have to go, so we worked together to stack pieces of broken concrete until we made a wall almost as tall as me.

I busted one of my knuckles building that wall.

I've been pushing at that knuckle and trying not to think about how hungry I am while those of us who are awake stay quiet and wait for the other kids to finish sleeping. Finally Natasha, the last one to wake up, starts stirring. She blinks her eyes open and pushes herself to sitting. Her hair is a mess and her dress is dirty and there are gray circles under her eyes.

We all look terrible.

"I'm sure they'll come for us," Natasha says, mostly to me and her sister. "Very soon."

CHAPTER FIFTEEN

"Be strong," Genevieve whispered on Thursday morning to the thick white mug containing her harvest spice latte.

She'd just settled upon a tall chair next to her sister at The Grind Coffee Shop. They sat facing a window overlooking Misty River's historic downtown square.

"Recovery update?" Natasha asked.

"Still clean."

Natasha pulled Genevieve to her in a congratulatory one-armed hug. Her sister had been monitoring Genevieve's recovery expertly. Checking on her, encouraging her, providing accountability, listening. But not beating the subject into a pulp.

Natasha had come straight from dropping her kids off at Mother's Day Out and could only spare thirty minutes for research before she needed to rush off to complete the one thousand things she hoped to squeeze into her kid-free hours.

"I have a gift for you," Natasha announced.

Let it not be knitted handicrafts.

"Mittens!" Natasha tugged a mass of pink yarn from her purse.

Knitted handicrafts.

"I couldn't figure out how to knit the thumb," Natasha said, "but then I thought, why do mittens need thumbs anyway? Why can't mittens just be like roomy socks for our hands?"

"Right!"

"I really think I might be on to something. I could open an Etsy shop and make a mint. Try them on!"

Bravely, Genevieve donned them. Unlike the hat Natasha had fashioned for her, the mittens were too loose. They gaped around her wrists like an old man's double chins. "Thank you!"

Natasha snickered. "Without thumbs, they make you look like you have hand wounds. People are going to love them!" Natasha whisked open her laptop as Genevieve stowed the mittens, which did indeed resemble enormous hand bandages, in her purse.

Together they bent over the computer while Natasha, no stranger to the law, looked up Angus Morehouse's arrest record. Genevieve was, as always, content to let her older sister be good at the things she was good at (knitting, not among those).

The end of Natasha's blond ponytail feathered against the shoulder of the tight-fitting exercise jacket she'd zipped up to her chin. "Ah. Here we are. I think this is the site that will allow me to access his arrests. If there's anything to find about you, Angus, we will." Her fingertips sped over the keys. "Voilà." Natasha pointed to the screen and read off each charge and the year.

Angus had been charged with misdemeanor battery three times, plus felony battery once. His felony conviction had sent him to jail.

"Angus doesn't exactly seem like a rosebud of a person," Genevieve commented.

"No."

"Is there any way to tell who he fought with on each of these occasions?"

Natasha shook her head. "The site doesn't give me that much detail."

"Well, we have reason to believe at least one of these arrests for assault may have been for the fight he had with Russell."

"If so, it would probably be this one." Natasha tapped a misdemeanor arrest that had occurred in the early spring of 1983. Russell had died later that summer.

"What if we look up Russell's arrest

366

record? If both men were arrested for the same fight, we'd be able to cross-check the dates and confirm, yes?"

"Yes."

While Natasha fed the website new information, Genevieve relished her latte and wondered if work was going smoothly for Sam over at The Kitchen this morning. It wasn't far from here. Just down a block and around the corner. Was he content? Irritated? Happy? Down?

She wished she knew his state of mind. Unfortunately, she didn't. It had been a week since their steak dinner. Their first interaction afterward had been at The Junction.

What a debacle that had been. Her, so falsely jolly. Her, so immaturely pleased that other men were hitting on her in front of Sam so that he couldn't assume that just because he didn't want to date her, nobody did. Him, saying so little. Him, with seething eyes that spoke a hundred things she couldn't decipher.

Two days ago, she'd banged around in his laundry room until he'd appeared. He'd spoken to her politely, but his face had been guarded and he'd kept the interaction brief. Yesterday, she'd joined him in his garden. After twelve minutes of small talk, he'd nodded to her the same way he'd nod to a stranger passing on the sidewalk, and left.

She'd known, when she'd launched herself at him, that she was recklessly crossing a line. In that moment, though, the recklessness had added to the spontaneous exhilaration.

Only now did she fully realize just how important the line between them had been to Sam. And how much she'd put at risk when she trampled over it.

She missed him. More than was logical or wise. She wanted to spend *real* time with him having *real* conversations. Combine missing him with the rough patch she'd hit in the writing of her study this week, and her mental state had been backsliding.

She'd made it to day sixty-five. More dopamine was supposed to be flooding back! Only twenty-five days left and she'd hit that crucial ninety-day goal.

Overall, she could acknowledge that she was improving. That said, the improvement wasn't like a consistent upward-slanting diagonal line. There were dips in her line. This week was a dip. This week she'd said "Not today, Satan" several times each day. She'd cried in the shower again last night, then put herself to sleep on wistful memories of how heavenly she'd felt when taking Oxy.

Oxy was her enemy. But, unfortunately, it didn't always feel that way. When she was at her lowest, Oxy seemed like a long-lost friend.

"Here's Russell's arrest record," Natasha said.

Genevieve had expected one arrest to pop up — from Russell's fistfight with Angus. Instead, she saw that Russell had just as many arrests as did Angus. Four. All for misdemeanor battery. "I'm surprised to see so many."

"I am, too." Natasha frowned. After a moment, she indicated the final entry. "This arrest occurred the same day as Angus's arrest. Early spring, 1983. So as we suspected, this is when they fought each other. Russell's first arrest would date back to his final year of high school and the middle two would have happened during his college years."

"If Russell was arrested four times, we can guess that he was probably in several other fights he didn't get arrested for," Genevieve said.

"No wonder he fought back when the Shoal Creek Killer attacked."

"No wonder. So . . . what else can we find out about Angus?"

369

"I don't know. I've already looked him up on genealogy sites and social media sites and come up empty. If I can think of anything else to try, I will."

"And I'll see if I can find anything online about Mom and Dad's years in Savannah."

"Will you be conducting that research before or after mooning over Sam?"

"Natasha! Can you please take pity on me and not mention his name?"

"Sam," she said, clinking her coffee mug with Genevieve's. "Sam, Sam, Sam, Sam, Sam."

The following Saturday, Genevieve created a scene.

The scene was not premeditated. In fact, it snuck up on Genevieve and surprised her the way a lioness surprises a gazelle.

Anna had asked for the first shift at today's Fall Fun Day. Her request had included something about a cute boy, plans to go to Amicalola Falls, and the word *please*. Genevieve had told Anna she'd happily take the second shift. Thus, she'd slept late and was catching up on Instagram when Anna's text arrived.

There are a lot of people here to see you.

Two seconds later, Anna added, *Bible study people.*

Genevieve, still in her pajamas, sprinted to the cottage's tiny bathroom to begin her morning prep.

She'd taken time during the last Fall Fun Day to stage shots of the event that showcased just the right mix of charm and farmhouse chic. She'd shared the photos on her platforms and mentioned how much she'd enjoyed volunteering. In each case, she'd tagged Sam's accounts (which she'd been working to bolster) and informed her followers of the day and time of the next Fall Fun Day.

Her intention: to give the farm a boost.

At no time had she mentioned that she'd be present at today's event. Unless she was participating in an event that offered security forethought, she didn't announce her future plans online. Maybe it was her mother's influence, but she was savvy enough — or anxious enough — to understand that if she announced to the world that she was planning to eat dinner at Pizza Hut in Misty River, she should then expect a gunman with religious views different from hers to show up at Pizza Hut in Misty River.

It sounded like her "Bible study people" had made their way to today's event just in case she showed.

After finishing her makeup and dressing in a pale blue sweater, a long necklace, and jeggings tucked into boots, she hurried toward the farm stand. Thirty or more people were milling about. She could see at a glance that Sam wasn't among them.

Sam.

Anna rushed up to her. "So." The girl's blond hair fell into place around her shoulders. "Most of the ladies saw your posts from the last Fun Day. But some had friends who came that day and took pictures with you. And they saw their friends' posts."

"Thanks for the heads-up." Genevieve's forward progress didn't slow.

"Yeah! I don't know where all they're from. I asked one and she said Alpharetta. And I was like, wow. I enjoy Alpharetta's North Point Mall. They have a Vans there."

"I see."

"Oliver's getting really overexcited by the crowd."

"Yikes."

"He's talking to a few women right now about horticulture, and I don't even know what that means. All I know is that it sounds like vultures. And they eat dead stuff, right?"

"Right. Although, horticulture means gardening. It doesn't have anything to do with vultures."

"Bummer. Vultures are kind of cool."

The crowd watched her approach with shy and excited expressions. In response, her professional persona came fully awake. Genevieve smiled, then had to work to keep the expression in place as a visceral memory split into her consciousness. Her, waking up in Sam's guesthouse, shaken because she didn't know where she was.

Her shiny exterior wasn't an accurate reflection of who she was.

Nope. This wasn't the time or place to go into a funk. A large group of women were waiting and watching.

Gathering her energy, she put on her public identity.

Genevieve Woodward, Christian author and speaker.

Later, when Sam exited his barn, he immediately noticed the crowd gathered near the farm stand. His steps slashed to a halt.

Genevieve. There wasn't a doubt in his mind that Gen must be the source of this crowd because if there was trouble on his farm or in his life, he could be sure to find Gen at the center of it.

He turned his steps in the direction of the farm stand, concern thinning his mouth.

When he'd opened the farm's front gate

373

an hour and a half ago, he'd noticed that a large number of cars waited on the side of the road. He'd chalked it up to luck and to the solid effort he and Genevieve had put into the last event. He'd thought that positive word of mouth had spread.

Now that he was drawing closer, he could see that the group of women surrounding Gen looked to fit into the "Christian women between the ages of eighteen and thirty-eight" demographic Natasha had told him about. Clearly, the extra visitors hadn't come because of luck or word of mouth. They'd come for the chance to meet Gen.

These people were probably all fans, just like the women at The Kitchen last month had been. But if her fans expected her to appear here today, then her detractors might also expect her to appear here.

He cut straight to the middle of the gathering and wrapped a hand around Gen's elbow. "Excuse us for a moment, please." He guided her several steps away and out of earshot.

Her hazel eyes and the feel of her delicate arm beneath his fingers derailed his train of thought.

What had he been about to say? That's right. "Hello." Then he added, "Trouble-maker."

"I've never in my life thought of myself as a troublemaker. It's actually quite thrilling."

"Since the day I met you, I've thought of you as nothing but a troublemaker." He forced himself to release her and put more space between them. "Did you tell people where you were going to be today?"

"I didn't. I simply posted about the farm on the last Fall Fun Day."

"Why?"

"To give your business a leg up."

"I'd never want you to give my business a leg up at the expense of your safety."

"These ladies simply saw that I was at the last Fall Fun Day, and they came by on the off-chance I'd be here again to say hi. And," she hurried to add, "to enjoy all the farm has to offer, of course."

The women seemed to care nothing for what the farm had to offer. "Your shift isn't supposed to start until one-thirty. Why don't you stay in the guesthouse until then, at least? I can handle this."

"Thank you, but no. I'm staying. I adore the women who do my studies."

He looked to the women, then back to Gen.

"I'm sure about this," she said. "Everything's fine."

Sam stuck his fingers in his mouth and

whistled. The sound cut through the chatter, and female faces swung in his direction. He raised his voice. "Kindly move this way."

The group migrated, which cleared the area around the farm stand.

"Welcome to Sugar Maple Farm," he said. "I'm Sam Turner, the owner. Thanks for visiting today."

A plump young woman looked between him and Gen, raised her phone, and snapped a picture.

He paused, not sure how to respond to that oddness. "If you're here to meet and speak with Genevieve Woodward, please raise your hand."

Every person raised their hand, except for a confused-looking man who he guessed was of Indian descent.

"Sir, please see the woman named Anna at the stand, just there, yes." He faced the women again. "Has anyone been waiting for Genevieve for more than an hour? Raise your hands, please."

Taking his time, he assembled a line based on how long people had been waiting. Then he stepped back and assessed each and every person. They all looked harmless.

He made his way to the farm stand, where Oliver and Anna stood.

"It's wonderful that these guests have read

Genevieve's books," Oliver crowed. "Literate people! If it's all right with you, I may treat them to some amusing historical anecdotes while they're in line."

"That would be terrific." He managed to keep every trace of sarcasm from his voice. The line didn't look like a fast mover, so Oliver would have a captive audience.

Oliver's chest swelled as he approached a foursome of women at the back of the line and made opening remarks. He braced one hand against his hip, gesturing grandly with the other.

"This situation is so cool," Anna said to Sam. "It reminds me of a food truck."

"How?"

"You know how food trucks just show up anywhere? Genevieve's like a food truck. A really popular one. That serves tacos. I'm starving. I could totally go for some tacos right now." She thrust her phone in her back pocket. "Can I ask you a personal question?"

"No." He wasn't in a smiling mood, but he gave the girl a small smile to soften his answer.

"In that case, I won't ask if you and Genevieve are a couple even though I'm dying to know."

"Thanks for practicing restraint."

"You guys would be great together. You're both older —"

"Excuse me?" He lifted an offended eyebrow.

"Oldish," she qualified. "She's down to earth and nice and pretty and . . ."

"Like a taco?"

"Yes! How can you resist tacos? I totally love them."

How *was* he supposed to resist Gen? He wished he knew.

He made a trip to the barn for more cider. Helped a couple who'd come to pick their own produce, then waited on some farm stand regulars. A family drifted up, interested in the next farm tour.

There was no way he was going to abandon Genevieve here, so outnumbered, while he took guests on a farm tour. Nor did he trust Oliver to drive a flatbed full of people. The older man might get sidetracked talking about Bogotá and drive them into an apple tree.

Five minutes before the tour's scheduled start time, Sam took up a position near Gen and announced, "Genevieve is going to take her lunch break now." She needed food. A chance to sit down. A rest from everyone's attention.

"I am?" She spoke with quiet amusement.

378

"You know, Sam, you're not the boss of me."

"I'm definitely not the boss of you. I'm a concerned friend who's not going to take people on a farm tour if it means leaving you here alone. Are you willing to take a break?"

"Yes, I'm willing. Have *you* had a lunch break?"

He let that pass. "I invite you to come on the tour I'm giving," he said to the women, "to the farm's orchard. Right around the time we return, Genevieve will be back."

After the tour, Anna and Oliver went home. For the rest of the afternoon, Sam and Genevieve worked together to juggle the farm's customers and her fans.

The whole time he was intensely aware of her. The timbre of her voice, the blue of her sweater, the sparkle of the three intertwined silver bands she wore on one finger. She had a way of making everyone feel at home in her presence. More than once, she'd teared up at the stories the women shared with her. Stories of loss and terminal illness and bitterness beaten by hope. They shared how her ministry had impacted them, and she told them how much they meant to her.

With every discussion he overhead, every laugh Gen gave, every woman who wiped her eyes with a tissue as she explained how

God had spoken to her through Gen's study, his admiration for Gen grew.

Her work meant something important to people. Not many could write and speak about the things of God like she could. No one else had her personality — confident and sweet, emotional and grounded, wry and real.

He could not do Genevieve's job. He wouldn't even want to.

He longed for the kind of quiet broken only by the sound of leaves in the trees and the kind of darkness interrupted only by stars. He wanted to grow things with his hands and leave these acres better than he'd found them. He was driven by excellence. But for him, excellence meant the poetry of a perfectly balanced omelet or an apple tree so healthy that its branches sagged with fruit.

He was simple. She was not.

He had no right to feel this ferocious protectiveness toward her and the gifts God had given her. But he did. Even more confusing, his protectiveness toward Gen had come into conflict today with his protectiveness toward her gifts. When he'd insisted that she take a break, he'd put Gen's well-being ahead of what might have been best for her ministry.

He didn't know if that was how God wanted it or not. He simply knew he'd choose the same way the next time. And the next.

When five o'clock finally arrived, he was glad to close the farm to the public. He and Gen stored the Fall Fun Day supplies in the barn, then he watched her drive away to have dinner with her parents.

He took refuge inside his house. But he couldn't hide from his feelings for her.

They followed him into the shower. They followed him downstairs.

Edgy and miserable, he did something he hadn't done in a long, long time: He sat in his living room in the twilight and swigged wine straight from the bottle with grim determination.

Genevieve

Tears press against my eyes every time I think about my mom and dad. My stomach is empty. My mouth is dry from thirst. I'm weak and dizzy and scared.

But since nobody else is complaining, I'm not.

I'm not going to ask if we're going to starve down here.

I'm not going to ask how long we can go without water.

I keep staring into the dim edges of our space, looking for a bag of chips, or some granola bars, or cookies. One of us would have seen those things by now if they'd been down here. Even so, I can't stop looking for them.

We're sitting in a line with our backs against the wall and our legs stretched out. It's better . . . so, so much better when we talk. But right now it's quiet.

I'm trying to think of something else to say. But it's hard to come up with stuff, because we've already talked about a lot. If I do come up with something, Luke probably won't answer, and whatever I say will irritate Sebastian.

This silence is the worst silence I've ever heard. It feels like a blanket that's trying to suffocate me.

CHAPTER SIXTEEN

Four nights later, Genevieve curled up in the cottage's love seat with her robe on backward to examine the photos she'd taken of Birdie Jean's scrapbook.

So far, Natasha had uncovered nothing more about Angus Morehouse. And Genevieve had uncovered nothing noteworthy about her mom and dad's years in Savannah.

Thus, she'd circled back to Birdie Jean's scrapbook.

Golden warmth burnished the air inside the cottage. Outside, gray clouds hung low on this second-to-last night of October. Wind buffeted the structure, occasionally tossing raindrops against the windows. The fire she'd lit this afternoon to brighten the final hours of her workday still crackled.

She'd uploaded the photos she'd taken at Birdie Jean's to her computer. After adjusting her laptop on her crossed legs, she increased the size of the first photo until it filled the whole screen.

Meticulously, she combed through the front page of the newspaper published the day after Russell's murder, then evaluated the following day's front page. In this case, the article about Russell continued on one of the paper's latter pages, so she brought up the picture she'd taken of the article's conclusion. A few ads bordered it. One for a dry cleaner. One for a repairman. A recruitment ad read, *Navy. It's not just a job, it's an adventure! At the Community Center tonight from 7:00–9:00 p.m., Seaman Derek O'Leary and Petty Officer Third Class Judson Woodward . . .*

What?

Her dad? She gave a huff of surprise at the unexpectedly wonderful discovery.

. . . will be available to share their experiences, the notice continued, *answer your questions, and discuss whether the United States Navy is right for you. Now is the time to invest in your future!*

What were the chances of coming across a piece of memorabilia like this from the year her dad had spent as a recruiter before law school? She could screenshot this and email it to him and mom. Or it might be fun to print it out and have it framed for him.

She skimmed the ad again. Her own father's name right next to an article detailing the facts of Russell Atwell's murder . . .

The happiness of her find began to slip. Then slip further. Until it evaporated into unease.

She'd wondered *What were the chances?* in a lighthearted way a moment ago. But now she had to ask herself that same question much more seriously.

Literally. What *were* the chances of this? That her mother's two husbands — one of whom had been kept secret from her and Natasha — had both been captured in print in the same issue of the *Camden Chronicle*?

The chances were astronomical. Such a tremendous coincidence that she had to doubt whether it was a coincidence at all.

Think, Genevieve.

Dad spoke positively about his stint as a recruiter. He'd liked it, in part, because he'd had some flexibility in choosing the locations of his recruiting stops. When possible, he'd used that flexibility to visit towns where his friends and family members lived.

In light of that, the convergence of her mom, dad, and Russell in the same small town the same weekend would make sense if . . .

Dad had known Russell prior to that week-end.

Or — her senses lurched unpleasantly — if Dad had known Mom prior to that week-end.

She whipped off her robe and began to pace. Dad had been three years older than Mom and Russell, but they'd all attended the same university, so it wasn't too difficult to imagine that Russell and Dad had met there. Perhaps they'd played intramural sports together? Lived near each other? Belonged to the same fraternity? She could picture her dad stopping in Camden to catch up with an old college friend.

It was much harder to picture Dad catching up with an old college friend who was female and happily married.

Her slippers whapped against the area rug, then the wood floor. Area rug. Wood floor. Anxiously, she fussed with her rolling ring.

It would also make sense for the three of them to have been in Camden the same weekend if Dad had met Mom that weekend through Russell.

Area rug, wood floor. Area rug, wood floor.

Her parents had told her they'd met more than a year after Russell's death. She wanted

387

to believe that, even knowing they'd lied by omission about Mom's first marriage.

They were the ones who'd told her that the sun was a star. That there wasn't a monster in her closet. That washing her hands would help her avoid the germs that cause sickness. That Reese Ashton was not dating material. That kindness and politeness matter. That they loved her. That God was real.

All those things had proved to be true. Her parents had poured the foundation upon which she'd built her life. They were the people she trusted most in the world.

Perhaps their proximity in Camden that weekend in 1983 really was a coincidence?

Yes. *No.*

Worry solidified in her midsection.

If she could take just one Oxy, it would crush the worry. She closed her eyes against a wave of longing for the relaxed, creative, confident buzz Oxy had given her.

She went to her mini-kitchen. With one sharp motion of her fingers, she opened a mini-pack of Jelly Bellies. Bright, sugary flavors exploded in her mouth as she chewed.

Sam had told her she could call him when tempted to take Oxy. But did she really want to disturb him, considering how convoluted things were between them?

She'd manage the worry on her own.

Too soon, she reached the bottom of the bag. She peered at it, disconsolate. She ordered the mini-packs specifically because they offered built-in portion control. But now, in order to manage her stress, her choices were either to lay waste to all her mini-packs of jelly beans or contact Sam.

She moaned. Why was it so hard for her to reach out to others for help?

Angry with her own pride, she texted him. *I'm struggling with a bout of worry. You invited me to let you know when I wanted to take Oxy, so I'm following through and letting you know.* She added two smiling emojis, then sent it before she could talk herself out of it.

As soon as she did, vulnerability besieged her. *What if he doesn't reply? What if he thinks I'm a head case? What if he's busy and my text is an annoyance to him?* Their friendship had been jagged since the kiss.

His text response came back more quickly than any text response she'd ever received from him. *I'm about to head to the super-market. Want to join me?*

Relief flooded her. She was struggling to think clearly about her dad's presence in Camden, but Sam would be able to. *Yes, please.*

She pulled boots over her leggings and a pink wool coat over her white dolman top. By the time his truck reached her cottage, she was waiting on the side of the road beneath her turquoise umbrella. She clambered into his passenger seat, storing her umbrella near her feet.

He did not send the truck forward but instead considered her watchfully. "What's going on?"

Oh, perish.

He was certifiably gorgeous in his black baseball cap, lightweight black jacket, work pants, and boots.

"I just found out that my dad was in the same town as my mom and Russell, the town of Camden, the weekend that Russell was murdered."

Seriousness settled into the creases at the corners of his eyes.

"You can drive while we talk," she said.

"Or I can sit here while we talk."

"No, it's okay. Drive." It would be easier to get this out without the full, swoony weight of his attention on her.

The truck jounced forward until it hit smooth road. She explained how she'd found the navy recruiting ad and the theories she'd come up with. "I just . . . I don't know what to think."

At a stop sign, he reached across to open the glove box. "Take a breath and drink this." He pulled out a bottle of water and handed it to her. "Hungry?" He motioned to the packages of almonds resting in the glove box.

"I'm okay." She refrained from saying she'd just inhaled jelly beans. "Thank you, though."

Since she'd met him, he'd supplied her with electrolyte water, protein shakes, muffins, steak, and more. It seemed he was prepared, even now, to dispense mobile sustenance from his truck. He'd been raised on an Australian cattle station. Every line and curve of him exemplified masculinity. But at heart, he was a caretaker.

Tenderness for him wrapped around her ribs so strongly that it stole her speech.

Sam was reserved and honorable. Guarded and good.

If she tried to tell him that he was a hero, he'd disagree. He'd disagree because he'd tried so hard to be Kayden's hero and failed.

His life experience had turned him into a reluctant hero, but he was a hero, just the same. She could see that as clearly as she could see the trees zipping past, clothed in autumn color.

He drove for a mile or more while she

took long, clarifying sips of water. She only wished the water were colder, because sitting this close to Sam was giving her a hot flash.

He doesn't want to kiss you, Genevieve! You can't be more than friends.

"You found a clue today," he finally said. "I don't want you to lose sight of the fact that that's a good thing."

"It doesn't feel like a good thing at the moment."

He mulled that over. "What's your goal concerning this search?"

"To find out what the letter writer knows about my parents."

"Each clue leads you closer to that goal."

"It's just . . . I didn't really want to find upsetting clues."

"This clue doesn't have to be upsetting," he said reasonably. "You don't know yet whether your dad's visit to Camden means anything or not. Until you know more, there's no sense worrying."

"True."

Companionable quiet coasted over them.

"Feeling any better?" he asked.

"Yes." He'd had precisely the comforting effect on her she'd known he would. Resting her head against the seat back, she concentrated on softening her tense muscles and finishing her water. She wasn't alone. Sam was here.

Ordinarily, she didn't enjoy grocery store runs. But the unexpected chance to spend time with him felt far more valuable to her than a ticket to a Broadway musical. If they'd been on their way to a dump, she'd have been thrilled.

"This past Fall Fun Day," he said, "reminded me that you're a celebrity."

"I'm not a celebrity," she said with automatic modesty. "My studies have been well received in some circles. That's all."

"*You're* well received, Gen. By my count, more than a hundred people came out to meet you."

She fiddled with the water bottle's lid. "I'm hoping they bought quite a bit of produce from the stand. Did they?"

"I don't care how they affected my produce sales. I care about how they affected you."

"I thoroughly enjoyed speaking to them."

"You're not uncomfortable with the attention?"

She resisted her inclination to answer with a simple no, forcing herself to be honest with him. "I'm ninety percent fine with it. Ten percent uncomfortable with it."

"Why ten percent uncomfortable?"

"Because I'm aware that I'm not deserving of it. It's strange to be known for two things you didn't control. An earthquake. And the sales of Bible studies."

"Do you think your notoriety from the earthquake increased the sales of your Bible studies?"

"Yes. People still remember the Miracle Five."

"Did the earthquake have any other upsides?"

She thought through her response. "When God saves you in a miraculous way, He becomes incredibly real."

"Other upsides?"

"I got to travel the world, telling people what He'd done for us. For a brief moment in time, we had a pretty profound impact."

"Other upsides?"

"The earthquake matured all of us. It deepened my relationship with my sister and gave me lifelong friendships."

He pulled into the grocery store parking lot, and they made their way through the front doors. He selected a shopping cart. She opted for a handheld basket.

He shook his head pityingly at her basket.

Clearly, Sam didn't need a list. He loaded fruit and vegetables into his cart with speed and assurance but without consulting any-

394

thing. Genevieve stood beside him, uncertain what to purchase.

"What were the downsides of the earthquake?" He placed a package of organic strawberries in her basket. Then blueberries, then mango, then kale.

"The trauma of it," she said.

"Explain."

"Before we were trapped down there, Natasha and I were these two happy, secure, protected girls. The worst thing that had happened to us was the time my mom got rear-ended when I was in first grade."

He led her toward the dairy section. "And then?"

"And then I found myself buried beneath a pile of rubble. I knew we'd probably die and that others had probably already been crushed when the building collapsed. I can't describe to you how jarring it was to find myself in that awful predicament . . . to be that terrified."

He added eggs and coconut milk to her basket.

"I had nightmares," she continued. "Anxiety. Trouble sleeping. All of a sudden, school became a struggle. That's when I started seeing Dr. Quinley."

"Any other downsides?"

"Are you really interested in all this?"

"I wouldn't be asking if I wasn't." He turned in to the paper towel aisle.

"My mom became very overprotective," she said. "She'd almost lost both of her kids and was dealing with the aftermath of her own trauma. Her insecurity didn't help matters. It wasn't until I left for college that I realized I'd been carrying the burden of her mental health on my shoulders. She still calls me all the time. She still worries."

"Other downsides?"

They walked down one aisle and up another.

"Gen?" he asked.

She'd been reluctant to text him earlier, but then she'd been tremendously glad she did. Should she tell him more? Probably.

When her silence continued, Sam stopped. He lifted her basket from her, set it in the child seat of his cart, and parked the cart next to a display featuring several flavors of coffee beans.

They stood to the side so that shoppers would have room to pass. Facing her, he crossed his arms and waited for her to say more. It was as if he'd positioned his big body to protect her from hurricane winds.

"Over and over again after we came home," she told him, "friends and family and strangers and pastors told us that God had saved us for a reason. 'He must have big plans for you,' they'd say. And we'd smile and nod and agree, because He'd done something monumental to save us, so we obviously owed Him something monumental in return."

Her mouth quirked into a frown. "It can be hard to undo things you internalize when you're twelve. For goodness' sake —" she flung out a hand — "one of my studies is called *The Sacrifice You Can't Repay.* And yet in some way or another, I think I'm still trying to pay God back for saving me."

His hat rode low over those haunting, pale green eyes. Compassion lived in the angles of his face. An invisible force was drawing her to him, sizzling the air with awareness.

"No matter how much I've done for His glory," she confessed, "I've always felt as though it wasn't enough."

Time does not heal all wounds. Some things burrow into you like a splinter, and no amount of ignoring the splinter will help.

"I can't imagine what you went through while you were trapped," he said.

Memories seeped in, like black dye polluting clear water. Far worse than the nightmares she'd suffered afterward was the nightmare she'd lived. That was the one she hadn't had the luxury of waking up from.

Eighteen years had come and gone, and here she was, still grappling with the ramifications of what had happened to her. The bad. And the extraordinary. She'd done the hard work necessary to heal when she was a child, and again more recently with Dr. Quinley. Yet nothing could change the fact that she'd been marked by disaster. The earthquake was part of her story. So was her phenomenal God, whom she'd been unable to find for months now.

Pressure built behind her eyes. Silently, she willed the tears not to come. Not here, in the coffee aisle, in front of Sam, who was reliable in a way she respected and practical in a way she trusted.

Sam moved forward, shrinking the space between them.

She pulled a rough breath inward. What was he —

He pushed his hands into her hair and kissed her.

He . . . *They* . . .

His mouth was gentle and conquering at the same time. He smelled like an Australian summer, and he kissed the way a maestro leads an orchestra. Her brain cartwheeled with surprised joy. She placed her palms on his chest and felt his heat and taut strength.

The kiss tasted like destiny . . . as if she'd

been waiting, without knowing she'd been waiting. For him. For this. It felt more right than anything had felt in forever and a day.

Her body soared to life —

A deep, rusty chuckle intruded on her bliss.

She and Sam stepped apart, looking to the source of the sound.

An eighty-something-year-old man smiled at them good-naturedly, furrows creasing his skin. "I'm laughing at myself, not you, because see, if I didn't depend so much on my coffee, I would've turned right around when I saw you two and gone a different direction. But I depend on my coffee something terrible. Please excuse the interruption."

"No." A blush rolled up her cheeks. "Please excuse *us.*"

She and Sam moved away from one another to give him access, Sam on one side of the gentleman and she on the other.

The older man poured beans into a brown sack. "I sure do love my vanilla-flavored French roast. I'm very loyal to it." He dumped the beans into the grinder, positioned his sack below the chute, and flicked the machine on.

Bravely, she glanced at Sam. He stared back, his eyes unusually bright. His cheeks were flushed, and he looked painfully irresistible.

Her focus skittered back to the coffee grinder. The delicious scent of vanilla coffee beans enveloped her. "I'll need to get myself some of that flavor," she said, meaning it. If that vanilla coffee could keep the sensory details of their kiss alive in her memory, she'd drink five cups of it a day.

"I recommend it," the gentleman said. "I surely do." The grinder finished its job. The crinkling sound his bag made as he folded it seemed deafening. He raised his face to Sam. "How about those Falcons?"

Genevieve curbed the urge to release a peal of hysterical laughter.

"They're off to a good start," Sam answered.

"Defense wins games," the gentleman said.

"Yep."

"And now I'll let you two pick up where you left off." He pushed his cart, one wheel wobbling madly, away from them. "God bless y'all."

"God bless you," Sam and Genevieve said in unison. They watched until he vanished.

"Lovely man," Genevieve whispered.

"Lovely."

Needing to collect her composure, she followed the same steps — sack, coffee beans, grinder — the gentleman had just performed. "Can't wait to try this coffee."

"Is this your way of avoiding me?"

"Too right," she said merrily, borrowing one of the Aussie sayings she'd heard him use a couple of times.

Oh dear. She really liked him. Which was wonderful. Which was dismaying. He'd kissed her this time. Hadn't he? Yes. He'd very definitely kissed her. Yet, she was still concerned that he was about to lay down some somber pronouncements like he'd done after their last kiss.

She deposited the bag of coffee in her basket alongside several items she did not recall selecting. What on earth was she going to do with fruit, vegetables, and coconut milk? She cleared her throat, busying herself a moment by rearranging the food in her basket, before returning her gaze to him.

"It would be best for you not to get involved with me," he said gravely. "I don't have anything to offer you."

She sensed that the serious approach was not the approach to take at this juncture with this serious man. "I don't know about that." She smiled. "Men who've just done half a woman's grocery shopping can't claim that they don't have anything to offer."

"Is that so?"

"It's in the rule book. I still need the other half of my groceries, however. Meat and such. Right? I can't imagine a dinner of eggs and blueberries."

His lips — lips she'd just kissed — twitched a fraction.

A middle-aged woman drew near, giving them not-so-subtle glances.

Sam tugged the front of the cart toward himself, caught it, and started down the aisle. Genevieve fell in step beside him. He added things to his cart without even looking at them. Was he rattled?

"I have a lot of flaws," he announced, clearly wanting to expound on his earlier statement about having nothing to offer. "I'm stubborn, opinionated, and set in my ways."

"Point taken."

"I shut people out. I want things I shouldn't."

"Hmm. Anything else?"

"I hate baseball."

"That's a crying shame. The hot dogs and peanuts they sell at the stadiums are yummy."

He selected protein bars from a shelf.

"You may be shocked to learn that I, too, have flaws," she said. "I cry too easily, and I'm terrible about laying down boundaries with my mom and with other people, too."

"I see," he said, carefully neutral.

"I hate video games and yogurt."

"Ah."

"I have a weakness for prescription pain-killers, and I often procrastinate my writing by taking online quizzes that tell me important things like which flavor of cupcake I am."

"Anything else?"

"My sister is prettier than me."

That commanded his full attention. "She's not," he said emphatically.

"Of course she is. Everyone thinks so."

"Not me."

They reached the check-out line. He leaned and stretched as they unloaded items onto the belt, muscles playing beneath his clothing. As they inched forward in line, she noted the tawny brown of his short hair. The slope of his nose. His waist.

This very controlled man had just kissed her in the middle of a grocery store! She could hardly believe it.

Thanks to her efforts, they bantered back and forth on the drive home. She didn't want him to get too much into his own head.

At her cottage, he insisted on carrying the groceries inside for her. When he'd set the last bag down, he turned to her. Silence elongated.

"Thanks," she said. The last thing she wanted was to try to define anything or to put pressure on him. "Good night."

He dropped his usual shields — just for a second — and she could see the force of his desire in his eyes. Then he shook himself, as if coming to his senses, and made for the door. "Good night. I'll come by soon to explain all the things you can make with your groceries."

"You better. I'm a Starbucks girl, not a kale girl."

He shut the cottage's door behind him.

She pressed her hands against her cheeks and stared into the middle distance.

What did their kiss mean? Had it been a spontaneous thing he didn't intend to repeat? Or did he intend to repeat it again and again?

She and Sam had each had one serious relationship. Together, their record was 0–2.

He might still love Kayden.

And Genevieve couldn't afford to set herself up to experience the level of devastation she'd experienced after Thad had broken up with her. If she did, she might self-medicate by reaching for Oxy.

Which she could *not* do.

Today, Sam had helped her resist Oxy. But down the road, if things didn't work out with him . . . ?

It was too soon to angst about future heartbreak! There was no commitment between herself and Sam. Just friendship, a crush, and two fantastic kisses. She'd strive to live in the moment, without fretting over his intentions or the destination of their relationship.

He'd kissed her. And it had been magnificent.

Tonight, she wanted to cling to the jubilation of that.

Luke

"I'm wondering if one of those holds water." Sebastian points to the two pipes exposed by a section of broken wall about a foot off the floor.

We've been down here for a whole day now, but it feels like ten. The girls and Ben keep saying that we'll be rescued soon. But why would anybody care about five American kids in a basement when the entire city must be ruined? I don't hear the sound of helicopters or rescue dogs or people calling for us.

One of the pipes is bent where a connecting piece joins two lengths of pipe together. Sebastian tries kicking down on that point. Nothing happens, except that he winces in pain and says a cuss word.

Genevieve gives him a shocked look, as if she's afraid a teacher is going to send him to detention.

I watch Sebastian through gritty eyes. I don't care whether he finds water or not because if Ethan's dead, I might as well die down here, too.

CHAPTER SEVENTEEN

Sam was supposed to have met Kayden at the Sydney Museum, like they'd planned. He'd forgotten. He hadn't been there at the right time, and she'd been kidnapped while she was waiting outside for him. Now he had to get her back.

What had he done? How could he have been so careless?

He tried to run down dark city streets to rescue her, but his body wasn't following his demands. It was as if his feet were stuck in tar. He was too slow. Hopelessly slow.

Why hadn't he met her like he said he would? He hadn't been there when she needed him, she'd been taken, and she might die. He'd betrayed her.

Guilt and terror lodged in his chest, so heavy and painful he couldn't bear it.

Wildly, he looked from side to side, trying to catch sight of her. If he could find her, he could make up for his terrible mistake.

"Kayden!" he yelled.

No answer.

He tried to run and couldn't move. "Kayden!" He didn't see her anywhere. Where was she? What had he done —

Sam wrenched from sleep to consciousness. For a long moment, he lay in bed, heartbeat fast against his ribs, struggling to acclimate to reality.

It had been a dream.

He'd never stood Kayden up. Nor had she been kidnapped. Unfortunately, though, he couldn't comfort himself with the knowledge that she was safe and healthy. She wasn't.

There was no escaping the fact that he'd let both her and himself down. And in the end, darkness had carried Kayden away. Not against her will. But because she gave darkness permission.

The fear and shame of the dream dragged at him like chains.

He pushed his stack of books to the side to view his alarm clock. 4:52. His internal timer often woke him a few minutes before he had to get up for work, as it had today.

He groaned and bent an arm over his eyes.

He'd dreamed of Kayden because kissing Gen had stirred up all his old issues. His guilt and regret.

When she'd told him yesterday that she was still trying to pay God back for saving her, it had wrecked him.

After God showed up for you miraculously, he understood why a person would want to pay God back. Yet how could anyone pay God back for a miracle? Gen was only human. She didn't have the power to perform miracles.

Which hadn't stopped her from almost killing herself trying.

He was like a dam whose base had been ripped away. He no longer had the ability to hold himself back. His willpower could resist every harmful thing he'd once indulged in. But it could not resist Gen.

Their kiss last night had affected him like a collision with a locomotive. Afterward, his hands had tremored and blood had pounded in his ears. His thoughts had been in opposition to each other. Pleasure versus fear. Greediness versus humility. Satisfaction over what he'd done versus self-blame over what he'd done.

Beep. Beep. Beep.

He hit the off button on his alarm and began going through his morning routine.

What was he going to do about Gen? Part of him whispered that he must do *nothing* more. He'd already allowed too much. But that part of him was growing weaker by the hour, drowned by the much stronger part of him that could think of nothing other than how soon he could see her again.

The woman who'd slept in his guesthouse like Goldilocks had frightening power over him. She could turn his body to fire and his hardened heart to soft soil.

Natasha liked for things to make sense. If something made no sense to her, she couldn't let it go. She'd fixate on it until she understood it. While in the fixation phase, she had a habit of gnawing on crunchy foods the way a beaver gnaws a log.

Genevieve sat next to her sister at the desk in Natasha's front room. A few celery sticks lay jumbled on a paper towel. Natasha slathered peanut butter along one celery stick's trough, then rested the knife back on the open jar. "Sure you don't want one?" Natasha offered the snack to Genevieve.

"I'm sure."

Genevieve had called her sister this morning, the morning after her fateful grocery store run with Sam, to tell her about the navy recruitment ad. Natasha had been on an outing with her kids at the time. Genevieve had needed to work. They'd decided they'd meet later in the day to squeeze in a

411

micro-investigation. Now here they were, but they had little time. It was 4:05 on Halloween afternoon, and Genevieve could feel the expectant excitement building like a coming storm within Natasha's household. The kids were currently playing in the backyard with Wyatt, but soon they'd all need to get dressed for this evening's festivities.

"We have a theory that Dad may have known either Russell or Mom before his trip to Camden," Natasha said. "If that's the case, then Dad most likely got to know one or both of them during his senior year and Russell and Mom's freshman year at Mercer."

"Agreed."

"We need evidence." Natasha drummed her fingertips against the top of her desk. "How can we find evidence that proves they knew each other before 1983?"

"Mutual friends? If Dad knew Russell or Mom in college then someone else knows that he did."

"Do you remember the name of any of Dad's college friends?" Natasha asked.

Genevieve had met a few of them many years before, but those interactions had been brief. "No. You?"

"No. I wish we could ask Nanny and Pop

412

about Dad's Mercer friends."

Unfortunately, Pop had passed away a decade ago, and Nanny had dementia. "I'll go visit Nanny soon," Genevieve said. "It's time for me to check in on her anyway, and it could be that something about Dad will shake loose from her memory." She tipped the hook of her earring forward and back thoughtfully. "Dad's siblings might know who his college friends were."

"None of them went to Mercer, but you're right. They still might remember his friends from that time. Problem is, as soon as I call Aunt Connie, Aunt Jolene, or Uncle Colby, they'll tell Dad and then Dad will know we're researching him behind his back." Natasha loaded another celery stick with peanut butter and munched it loudly.

Genevieve stole a surreptitious peek at her phone for the three thousandth time that day.

Status: Sam still hadn't texted or called.

She'd determined that she would not obsess over what Sam was thinking or what might come next between them. That's what her head had decided, very firmly. Her hands, however, wouldn't stop reaching for her phone and checking it compulsively.

"A photograph would provide evidence," Natasha mused.

413

"What sort of photograph?"

"Of Dad with his college buddies that . . . I don't know, ran in the school newspaper?"

"What about a school yearbook?"

"That's genius!" Natasha's posture whipped straight. She faced her computer and began typing. "Remember all those photos I displayed at Wyatt's birthday dinner two years ago? One of them was of him on the JV basketball team in high school. I found that on a website. It's amazing how many yearbooks have been archived online."

"Dad was in a fraternity, and Mom was in a sorority. Both those organizations would be featured in a yearbook."

"Russell's obituary mentioned that he was in a fraternity, too," Natasha said. "But it wasn't the same fraternity as Dad's."

"Maybe something else connected them. Intramural sports occurred to me yesterday."

"Or a club of some sort? If we can find a picture or even a listing of names that proves that Dad was in the same organization the same year as Russell or Mom, we'll have our evidence."

Natasha journeyed to a site specializing in yearbook records and typed in *Russell Atwell, Mercer University, 1982*. Two results popped up. Genevieve held her breath as

414

Natasha clicked on the first link. It revealed a class photo nestled within a full page of class photos. They'd both seen this picture of Russell numerous times.

"Shoot," Natasha said. " 'In vain have I struggled. It will not do.' " She returned to the search results and clicked on the second and final link.

A yearbook page about Russell's fraternity appeared. They found him in a group picture that showed at least ten guys doing construction on a service project. Dad wasn't in the photo.

Natasha ran a search for Mom. Again, two hits. One for Mom's class photo and one for Mom's sorority. Mom's name was listed alongside the names of her sorority sisters, but she wasn't featured in any of the photos on the sorority's page.

They might be wasting their time, hunting for a college connection. Mercer had thousands of students.

Finally, Natasha ran a search for Dad. This time the site found three matches. The first led them to a page focused on a Christian student organization. Dad stood, the tallest of the bunch, clean-cut and smiling, in the back row of the photo. Russell wasn't listed as a member of the organization. The second match took them to Dad's class photo. The final match brought up his fraternity's page.

Genevieve drew in a sharp breath of astonishment. "There." She pointed.

They peered at the screen. Then at each other, speaking volumes through the look they shared. Then at the screen.

The photo on the left center of the page revealed their dad . . . with Mom on his arm.

The two of them together, in college. Five years before they'd said they met.

Mom wore a formal gown and a feathered hairstyle. Dad, his gangly body garbed in a tuxedo, looked down at Mom with an enamored smile on his face. His hand clasped hers securely. Mom gazed straight at the photographer, laughter twinkling in her eyes. The caption below read, *Fraternity treasurer Judson Woodward enjoys a night out with his date.*

Natasha consumed another celery stick the way a glue gun consumes glue sticks.

"I can't believe we actually found evidence," Genevieve whispered shakily. She'd been right when she'd deduced that Dad might have known either Russell or Mom before coming to Camden. But she'd been fairly sure that Russell was the one Dad would have known.

No. It had been Mom.

Natasha spun her desk chair to face Genevieve. "Not only did they know each other in college, they were in love with each other in college."

"We don't know that they were in love," Genevieve felt honor-bound to say. "We only know that they went to one function together."

"Look at his face, Gen! He's got that soft, smitten look."

True. The young man in the photo had thick dark hair unmarked by silver and no beard. A pair of '80s-style glasses fit securely on his nose. His ears and Adam's apple had both been a little more prominent back then, when he'd been skinnier. However, a few things about her father had remained exactly the same: the kindness in his demeanor and the expression on his face. Her older, more weathered father still looked at Mom that very same way.

"Mom's beaming like I've never seen before," Natasha said.

Right, because after this her first husband was killed. Later, her daughters were almost killed. Life had made her nervous, which had prevented her from experiencing the type of undiluted happiness captured in this old yearbook picture.

417

"Hon?" Wyatt called from the region of the back door. "Is it time to change into costumes?"

"Not quite yet. Five more minutes."

The back door closed in response.

"So," Genevieve said, "let's say that Mom and Dad were a couple in college. But then something happened to break them up."

"Most likely Dad's enlistment in the navy broke them up. When he graduated and left, Mom still had three years of college ahead of her."

"So then Mom starts dating other people. She meets and falls in love with Russell. After graduation, Mom and Russell marry."

"Then Dad makes a stop in Camden, where the newlyweds were living. Ostensibly, to recruit. But also, to say hello to his old girlfriend." Natasha wrinkled her nose. "Why? It seems weird that he'd reach out to an ex-girlfriend after she's married."

"Perhaps they remained friends after their breakup?" Genevieve suggested.

"Are you friends with any of your ex-boyfriends?"

"No."

"Me neither."

"That doesn't mean that it couldn't have gone down that way for Mom and Dad," Genevieve said.

Natasha chewed the side of her bottom lip.

A shiver of premonition ran between Genevieve's shoulder blades, because she knew what her sister was about to say before she said it.

"What if Mom and Dad still had a thing for each other?" Natasha asked. "What if Mom cheated on Russell with Dad that weekend?"

The possibility jangled.

"The person who wrote the letter said that Mom and Dad weren't going to 'get away with it,' " Natasha continued. "What if someone saw them kiss? Or found them in bed together?"

"On the weekend of Mom's husband's murder?"

"That would have been scandalous enough to motivate someone to write a letter."

"Yes," Genevieve said. "But I just can't believe that Mom would have cheated on Russell or that Dad would have participated in that, either." A marital affair didn't square with her parents' character. "Mom and Russell looked incredibly happy in their wedding announcement photo."

"Okay, so, what other scandalous thing

could Mom and Dad have done?" Natasha asked.

In the silence, the dishwasher chugged.

"I don't know," Genevieve said.

The back door banged. Half a second later, Millie spilled into the room. "Daddy says it's time to put on my costume!"

The Fellowship Hall at The Vine Church hadn't been constructed with the type of sound-dampening materials needed to handle the din generated by a hundred children and their entourages. Especially when those children were enjoying their first round of overstimulation and candy right before their second round of overstimulation and candy.

Genevieve and Natasha's family had arrived thirty minutes ago for the Light the Night event at Natasha's church. They'd meet up with their parents shortly, then take the kids out trick-or-treating, which, blessedly, would be quieter. A volcanic explosion would be quieter.

"What a darling little Spider-Man," the lady at the Go Fish station said to Genevieve. She handed Owen a makeshift fishing pole with a clothespin dangling from the end of its line. He tossed the line over the partition painted to resemble the ocean.

"He looks just like you, Mama," the woman told Genevieve.

"Thank you, but I'm not his mommy. I'm his aunt." His unmarried, childless aunt.

"What a good auntie you are," she said. Then, to Owen, "Move your fishing pole around to see if you catch anything."

Genevieve glanced down the length of the large space at the kaleidoscope of activity —

And spotted Sam.

A dazzled stillness fell over her as memories of yesterday's kiss replayed in her imagination.

As if she'd called out to him, he looked up.

The electricity that snapped between them was so powerful Genevieve was surprised everyone in the room didn't duck for cover.

Warmth contracted her abdomen.

He gave her a small, affectionate smile and nodded.

She returned his smile and nod, then startled when Owen tapped her thigh. The woman working the booth had knelt down to help Owen free his prize (a tiny box of crayons) because Genevieve had been unable to hear, see, or sense anything else while ogling Sam.

"Way to go, buddy," Genevieve said.

Sam was here. *Sam* was *here*.

Owen dropped the crayons into the favor bag she was carrying for him, then outstretched his arms.

Genevieve swept him onto her right hip. "Can you say thank you for the crayons?"

"Tankoo."

"You're welcome, sweetheart," the older woman said.

Would Sam approach her now?

She'd been sure that her chances of seeing him today were shot when she'd left the farm.

Her chin kept wanting to tug back in his direction and sneak another peek. It took physical effort to resist the gravitational pull.

She carried Owen to an art station that provided dot markers plus coloring pages featuring pumpkins and scarecrows. Once she got him situated on a chair, he released the two soggy Goldfish he'd been protecting in one hand and went to work.

"Happy Halloween." Sam's voice. His Australian accent rippled over her like satin.

She twisted to find him standing nearby, fingers pushed into the front pockets of his jeans, a gray athletic shirt hugging his shoulders.

"Happy Halloween." She looped a finger inside the neck of Owen's Spider-Man costume. She didn't want to get sucked into

422

a Sam vortex and fail to notice her nephew toddling out of the church toward the nearest busy street.

"Are you dressed as a . . ." He pushed his lips to the side, considering. "Russian folk singer?"

She laughed, which felt like a gift in the face of the uneasy feeling she'd been carrying since she'd seen the yearbook photo of her parents. She indicated her braids, jewel-toned cape, full skirt, lace-up boots. "Really? You don't know who I am?"

"Nope."

"I'm Anna from the movie *Frozen.*" Her costume wasn't a cheap knock-off. It was legit. After she and Natasha had decided to dress as Elsa and Anna, her sister had rented these costumes for them.

"Never saw it."

"*Frozen* was something of a cultural phenomenon."

"Among who?"

"Females worldwide."

"Anna!" a little girl called, pointing at Genevieve as she ran past.

"See?" Genevieve said wryly.

"Red!" Owen sang, stabbing his coloring page with a red dot marker.

"Is this your nephew?" Sam asked.

"Yes, this is Natasha's son, Owen." Owen

423

spared Sam a skeptical glance. "Owen, this is Mr. Turner."

"Sam."

Owen returned to his art.

Genevieve regarded Sam. "If Owen could talk and had manners, he'd say that it's nice to meet you."

She swallowed. She hadn't told anyone about yesterday's kiss, so it was strange to stand here with him in public, very circumspect, but with this blazing private knowledge between them.

"What brings you here tonight?" she asked.

"I go to church here."

"You do? So does Natasha." Her sister had never mentioned that he attended The Vine.

"I go Saturday nights."

"Ah. She goes Sundays."

"They needed volunteers, so I offered to help with the putting green."

"That's very sacrificial of you."

"You volunteer at the farm a lot."

"Yes, but I had mercenary motives when I agreed to volunteer at the farm. I wanted your cottage."

His mouth took on a lopsided curve. She could see his reserve battling against his desire for connection. "I don't think you're very mercenary," he said.

424

"Oh, but I am. Where chives are concerned."

He chuckled, and it went to her head like vodka.

"I'm impressed that someone not related to any of these children would brave this," she said.

"It's good for me not to spend all my free time alone."

A visual of him inside his farmhouse cooking dinner for one plucked a cord of sympathy in her, which ended up making the visual unreasonably sexy.

"I better get back." He gestured to the line forming at the putting green. "I abandoned my mate Eli."

"You have a friend?" she asked with exaggerated surprise, only half kidding.

He grinned, and his face creased in that endearing way. "I have one friend."

"Two," she corrected breathlessly, tightening her hold on Owen to ensure he was still in the vicinity.

"Would you like me to drop in later?" he asked. "To explain what to do with the groceries I chose for you?"

Inside, she was salsa dancing. "Sure."

"What time?"

"Natasha's kids have to go to bed early or they turn into monsters, and not the cute

425

Halloween kind. I expect to be home by nine."

"See ya then."

She watched him weave through the crowd. He stepped to the side to let a family pass and corrected a kid's course when the kid would have barreled into his legs.

He was coming over later.

Natasha stepped directly into her line of sight. "Are you using my child as a dude magnet?"

"How could you think so little of me?"

"How could I think so *much* of you, you mean. If you're using my child as a dude magnet, I was going to compliment you."

"Actually, I discovered that kids don't really provide a very romantic ambiance."

"You don't say," Natasha said dryly. She resettled the train of her Elsa dress. "Luckily, it didn't appear that you two need any help in the romance department. Sam was looking at you like he was a puma and you were dinner."

"He was?"

"Have you kissed that man again?"

Genevieve paused.

"When?" Natasha demanded. "When did you kiss him?"

"Yesterday. This time he kissed me."

Natasha crowed. "I'm jealous! You're having first kisses and all I'm having is PMS."

Owen abandoned his chair. Natasha took his hand, Genevieve straightened the area Owen left behind, and they made their way to the cakewalk. Millie and Wyatt were already there, moving in a circle over masking-tape numbers as "Monster Mash" played.

Genevieve took out her phone and snapped photos of her niece and nephew.

Sam was coming over later.

"Honey girl." Dad approached wearing a hideous beige scarf Natasha had knitted for him over his button-down shirt. No doubt, the long brown dog ears perched on his head had been Mom's idea and he'd good-naturedly gone along.

Mom had on dog ears, too. Hers were lighter brown, shorter, and bent over at the top.

Genevieve hugged them, but when they stepped apart, she couldn't quite meet their eyes. They'd lied to her and Natasha about when they'd met. Why would they lie about that?

"Doing okay?" Mom asked her.

"Yes. I think the kids are having a great time."

"Good, good. You look adorable, sweetie."

"Thanks!"

Mom intertwined her fingers with Genevieve's and heaved a sentimental sigh. "Halloween night. What a moment to treasure."

"It really is."

"Millie and Owen won't stay little for long, sadly. They'll grow so fast." She squeezed Genevieve's hand as they watched Millie circling. "The best years of my life were the years when I had you and Natasha at home with me. When you were small and I had you all to myself, we'd play and cuddle all day."

"They did the mash," the song's chorus sang. "They did the monster mash."

"I blinked," Mom went on, "and you and Natasha were adults. In the place where my babies had been, only precious memories remained."

Tears were piling onto Mom's lower lashes.

Uh-oh. "Mom," Genevieve said.

"I'm thankful, of course, that you and your sister have turned out wonderfully. Because you have. You're my life's best work."

Sam is coming over later.

"I know that events like this one can be lonely for single women," Mom said. "If you're feeling that way, I want to be sensitive to it."

"I'm not feeling that way. I'm happy."

"There are a lot of young families here. Which can be hard."

"She's happy, Caroline," Dad said, winking at Genevieve.

"It's just . . . I want you to know I understand your sorrow," Mom told her.

"Thanks, Mom."

"You have Dad and me, sweetie. We love you to the moon and back."

"I love you, too."

"And we'll always be here. For anything and everything you need."

"I appreciate that. Very much."

"Have you had enough to eat tonight?"

"Yep."

The music cut away. Neither Millie nor Wyatt had landed on the correct number. Consternation stamped Millie's face. Wyatt counteracted that by sweeping his daughter upside down until she laughed.

"I'll make you a cake," Mom assured Millie as she bent to christen the little girl's face with kisses.

Dad took Owen into his arms and ruffled his hair. "How are you, buddy?"

What despicable thing could these two people — who wore dog ears on Halloween and cherished their grandchildren — have done all those years ago?

Natasha

I think Sebastian's lost his mind.

He picked up a rock, and he keeps dropping it on the bent area of the pipe. *Crash.* He lifts it again. *Crash. Crash Crash.* Metal creaks.

How many times has he dropped the rock on that pipe? Thirty? Fifty? He's grunting and sweating. What if he spends all his energy on this pipe only to find out that it's empty or that it carries sewage?

Crash. This time, he doesn't pick the rock back up. Instead, he raises his knee and lets out a yell as he kicks down on the pipe with his heel.

It doesn't break.

I come to stand next to him. "I'll help."

"We'll all help," Ben says.

"No. I can do it myself."

Suddenly, he's not the only one who's angry. I'm angry, too, because he's so

430

rude. Why would anybody be rude in this situation? It's hard enough to be stuck down here. We're all worried. We need to be kind to one another.

Sebastian lifts his rock again. All of us except for Luke hunt around for the next biggest rocks we can find. When Genevieve stands, she has to put out a hand to steady herself and fear kicks me in the gut. She's weak and moving slow.

She needs food and water and a bed.

God, please come get us out before nightfall. Please, God. I can't face another black night in this hole.

"I *said* I can do it myself," Sebastian snarls as I near him with my rock.

"I heard you. But I'm going to drop this rock one way or another, and if you don't move to the side I might drop it on your head."

Sebastian takes one step back, breathing hard.

We take turns hammering the bend in the pipe with our rocks.

Nothing.

CHAPTER EIGHTEEN

Sam knocked on Gen's door at nine that night. He shouldn't have invited himself over. He was chasing after something that he wanted too much, that was too dangerous to him.

Yet here he was.

She opened the door. "Hi."

"Hi." He just stood there, unable to move.

She'd changed out of her costume into jeans and a casual sweater. Her thick hair flowed over one shoulder and her long earrings swung against her throat. Her hazel eyes were so much clearer than they had been, back when she'd been using. Every day they were sharper and brighter.

"Come in," she said easily. "I lit a fire."

It didn't feel like he was coming in from the cold of one autumn night. It felt like he was coming in from seven years of cold.

He settled onto her love seat. She settled beside him, their bodies close but not touching.

"The groceries?" he asked.

"Can wait a little while." She asked him questions about Halloween in Australia. He asked about the Halloweens of her childhood. Which led to stories about their best and worst family holidays.

Her company was like diamonds to him.

When he looked at his watch it was ten. He hated to leave but he needed to leave. His alarm clock would wake him in just seven hours. Lack of sleep wasn't his primary concern, though. If it had been, he wouldn't have come tonight, because he knew even this short visit would keep him awake for a long time. His primary concern was that he didn't trust himself with her. He'd exerted his control for as long as he could, and now it was crumbling in his hands.

He pushed to his feet. "It's late. Can the groceries wait one more day?"

"Of course."

"I'll see you tomorrow."

She trailed him to the front door. "See you then."

He walked four paces away from the guesthouse. Stopped. *Don't look back.* His heart was burning.

He looked back.

With a growl, he returned to her. Sweeping her body against the lean length of his, he kissed her the way he'd been aching to. She responded immediately, passionately, her arms locking behind his neck.

If this kiss were an ocean, he'd willingly let himself sink down, down, down until he drowned.

Where was his sense of self-preservation?

At the bottom of the ocean. Far, far away.

He kissed her for as long as he dared. Deep kisses. Soft and slow kisses. He told her a million things through those kisses about his devotion and his inner struggle.

He separated from her, scared to think what his feelings for her might cost him. But at the same time, he wasn't sorry for his actions.

"Good night." She grinned, seeming neither to want nor expect an explanation from him.

" 'Night."

When Genevieve's phone beeped to signal an incoming text the following day, she lunged for it like a sprinter off the blocks. *It might be easier to explain what to do with your groceries if I can talk about it while I make you dessert at my place tonight,* Sam's text read.

434

A rosy glow infused every particle of her. How could one text from a man generate such a strong physical reaction?

She sat at the desk in the cottage, beaming at her phone. Not wanting to respond so quickly that she'd appear overeager, she put on "Super Bass" by Nicki Minaj, then danced around the interior of the space, singing along.

She'd been floating through life since he'd kissed her last night. He'd told her that he thought it would be best for her not to get involved with him. Certainly, he also thought it would be best for him not to get involved with her. Thus kissing her ran against his will to a certain degree.

Yet he'd done it anyway — at the grocery store and again last night — which left her feeling *ridiculously* pleased with herself.

Sam was not an easy fortress to breach. However, she'd miraculously managed to tap a tiny fissure into the wall of his defenses. He was letting her in, which made her hope all kinds of crazy things.

For now, though, the tiny fissure was enough. Indeed, the thought of continuing exactly as they were filled her with tingling excitement.

It wasn't that she could no longer hear the voices of her misgivings. She could still hear them. The path she'd set out on was a scary one. Kissing Sam might be ill-advised at this precarious point in her life. And it might lead to catastrophe. It's just that the joy of kissing him was so strong that she was willing to risk *a lot* in exchange for it.

Do you make apple crisp? she texted him back. *I feel that I might be able to absorb all this new information about my groceries best while eating apple crisp.*

I'll make it for you, but only if you agree to call it by its proper name, apple crumble.

Sam was a gift that God had dropped in her lap at one of the lowest moments of her life, right when she'd deserved a gift the least. She was grateful, simply and deeply grateful, for the gift.

That night, they ate apple crisp and they kissed.

The kisses were the sweeter of the two.

No one mentioned a word about Genevieve's groceries.

A knock sounded on Sam's door the next afternoon, shortly after he'd returned home from work. Genevieve stood on his porch wearing an athletic outfit, spotless blue tennis shoes, and her hair in a ponytail.

Joy shot through him at the sight of her.

Less than twelve hours had passed since

436

he'd seen her last. Even so, he'd missed her.

"I'm heading out on my daily walk," she said. "If you're free, I thought this might be a good time for you to explain what I should do with all those groceries you bought me."

They walked two miles. They held hands part of the time. They laughed most of the time.

He said nothing to her about her groceries.

I'll be working in the garden later, Sam texted her the next day. *I can explain then what to do with your groceries.*

They gardened.

But they did not talk about groceries.

You home? he texted her the following afternoon.

Her pulse leapt happily. *Yes.*

Would you mind helping me with something in the barn? While you're here, we'll talk about your groceries.

Coming right over.

Minutes later, she neared the barn. He'd told her that he'd had it repaired, then sanded, before painting it gray and topping it with its sleek new metal roof.

She loved his house. But she loved the barn, too, especially against the backdrop of fall foliage.

437

She loved this whole farm, in fact. The apple orchard. The pond. The paths meandering through dense trees. This place charmed her and calmed her. Somehow, her soul could rest here more easily than it had been able to rest anywhere.

It took her eyes a moment to adjust to the darkness inside the barn. Where was Sam?

She yelped and startled backward. He was immediately to her right, standing a few rungs up a ladder, striking a pose.

He held a gray kitten against his torso, one arm beneath it, one arm supporting it from the side. He braced his legs apart and smiled winningly into the distance.

He was reenacting the August photo from her *Firefighters and Kittens* calendar.

She burst out laughing. Her only sorrow — that he wasn't shirtless like Mr. August.

The kitten wiggled. The tiny mite wasn't dozing in Sam's arms the way the kitten in the calendar photo had.

She laughed harder.

His gaze flicked to hers. Amusement warmed his features. "Well?" he asked. "Do I look like Mr. August?"

"Better."

"Better?"

"So much better."

"Because this doesn't feel very sexy. This

438

beast is scratching me up."

"Extreme sexiness comes at a price."

"A high price," he agreed, breaking the pose and moving the kitten to his shoulder, trying to position him like a parent would a baby who needed burping. The animal scrabbled madly for purchase. "What woman could resist this?"

"Not me." She extended her hands. "Here. Want me to take him?"

"Please."

She lifted the kitten from him. "Aw. He's more fluff than substance."

"And more anger than fluff."

She repeatedly stroked a fingertip down the animal's forehead. "Did you adopt a kitten?"

"No, Eli's girlfriend did. They're both out of town for a night and they asked me if I'd babysit."

"Isn't *kittensit* the proper term?"

"I should have said no."

But, of course, he'd said yes. Because, at heart, he was a protector.

"What's his name?"

"Abner."

She raised the animal so that she could smile at him eye to eye. "Hi, Abner."

"Hi, Gen," Sam whispered in a raspy voice.

439

"Is that your Abner voice?"

He nodded.

She cradled Abner against her, and the cat settled. "He likes me best."

"So do I."

She fisted a hand into the front of Sam's down vest and pulled him to her for a kiss, the kitten between them.

They played with Abner at length.

No one mentioned groceries.

"Tonight's the night," Sam said to her the following evening. "I'm here to talk to you about your groceries."

"Seriously?" she asked with a note of incredulity.

He entered her cottage and set down two new bags of groceries. "Yes."

"I ate most of the old groceries."

"Which is why I brought new groceries. I'll make you dinner, if you're hungry."

"I am."

Gently, he wound a strand of her hair around his finger, then let it glide between his thumb and forefinger. She saw heat in the green depths of his irises before he cupped the back of her neck and tipped his forehead against hers. "Have you had a good day?"

Her throat went dry. She loved the proportions of his body, its sturdiness and vitality. "Yep."

Together, they unpacked the sacks. He cooked and, as he did, explained what he was doing. She wrote each step of the recipe down in a notebook. Admired his skills. Passed him utensils and pans and ingredients.

When he came to the end of the process, he handed her a bowl filled with a deconstructed enchilada. It had no tortillas in it. Just poblano pepper and butternut squash, beef, and avocado sauce.

Since she didn't have a true table in the cottage, they sat on the rug facing the fire, their backs against the love seat.

As usual when she ate Sam's food, it caused something tightly wound within her to loosen. It was the best kind of medicine, his food. "This is awesome."

He finished chewing and swallowed. "Thank you."

"However, there's no way that I can recreate this. I'm incredibly flattered that you think I can, but I'm afraid that your lesson may have been wasted on me the way a — a trigonometry lesson would be wasted on a five-year-old."

"I dictated the recipe to you. You wrote everything down."

"Yes, and yet I'm going to need to start off at a much easier level."

"Define easy."

"Three-ingredient easy."

After they completed dinner cleanup, Sam showed her what to do with each and every one of her new grocery store staples. She ended up with three simple breakfast ideas, three simple lunch ideas, three simple dinner ideas.

"What do you reckon?" he asked in conclusion. "Still like teaching trigonometry to a five-year-old?"

"No. I now believe I'll be able to pull off two of these nine dishes."

He grinned wolfishly. "You can pull off all nine of the dishes," he said with so much unshakable confidence that she didn't dare protest.

"That's what I said."

Genevieve had always liked field trips.

The more things changed, the more they stayed the same, because she and Dr. Quinley had taken a field trip for today's session — from the psychologist's office to the atrium outside — and she found that she liked field trips still.

They sat at a little round table drinking the tea the doctor had brewed and enjoying the perfection of the sunny sixty-eight-degree day. The dark trunks and branches of the maple trees around them played hide-and-seek behind foliage that blazed a deep, bright red. The trees were so eerily vivid, they were otherworldly. They made Genevieve feel as though she and the doctor had been transported into the center of a fantasy novel.

"I still catch myself thinking about Oxy fondly," Genevieve told her. "Almost with this sense of . . . loss and nostalgia."

"There were things about the pills you enjoyed."

"Very much," Genevieve confirmed.

The doctor settled a flap of her knee-length sweater over the other flap. In her aging face, her dark eyes were as kind and bright as those of a girl. "When we long for something that isn't good for us, it can be instructive to think about the things we want more."

"I'm not sure I know what you mean."

"What do you want for yourself, Gene-vieve?"

She took a sip of tea. "What blend is this?"

"Nettle leaf."

"It tastes like hay."

The older woman laughed richly. " 'Hey, hey, we're the Monkees,' " she sang. " 'Peo-

443

ple say we monkey around.' "

"It tastes like hay, and I find that I like it, even so. What does that say about me, doctor?"

"That you can appreciate unconventional flavors."

Sam was a bit of an unconventional flavor. In the past, she'd always gone for Southern men who dressed hip, had been raised by their mommas to have impeccable manners, and were ambitiously scaling the corporate ladder. Remembering them, especially Thad, she found that she could appreciate Sam very, very much.

The doctor tilted her head back to admire the leaves and waited for Genevieve's honest answer to her difficult question.

"What do you want for yourself, Genevieve?"

"I want more for myself than a life in which I have to depend on painkillers." Painkillers would never be able to love or comfort her. Like every other human on the planet, she'd been wired to be loved and comforted by God. And Oxy was no substitute.

Recently, she'd begun to feel as if she was drawing nearer to God as she worked to break free of her shame and put an end to her lies. Yet, she still couldn't feel His presence.

444

"I want to have a clear head," Genevieve continued. "I want peace. I want deep relationships and satisfying work. I don't ever again want to break promises to myself."

"When you start to think fondly of Oxy, experiment. See if you can't reroute your thoughts to those very excellent goals."

"Will do." Genevieve wrapped her hands around her mug.

"Last week you told me that you'd started dating Sam. How's that going?"

"What's an adjective that's better than fabulous? That's how it's going."

"Marvelous?" the doctor offered.

"Tremendous?"

"Extraordinary?"

"Magnificent," Genevieve declared. "It's going magnificently."

"Personally, I've always been a sucker for a foreign accent. I once dated a man named Arturo from Argentina. He wore a gold necklace with a saint on it and he could *tap dance.*" She rested one ringed hand on her chest. "He was magnificent."

"But?" Genevieve hadn't started therapy yesterday. She knew that undertaking a romance during the first ninety days was often a Very Bad Idea. She'd known it when she'd kissed Sam after their steak dinner.

She'd known it when he'd kissed her in the grocery store.

It seemed to take Dr. Quinley a moment to recover from her Arturo-haze. "*But* dating comes with some pitfalls I want to make sure you're aware of. We've talked at length about the void that painkiller addiction leaves. You wouldn't want to allow yourself to fill that hole with Sam."

"Point taken." The doctor was right, of course.

"Co-dependency is unhealthy for anyone. But for you, it carries a different sort of danger, given that you're in recovery."

"I couldn't agree more. In fact, you're articulating things I've thought about a lot. I definitely don't want to become co-dependent on Sam."

"He can be *one* of the things in your life."

"But he can't be my everything."

"Precisely."

Who cared if a man could golf or fish or play baseball? The most seductive (and practical) talent any man could have was a talent for cooking.

Last night, after her session with Dr. Quinley, Sam had made her a divine dinner. And now, sitting across from Natasha this morning at The Kitchen, she was getting positively misty over his equally divine paleo donut.

Natasha had been talking about her hunt for information on Russell's family for a while now. Genevieve was finding it hard to concentrate on her sister's monologue when she could concentrate on thoughts of Sam and his donut instead.

"Genevieve."

She jerked straight.

"Did you hear anything I just said?"

"Um . . . something about the Atwell family?"

Natasha rolled her eyes. "You're so infatuated with your new boyfriend that you're incapable of focusing on anything else."

"Shhh." Genevieve leaned quickly toward her sister and lowered her voice. "He's not my boyfriend." The last thing she wanted was for one of Sam's employees to overhear and inform Sam that she'd given him that title.

"If he's not your boyfriend, then what is he?"

She didn't want to go there, either within the quiet of her own mind or verbally with Natasha. "He's Sam," she answered. "And he's great."

" 'A lady's imagination is very rapid . . .' " Natasha dangled the quote from *Pride and*

Prejudice, brows lifted meaningfully.

" 'It jumps from admiration to love, from love to matrimony in a moment,' " Genevieve finished grudgingly. "Except, not in this case."

"Then what *is* happening between you two? In this case?"

"When I know, you'll be the first person I tell."

Natasha leveled a troubled look at her.

Genevieve waved a hand. "I'm on cloud nine. I don't need to give Sam a label."

"Bull."

"Anyhoo, will you look at that. He just emerged from the back."

Never the queen of subtlety, Natasha twisted in her chair and waved.

He immediately crossed to their table.

The stark details of him — simple black T-shirt, wide chest, short hair slightly mussed — flashed a thrill through her.

"Good morning," he said to them both.

His serious eyes with their frame of dark lashes met hers. She could disappear into those eyes like Alice down the rabbit hole. The quick, searching look he gave her held tenderness. Communication passed between them. *How are you?* he asked.

I'm doing well, she assured him. *You?*

I'm doing well, too.

Natasha asked him friendly questions while Genevieve got lost in memories of their kisses and the sweep and swirl of her emotions.

"Anyone need more coffee?" he asked.

"I'd love another latte," Genevieve said.

"I'm still working on my tea," Natasha told him.

He moved toward the coffee bar.

"As I was saying," Natasha said. "Russell's family moved to Atlanta after his death. His father died there in 1986. As far as I can tell, his mother and his two younger sisters still live there. I searched and searched. I made a few phone calls. But I haven't been able to find out anything about them online. I'm guessing that they lead quiet lives."

"Hmm." Genevieve's attention tracked Sam as he worked the espresso machine. The woman who stood behind the to-go line cash register, Star, slid glances at him from beneath her lashes when he wasn't looking. If Star could have shot love beams out of her eyes, Sam would have been reduced to vapor.

"Genevieve." Once again, Natasha broke into her reverie. "Honestly!"

"Sorry!" She grinned apologetically. "What's our plan going forward?"

"I'm going to see if I can find an address

for Russell's mother. If I can, I thought I might reach out and ask for a meeting. She may be able to shed more light on what Mom and Dad and Russell were up to the weekend of Russell's death."

"I don't know, Natasha. Alice Atwell lost her son. I'd hate to stir up her grief. I can't imagine we'll comfort her if we show up and announce that our dad once dated her son's wife in college."

Natasha exhaled with frustration. "I'm not sure what else to do, then. The yearbook picture of Mom and Dad is the only shred of evidence I can find linking the two of them prior to when they started dating years later in Savannah. You and I have both hunted for information on their time in Savannah, and nothing unusual has come up. It seems that everything that happened in Savannah happened just the way Mom and Dad always said it did."

Genevieve had come to Misty River because of the first letter. For the past several days, though, the mystery involving her parents had lessened in urgency for her as Sam had overtaken the top spot in her list of priorities. "Don't forget that I'm going to see Nanny." She'd called Aunt Jolene and set up an appointment to stop by and see her dad's mom day after tomorrow. "Who

450

knows? Nanny may have a lucid moment and be able to tell me something about Dad's relationship with Mom while he was in college."

"She's a sweetheart. Unfortunately, I don't think she has many lucid moments anymore." Natasha tightened her ponytail. "I took her to an outdoor class last summer where instructors were teaching the steps of a quadrille. I wanted to get her out of the house, and Wyatt and I were terrible at the quadrille, so I'm sure we were extremely entertaining to watch. She seemed miserable the whole time."

"She was probably highly confused to find herself surrounded by Americans twirling to the steps of an English dance."

"If you don't find anything out from Nanny, and we decide not to pursue a meeting with Alice Atwell, then we might need to admit that we're done . . . that we've found all the information we can."

"What about reopening our investigation into Angus Morehouse?"

"We researched him as much as we could and didn't come across a single clue."

"Perhaps we can find a friend or family member of his that we could talk to?" Genevieve suggested.

"I'm not opposed to that."

"I'll make a note to call Birdie Jean and ask her if she could suggest someone. What if that doesn't pan out?"

"Then I think it's time to confront Mom and Dad."

Sebastian

We need water, and this pipe might hold water — so no matter what, I'm going to break it.

When it's my turn again to hit the pipe, I raise my rock over my head and throw it at the pipe with all my strength.

A metallic sound explodes through the space. The pipe cracks. Instantly, water gushes from its broken end. The girls and Ben cheer.

Water's coming out fast, spilling all over the floor.

I lift the broken end up as high as I can. Water continues to bubble from the top, drenching me.

Gradually, it slows to a trickle. "Girls, come have a drink."

The sisters approach. Natasha pushes Genevieve forward. I tip the pipe down carefully and let her have a turn drinking from it. Then Natasha.

"Now you," I tell Ben. I hold the pipe for him, too.

"Now you," I say to Luke.

"I don't want any." His brother's probably dead, so Luke's willing to die, too. I hate him — this boy who has everything that I don't have.

I narrow my eyes. "Get over here and drink some water."

"Or?"

"Or I'm going to make you." I'm big for my grade, but Luke's a year older and stronger than me. I don't care. If I have to fight him over this, I will.

An awful smile breaks across Luke's face. He stands and takes hold of the pipe. "Save your energy, Sebastian. You might need it." He drinks.

CHAPTER NINETEEN

Two weeks had passed since he'd kissed her in the grocery store coffee aisle. Every day of those two weeks had been paradise for Sam. Every one of them torture, too.

He stood at the far end of his dining room, staring out the window at the dark of early morning. The exterior lights revealed frost crusting the contours of his land. Mist hovered above it like an overprotective mother.

Exactly the thing he'd known he couldn't let happen was happening.

All his focus, passion, and meaning were narrowing and narrowing to one small person.

It left him feeling stupid. He had no idea what she felt for him and no sense of their future, which meant that he couldn't adjust his own emotions accordingly.

He made a rough scoffing sound.

Even if he did know how she felt about

him and had a sense of their future, what chance did he have of adjusting his own emotions? He'd already been trying his best to hold them back. He'd already kept himself apart from her as much as he could stand.

He didn't want to keep himself apart from her.

She was the best thing in his days. She was the joy in his dull, gray, lonely life.

He refused to stop what they had.

Yet his gut kept whispering to him over and over that he was setting himself up for a fall.

"What time is it?" Grandma Woodward asked Genevieve the next day.

It was the third time Nanny had asked the question since Genevieve had arrived for their visit. "It's 11:40."

"What time is my appointment?"

"Let's take a look at your schedule." Genevieve rose from where she'd been sitting near her grandmother's wheelchair. She drew the older woman's attention to the small whiteboard resting on top of the bureau in her aunt and uncle's living room.

Months ago, her grandmother's caregivers had begun listing her daily schedule on the whiteboard. Not only did it keep everyone on the same page as to the day's calendar, it calmed Nanny's anxiety to know how her day was constructed.

Both Genevieve and her paternal grandmother depended on their daily schedules, it seemed.

Nanny didn't respond to the whiteboard with either an affirming word or gesture. Her expression went blank.

Genevieve returned to her chair.

Her dad had taken after his mother in many ways. Both were wise, mellow, friendly. Genevieve had never seen either one of them fly off the handle and lose their temper. Never.

Tall, willowy Gloria Woodward had married a comptroller at a paper factory, raised four children, and taught at her church's preschool for fifty years. Through it all, she'd dressed sensibly and comported herself humbly.

The death of her husband a decade ago followed by a dementia diagnosis several years later had eventually landed her here, in the home of her oldest child, Jolene.

A pale pink scarf encircled Nanny's neck. A cream sweater and a pair of brown slacks swathed her body. She wore her white hair trimmed short. Always on the slender and stiff side, Nanny had become both of those things to a painful degree over the last two years.

Genevieve could still smell and taste the butterscotch pudding Nanny had made for her every time she'd come to stay at her house when she'd been young.

Nanny's memories had deserted her. But Genevieve remembered.

"May I hold your hand?" She'd learned not to take Nanny's hand without asking first. The older woman didn't have many opportunities to express her will these days. Genevieve wanted to give her as many chances to do so as possible.

Nanny turned her chin to Genevieve slowly.

Genevieve rested her hand on top her grandmother's wheelchair armrest, should she want to take it.

Grandma looked at her as if she couldn't place her.

"I'm Genevieve. Judson's younger daughter."

"Judson." Recognition sparked in her face.

"Yes." She'd stated her identity when she'd first arrived, but this time it seemed to penetrate better. "Your son, Judson. He's doing well, and I'm doing well. And you're doing well, too, here at Jolene's house. You're safe and well cared for."

Her grandmother wrapped her bony hand around Genevieve's.

Genevieve tried to pour all her affection into the simple touch. "Do you recall Judson's college years, Nanny?"

No answer.

"He went to Mercer," Genevieve said. "I'm guessing he occasionally introduced you to friends and girlfriends."

Nothing.

"Perhaps you met my mother then? Caroline?"

No reply.

So much for the hope that a memory of her parents' college romance might shake loose from Nanny's brain.

They'd learned that they could sometimes connect with Nanny through songs, so Genevieve started singing "Amazing Grace." She moved her grandmother's hand gently from side to side in rhythm with the song.

Nanny's attention stayed on Genevieve the whole first verse before it drifted away. Across the second and third verses, her grandmother's lips moved every so often, framing one of the familiar words.

Tears sheened Genevieve's eyes. It was beautiful to sing of God's grace with Nanny and so difficult, at the same time, to see her in this condition.

Nanny's caregiver was preparing lunch in the kitchen. The sounds of her movements formed a backdrop as Genevieve sang "The Old Rugged Cross" and then "How Great Thou Art."

Near the end of "How Great Thou Art," her grandmother slipped her hand from Genevieve's and returned it to her lap.

"Are you feeling all right?" Genevieve asked when she finished the song.

"Yes."

"Is there anything I can get you?"

No answer.

"Judson, did you say?" Nanny asked.

"Yes. My father is your son, Judson."

"So tidy."

"Yes. He's still tidy. He helped me clean up two nights ago when we had dessert at the cottage where I'm staying."

A long pause.

"What time is it?" Nanny asked.

Genevieve stayed until her grandmother sat down to eat lunch, then drove back to Misty River tinged with melancholy. She envisioned Nanny and Pop Woodward singing to her on her birthday the year she'd had the unicorn cake, clapping for her after the fifth-grade school play, driving her and Natasha to the community pool in their wide Lincoln Continental.

460

She'd choose to focus on those times and on the positive things that had happened during today's visit. Nanny had sung a little with her. And she'd not only remembered her son but also remembered that he was her tidy one.

Nanny had always been complimentary of her son's tidiness. In fact, back when Genevieve had looked through her parents' family photo albums shortly after arriving in Misty River, she'd come across several photos of her father's boyhood bedroom that Nanny had taken. Her father in his tidy room. His books, meticulously shelved. Bed tightly made. Floor clean. Toy action figures . . .

Her stomach gave a slow, sickening roll as a thought occurred to her.

Her immediate response was to thrust the thought far, far away. It didn't mean anything. It was nonsense.

Yet, her anxiety wouldn't listen. It grew and grew.

Genevieve turned her Volvo in the direction of her parents' house. She'd take another look at those albums. Her dad would be at work, of course. Her mom may or may not be home; she spent a good portion of every day outside the house meeting friends, volunteering, spending time with

Millie and Owen, playing mah-jongg.

When she reached the house on Swallowtail Lane and clicked the garage door opener, she saw that, blessedly, her mother's car wasn't parked within. She let herself into the house, feeling more like a thief than she ever had before upon entering her childhood home.

Upstairs, she had no difficulty locating the albums Nanny had made. She selected an album, paged through it — nope. This wasn't the right one. She slotted it back into its place and pulled free the next album. About a third of the way through, she came upon the set of bedroom pictures she'd been seeking.

The specific picture she'd recalled in the car just now was situated in the center of its page. A shallow wooden box held nothing but Dad's boyhood collection of action figures. He hadn't tossed them inside. He'd carefully placed them within, every one of them facedown, arms at their sides, legs straight and centered at hip width.

It was as if she was looking at an old, old omen. Each small inanimate object prophesied the future positioning of Russell Atwell's dead body exactly.

She couldn't take her eyes off the picture. Dizziness beckoned at the fringes of her vision. Her mother might return home at any second. Yet her brain failed to send her muscles the command to move.

It was a coincidence that her father's action figures so perfectly mirrored the positioning of Russell's body.

Except . . . She knew that her parents had lied to her about when and how they'd met. And she knew they'd covered up Mom's first marriage. Why do that unless they had something to hide?

Her father had been in Camden the weekend of Russell's murder.

Also, Russell's body had been found in a pose unlike that of the Shoal Creek Killer's other victims. Facedown, with arms at his sides, legs straight and centered at hip width.

Lord God.

She'd just been thinking earlier today that she'd never seen her father lose his temper. The most controlled man, the best man, the most trustworthy man in her life could not have been mixed up with Russell's death in any way. It made no sense. Yet suspicion was growing deep inside, like a seed splintering open and extending its roots. This seed was confusion and its roots were fear.

Her hands seemed to belong to a stranger as she returned the album to its place.

Typically, she grabbed lunch at this time of day, then worked for the rest of the afternoon at the library, a coffee shop, or a bookstore. But today's schedule was now hopelessly lost to her. The very last thing she could deal with? Public scrutiny.

She drove to her cottage and clicked on two lamps. Set her teakettle to boiling. Checked her phone and email. Started a fire. The kindling didn't want to catch. She tried twice before throwing down the box of matches.

She paced, her body's movement tense with desperation.

Even imagining that her father — *her father!* — had somehow arranged Russell's dead body felt like a betrayal of him. He'd read *Chrysanthemum* by Kevin Henkes to her approximately a million times. He'd coached her terrible first-grade soccer team, of which she'd been the most terrible player. He'd escorted her to a father-daughter Valentine's Day dance in seventh grade and convinced her that she was beautiful even though she'd been an awkward girl with tragic bangs.

Over and over, she pulled up Natasha's number on her phone. Each time, she hesitated before activating the call. She needed more time to consider her concerns

464

and determine whether or not she was crazy before calling Natasha.

She sat at her desk and tried to work on her Bible study. Failed. Tried to post to social media. Couldn't. Tried to do the busywork at the bottom of her to-do list. No luck.

She opened her Bible. However, her mind kept starting sentences with the printed words and finishing them with *What did my father do?*

Around four in the afternoon, she realized that she hadn't eaten since breakfast. She wasn't hungry but made herself a salad because Dr. Quinley had repeatedly emphasized the importance of prioritizing her physical health. Especially when one of her triggers had been pulled.

After eating, she stood on her porch, relishing the chill bite of the November wind against her face. She was in dire need of a distraction. Ideally, a calming distraction. She peered toward Sam's farmhouse.

She'd stopped by The Kitchen on her way to Nanny's earlier. They'd hung out in his office for thirty minutes, laughing, talking, kissing. He was scheduled to attend a half-day mini-conference and dinner for local business owners this evening. Thus, he wouldn't be at home. That fact didn't stop her from climbing into her car and driving by his house.

The absence of his truck and the lifeless windows rendered her more bereft than they should have. Technically, he wasn't her boyfriend. Even if he had been, he wasn't available to help her at present. His world did not revolve around her. And she could not become co-dependent on him.

Which was fine! She didn't need his help because she was perfectly capable of handling this herself. Her family issue wasn't his problem. He didn't need to know that her sky was falling.

Temptation whispered to her, reminding her how calm and in control Oxy would make her feel. She steered toward town, her desire for Oxy clawing at her like hunger pangs.

A prescription for Oxy still awaited her at the Riverside Pharmacy. She had only to notify them that she wanted it filled. No one else had to know. In less than an hour, she could pop a few pills and let peacefulness lap over her. With Oxy's help, she wouldn't have to feel so panicky.

She drove to Buttercup Boutique and tried on clothes. It helped slightly to surround herself with outgoing people. She left with a bulging bag of new clothes she wasn't at all convinced that she either wanted or needed.

When she drove past the pharmacy, she didn't even allow herself to peek at its storefront. "Not today, Satan."

Sam's truck passed her cottage at 12:02 a.m. She marked the time because, though she was lying in bed with the lights out, she could not have been more awake. The night didn't surround her with soft sweetness. It surrounded her with sinister peril.

Perhaps she should go to his place now, to see him. He'd invited her, quite seriously, to confide in him.

Only, he'd be tired.

And she didn't need his help!

Not tonight, anyway. This could wait until tomorrow.

12:27. She prayed, lungs tight because she didn't want her parents to be mixed up in anything dishonorable and because she couldn't trust them *not* to have been mixed up in something dishonorable.

12:50. Sam would be asleep at this point, so she'd missed her window to visit him.

12:55. Which was for the best because she didn't need his help.

12:58. She'd feel *so* much better inside his house. Just that. She wouldn't wake him, she'd simply relocate and attempt a secret sleepover on his laundry room floor.

She changed out of her pajamas and into yoga pants and a sweatshirt. Too scared to walk all the way to his farmhouse alone at this hour, she drove most of the distance before parking far enough away so he wouldn't hear her engine. A single exterior light provided dim illumination as she tiptoed into the laundry room.

She checked the door that led to the rest of the house. Open. God bless him. Ever since the grocery store kiss, in a display of trust, he'd only been locking his back door, not the door from the laundry room to his hallway.

She folded the comforter she'd brought over on itself a few times, laid her pillow on top, then slipped her robe on backward and rested into the nest she'd made.

Just as she'd suspected it would, the fact that she was no longer so alone began to hush her anxiety. Sam was strong and principled and more than a little unattainable, and he was sleeping just one floor above.

Hopefully, their relationship would progress, and she wouldn't always be relegated to the metaphorical laundry room of it, with him one floor above. But for tonight, this setup was more than satisfactory —

The door to the hallway opened. Sam filled the portal, silhouetted by gentle light from behind him. His hair was askew, his feet bare. He'd donned a rumpled T-shirt over pajama pants.

"Did I wake you?" she asked. "I'm so sorry."

"I'm not." He reached down with both hands. She grabbed on. He pulled her to her feet, then wrapped her against him in a hug. "I missed you," he whispered against her hair.

She loved him.

Perish. The. Thought.

They hadn't even talked about making their relationship exclusive. He was solitary and extraordinarily protective of his heart. He might never be able to love anyone the way that he'd loved Kayden.

Regardless, she loved him and couldn't stop herself from loving him, even if it spelled her complete and utter doom.

Lifting her off the floor, he carried her toward the kitchen. He turned on more lights with his elbow as he passed sets of switches. "Were you having a late-night laundry emergency?" he asked.

"Yes."

"That required blankets and pillows?"

"Yes."

"You just wanted to see me," he accused teasingly.

"I was having a very dire laundry emergency," she insisted.

"Then how come the washing machine wasn't going?"

"An excellent question." She tightened her grip around his neck. "To be honest, I was planning to camp out in your laundry room tonight because I couldn't fall asleep at my place. However, I intended to be as silent as a Navy SEAL so that I wouldn't wake you."

"You were very quiet. Luckily for me, I can sense you even when I can't hear you." He seated her on his kitchen countertop.

She coasted a fingertip down the side of his rugged face. The better she knew him, the more and more appealing he'd become. In his eyes, narrowed against the brightness, she saw his intelligence. In his forehead, she saw the creases that Kayden's death had chiseled. In his olive skin, she saw the hours he spent working outside. In his blunt jaw, she saw his humility and his centeredness on the things that mattered.

A hundred painters could never do him justice.

"If I sense that you're in my house, there's no way I can sleep," he told her.

"I'll leave," she offered, hoping he wouldn't take her up on it.

"Not a chance."

"You have that big order to fill for the school fundraiser tomorrow," she reminded him. Ben and several of the other teachers at Misty River High School had helped the senior class organize a dinner and silent auction to raise money for an educational trip to Washington, DC. Sam had agreed to donate dessert for their event. "I don't want you to be tired in the morning on my account."

"I don't care if I'm tired tomorrow. I only care about you."

Joy plucked at the corners of her lips.

His hands gripped the front edge of the counter on either side of her. "I like your robe."

She looked down at herself sheepishly. "And my lack of makeup? And my sleep ponytail?"

"Yes and yes. You look beautiful."

"So do you."

"How come you couldn't fall asleep at your place?" he asked.

"Because I had a really awful thought about my dad today."

He considered her. "Did you have anything to eat for dinner?"

"A Diet Coke."

His grimace communicated extreme pain. He opened his refrigerator.

"I don't need you to make me anything," she hurried to say. "I'm not hungry. If I get hungry, I have all kinds of healthy things to eat back at my cottage —"

"Who said I was making anything for you? I'm hungry."

But, of course, he was going to make food for her.

While she told him about Nanny's comment about her dad's tidiness and the photos of Judson's childhood bedroom, he whipped up some paleo pancake batter with cinnamon and walnuts, then poured a circle of it into a sizzling skillet.

Sam asked a few questions. Mostly, though, he listened.

He handed her two pancakes stacked on a plate. They tasted the way she imagined the food served in heaven (accompanied by harp music) tasted. A sense of security melted into her as surely as the pat of butter melted into her topmost pancake.

Sam chewed a bite of pancake. "What're you going to do?"

"Discuss it with Natasha tomorrow. Then settle on a plan of action." She set down her fork and took a long drink of ice water.

"It's crazy, though, right? To see a connection between my dad's action figures and Russell's body? It sounds crazy when I say it out loud."

"Do *you* think it's crazy?"

"I wish I did." She took her time swallowing her mouthful of pancake. "Something about it, though . . . about Russell's body arranged just that way . . . It seems like something my dad would do. He really is very tidy. Automatically so. It's kind of his calling card."

"It's too early to jump to the conclusion that your dad had anything to do with Russell's death."

"Agreed."

"Talking to your sister seems to me like the right play."

She polished off her final bite, tasting the balance of cinnamon and nuts. "I think I'll be able to sleep now."

"Good. Want me to take you back to the guesthouse?"

"Are you referring to the cottage?"

His dimples warmed her cold corners. "I'm referring to my guesthouse."

She suddenly felt utterly exhausted. "I'll accept your offer to escort me there."

"I'll stay with you until you fall asleep."

"You don't have to do that."

473

"I know." He picked up one of her hands and kissed her palm. "But I will."

Ben

Two days have passed since the earthquake.

Only three of us have watches, so I took mine off and laid it on the floor so that the two without watches can check the time whenever they want. I try not to check it. Every time I do, I'm upset by how slowly time's passing.

I knotted my shirt into a circle and made a sling for the water pipe. I tilted the pipe up and hung the sling on a jagged piece of wall so that the water stays down in the pipe. The earthquake must have broken the pipe somewhere, because no new water is flowing from it. We have to dip the pipe a little lower each time to get water to pour into our mouths, so we're trying to conserve.

"Let's pray," I suggest when we reach forty-eight hours after the earthquake.

Sebastian makes a rude noise and Luke looks away.

"Let's do," Genevieve says.

"Who's going to do it?" I ask. I hate to pray out loud.

"Me," Genevieve answers. I'm kind of surprised, because she's the youngest one here.

She bows her head and prays the prettiest and most powerful prayer I've ever heard in my life. She's saying all the things I want to say, the way I want to say them, and tears fill my eyes.

God, is all I can think. *God.*

Please rescue us.

CHAPTER TWENTY

It had become Sebastian Grant's habit to fly his private plane from Atlanta, where he worked, to Misty River any time he had three days off in a row.

He'd achieved his pilot's license five years ago and purchased his twin engine plane a year ago. He liked the challenge, adventure, beauty, and quiet of flying. The forty-five-minute trip from Atlanta's Fulton County Airport never felt like inconvenient travel time. It felt like a hobby he enjoyed.

The drive from the airstrip outside Clayton to his house in the mountains north of Misty River — less enjoyable. Especially on this particular Friday morning because fog lay thick at ground level. Grimly, he steered his Range Rover along winding two-lane roads.

Now that no hospital administrators, physicians, nurses, or patients needed him for anything, weariness was beginning to weigh his body down. Like many doctors, he could function on a small amount of sleep. He could also fall asleep at will and wake up fully when necessary.

Leaning forward slightly in the driver's seat, he rolled his shoulders, then angled his head to the right and left. When he reached his house, he'd sleep for two or three hours. After that, he'd work out, shower, then take Ben's parents to the dinner and silent auction for the high school's seniors. He'd marked this Friday off his schedule so that he could attend the event.

He wasn't married. He had no children. No biological parents or biological siblings. His career consumed most of his focus, time, and passion. Only one thing, apart from it, meant anything to him: the Colemans.

A long curve melded into a straightaway. The music on the Siriusly Sinatra station was so relaxing that it was putting him to sleep, so he punched the button for the classic rock station. Just as he refocused on the road, a beat-up sports car swerved out of the mist into his lane.

Sebastian wrenched his wheel to the right. Horn blaring, the car veered past, inches away, and continued down the road in the opposite direction.

Sebastian tried to correct by jerking the wheel back to the left, but speed and momentum thrust him into a skid. His Range Rover shot off the road's shoulder. He flattened the brake, and the car screeched. Then earth fell away into a drainage ditch. The front end of his car impacted the bottom of the ditch, crushing metal. Sebastian's body rammed forward.

Pain flashed, blinding, in his skull.

Then his consciousness yanked away.

"Sir?"

Sebastian heard the feminine voice as if he were at the bottom of a hole. Chuck Berry's "Downbound Train" played.

"Can you hear me?" she asked, sounding worried and faintly out of breath. "Are you all right?"

Her voice was smooth and sweet like honey. He didn't want the woman with the voice like honey to be worried. Also, he didn't want to wake up, because his head ached with dull, fierce pain.

"Sir," she said. "Can you hear me?"

"Yes," he said hoarsely.

"He fell on his knees," Chuck Berry sang, "on the bar room floor and prayed a prayer like never before."

Sebastian slit his eyes open. Pinpricks

479

punctured his vision. He was inside his car, his seat belt cutting against his chest diagonally. What had happened?

Wincing, he lifted his chin. Cracks scarred his windshield. Beyond the hood, he could see nothing but dirt and torn grass. A pair of sapling trees wedged against his driver's side door.

He'd been in a car crash.

How long ago? Why?

He didn't know. He'd flown to the airstrip. He . . . he remembered getting into his car and pulling out onto the road in the fog. That's all.

He'd lost time.

Experimentally, he moved his fingers and toes. Everything was working fine except for the splitting pain in his head.

The one with the beautiful voice clicked off the radio. "Downbound Train" disappeared, leaving only a faint ringing in his ears.

"I'm relieved that you came to," she said.

The tone of her words softened the agony inside his skull.

Slowly, he turned his chin in her direction. He'd lost his tolerance for light and the pinpricks wouldn't go away. He squeezed his eyes shut against the disorienting sensation, then opened them and con-

480

centrated hard so that he could focus on her.

She . . . had the face of an angel.

An unforgettable face. A heartbreaking face, both hopeful and world-weary. He guessed her to be a year or two younger than he was but she didn't look sheltered or naïve.

Long eyelashes framed gray-blue eyes as deep as they were soft. She had full lips with a defined groove at the top. Blond hair, parted on the side. Neither curly nor straight, it had a natural, faintly messy look to it. She'd cut it so that it ended halfway between her small, determined chin and her shoulders.

Had he died? Was she an angel? She was here, which made him think he'd died. But his head hurt, which made him think he hadn't.

"Are you injured?" she asked.

"I'm fine. Except for my head."

Concern flickered in her expression. At least, he thought it did. He struggled to see her more clearly, furious that he couldn't look at her with his usual powers of observation.

She knelt on the passenger seat, the door behind her gaping open. "I've already called 9-1-1. Hopefully they'll be here soon."

"I hope not."

"Hmm?"

"I don't want them to take me away from you."

Her brows lifted. "I . . ." She gestured. "I was behind you on the road. I came around the bend just in time to see your car go off the edge. I pulled over and dialed 9-1-1."

"How long was I out?"

"Just a few minutes. Is there anything I can do for you?"

He extended his right hand to her. "Hold my hand?"

"Of course." She wrapped both of her hands around his. The heat of her touch had the same effect on him as her voice and appearance.

He suspected he'd cracked his head on his side window, which had knocked him out and likely given him a severe concussion.

"Would it help if I unfastened your seatbelt?" she asked.

"Yeah." He was capable of freeing it using his left hand. But if she was offering to do it for him, he wasn't about to say no.

She let go of his hand to accomplish the task, and he cursed himself for making a tactical error. But then she braced one hand against the center console and reached across him, bringing her hair within a few inches of his nose. He drew air in and registered the scent of lavender.

Dark satisfaction curved his lips. He hadn't made a tactical error. His brainpower remained intact, and he was going to be just fine. The constriction of his seat belt released.

She arched back and resumed her earlier position.

He extended his hand.

She took it. "Better?"

"Much."

The sound of sirens reached him. In response, resistance sharpened inside him. He didn't want to be parted from her.

Twice before in his life, he hadn't wanted to be parted from people. When he was eight. When he was thirteen. Both times, his desires hadn't mattered.

"Is there anything else I can do for you?" she asked. "I'd be happy to call someone."

"No. I'm not the type . . . to alarm people . . . before I have solid facts." He paused for a moment to gather his strength. The pinpricks still wouldn't go away.

The sirens drew nearer. Louder.

He rested the back of his skull against his headrest but kept his face turned fully to the right, his concentration trained on her.

483

"After I speak with the doctors . . . I'll make calls. To tell people what's happened."

"Okay."

The sirens grew so loud that they made conversation impossible.

She craned her neck to look toward the road.

Idiot sirens. Violently, he wished he could take back her 9-1-1 call.

He had to remember that he was a stranger to her. He couldn't expect her to feel about him the way he felt about her. She hadn't been in a crash. Her head was clear.

The noise of the ambulance cut away. Its lights continued to revolve, sending rays of red and blue against her face. She gave him a small, encouraging smile. "They'll be here in just a second."

He gripped her hand more tightly, holding her with him. He memorized the curves and lines of her forehead, cheeks, hair, neck, arms.

Men's voices neared.

She moved to exit his car.

He didn't release her hand. "Don't go," he said.

She leveled a bemused look on him. "I need to get out of their way. It's all right. They're going to take great care of you."

484

Gently, she slipped her hand from his and scooted away.

All he could think was, *No. Don't go.* But he'd already said that, and it hadn't worked. He couldn't force her to remain with him.

"You're going to be just fine," she said.

He was not going to be just fine without her.

Two men in EMT uniforms filled the passenger-side doorway. They were leaning in, talking to him.

Sebastian twisted, trying to keep sight of her, but in an instant, the fog stole her from view.

She hated to be late.

But in this case, she'd had no other option. She'd stopped immediately after she'd seen a sports car whip past her just as a Range Rover hurtled into a ditch. After parking, she'd scrambled down the embankment, heaved the SUV's passenger-side door open, and found a handsome, dark-haired man slumped unconscious against his seat belt. The stranger's emergency had, rightfully, taken precedence over everything.

A truck waited in the fog on the road outside her house. She parked her old Honda Pilot in her driveway and hurried toward the truck.

The driver rolled his window down.

"Sam Turner?" she asked.

"Yes."

"I'm Leah Montgomery." They shook hands through the window. "I'm really sorry that I'm late. I apologize."

"No worries." He spoke with a fabulous accent. "Good to meet you."

"Nice to meet you, too."

He killed the ignition, stepped out, and pulled a stack of white boxes toward him.

"I would have called to let you know I was running late," she told him. "But one of my students set up your donation and this drop-off time. I didn't have your number."

"Not a problem."

"May I help carry those inside?"

"Sure. It's going to take two trips." He gave her two of the white boxes and hefted five more. Together they climbed the short, steep walkway leading to her front door.

Her tiny mid-century modern house looked like a rectangular Lego. Embedded into a hillside, it had a flat roof and an equally flat front composed mostly of glass to take advantage of the valley views.

"Thank you for donating these to our fundraiser," she said. "That was very generous of you."

"Happy to help."

486

"I love your restaurant. I'm the one who suggested the kids contact you to ask if you'd be willing to make your paleo lemon cheesecakes for us. They're incredible."

"I hope you reach your fundraising goal."

"So do I. If we don't, it won't be because we didn't serve an excellent dessert."

Across town, Genevieve arrived at Natasha's neighborhood playground toting a cup of coffee in one hand and tea in the other. As she made her way through dissipating swaths of fog, her sister and the play equipment came into view, floating like islands in the white.

"I've got the worst indigestion," Natasha declared.

"Luckily, your dispenser of tea and mercy has arrived." Genevieve passed Natasha's cup to her.

"God bless you very much."

"Millie and Owen!" Genevieve called, waving. "Hi, sweethearts."

"Hi, Aunt Gen!" Millie waved back from her position on top of the play structure. Owen smiled at her from the bottom of the slide.

"I'm impressed that the fog and the cold didn't keep you guys inside," Genevieve said.

"It's not physically, mentally, or emotionally possible for me to keep my kids cooped up inside our house all morning. I'd brave a typhoon before I'd stay indoors with them."

"I see."

"That woman across from us?" Natasha indicated the figure standing on the other side of the park next to a small boy. "She knows. She and I are here because . . . necessities."

Genevieve admired Millie and Owen's pink cheeks and glowing, healthy skin. Natasha had bundled them in jackets and ill-made knitwear.

Sipping her latte, Genevieve reflected on just how far she and Natasha had come since the rubble of El Salvador. The earthquake that had snatched the lives of so many had inflicted inner wounds on them but very few outer scars.

Here they stood, in their thirties now, watching her sister's children shriek and climb and run.

Anyone who saw the three generations of the Woodwards would probably view them as a shining example of a close-knit, richly blessed family. Practically perfect. What exactly, in addition to Genevieve's reliance on OxyContin, did that "practically perfect" veneer hide?

"You said in your text that you have a new theory about Dad," Natasha said.

"It isn't a very nice theory. Not to mention it might be totally wrong."

"No need to make further opening statements. Just dive right in and tell me your not-very-nice theory."

Genevieve relayed Nanny's comment about their dad's tidiness. Then she explained how that comment had jogged her memory regarding the photos in the album, and how one specific photo had precisely forecast the positioning of Russell's dead body.

When Genevieve finished, Natasha somberly looked down the line of her shoulder at her. Wind blew a piece of Natasha's light hair across her cheekbone.

Heavyhearted, Genevieve pulled up the picture she'd taken yesterday of the photo of their dad's action figures. She passed the phone to Natasha and gave her time to study it while she watched over the kids.

"This gives me a bad feeling," Natasha said at length, handing back the phone.

"We know Dad was in town the weekend Russell died. Do you think he could've been inside Mom and Russell's house?"

"I suppose it's possible. But why?"

Millie ran up to them, Owen toddling

after her. Her niece's knit cap was so loose it was now dangling from her ponytail. Owen's scarf had ridden up almost to his forehead. They were in need of a drink and snack, so Natasha extracted both from her enormous mommy tote bag. In under three minutes, the kids ran off again, Owen protecting several multicolored Goldfish inside his chubby fist.

"We know that Mom and Russell's sister discovered Russell's body when they came home from an evening Bible study," Genevieve said. "What if Dad was with them when they walked in? They find Russell, and Dad steps in and turns the body over, straightening it."

"He must have known touching the body would disrupt the evidence."

"He would have been rattled though, right? Not thinking clearly?"

Natasha made a doubtful sound.

The kids' voices carried on the air as Millie situated Owen on the slide in front of her. They slid down together.

"Also," Natasha said, "what would Dad have been doing at a Bible study?"

"Maybe Mom and her sister-in-law stopped somewhere after Bible study, ran into Dad, and Mom invited him to come by the house."

"If that were the case, why didn't Mom and her sister-in-law tell that to the police and the reporters?"

Genevieve rubbed her thumb against the sharp edge of her coffee cup's lid. "I don't know." She let the possibilities descend through her like sand through water.

"I think we need to sit down with Mom and Dad, tell them everything we know, and force them to have an honest conversation."

Genevieve's soul shriveled at the prospect. "When?"

"I'd say tomorrow, but we're going to the kids' preschool autumn festival tomorrow."

"And I'm working at the farm's Fall Fun Day."

"Let's do it Sunday after church."

Both Genevieve's and Natasha's phones chimed at the same time, signaling incoming text messages.

They checked their phones.

Ben had sent them a group text. *Sebastian was in a car accident this morning. He has a nasty concussion, and the doctors want to hold him overnight for observation and additional scans. They think he's going to be fine.*

"Oh man," Genevieve whispered. Her body had leapt into alarm mode when she'd read the first words of Ben's message. Her

491

fingers flew over the screen's keyboard. Natasha, too, tapped her phone.

Is he in Atlanta? Natasha texted.

Thank God he's okay, Genevieve responded.

In seconds, Ben's response came through. *He flew to Misty River this morning. He's at General.*

Is the concussion his only injury? Natasha asked.

Yes. I'm thankful that his injuries aren't worse. His car's totaled.

"I'll drive over to General," Genevieve said, "and check on him."

Late the next afternoon, Sam's sixth sense picked up a change in the atmosphere of his barn.

Gen was here.

He straightened from checking the oil on his tractor and turned toward the open barn doors.

Gen's long earrings swung as she walked closer. Her eyes gleamed with affection.

He closed the distance between them, his big hands tunneling into her hair as he kissed her. Their chemistry flashed. His body shielded hers as he communicated the thing he'd never spoken to her in words — the depth of his devotion.

When she pulled back, she slid one palm down to cover his heart. He could feel it drumming beneath her touch.

They'd just completed the last of their Fall Fun Days. During today's event, they'd had very little time to talk and no time alone.

"I stopped by to let you know I'm taking off," she said. "They released Sebastian from the hospital today, so Ben and I are taking dinner to his house."

"I hope he's feeling better."

"He'll be fine." She studied him for a long moment. "You look concerned."

That's because he was concerned. It was idiotic to put so much stock in her.

"You're concerned about us," she correctly guessed. "What we have is a very good thing, Sam."

"I know."

"What is it about us that's worrying you?"

His jaw hardened.

"You've always wanted me to be open with you, right?"

"Yeah."

"I've been trying. Can you try to be open with me?"

It was only fair. He'd demanded honesty from her, but he hadn't been honest about his feelings for her in return. It was . . .

brutally difficult for him to put himself out there.

"What is it about us that's worrying you?" she repeated.

"I'm worried that this has become too important to lose."

"Ah. Well." A few seconds slid by. "I agree. This *has* become too important to lose."

He considered her for a long moment, then drew her to him in a hug, closing her against his frame.

"You said you thought she might have been an angel," Ben said an hour later. "Maybe she was."

He was referring to the mystery woman who'd stayed with Sebastian after his accident. "No," Sebastian answered. "I said she looked like an angel. She was real."

Sebastian sat in a chair, his head throbbing, watching Ben and Genevieve move around his kitchen island, preparing dinner. It was probably time for more meds.

He'd spent yesterday and most of today at the hospital, lying in bed, thinking of the mystery woman. Having his head scanned, he'd thought of her. Trying to fall asleep, he'd thought of her. Talking to his nurses, he'd thought of her. Never had he had such a strong reaction to someone he'd

494

just met.

" 'Ba-aa-aa-by, you're my angel,' " Ben sang, quoting the lyrics from the Aerosmith song.

"Usually," Genevieve said, "real, non-angel men ask the real, non-angel women they're interested in what their name is."

"Thanks for that enlightening piece of information. If I hadn't just crashed my car, I'm confident that it would have occurred to me to ask her name. Would you mind turning off this light?" The fixture over the table was shooting pain into his skull.

Ben immediately flipped the switch. After turning on the lights mounted on the under-side of the cabinets, he switched off the kitchen's recessed lighting, too. "That better?"

"Much."

"How long do your doctors think it will be before your concussion resolves?" Genevieve asked.

"Who cares what they think? I think it should resolve in seven to ten days. These country doctors wouldn't know a concussion from a diffuse axonal injury."

Her lips twitched as if she were trying not to laugh. "Is it humbling to find yourself at the mercy of lesser mortals, Sebastian?"

"Why do you seem to be enjoying this?"

"I have faith that the country doctors have seen a concussion before and know exactly what to do. Wow, this mood lighting is very moody. Do you have candles somewhere? We can eat by candlelight."

"I'm male," Sebastian said. "I don't have candles."

Ben laughed.

Genevieve rolled her eyes, opened the oven, and lifted out a loaf of French bread. "Did you see the mystery woman's car at least?"

"No."

"It's kind of romantic, actually," Genevieve said. "Handsome doctor meets woman under dramatic circumstances. Becomes enamored. But is parted from her before he can learn her identity."

"Then prowls around his house in a bad mood." Ben grinned as he tossed the salad.

Genevieve cut the lasagna into squares. "Do you feel about the mystery woman the way that Ben feels about Leah?"

"Yes," Sebastian answered in the exact same moment that Ben answered, "No."

Ben gave him a look that said he couldn't believe his ears. "I've known Leah for more than a year. You spent ten minutes with that woman. You can't feel about her the way that I feel about Leah."

"Yes I can."

"Whatever, dude," Ben said good-naturedly.

Sebastian went after the things he wanted. In part, because of his own powerful inner drive. In part, because he knew he could die at any time. He'd learned that truth after Luke's brother, Ethan, who'd been with their group one moment and crushed the next moment, had died in the earthquake. The crash yesterday only confirmed Sebastian's mortality.

It might be that his head trauma was to blame for his inability to focus on anything but the woman who'd been beside him in his car when he regained consciousness. Perhaps he'd see her the next time and find her ordinary.

Even so, there *would* be a next time, because he needed the chance to find out.

Genevieve

We've been stuck down here for four days now.

I'm sure that my parents are doing everything they can to find us. But no one's come. Still. I never imagined we'd be trapped, alone, for this long.

What if they can't get to us?

Ben and Natasha and I are doing our best to keep everyone's spirits up. We talk and tell stories and play games and laugh sometimes, even though we all know it's not real laughter.

We look bad and we smell bad and we're weak because we haven't had anything to eat. We sleep to pass the time. I dream of my mom's buttermilk chess pie, her lullabies, her perfume. I dream of my dad's hugs, his voice reading out loud to me, the way he dances when he wants to make us laugh.

If it's the middle of the night when I wake from those dreams and the darkness hides me, I cry. If it's light, I don't cry. I pretend to be strong and I pretend to have hope, even though I feel small and forgotten here. Like a prisoner in a dungeon.

I'm scared that my parents won't be able to find us. But I know for sure that God already has.

I pray and pray and pray.

The God I know rescues prisoners from dungeons.

CHAPTER TWENTY-ONE

Genevieve found it excruciating to act normally with her mom and dad while sitting on an enormous secret she and her sister were just minutes from debuting. It felt akin to having a tea party on top of a land mine.

When she and Natasha had arrived at the house on Swallowtail Lane a few minutes ago, they'd discovered that Mom — who'd never met a simple occasion she couldn't turn into something fancy — had made a buttermilk chess pie in honor of their visit.

Dad had greeted them, then became absorbed with something on his phone that no doubt pertained to Mercer football. Genevieve was stacking the few dishes that had been in the sink into the dishwasher. Natasha was pouring them all cups of coffee, and Mom was placing wedges of pie onto china plates while gushing about the creativity award Millie had received at yesterday's preschool autumn festival.

"I was telling your father just last week that Millie has exceptional artistic skill. I don't have any doubt that she's going to grow up to be every bit as impressive as you two. I just hope I live long enough to congratulate her at her first New York City gallery showing."

"We might want to recalibrate our expectations of Millie," Natasha noted. "Right now my highest goal for her is that she allow me to brush her hair without throwing a screaming fit and learn to like at least one vegetable."

Mom waxed philosophic about the benefits of high expectations on a child's formation.

"Huh" was the best Genevieve could muster.

She'd been adept at pretending even before she'd had to cover up her Oxy use. For ages, she'd been working to come across as the most loving, the most humble, the most bulletproof, the most down-to-earth version of herself. It seemed, though, that she was reaching the end of her ability to pretend.

Without Oxy to take the edge off, she was feeling physically sick with nerves. If she tried to eat pie, she'd throw up. If she

501

declined it, Mom would take it personally.

When Genevieve had started to investigate her parents' past, she'd been fueled by unease and curiosity. She'd had no way of knowing then just how convoluted and upsetting the past would prove to be.

In fact, no person could ever discern where a particular path might lead until they walked it.

She hadn't known when she'd agreed to the mission trip in El Salvador that she'd end up stuck in a cave of destruction. She hadn't known when she'd started dating Thad that he would obliterate her heart. She hadn't known when she started taking Oxy that it would lead to a crippling dependence.

The only One who could know where a path might lead was God Himself. She'd prayed before she'd started investigating her parents. Yet she hadn't had a dependable line of communication with God in what felt like a really long time. Consequently, she hadn't heard a firm yes or a firm no. Which hadn't stopped her from wading into her parents' past. Perhaps doing so, like taking Oxy, had been a big mistake.

"It's ready, everyone," Mom announced.

They took their places around the circular kitchen table where they'd eaten countless meals back when she and Natasha lived at home.

Natasha had once refused to eat a bowl of oatmeal at this table. Dad had calmly said that it was nourishing and that it cost money, and if she wouldn't eat it, she'd have to sit there for an hour thinking about how important it was to be grateful.

Natasha had sat there for an hour.

She and her sister had consumed the pink waffles their mom made for them on Valentine's Day at this table. They'd embellished them with whipped cream, powdered sugar, and rainbow sprinkles.

On Sundays they'd eaten club sandwiches for lunch at this table. On those occasions, just like today, all four of them had still been dressed in their church clothes. Club sandwiches were Dad's specialty, and he'd layer mayonnaise, lettuce, bacon, bread, tomato, turkey, and mustard — always in that order — between two outer slices of toasted bread that he cut into precise triangles.

So many nights they'd gathered around this table for dinner. Light had poured in through the windows to illuminate their summertime dinners. A tapestry of changing leaves had watched over their fall dinners. Darkness had turned the windows to flat black geometric shapes during their winter dinners. Green buds and colorful flowers had blanketed the yard during their spring dinners.

Her mother and father were interwoven into her lifetime of memories.

How were they going to take this?

She and Natasha had been rule-following girls. They'd never done anything to make their parents as angry as these revelations had the potential to make them.

"This is just like old times," Mom said. "The original four." She wore a gauzy pearl gray dress. Dad's subtly patterned tie remained snugly fastened around the neck of his starched white dress shirt.

"I've been hoping and hoping for the chance to get together," Mom continued. "The four of us like this. But you girls are always so busy, and I didn't want to intrude."

Natasha curled her hand around the base of her coffee cup as if it were an anchor. "Genevieve and I wanted to talk to you without the rest of the family present." She had the good grace to look tense.

"Are you expecting a third baby?" Mom asked Natasha excitedly.

"No."

"Are you engaged?" Dad asked Genevieve.

Mom let out a scandalized gasp. "No! Sam seems like a wonderful, God-fearing man, but it's too early for an engagement. My goodness." She fanned herself. "Genevieve and I haven't even had a chance to have a long discussion about Sam yet."

"The whole town's talking about your romance," Dad told Genevieve.

"Sam and I are definitely not engaged."

"In fact, we're not here to offer happy news," Natasha said. "It's probably for the best that you're both sitting down."

Instantly, seriousness descended.

Lord, cover us with grace. Painfully, Genevieve cleared her throat. "We're here to talk about the anonymous letters I've received."

Mom sat back in her chair, her chin tucking against her neck in a way that indicated that they'd hurt her feelings. "We told you that was nothing, sweetie. A hoax —"

"We know about your first marriage," Natasha said bluntly.

Silence unwound through the kitchen like a ball of yarn. Mom's face drained of color.

Dad's eyebrows lowered behind the lenses of his glasses.

Genevieve held her tongue, giving them time to process.

"How did you learn about the marriage?" Dad finally asked.

"If either of you had any secrets," Genevieve answered, "we guessed that they originated before you moved to Misty River. Mom grew up in Athens and since it's relatively close, I drove to the courthouse there and pulled her records."

"Without talking to me?" Mom asked.

"After you claimed to know nothing about the first letter," Natasha said, "Gen and I decided to learn everything we could before broaching this subject with you again. Here we are, broaching this subject with you again."

"But . . ." The lines around Mom's mouth deepened. "Genevieve came home almost three months ago. How long have you been researching us?"

"That whole time." Natasha's features broadcast honesty and compassion. "We know a lot. For example, we know that you two dated in college, because we saw a photo from a fraternity function in the Mercer University yearbook."

Dad and Mom exchanged a long look Genevieve couldn't interpret.

"After Dad graduated, he went into the navy and you finished school." Genevieve picked up the tale. "In 1982, you married Russell Atwell, and about a year later, he was murdered by a serial killer."

In response to their daughters' blindside, her parents' posture had gone rigid. Beneath that, Genevieve sensed a sharp sort of alertness in them, as if they were scrambling mentally to concoct defensive strategies.

"We studied issues of the *Camden Chronicle* that ran the week of Russell's death and saw a navy recruiting ad that listed you by name," Natasha told Dad. "So we know that you were in town the weekend Russell died. And we suspect you were inside the house the night of the murder."

"Why?" Dad asked quietly.

"Because Russell's body was arranged exactly the way you used to arrange your action figures when you cleaned your room," Natasha said. "Which made that crime scene different from the Shoal Creek Killer's other crime scenes."

Neither parent spoke. In the unnatural silence, Genevieve listened to her own apprehensive breathing.

"What is it you think happened?" Dad asked. He was far too smart to reveal his hand before they revealed theirs.

"We think you planned a stop in Camden to visit Mom or Russell or both," Natasha replied. "After finding Russell dead, you turned him over and straightened his arms and legs."

Pain seared his expression. "How come you don't suspect me of killing him?"

"Because we know you," Natasha said firmly.

"And love you," Genevieve added.

He pulled off his glasses and set them aside, then planted his elbows on the table and clasped his head in his hands.

Mom wrapped a protective hand around his shoulder.

"Tell us what happened," Natasha pleaded, her attention on their dad. "Please. We need to know so we can do whatever's needed to help."

Wounded anger flowed from their mother in waves, making Genevieve feel like Judas for pursuing this investigation behind their backs. She straightened the already-straight hem of the cropped jacket she wore with her wide-skirted dress —

Dad stood, his chair scraping against the wooden floor. Agitated, he paced the length of the kitchen. He stood in the opening that led to the formal living and dining space, his back to them. One excruciating minute passed.

Mom twisted in her chair to focus on her husband. "Judson." The syllables carried entreaty and warning.

He returned. Still standing, he faced

Mom. "I can't have them think I'm innocent in this."

Genevieve's stomach twisted.

"Judson," Mom said.

He addressed his daughters. "I can't have you thinking that."

"Then tell us what happened," Natasha said.

He always looked vulnerable and a little unfamiliar to Genevieve without his glasses. Her dad might be vulnerable in this moment, but he wasn't unfamiliar. He was her daddy. Her first, best-trusted love.

He paced along the kitchen again.

"Girls," Mom said accusingly. "This is all *so* upsetting. This is all such ancient history."

"Ancient history that has come back to haunt you," Natasha returned calmly. "We need to face it now."

"I think it best that we stop this discussion right here," Mom said. "Let's leave the past in the past."

"I can't," Dad said. This time, when he approached, Genevieve read resignation in him. He put his glasses back on and looked to his wife. "I can't anymore, Caroline."

Mom reached for his hand. "Honey. I think —"

He squeezed Mom's hand lovingly, and

her words halted. "I was inside the house that night," Dad said to her and Natasha. "You're right about that."

Mom bit her bottom lip.

"I've loved your mother since the first time I went on a date with her, when I was twenty-two years old. She broke up with me seven months later, two months after I entered the navy. She was nineteen then, and I understood why she did it. But my feelings for her never changed. Not at all. When I came back stateside to recruit, I scheduled a trip to Camden so that I could see her. That's all I wanted, just to see her and talk with her. To know that she was happy."

Genevieve braced herself.

"Your mom met me at a diner in Camden, and I bought her a milkshake. She put on a good front. But back when we were dating, I'd gotten to know her well, and I could tell something was wrong. I asked her about Russell."

"I didn't say a single negative thing about him," Mom said to him.

"That's true." It seemed that the memory of that long-ago conversation at the diner was arcing back and forth between them. "But there was pain in your eyes." He regarded his daughters. "I couldn't get her to confide in me. We said good-bye, and we went our separate ways."

"Someone told Russell that they'd seen me speaking with another man at the diner," Mom said stiffly. "Russell could be funny, sweet, decent. Unfortunately, he could also become very angry. When he got angry, he was . . . abusive."

"I'm so sorry," Genevieve whispered, feeling like the wind had been kicked out of her. Russell had beaten Mom? "We . . . saw Russell's record. We know he was arrested several times for assault."

"We never imagined that he'd assault you, though," Natasha said. "That's awful."

She'd only ever seen her mom and dad fight fair, without raised voices or hurtful words. Certainly without violence. In her current marriage, Mom was cherished. It sickened Genevieve to think that Russell had raised his hands against her.

"After I left your mother at the diner," Dad told them, "I was so worried that I drove to the house she shared with Russell. Caroline's car was out front. I parked a good distance away and waited for a few hours until Russell pulled into the driveway. I watched him storm inside."

"Russell was furious," Mom said.

The house was clean and orderly. The air

smelled pleasantly of apples and cloves. Yet, the story her parents were painting was infiltrating what should have been a cozy environment with tentacles of menacing cold.

"A few minutes after Russell returned home," Dad said, "I drove by their house. I couldn't see anything, so I got out of the car and doubled back on foot. When I got close, I saw them both clearly through the front bedroom window. Russell slapped your mother, then threw her down on the bed and began to rip off her clothing."

Mom remained motionless.

Dad looked bleaker than Genevieve had ever seen him look. "I'd never been that mad in my life. The front door wasn't locked, so I ran inside."

"Russell heard the door bang against the wall," Mom said. "He left me to see who'd entered."

"He yelled at me and threatened me." Dad ran his fingers through his graying hair. "I punched him in the face. He punched me back. He was strong, and his hatred was so deep that it made him stronger. He was a better fighter than I was. But I'd just seen how he'd treated your mother, so I was even angrier than he was."

Genevieve was scared to hear more. She

wanted her father to continue to be the man she knew.

"I followed Russell into the living room," Mom said. "I begged them to stop, but neither seemed to hear me."

"Your mother later told me she'd been sweeping when Russell entered the house. As soon as I was able to push Russell away from me, he grabbed the broom that was leaning against the fireplace and rammed the tip of the handle into my face. It sank into my left eye. As he pulled the broom back, I caught it in my hands and twisted it away from him. Then I swung it as hard as I could. It caught him in the temple."

"He didn't go down." Lines furrowed Mom's forehead. "He paused, then he came at your father again."

"So I hit him in the head again, equally hard, in the same place. That time, it knocked him out cold."

"We thought at first that he was only unconscious."

"But he never came to. Within a short period of time, he was dead."

Mom rose and went to the windows, where she peered at her backyard garden. "Your father acted in self-defense."

"The first time I hit him, I did so in self-defense because I believed he would have killed me if he'd had the chance. But after that first strike, I knew I'd hurt him. I should have dropped the broom and tried to wrestle him to the ground."

"It was self-defense, Judson." Mom spoke to the glass. Her words did not invite argument.

My father killed Russell Atwell. Genevieve's numb brain couldn't accept it. *Russell was the one who ruined Dad's left eye.*

"Why didn't you call the police?" Natasha asked.

"It took a while before we were calm enough to think straight," Mom said. "I was beside myself. Russell was dead, and your father's eye was seriously injured. He didn't complain about it, but I knew it was hurting him terribly. I taped a washcloth over his eye. I didn't know what else to do. Obviously, he needed to go to the hospital, but he wouldn't hear of leaving until we'd decided what to do about Russell."

"We worried how it would look. Essentially, I'd entered my ex-girlfriend's home, then killed her husband."

"But Mom saw everything," Natasha said. "She was a corroborating witness."

"Yes. I've wished every day since that we *had* called the police and taken our chances with the judicial system. If my actions resulted in jail time, then I should have stood up to my sentence and done the time."

"Camden is a close-knit town." Mom rotated to them, arms crossed. The joints in her hands were pointed and white. "Russell was one of their favorites. The people of that town doted on him, but very few of them knew me. I didn't think they'd accept my word if I tried to tell them what had happened between Russell and your father. They'd have believed that I was in on it, too. That together, Judson and I wanted Russell dead." She ratcheted her hands even tighter. "I wanted peace, and I wanted to be free of Russell. But I didn't want him dead."

"In those days, the Shoal Creek Killer was receiving constant attention in the media," Dad said. "It was all anyone could talk about."

"So we tried to make the scene look like it would have looked if the Shoal Creek Killer had committed the murder."

"Russell fell onto his chest with his face to the side. I turned his face down because I didn't want your mother to have to look at it. I straightened his limbs because that position was more dignified than leaving him how he'd fallen. At the time, I didn't know that the other bodies had been left in

515

a heap. The police hadn't released details about the positioning of the victims' bodies."

Genevieve's mind reeled sluggishly. "But Terry Paul Richards later confessed to killing Russell."

"Yes." Dad nodded. "At that point, he'd been convicted of three of the murders and was facing execution. Nothing could have made his situation worse than it was. I think he took responsibility for Russell's death in order to increase his own fame."

"Who else knows about this?" Natasha asked. "Someone does, because someone sent Gen those letters."

Dad frowned. "Russell's sister, Sandra, knows. She walked in when we were almost finished staging the scene. She saw everything."

"Sandra and I had plans to go to Bible study together," Mom told them. "She'd come to pick me up and was running ahead of schedule."

"Your mother told Sandra what had happened. One side of your mom's shirt was ripped, and her face was pink from where Russell had slapped her. Even so, I thought Sandra would immediately turn us in. Instead, she helped us make it look like the Shoal Creek Killer had committed the murder."

"Why?" Genevieve asked.

"Because she knew how he was," Mom answered. "Russell had beaten her, too, when she was a kid."

"Sandra told your mother to clean herself up and leave with her for Bible study. So we put Caroline's ripped clothing and the broom and anything else that we thought might incriminate me in a black garbage bag. Sandra took your mother to Bible study, and I drove the garbage bag to a public dumpster a half hour away. Then I drove half an hour in another direction and ran my car into a tree near a field where some kids were playing. I went to them for help, and one of their mothers drove me to a rural hospital. I claimed that the accident had caused the eye injury."

"No one questioned your claim?" Genevieve asked.

"No. They were focused on trying to save my eye. But they were unsuccessful."

"What happened next with you, Mom?" Natasha asked.

"Sandra took me home after the study. She dialed the police, then handed me the phone."

"Were the two of you in contact immediately after that?" Natasha motioned between them.

"Not for the month that I remained in Camden." Weariness had begun to drain some of the rigidity from Mom's posture. "That month was a nightmare. The funeral. The media attention. I was grieving for a man I'd loved very much at one time. I was terrified that your father and I would be arrested. It wasn't until after I moved back to my parents' house that I called your father."

"We agreed that we'd relocate to Savannah," Dad said.

"You wanted to be close to each other," Genevieve guessed.

"Yes," Dad answered. "We wanted a chance to get to know each other again in a place that could offer us a fresh start. Savannah was far from where either of us had lived."

"Your family members never mentioned your first marriage to us," Natasha said to Mom.

"Before I married your dad, I asked them not to speak to me or to anyone else about Russell again. Before you girls were born, I made it especially clear that I didn't want anyone telling you about my first marriage or the murder. My relatives didn't want to saddle you girls with that ugliness, either."

Genevieve pushed her hair behind her

ears. "So Sandra's the one who sent me the letters."

Dad inclined his chin.

"She was your accomplice at the time," Genevieve said, "but the letters were threatening. Why the change of heart?"

"With Russell for a brother, her life had never been easy," Mom said. "But it became even more challenging in some ways after Russell's death. Her father drank himself into a grave. She, her mother, and her sister struggled financially. She's had three husbands. As time passed, I think she became bitter."

"Two weeks before she sent you the first letter, she asked us for one hundred thousand dollars to buy her silence," Dad said. "We told her no. The letter she sent you was her way of applying pressure to force us to change our minds."

"And?" Natasha asked. "Have you changed your minds?"

"We haven't paid her anything yet," Mom said. "But we haven't ruled out the possibility of paying her, either. We met with our financial planner to see if there's a way to come up with that sum."

"If we pay her now," Dad said, "I'm convinced that she'll ask for more in the future."

"You can't pay her." Natasha's jaw hardened. "She's blackmailing you, and blackmail is illegal."

"She wouldn't be able to blackmail us if we hadn't done illegal things, too." Mom's words were brittle. Irrefutable. "We have two terrible options. Pay her. Refuse to pay her. We can't afford to do either."

Genevieve's brain searched for avenues of escape. Mom and Dad couldn't pay this woman again and again in an effort to guarantee her silence. But the alternative — not paying her and then having Sandra go to the nearest news station with her story — was even worse.

Natasha and Dad were the two attorneys in the room, but even Genevieve knew that there was no statute of limitations on murder.

If Dad was charged with murder, the only eyewitness would be biased Mom. Sandra hadn't actually seen Dad's altercation with Russell.

If Sandra's heart really had hardened over the years, would she testify to Russell's abuse when she was a child? Would she testify that she knew her brother had been abusing his wife? Or might she throw Mom and Dad under the bus?

The Shoal Creek Killer had been featured

in a recent Netflix series, true crime books, and conspiracy theory blog posts. If word got out that her parents had pinned Russell's death on Terry Paul Richards, the story would likely become national or world news.

Her . . . her ministry had earned quite a huge sum of money. She'd only felt comfortable living off a small percentage. She'd given much of it away. The rest she'd invested, because she'd never had any sense of how long her ministry might last.

Her parents couldn't afford to pay Sandra off time and time again.

But she could.

"I'll pay Sandra."

"No," Natasha and Dad said in unison.

"I was finally able to get my hands on an address for Russell's mother a few days ago," Natasha announced. "Gen didn't want to reach out to her. But that was before Gen and I knew all of this." She met each of their gazes in turn, as if seeking to gain consensus. "Now I think we have to meet with Russell's remaining family members and tell them everything."

"I disagree." Mom spoke at once. "Think of the ramifications of what you're suggesting."

"What I'm suggesting is that we *do the*

right thing." Natasha held her head high, unwavering. "Dad already said he wishes he'd admitted everything all those years ago instead of covering things up. We have a chance to rectify that. It's not too late."

"We had a great deal to lose then." Mom's volume was rising, her syllables trembling. "We have far more to lose now."

"Natasha's right." The implacable assurance in Dad's statement cut through the room, through Genevieve, like a scalpel.

"Judson," Mom whispered. Moisture gathered in her eyes.

"Natasha's right." He gazed at his older daughter.

Natasha and Dad. The two of them had always been the most alike. Even-tempered, more practical, less emotional. Both had a powerful sense of right and wrong.

Mom took several steps away. "No."

Dad regarded his wife with apology for the grief he was destined to cause her. "It's time, Caroline. I've been carrying the guilt of this for thirty-seven years. I need to do this."

"Are you hearing me say *no,* Judson?" A tear flowed down her cheek.

"I'm ready to go and talk with Sandra and her mother and her sister," he said gently. "It's going to be all right."

"How can anything ever be all right again after you tell them?"

"Caro—"

She swept from the kitchen. The door to the master bedroom slammed.

Genevieve realized she'd been holding her breath and released it with a sigh.

"I'll talk to her," Dad said. "She needs time, but she'll come around. She's scared to admit it, but she knows this is the right path."

"Do you want me to call Russell's mother, Alice?" Natasha asked. "I can simply introduce myself as Caroline's daughter and ask if my family can come by and speak with her and her daughters."

"Give me the rest of the day to talk with your mother. I'll call you in the morning and hopefully give you the go-ahead then."

"Okay."

"I'd rather meet with them soon," he said. "The longer we drag this out, the worse it will be."

"I agree," Natasha said. "When Mom has time to worry over something, it grows bigger and worse in her imagination."

"I'm tired of living with this secret." Indeed, he looked tired.

They stood, and Natasha gave Dad a hug.

"I love you, cupcake," he murmured to

her sister.

Then he engulfed Genevieve in his secure embrace. "I love you, honey girl."

She wanted to weep because he smelled like Irish Spring soap, same as ever. He'd done a terrible thing, but he'd been a wonderful father. "I love you, too."

"I'm sorry," he said to them both when they'd stepped apart. "For what I did. I wish I could shield you from this."

"It's okay, Dad," Natasha answered.

Genevieve nodded, because her mouth was shaking.

He disappeared toward the master bedroom.

Genevieve took Natasha's hand and squeezed, then the sisters let themselves out. Without a word, they set off for their houses in their respective cars.

The road rose and fell beneath the tires of her Volvo.

Natasha and Dad had come to the decision to confess. Mom had been against it. Genevieve hadn't provided her opinion, nor had anyone asked for it.

Her opinion was torn down the middle between her mom's stance and her dad's. She understood her mother's reaction because no part of her wanted the truth of Russell's death to come to light. She'd prefer to continue on with her life as if everything were fine and normal. As if she didn't know how Russell had died.

However, she could acknowledge that Dad's approach was the ethical approach.

There'd been a time when her right vs. wrong meter had been almost as strong as her sister's. Then her ministry had grown. The stakes of her actions had increased. Layers of silt covered her meter as it became more and more important to maintain the image of the funny, wry, girl-next-door Bible teacher with a flair for clothing and interior design and Instagram photos.

Her old, neglected meter was telling her that Natasha and Dad were correct. Confessing to Russell's family was the right thing to do.

It was also the thing that would bring destruction down on herself, her sister, her mother, and her father.

Luke

The sisters and Ben keep praying out loud. Every time they do, my chest burns with anger. My parents have taken my brother and me to church all our lives. They sent us on this trip because they wanted us to follow the Bible and help others. They trusted God. They believed that we'd be safe.

God reacted by sending an earthquake because He obviously doesn't care anything about us.

We've been down here for six days now. Either Ethan turned and escaped the building when it started to shake, the concrete crushed him, or he found a space like our space. We've survived in this room because we have water. Even if he was able to find space, he won't have water.

The only way he could be alive is if he turned and escaped.

A small part of me won't give up the hope that he turned and escaped. But in my bones, I know that he didn't.

I know that he's dead.

I keep trying to blame God for Ethan's death, but I can't.

Because if Ethan's dead, I know that I'm the one who killed him.

CHAPTER TWENTY-TWO

How did it go with your parents? Sam texted Gen that afternoon. She'd told him that she and Natasha were planning to confront their parents today, and he'd seen her car at the guesthouse when he'd arrived home a few minutes ago.

Scrolling dots appeared, letting him know that she was typing.

Then the scrolling dots vanished without a reply.

His mood darkening, he went to the orchard to continue pruning the apple trees of diseased and overcrowded growth. Why was Gen avoiding his question?

Finally, a *bing* sounded to signal a new text. Ripping off one of his gloves, he reached for his phone.

It's not good, Sam, what happened all those years ago.

His heart sank. *I'll be right there.* He took off his other glove and set his boot on the

528

rung below, then stopped as another text arrived.

I think it's best if you wait. I'm trying to adjust to what I learned, and I feel like I need a little time alone.

She didn't want to see him? Tension snaked across his shoulders.

You told me once, she wrote, *that if I wasn't ready to tell you something, I should simply say that to you outright. Is that offer still open?*

Yes.

Thank you, she texted. *And I'm sorry to be so cryptic. I'm really sorry. See you tomorrow evening?*

Sure.

He waited for another response from her. None came.

After pocketing the phone, he interlaced his hands behind his head and tilted his face to the branches and the backdrop of sky.

Since coming to Misty River, he'd given everyone space and expected everyone to give him space in return. That's how he'd wanted things, so that's how things had been.

However, it was no longer in his nature to give Gen space. Clearly, she'd learned something terrible today. He wanted her to tell him about it. Not just for his sake, but for hers. If she was anxious or depressed, keeping quiet and shutting herself off from everyone was the worst thing she could do.

She'd gone eighty-six days without Oxy. *Eighty-six days.*

However, he knew from experience that no matter how much time had passed, when an addict was miserable, they were also susceptible. If she was in enough pain, she might sabotage herself by taking Oxy.

His blood chilled at the thought.

He could wait until she drove away, search her house, and make sure she didn't have Oxy —

No. If he wanted her trust, which he did, he'd have to earn it. He'd never earn it by standing in judgment of her, only by coming alongside in support.

To gain her trust, he first needed to give his trust.

She'd told him the last time he'd let himself into her guesthouse, back before they started dating, that it had hurt her to know he'd searched her things. It would hurt her much worse now, so he refused to do it.

At ten o'clock that night, Genevieve sat cross-legged on the small patch of floor at the end of her bed, her back propped against the wall. Her candle flickered, and a mug of tea waited within arm's reach. Her laptop sat on the floor before her, playing one of her fluffy romantic comedies.

Unfortunately, all her bids at comforting herself were falling short.

She felt both covered in a blanket of desolation and stripped naked. Her mind couldn't focus on the movie, because it was too busy gnawing on fears over her family's future.

When it became known that her parents had framed the Shoal Creek Killer for Russell's murder, the court of public opinion would be brutal. The fact that Mom and Dad had gone on to marry, have two daughters, and raise them as if Russell Atwell had been nothing more than a bump in the road would lead people to conclude that they were heartless and guilty.

She could picture herself on camera saying, *"I know them! That's how I know they're telling the truth about what happened. Neither of them could have planned to murder Russell."* Strangers from coast to coast would think her impossibly naïve.

Even if, by some miracle, Dad was charged, tried, and acquitted because he'd acted in self-defense, his reputation and career could never, ever be salvaged. He was the county DA, for heaven's sake. An elected official.

The scandal would ruin her mother just as thoroughly. Mom was deeply proud of the family she'd raised. She basked in the respect of her peers, her identity as a community volunteer, her daughters' success, and her flourishing grandchildren.

This time moving to a fresh city wouldn't solve her parents' problems the way it had when they'd moved to Savannah. This time they'd be known anywhere they tried to hide. The fallout would cage them as surely as rubble had once caged her and Natasha.

As soon as she'd returned to the cottage today, she'd knelt and prayed over the situation. She'd pled with God, cried, bent her head low and begged.

She hadn't sensed His mercy. She hadn't been able to grab hold of His unconditional love. Even that word, *unconditional,* had become head knowledge for her, not heart knowledge, because her mistakes and her parents' mistakes were so close and enormous.

Her failure to keep her relationship with the Lord vibrant, and her dependence on painkillers, and her secrecy concerning all of it rendered her a fake. She had absolutely no business serving the Lord as a Bible teacher.

She shut her laptop, silencing the movie. Drawing her knees toward her torso, she banded her arms around them as if to hold herself together.

She'd put Sam off by telling him that she'd see him tomorrow. The woman who'd had the courage to stand in front of thousands and preach the Gospel was now faltering at the prospect of having to speak to just one man. If she told Sam about her parents, she'd be giving him enormous power over them. He could go to the nearest police station and tell them everything.

Which he'd never do!

So then, why? Why couldn't she bring herself to tell him?

Was she really this full of stupid pride?

No. She *would* tell him. It's just that she hadn't even begun to digest the truth about Russell's death herself. Her thoughts were shooting in a million different directions.

Closing her eyes, she pushed the heels of her hands against her forehead.

God.

God, please help me. Please lift this feeling of impending catastrophe off of me. Make yourself known and real to me again like you once were.

Come in power, I beg you. Calm my mind. Help me to trust you wholly, so that I can face what's coming for my family and for me. If it's your will for disapproval to rain down on us, then you'll make a way for us to bear up under it. And, ultimately, you'll redeem the suffering you allow.

That's what I believe. That's what is true.

She poured out all of her praises and worries and pleas. Then she strained to hear His response.

Long minutes passed.

She waited and waited, ears and senses pining for Him.

"Where are you?" Her question sounded small and raspy in the empty space.

She couldn't stand to feel this way — so anxious that she wanted to claw out of her skin.

She pounded both fists into the hardwood floor. "Where are you?" she yelled.

She discerned no answer.

Her heart drummed with deep-seated panic.

God had abandoned her.

He missed Gen far more than he should.

Sam crossed the distance from his truck to the front door of the guesthouse and knocked. After receiving her texts yesterday

534

at the apple orchard, he'd hardly slept. He'd been distracted during his work on the farm today and during his basketball game with Eli and the others. After showering at the gym, he'd headed straight here.

Now that daylight savings time was done, darkness fell early in the mountains. Sunset was perhaps only half an hour away, but the storm bruising the sky would get here even sooner.

The door swung open, and Gen filled the opening. Wind lifted her hair, whipping strands of it away from her pale pink cheeks. He simply stood on the threshold, over-whelmed with tenderness, adjusting to the power of her nearness.

She slid her hands around his neck. "Hi."

"Hi."

She looked like she'd been fighting her demons with everything she had and losing.

He hated that he couldn't shield her from what she was going through. He was a fixer. Give him a goal — run a farm, open a restaurant — and he'd take every action needed to achieve that goal. But this? "Gen —"

She drew his profile to hers. Their lips met, and his longing for her answered instantly. Their kiss held an edge of desperation.

"It's good to see you," she whispered when they broke apart.

"You too."

They hadn't even made it through the front door.

She rested her ear against his chest.

"Your parents?" he asked. He didn't need to say more. They both knew what he was asking.

She kept her face where it was, saying nothing.

Turn to me, he begged her silently. How could he show her that she could depend on him if she wouldn't give him a chance?

"My family's decided to speak with Russell Atwell's mother and sisters," she finally said. "I was hoping that we could make it happen today, because I'm dreading it. But my mom didn't give her approval until a few hours ago. So Natasha set up a visit with them for tomorrow morning."

"What did you find out —"

She launched herself into his arms, and they were kissing again. He walked her backward toward her makeshift kitchen. If she wanted to distract him from asking about her parents, she'd chosen the most effective way possible. Need gathered within him, an insistent storm.

Her hip bumped against her butcher block

island and immediately after, a clanging sound reached his ears.

She gave a huff of amusement against his lips. "Are you tearing up my cottage?"

"Guesthouse," he corrected, glancing to see what had fallen. A square metal canister. Its lid had popped off, fanning tea bags onto the floor and causing a small bottle — a prescription bottle — to roll free. It turned, label side up, label side down before coming to a stop.

She continued their interrupted kiss.

A prescription bottle.

His body reacted before his mind could, turning to stone. "Your tea fell."

"Mmm?"

"Your tea."

"Oh!" In the next second, she separated from him and bent over the floor, blocking his view of the bottle with her body. She swept everything into the canister.

That prescription bottle could be for anything.

Allergies. Iron supplements. Anything.

"There we are," she said, her tone bright, as she set the canister back on the butcher block. "I've fixed the damage you're responsible for." She grinned.

The air blowing through the gaping doorway had turned colder. "What about the

537

damage you're responsible for?" he asked in a level tone.

She cocked her head, as if confused by his question.

"I saw the pills, Gen."

Her expression went too smooth, and in that instant he knew the pills weren't allergy meds or iron supplements.

His insides hollowed out. He held out a hand and noticed that it was shaking slightly. "May I see them?"

"Sam."

"Please."

She jutted out her chin, lifted the prescription bottle from the container, and handed it to him. The label read *Genevieve Woodward. 20mg OxyContin.*

"I didn't take any," she said.

He dragged his gaze to hers, anger multiplying inside him. "When did you get these?"

"Last night."

"Where?"

"Riverside Pharmacy. I'd . . . asked my doctor in Nashville to put a prescription into the system for me back in August when I was going through detox."

"Why?"

"Because I was so sick at the time. And unsure if I could make it." A line notched the skin between her brows. "I was in a bad place mentally last night, and it helped me feel better, somehow, to know that the pills were nearby. If necessary."

"It made you feel better," he said with tight control, "to know that poison was nearby if necessary?"

She set her mouth. "I didn't take any."

"Genevieve," he growled.

"Yes, Sam? Are you going to kick me out of the cottage now?" Irritation rolled off her as she drew herself tall.

"Of course not."

"That's what you said you'd do."

"That's what I said I'd do months ago. Now I couldn't stand it if you left." He *hated* these pills. His fingers curled around the bottle, and he wished he could crush it in his grip. "As long as you keep hiding your addiction to Oxy, you are never going to beat it."

"I am beating it!"

Kayden's addiction had been dangerous, and he and Kayden had both kept silent about it. At the time, he'd labeled his silence as loyalty. In truth, he'd betrayed Kayden with his silence, just as much as she'd betrayed herself with it. Hiding her struggle hadn't helped her. Hiding it had ended in her death.

"The next step is taking pills in secret," he said, his pulse throbbing. "And the next step is you wasting away."

Outraged color swept up her face. "No. *Kayden's* next step was taking pills in secret. Kayden's next step was wasting away." She planted her hands on her hips. "Are — are you comparing me to Kayden every time you're around me?"

"No."

"Are you trying to help me because you wish you could go back and help her?"

"Of course not."

"I don't want to be your do-over, Sam."

Her words slapped him. "You aren't my do-over."

"Do you still love her?" she demanded.

"I love *you,*" he said furiously, almost shouting. "You're the one I go to sleep thinking about and wake up thinking about. I've been lonely for years, and you're the one who's changed that. You're everything to me, which is why it terrifies me that you turned to painkillers last night instead of to me."

She opened her mouth to speak but words didn't come.

Hopelessness made a grab for his heart. He pushed his palm against his chest as if doing so might keep it intact. He couldn't remember the last time he'd been this upset or desperate. He needed to go. He didn't trust himself to say one more word.

As he stalked from the guesthouse, fat raindrops blew against him sideways. Then thunder crashed. Water wet his shirt, his hair, his neck.

He drove his truck to his house. As soon as he reached his kitchen, he checked the label for the number of pills that had been prescribed. Sixty. He dumped the pills onto the dining room table and counted them.

Twelve, thirteen, fourteen. Tremors racked his body. He'd understood all along that he couldn't deal with Genevieve going back to pills again and again and again.

In your weakness I am strong.

Lightning sent brightness flashing through the room.

Horrible memories from the past pulled at him. Grimly, he continued counting.

Fifty-seven. Fifty-eight. Fifty-nine. Sixty.

He counted them a second time, to be sure. Then a third time.

They were all here. Just like she'd said, she hadn't taken any.

He slid the pills into his palm. At the sink, he flicked on the water, then poured them down the garbage disposal.

The destruction of her pills made him feel

no better.

She could always get more. Hide more. Take more.

Natasha

"Did you hear that?" I ask the others on our eighth day in our underground room that smells like a sewer. I was trying to French-braid Genevieve's hair, but now I cock my head to the side to listen.

"What?" Genevieve asks.

"Shh," I say.

There it is again, the grinding sound of a big machine. Then comes a far-off groaning, scraping noise . . . as if pieces of our building are being lifted away.

"What is it?" Ben asks.

Genevieve looks at me excitedly.

"I think," I say, "that might be the sound of our rescue."

CHAPTER TWENTY-THREE

The drive to Atlanta to confront Alice Atwell was worsening Genevieve's state of mind, which had been dismal since her fight with Sam the night before.

Heartsick, she propped her chin in her hand and watched the scenery fly past from within the backseat of her dad's BMW. The tension inside the car was so thick that, had she scissors, she'd have been able to cut it to pieces.

Sam had found her pills.

In fact, the way things had unfolded, it was almost as if God had *wanted* him to find them.

Sam had accused her of hiding her addiction, and he'd been right. She'd literally been hiding that bottle of Oxy in that canister.

Hiding . . . still.

Even after all the effort she'd made the past three months to be open with herself,

Sam, and Natasha, he'd caught her red-handed, and she'd been horrified. Then he'd chosen that moment — when her very worst flaw had been on display — to tell her that he loved her.

She still couldn't believe he'd said that. A few times since last night, she'd questioned her recollection of his *"I love you"* because it seemed so impossible that he'd said that.

But no, it had been real. Had he spoken those words to her a different day under a sweeter circumstance, she'd have been elated. As it was, she'd been wondering if she'd forced the declaration from him the way a person might force a bear to attack by poking it with a stick.

Had he meant it? Did he love her? Really? And if he had loved her last night, did he love her still, after finding Oxy in her cottage?

Her actions last night had woken the ghost of Kayden, which had probably made him doubt whether he had the heart to continue dating her.

After Sam left last night, she'd paced endlessly, her distress oscillating between remorse over their fight and fear for her family. Sam hadn't come back to the cottage or texted or called. Nor had she reached out to him.

She hadn't taken a pill in almost three months. Regardless, her life seemed to be spinning out of control, just like it had been the day she'd awoken in an unfamiliar cottage with a stranger standing over her.

Genevieve's focus settled on her parents in the front two seats. Mom was pretending to read, but Genevieve hadn't seen her turn a single page. Dad had turned on instrumental music and passed the drive in silence, his profile strained. Natasha sat next to Genevieve in the back, tapping on her computer with a drawn expression. Over the past hour and forty minutes, Genevieve had periodically attempted to catch up with social media on her phone. Mostly, though, she'd stewed about Sam and hovered on the precipice of tears.

"I think we're coming up on it," Dad said.

Natasha, family navigator, checked her phone. "Yes. It's the next left."

They turned into a mobile home community. Timberland Village's freshly paved roads took them by neat, modest homes set between towering trees.

"Just here." Natasha pointed. "That's the one."

Dad pulled onto a concrete slab behind a Buick and a Kia. Alice's white rectangular house loomed alongside them. Spiky plants dotted the mulch at its base. The dark green stair rail leading to the front door's landing matched the home's green shutters.

After extracting his keys from the ignition, Dad simply sat, staring out the windshield at the house. Mom, who was far too pale, watched Dad.

Her father had been the one who'd advocated for this meeting. Yet wanting to do this in the abstract didn't mean he was looking forward to this in actuality.

Would their family be the same after this? Or would this fracture everything? Dread boxed Genevieve in on every side.

Dad led the way to the door and, soon after, a woman near her parents' age answered their knock. She wore a blue sweater and short blond hair. "I'm Dawn." Russell's youngest sister. Russell had been the eldest sibling. Followed two years later by Sandra, the one who'd sent the letters, then two years later by Dawn.

"It's been a long time." Mom made an attempt at a smile.

"It has." Dawn's manner communicated politeness. "Come in."

They followed Dawn into a living area adjoining a kitchen. Dawn indicated the elderly woman occupying the sofa. "My mother, Alice." Then she lifted her hand toward the figure standing straight and hostile near the sofa's end. "My sister, Sandra."

Mom introduced her family members to the Atwells.

"Caroline, dear," Alice said, extending both arms, "let me hug you."

Mom bent to hug Alice while Sandra remained motionless. She'd crossed her arms over a long-sleeved T-shirt with a faded picture of a hot air balloon on the front. Even in belted jeans and Nikes, Sandra had the demeanor of a judge about to hand down a prison sentence.

Genevieve, Natasha, and Dad helped Dawn bring over chairs while Mom and Alice murmured about how fast time flies.

Russell's two sisters resembled each other strongly. Both were thin, with sharp chins and noses. Sandra's hair was highlighted like Dawn's, though Sandra's was longer. It fell in a no-nonsense style to her shoulders.

Alice Atwell, eighty-three, had a sturdier build than either of her daughters, yet appeared frail of health. A walker waited near her, as did an oxygen tank on wheels. The older woman had secured her long white-gray hair into a twist using a double-pointed wooden hair prong. The dusky pink housedress she wore matched the shades of her decor.

Walls of stark white hemmed gray carpeting and gray furniture that smelled of baby powder. Throw pillows integrated bursts of pink and teal.

Dawn took a seat on the sofa next to her mother. Sandra perched on the armrest on her mother's other side.

Bile climbed Genevieve's throat as she sat, facing them.

"I've thought of you many times," Alice said to Mom. She dispensed her words carefully, as if each one required effort.

"And I you."

"You left Camden so shortly after Russell's death."

"I did, yes."

"After a time, we found that we couldn't stay in Camden, either, and we moved to Atlanta. I've often regretted that I lost touch with you."

Genevieve suspected that Mom had made a concerted effort to distance herself from everything connected to her Russell Atwell years. Alice may not have been able to keep in touch with Mom even if she'd tried hard to do so.

"It's wonderful to see you," Alice continued, "and your new husband and your grown daughters. You're all so beautiful."

We're all so guilty! Genevieve wanted to say. She really didn't know how she'd be able to watch Alice's current graciousness turn into anger and then condemnation.

"Thank you very much for inviting us to visit," Mom said.

"When Natasha explained over the phone that she'd been looking for me, I asked her to bring you all over straightaway. Didn't I, Natasha?"

"You did."

A becoming peachy undertone lit Alice's skin. Hers was not a bitter face, as Genevieve had been expecting, considering what had happened to her son and husband. Alice's wrinkles, furrows, and lines gave evidence of her years and her sorrows, yes. But she had a calm and perceptive demeanor.

"Gordon passed away more than thirty years ago," Alice said to Mom. "Did you know that?"

"Yes. I was very sorry to hear it."

"Sandra lives with me here and takes good care of me. Dawn works for the United States Postal Service. She and her husband have two boys. One's a police officer and the other restores old motorcycles. We're very proud of them."

"As you should be." For once, Mom resisted the urge to play a game of "my children are more impressive than yours." She cleared her throat. "In addition to our desire to . . . reconnect with you, we looked you up because we wanted to discuss something with you. The night of Russell's death, actually. That's what we'd like to discuss."

"Oh?" Sandra said, the sound critical and mocking.

"We know the facts of what happened," Dad told Alice. "I wish we'd shared them with you much sooner."

"Then why didn't you?" Sandra asked.

"Sandra," Alice murmured disapprovingly.

"We didn't share the details with you sooner," Dad said to Alice, "because we were afraid."

Alice considered that. "Go on."

Mom told them about the relationship she'd had with Dad in college. Then about her relationship with Russell. She outlined the abuse she'd suffered at Russell's hands, keeping the details clinical. No blame rang from them.

Even so, Sandra and Dawn stiffened. Genevieve didn't blame them. Mom was speaking ill of the dead, and the dead was their sibling.

Dad told them about traveling to Camden

551

to recruit for the Navy.

Alice listened with great concentration, as though her ears had been hungry for this information a very, very long time.

Mom and Dad took turns recounting the day of the murder.

At last, Dad described entering Mom and Russell's home and his fight with Russell. Pain drew Alice's eyebrows low.

After Dad explained her son's final moments, a crushing quiet descended.

Alice shifted her gaze from Dad to Sandra. Finally she said, "Caroline was with you that night."

Sandra held her mother's regard for a long moment. Would Sandra confirm or contradict her parents' story?

"Yes," Sandra replied.

"And? Are they telling the truth?"

"I have no idea whether they're telling the truth about the things that happened before I arrived. When I got there to take Caroline to Bible study, Russell was already dead."

"Did you find everything in the house as they've just described?" Alice asked.

Sandra frowned. Gave a short nod.

"You helped them arrange things so that suspicion would fall on the Shoal Creek Killer," Alice said, connecting the dots. "And then you took Caroline to Bible study, so she'd have an alibi."

Dawn's fingers crept up to cover her mouth. "Oh, Sandra."

"If I had it to do over again," Sandra told her sister, "I wouldn't have helped them."

"What happened afterward?" Alice asked Dad.

"Ma'am?"

"You said the broom handle sank into your eye. What happened to your eye?"

"It couldn't be salvaged. I've had an artificial eye ever since."

She paused. "Did you continue to work as a recruiter?"

"No, ma'am. Soon afterward, I attended law school."

"Are you still practicing law?"

"I am. I'm the district attorney for Rabun County, which I realize must seem like a great injustice to you. I've led a life that I had no right to lead."

Genevieve knotted her hands in her lap as she watched her dad's mouth quiver. She had never, *never* seen her father lose his grip on his composure —

Clarity opened inside her.

Of course, she thought. Of course. Her brainy, easygoing father had been overcome with passion and rage on the night he'd killed Russell. The consequences had been severe and nonnegotiable. There'd been no way to make it right, to bring Russell back from the dead. So he'd avoided situations that might goad his temper, because he knew the damage he was capable of inflicting.

"Come closer," Alice said to Dad, beckoning.

"Mom," Sandra warned.

"Come closer," the older woman repeated.

"I really don't think . . ." Sandra began.

But Dad was already crossing the space and kneeling before Alice. "I'm sorry," he said to her, his voice unsteady.

Genevieve had staggered under her guilt and regrets for the past year. Her dad had been staggering under his regrets for *thirty-seven years*. She couldn't fathom the weight of them.

"*Sorry* can't undo what you did," Sandra said.

"I know," Dad said to Alice. "Nonetheless, I'm incredibly sorry. Russell was your son, and I won't blame you for turning me in. I'll tell the authorities what I've told you. I'll cooperate."

Alice looked into him, as if searching his soul. "I believe you will." She laid a crooked hand on his shoulder. Nostalgia lingered in her face as she studied the man so near to the age her son would have been, had he lived.

"I gave birth to Russell. I *loved* him. I did . . . and still do . . . love him."

"Yes, ma'am."

"No one's entitled to take the life of another. You shouldn't have taken his life. Not under any circumstances." Alice's attention rested on Mom, Sandra, then back to Dad. "All three of you did wrong when you failed to call the police and when you schemed and lied about it afterward."

"Yes, ma'am," Dad said.

"I feel strongly . . ." The weakness of Alice's lungs stole much of her air on a wheeze. "That it's my right to turn you in."

"I agree," Dad said.

"I'm the one who brought Russell into this world, who cared for him and taught him, who prayed for him and watched him grow." Sorrow reverberated in every word.

Dad nodded. He pushed a tear from his own cheek with the heel of his large hand. He remained kneeling.

Alice's grip had not left his shoulder. Her forehead was lined with intensity and determination. "It's my right to turn you in, young man. But I will not do it. And since I will not, I can say with confidence that no one will."

Her father looked at Alice uncomprehend-
ingly.

Astonishment tumbled within Genevieve.
What?

Sandra rushed to her feet. "No! *Mother.*"

Alice's rheumy eyes remained on Dad.
They held a wisdom as old as the valleys
and hills of the Blue Ridge Mountains.

Goose bumps arose over Genevieve's skin.
Alice knew. Alice knew of her son's violence. Mothers always know, and this one
knew about her child's flaws, his terrible
temper. Perhaps she'd known at the time
that Russell had abused her daughters and
his young wife, too. Alice hadn't asked
Sandra to explain why she'd helped cover
up her brother's murder. Likely because Alice understood exactly why Sandra had
done what she'd done.

"Mother!" Sandra said urgently. Her
fingers curled into fists.

Alice observed her older daughter. "You
were content to let him go the night your
brother died."

"Yes, but every year since then I've
checked up on Judson, and I've seen how
he's succeeded." Sandra jabbed a finger
toward Genevieve. "How they've all gone
on as if nothing bad ever happened. None
of them paid the smallest price."

"He was injured that night," Alice said. "He's harbored remorse for a long time. He's spent his career putting guilty people behind bars."

"He's lived large in his big house with his wife and his daughters. How can you think about letting him go now?"

"I agree with Sandra," Dawn spoke up. "Letting him go isn't justice."

"Some things are more important to me than justice," Alice answered. "He's suffered. I've suffered. You girls" — she looked at both her daughters — "have suffered. Every one of us has suffered enough."

The older woman's hand on Dad's shoulder hadn't wavered. She was the one who'd been dealt a shock today, the one whose body was feeble. But it seemed to Genevieve that Alice was also the one centering her father through the strength of her touch. Small indentations formed on the fabric of his shirt beneath Alice's fingertips.

"You told me that you were sorry," Alice said to him.

"I am."

"Then I forgive you."

"No," Sandra said.

"Yes," Alice responded.

"You forgive me?" Dad rasped.

"I forgive you for killing my son. I forgive

you fully and completely. Do you understand?"

He searched her face.

It made *no sense* to Genevieve that Alice
should give him — a man she'd never met
— this astounding gift. Against the will of
her daughters. Regardless of the fact that
Dad had taken something precious from
her.

"Do you understand?" she repeated.

"Yes, ma'am."

"It's done."

"I don't think —" Dawn said.

Alice interrupted. "We'll talk about it
later. Not another word about it right now,
girls. *Not another word.*"

Sandra snatched up her purse and
stormed from the house. Only vaguely did
Genevieve register the sound of Sandra's
footsteps on the steps outside or her car
engine starting.

Genevieve had been looking for God for
such a long time. And here He was, in this
mobile home in Atlanta, in the form of a
woman who'd lived eighty-three years.

Here He was, *at last.*

The book of John said that Jesus had been
full of grace and truth. That's exactly what
Genevieve had seen just now. Unmitigated

558

truth. And in response to it, undeserved grace.

Her dad's head lowered, and he began to weep. His wide shoulders shook with the force of it.

Genevieve finally allowed the tears she'd been fighting all morning to come. She didn't cry because of anguish. She cried because of the outright beauty of what Alice had done and because Genevieve had finally found the God she'd been looking for and missing and needing.

His spirit settled over her like warm, soft rain.

Natasha reached over and squeezed Genevieve's hand. Genevieve squeezed back, indicating that she was okay. And she was. God had not abandoned her. She could sense Him and what she sensed, very strongly, was truth and grace.

Grace and truth.

Until her dad had trusted Alice with the truth, Alice had been unable to dispense grace. If Genevieve stifled her truth, then she stifled the Lord's ability to show her grace.

Natasha had been right when she'd insisted that Dad come here and confess.

Sam had been right when he'd told her she'd never beat Oxy if she continued to keep it a secret.

She'd been wrong. Wrong about so many things.

When Alice moved to rise, Dawn quickly took hold of her mother's arm and assisted her to her feet. The older woman gestured for Dad to stand, then encompassed his much taller frame in her arms.

A stranger looking at Alice's outward appearance could have no idea of the dignity and power God had seen fit to bestow upon her. She was a missionary in a housedress and terry cloth slippers.

Because of her, the Woodward family was free.

Because of Christ, Genevieve was free.

And she would never be the same.

Sebastian

For the past couple of days, my head has been full of nothing except thoughts of how to get us out. I've examined every wall. I piled stones and climbed on top of them and tried to break out the window. I ran my hands along the ceiling. I worked to clear a path for us down each hallway.

All my attempts failed.

I'm not strong enough to move chunks of building bigger than I am. Just when I was trying to force myself to accept that we're all going to die down here, we started to hear machinery.

I think someone might be coming for us.

"You see?" Genevieve asks me with a smile. "God heard our prayers, and He's going to get us out."

"We're not out yet," I say.

"He's coming," she says firmly. "You'll see."

Our room shakes and dust shivers over us. "Let's sit against one of the walls," I suggest. The two leaning walls seem to offer a little bit of protection.

"Which wall?" Ben asks.

I pull a quarter from my pocket. "Heads that wall." I point. "Tails that wall." I flick the quarter into the dim air. It spins and lands on heads.

We all move to sit against the winning wall.

CHAPTER TWENTY-FOUR

Late that night, Sam stared out his bedroom window, exactly as he'd done so many times since Gen's arrival.

Only the porch light was on at the guesthouse, which meant that she was asleep.

He wished he could sleep. But his frustration and doubt wouldn't allow him to.

In the black glass before him, he didn't see his own reflection. Instead, he saw the flat he'd shared with Kayden in Melbourne.

The night he'd moved out, he'd tossed his clothing into a duffel bag. His thoughts were red with anger, his spirit howling with betrayal. "You're using again," he bit out. "And you're lying to me about it. Again. I've done everything I can for you, Kayden." He straightened. "Do you have a death wish?"

"Of course not!" Her blond hair tumbled around her too-thin shoulders. She wore her old, carefree clothing. A tank top and surfer shorts and bare feet. But there was nothing carefree about her face anymore. Nor anything carefree about his personality. "I had a migraine! You've never had a migraine, so you can't know how unbelievably painful they are. I took just enough to manage the pain."

"And then didn't meet your sister for dinner, which is what you told me you'd be doing."

"I . . . went to the beach and caught a few waves."

"With a migraine?" Whenever Kayden told him she was going to spend time with someone, he'd taken to calling that person to fact-check. Her sister had informed him that Kayden hadn't shown. At which time, he'd called Kayden, who hadn't answered. He'd taken off work early and driven home, terrified. He'd found her listening to The Doors records and snacking on a brownie. Her eyes were dull in her head, her voice fuzzed the way it fuzzed when she'd been using.

"You're overreacting," she accused.

"No. I've underreacted every time before this time. I'm finally getting my response exactly right. I'm moving out." He zipped his duffel and hauled it onto his shoulder.

"You've threatened that before, Sam."

564

He stormed past her on the way to the door. "This time I'm not threatening. I'm doing."

She scrambled after him. "You'll be back."

"I won't." His fingers gripped the front doorknob. Half of his instincts were begging him to stay. He loved her. The other half of his instincts were ordering him to leave. She'd let pills ruin their relationship. "I can't watch you kill yourself."

Her eyes narrowed. "You're such a self-righteous jerk, Sam. Throwing a fit because I took medicine for a migraine. Nagging me day and night. I'm so over it."

"So am I."

"Then leave," she'd shouted. "And don't come back."

He hadn't come back.

Wrenching himself away from the window, Sam pulled on a sweater and pushed his feet into boots. Desperate to escape the house in order to escape the memories, he let himself outside and walked deep into the meadow. He drew in breaths of cold mountain air and struggled to calm himself.

To this day, he believed he'd made the wrong decision when he'd left Kayden. At the time, separating himself from her had seemed necessary. Maybe he would have felt he'd done the right thing if she'd gotten clean and moved on with her life. But because she'd died, he'd been unable to avoid the certainty that he'd quit right at the moment when he should have dug in his heels. If he'd stayed, she might have found freedom from Percocet and recovered and lived.

He'd chosen wrong.

He'd screwed up. He'd failed her and himself.

But what he could not do any longer was hang on to his guilt. He'd said good-bye to Kayden the night he'd walked out of their flat in Melbourne. But now he needed to live out that good-bye.

Loyalty formed the bedrock of his personality. For him, keeping her with him by stewing and beating himself up came far more easily than opening his hands and letting her go.

Yet he had to let her go. He had to.

I'm sorry formed in his mind. *I'm sorry for the ways I let you down.* She'd been incredibly important to him. The joy of her love and the sadness of her death would always remain with him. What had been done couldn't be undone or changed.

Ultimately, he hadn't been able to control Kayden. Nor could he control Gen. As much as he wished it was different, he didn't have the power to save anyone.

The only one he could control was himself.

His chin tilted upward. Hundreds of glittering stars lit the dark night. The sounds of nature sang an eternal song. He could feel God's nearness, and his muscles began to relax. The chaos of his mind gradually stilled.

He stood for long moments, thinking and praying and shivering.

Since he'd found Gen's pills yesterday, he'd been raking through his options. He'd remembered his history and considered his future. He'd confronted both God and the isolated way he'd been living his life since Kayden had taken hers.

He'd come to no conclusion. . . .

Until now. Certainty slid into his soul, as cool and deep as water.

Ever since he'd met Gen, he'd been telling himself that he couldn't deal with it if she returned to Oxy. For more than twenty-four hours, he'd been standing by that statement, telling himself again and again, *I can't do this.*

And each time, God had countered that thought with *In your weakness, I am strong.*

He hadn't been able to handle Kayden's downward spiral. He didn't feel able to

567

handle Gen's downward spiral, either. But when he said *"I can't,"* he was lying. He *could.* Regardless of his weakness, in God's strength he could do the one thing within his ability.

He could stay.

God had brought him to another fork in the road. Once again, he could turn his back, or he could hold on and refuse to give up.

Leaving Kayden had been a mistake.

He'd probably make lots of new mistakes with Gen, but he *would not make* that same one again.

He wasn't going to let Oxy take Gen without a fight. If he went down, he was going to go down swinging. If she broke his heart, then at least he'd know he'd done all he could. He'd know that his silence and inaction weren't to blame because, this time, he would not be silent or inactive.

Oxy was stronger than he was. But he was convinced that Oxy was not stronger than God.

The sky seemed to glow with approval. A feeling of rightness solidified within him.

He'd given himself the illusion of safety by regulating his diet, exercise, sleep, restaurant, farm. But he hadn't found safety in a life protected from problematic people.

He'd only found loneliness.

God hadn't left him here, alone, on this land. Instead, He'd chipped away at him through Gen and forced him to acknowledge that, just like everyone else, he'd been made for community.

Relationships were painful and messy and beautiful and important. The mess came with the beauty. The pain came with the importance.

That was life. And God was calling him to live it.

Whoever had said that the center of God's will was the safest place to be had either been a fool or hadn't known God very well.

On the drive back from Atlanta yesterday afternoon, then last night as she'd read Scripture, and this morning as she'd prayed, God's will for Genevieve had become louder and more distinct.

At last, she could hear Him. And what she heard Him saying was that no matter the cost, she needed to confess her issues with painkillers. To everyone.

Grace and truth.

At present, she was sitting with her family in her mom and dad's living room. She and Natasha occupied the sofa, her parents the side-by-side armchairs across the coffee table. They'd started off drinking peppermint tea, marveling over yesterday's events, and complimenting the mantel covered in a Thanksgiving garland, tiny white pumpkins, and two miniature bundles of wheat. After everything that had gone down the day before, their gathering felt very much like a gathering of people who'd survived a catastrophe that should have killed them. They were shell-shocked and sobered and stunned and grateful.

Genevieve would have liked to continue to float in that feel-good pool for the remainder of her visit. Instead, the Holy Spirit had pressed against her from the inside, compelling her to speak. She'd forced herself to tell her mom and dad about the Oxy.

Her parents' secrets had ripped down their façade of false goodness. Now she was ripping down her own façade. It was as if the four of them were looking at one another straight in the face at long last, instead of through distorting glass.

Inside Alice's home yesterday, her dad's worst mistake had been exposed. He hadn't been able to bring his perfection to Alice's table. Afterward, it had hit her. Like her dad, she had *no* perfection to bring to God's table.

She'd been rescued miraculously in El Salvador and lived the rest of her life striving to execute the big plans she'd believed God had saved her to accomplish. She'd written Bible study after Bible study. She'd taken terrifying flights all over the world to preach and proclaim His glory. She'd worked and worked and tried and tried, pushing herself to her limits. Somewhere along the line, she'd become known as someone who was righteous and honorable.

But even after all that, all those years of service, the only thing she had to bring to God's table was the sin that made His grace so necessary.

The verse in Isaiah that equated righteous acts to filthy rags had never been more appropriate.

It was like the unfastening of a dungeon's lock to let go of the idea that God had saved her because He had big plans for her. The people who'd told her that had been well-meaning, but mistaken.

In all honesty, she didn't know why God had chosen to save the five of them.

Because of their prayers? Because He loved them?

Maybe. But He sometimes said no to prayers. He sometimes took the people He loved to heaven rather than preserving their lives on earth.

What she did know was that He had not saved her so she could work herself into an early grave attempting to pay Him back. He hadn't saved her so she could perpetuate the illusion of perfection. He hadn't saved her so she could build a life so demanding that she'd have to swallow Oxy to cope.

She could not pay God back for saving her. Goodness knows, she'd tried.

I cannot pay Him back.

And praise God for that. *Praise God!* Because that meant she could quit trying so very hard.

She'd rather be known as a woman who'd wrecked her life and was nonetheless loved by Him than as a woman who was good.

After today, she'd lose the respect of many. But she would still have *Him.*

And He was everything.

Before she started taking Oxy, she'd thought she understood grace. But now that she'd failed in such a flagrant way and been so thoroughly humbled, she grasped grace — and just how much it was worth — far, far better than she had before.

"As of tomorrow," she told her parents, after answering all their concerned questions, "I'll have been clean for ninety days. That's a pretty big milestone. But it's not a milestone that means I'm cured. There's no cure. I mean, I almost took Oxy a few nights ago after finding out what happened to Russell. So I'm always going to have to be vigilant and careful. As time goes on, though, I'll continue to feel more and more like myself. Stronger. Healthier."

"Oh, sweetie." Mom gave her a look of melodramatic tenderness. "Thank the Lord that you're all right."

"I intend to stay clean," Genevieve told them. "I also intend to be more transparent. I've decided to admit my struggle publicly. I wanted to tell you first, before I make the announcement, so that you can brace yourselves."

"Way to go, Gen," Natasha said.

"I understand why you feel the need to be transparent," Dad said. "We support you."

"Yes," Mom added. "We do support you, of course. I'm glad that you *finally* told us this. We're family." She hesitated. "Do you . . ." Her nose wrinkled slightly. "Do you really think, though, that it's necessary to tell *everyone* that you used opioids? Think of the damage that will do." No one was more enamored with Genevieve's career than Mom.

"I do think it's necessary to tell everyone," Genevieve answered, "because that's what the Lord's leading me to do. To be honest, I'm scared of the damage it will do. But I'm more scared of the damage that silence will do."

"Gen —" Mom began.

"Mom," Genevieve said firmly. "I know that your protectiveness of me stems from a good heart —"

"Of course! I want nothing but your very best."

Genevieve dipped her chin in acknowledgment. "I believe that's true. However, your protectiveness overwhelms me at times. A lot of the time, actually."

Mom drew back as if she'd just been stung by a bee. "I'm only trying to help."

"I know."

"I . . ." Mom looked wounded. At a loss.

Genevieve had always known where her mother's overprotectiveness had been born: in the wreckage of the earthquake. She, Natasha, Ben, Sebastian, Luke — they'd all experienced trauma. But they weren't the only ones. The earthquake had inflicted trauma on their parents, too.

"Mom," she said quietly, empathy welling inside her. As awful as it had been to be trapped underground, she'd choose what she'd gone through over what her mother had gone through. Her mom's much-loved

574

children — her only two children, the ones in which she'd invested her adult life — had been missing for days. The experts had told Mom she and Natasha would most likely die.

"We lived." Genevieve held eye contact with her mom, willing her to let the words, the reality, soak into her soul. "Natasha and I survived the earthquake. It's not an event any of us would have chosen. But it's what happened, and we all came out of it alive. I'm thirty years old. Natasha's thirty-two. We're adult women. Independent. Able to support ourselves. Able to *protect* ourselves. We might make mistakes from time to time —"

Natasha cleared her throat.

"Well," Genevieve amended, "Natasha never makes mistakes, but I sometimes do. Even so, overall, I think we're doing really well."

"You can afford to relax a little." Natasha smiled at Mom to cushion her words. "Sit back. Enjoy the hard work you put in when you were raising us. There's no need, anymore, to hold on quite so tight."

Dad interlaced his fingers with Mom's on the armrest of her chair. He wore the familiar I'm-the-luckiest-man-in-the-world expression. From behind his glasses, he shot her a reassuring wink.

Mom's pretty mouth tightened.

"Mom?" Genevieve asked.

"Ready to cut the apron strings?" Natasha added.

Mom sniffed. "I'll never cut the apron strings."

"Are you ready to *trim* the apron strings?" Natasha said coaxingly.

"It may be . . ." Mom finally replied grudgingly, "that I could benefit from letting go . . . a little bit more than I have."

Genevieve decided to chalk that response up as a win and broke into spontaneous applause.

"Felicitations!" Natasha crowed in true Jane Austen style, joining in the applause.

Genevieve pushed from her chair and motioned the rest of the family to their feet for a group hug.

"I love you," Dad said once they formed a Woodward family huddle.

"I love you, too," the rest of them echoed.

"We'll help you in any way we can," Mom told Genevieve.

"And I'll help you," Genevieve replied staunchly, *to abstain from smothering me.*

"This is a moment to treasure," Mom cooed.

Before all was said and done, Natasha

promised to knit Genevieve a sweater. Dad mentioned a player on the Mercer football team who'd kicked his prescription drug habit. Mom suggested taking Genevieve to the hair salon next week.

If Natasha was motivated to knit and Dad was thinking about football and Mom was wanting to change her hair, then everything really was going to be okay.

That afternoon, Genevieve sat at her desk in the cottage watching light rain christen the undulating land of Sugar Maple Farm. It nicked the pond with hundreds of increasing circles and pattered against the leaves of the morning glory vine framing her window.

She hadn't seen Sam's truck return from work yet today.

Sam. The thought of him prodded a tender, painful corner of her heart. She loved him, but she couldn't let herself think of him or how things had been left between them at this particular point in time. Thinking on those things had the power to liquefy her bravery. And in order to do what she had to do before she'd be able to look Sam in the face again, she needed to be brave.

She'd decided to give herself a few days to catch her breath and think before approaching him. Tomorrow, day ninety post-

Oxy, she'd spend alone at Misty River's spa, relaxing and reflecting. No doubt Sam also needed time to catch his breath and think. Also, to figure out whether or not she was worth the effort. The tender corner of her heart throbbed again —

She drew in several courage-building inhales. She'd survived admitting her addiction to her parents. She could survive this.

She shook out her hands, then rested her fingertips on her computer's keyboard and composed an email to her agent. Sent it. Composed an email to her publisher. Sent it. Composed an email to the coordinators of the conferences she had on her calendar. Sent it.

In each case, she explained her issue candidly and informed them how she planned to alter her schedule. She told them she'd be letting her followers know immediately and finished by asking them for their forgiveness.

Sniffling as tears snaked over her lashes, she began to compose an open letter.

To those of you who've done my studies, heard me speak, supported me . . .
I hope you know how much I love you. I love you dearly.
One of the most fervent desires of my

heart has been to serve you. I'm incredibly honored to have been a part of the writing and speaking ministry the Lord entrusted to me for the past ten years. I've been very, very passionate about leading you forward as we chase hard after Christ.

Lately, though, I no longer feel capable of leadership.

I started taking an opioid painkiller more than a year ago. At first, I took it for a medical reason. But I continued taking it for mental and emotional reasons. My dependence on painkillers became so powerful that I needed them every day simply to get by. I made bad decisions that endangered myself and others. I lied repeatedly to cover up my secret. Twice, I tried to quit and failed.

A few months ago, I was finally able to stop taking the pills. Since then, I've been attempting to maintain my full workload. I've wholeheartedly wanted to continue speaking. I've wholeheartedly wanted my next study to release when I told you it would. I've wholeheartedly wanted to be healthy.

However, I've realized that I can't have everything I want. I need to choose, and God's let me know that, in this season,

He would have me lay down my writing and speaking.

I was obedient to Him when He first called me to those things. I'm going to be obedient to Him now and step away from those things. I feel called to make my life smaller. Less loud. Less filled with stress.

I've canceled my upcoming speaking engagements, and I will not be completing my next Bible study on schedule, if at all. I know that many of you were counting on me, and I'm profoundly sorry to disappoint you.

As I write this, I'm aware of how many things can be taken away from us in this life. Career. Reputation. Wellness. Truthfulness.

For the next several months, I plan to embrace the one thing that can't be taken away: my identity as a child of God. It's that identity that has freed me to be honest with you.

While in the dark cave of addiction and recovery, it has comforted me to remember that Jesus's body spent time in a dark cave, too. He did not remain there, however. At the appointed time, God called Jesus out of the cave, back to life and light. God hasn't forgotten those of us who are languishing in dark caves. He's calling us back to life and light, too.

Instead of leading you forward as we chase hard after Christ, I'm simply hoping for the chance to walk beside you.

I'm very, very grateful for you.

Love, Genevieve

She posted the letter on the front page of her website. Methodically, she visited each of her social media platforms. On Instagram and Facebook, she posted the entire letter. On Twitter, she linked to the letter.

After that frenzy of emotion and typing, she shut her computer and set her phone to Do Not Disturb.

The calm surrounding her took her by surprise. She'd just incited her own personal calamity, and it seemed that should come with shrieking sirens and the roar of a train and the smashing of glass and a whirlwind of air.

Instead, she was sitting safe and warm inside her cottage. Smoke slipped into the sky from a distant chimney. A bird soared against the backdrop of charcoal-edged clouds.

She could sense the furor she'd created. It was large and would grow larger in the coming days. There would be reactions and judgment and controversy and differing opinions.

And yet . . . she didn't feel the need to wade into any of it. At least not yet. Maybe never.

For now, she just wanted to rest, bathed in God's approval and in the certainty that, for better or for worse, she'd done the irrevocable thing He'd called her to do.

When she stood, it felt as though shackles of guilt were cracking open and dropping away from wrists and ankles. Jesus Himself had bought and paid for her freedom.

Ben

Our rescuers are close.

Their machines have been lifting away layers of this building for most of the day. I've been drumming my fingers on the concrete for what seems like hours, because I'm so desperate to be free.

Suddenly a grinding, scraping noise fills the air, so loud that we all jump and cover our ears. Our floor jolts, the way it did during the earthquake. Fear slams me.

No! We can't die now. They're so close. So close!

The wall across from us releases from its position. The girls scream as it crashes down. I duck and protect my head. The heavy slab lands just a few feet away from my legs. The wall at my back and the floor below shudder.

No!

Noise like thunder. A cloud of dust all around.

I wait, without breathing, for the wall behind us to flatten us.

Instead . . .

It holds, protecting us from the falling debris above.

It holds.

It holds.

CHAPTER TWENTY-FIVE

The world was a much, much quieter place when one only used one's phone to accomplish the bare minimum. Genevieve had noted this fact approximately a million times over the past two days since announcing her flaws to the world.

She'd donned layers beneath her jacket in preparation for the brisk temperature she could expect on today's morning walk. After lacing up her blue tennis shoes, she let herself out of the cottage and looked up —

She came to an immediate stop on her small porch.

Sam's truck was parked out front. He was waiting for her, leaning against the side door, ankles and arms crossed. The clear, cold November day formed a crystalline backdrop.

Her breath snagged in her chest.

Sam.

He regarded her in his usual serious way.

Not happy but not unhappy, either. He had on jeans and a quilted navy jacket open over an unbuttoned flannel shirt and, below that, a snowy white T-shirt. Love for him coalesced inside her. She'd been a world-class idiot to risk her relationship with him. How could she ever, ever, have done that? If given the chance, she'd never risk their relationship again.

She raised a finger. "Can you wait there one second?" she called, then scrambled back inside to retrieve the gift she'd purchased in town for him yesterday. She ran to the restroom to spritz on one pump of perfume and check her hair, which was, surprisingly, in the mood to behave.

As she walked toward him across the grass, he pushed away from the truck's side.

Don't mess this up rattled across her brain. That and, *He's true and trustworthy and gorgeous, and it's impossible that he likes me. But he does. And he might even love me. So don't mess this up.*

He hadn't been parked here earlier, when she'd been eating her breakfast. Clearly, he knew her weekday schedule well enough to know when she left on her walks. It was a good sign, surely, that he'd sought her out. Surely?

Don't mess this up.

586

She halted a few feet from him. That olive skin. That thick hair. That solemn chin. She could feel the attention he leveled on her through every inch of her body.

"I come bearing gifts." She lifted the one-pound plastic tub she held. "There are enough organic, non-GMO chive seeds in this container to satisfy baked potatoes all across the country." What was she saying? Those were not the words she'd prepared. "To make amends for the chives I murdered, I bought you more than a quarter million new seeds." Alert! This wasn't going well. "Will these keep you stocked for a while?" She tested a smile.

After a few seconds that felt like months, one side of his mouth hitched up. A dimple dug into his cheek. "Yes."

She was so relieved, she considered fainting. "This is just a small token of how sorry I am." She extended the seeds.

He took them from her, the emerald power of spring lighting his eyes.

"Because I am," she continued, "very sorry for filling that stupid prescription and for shutting you out."

"I read the letter you posted on your website."

"You did?"

587

He nodded. "I want to show you something."

"Okay."

He set the chives in his truck, and they walked toward his farmhouse. As they went, she told him about her parents' involvement in Russell's death and why that had sent her sinking into such a black hole of anxiety. She told him, too, about their visit with Alice Atwell.

He listened carefully but said almost nothing.

A few days ago, before their fight, they'd either have held hands on this walk or her arm would have been wrapped around his elbow, their shoulders rubbing. The physical separation between them now felt painfully obvious.

"Have you seen any of the responses to the letter you posted?" he asked.

"No. I've purposely stayed away from all of it."

They climbed the steps to his front door, which he held open for her. She passed inside and . . .

Flowers greeted her. *So many* flowers.

Slowing, her jaw dropped. Flower arrangements and gift baskets and cookie bouquets lined the walls of the foyer. They covered his desk. They jutted upward from his dining room table. More of them buried his living room coffee table.

"These started arriving for you yesterday," he said.

Struck with wonder, her hands rose to cover her mouth.

"One of my employees at The Kitchen spent his work hours at the gate yesterday, receiving all of them. I didn't want the trucks and delivery men disturbing you."

"I had no idea. I was gone most of the day yesterday."

"By the time you got back, I'd brought them all here. I hauled more of them up this morning."

"I had no idea," she repeated, dropping her hands.

"You have over three thousand comments on your website, Gen. Thousands more on your social media sites. The people who sent these did so because they support you."

"And the people who don't support me?"

"Have been venting their disappointment," he admitted. His expression challenged her to look on the bright side. "But some people are always going to be disappointed and unhappy. The majority care about you. A lot."

"They do?"

"Yes." He spoke with so much certainty

that she didn't dare question him. "You're more real to them now because they know that, like them, you sometimes fall short. And you're brave enough to admit it when you do."

"I regret that I fell short with you, Sam." Gently, he took hold of her upper arms and turned her to face him. His masculine features sharpened with concentration. "You told me once that you believed that I was like the caravan that rescued Joseph from the pit. You thought that God brought you here because of what you were going through. Remember?"

"Yes." Her heart thundered.

"It's the opposite, Gen. I think God brought you here because of me."

She blinked.

"You'd have figured out your problems," he said, "with or without my help —"

"No. I wouldn't —"

"— but I was never going to. Without you."

She was speechless.

"I love you," he said. "I will always love you. And I will never walk out on you again. It's me who's sorry that I fell short."

"You didn't fall short."

"I love you." Fervent color stained his cheeks. "No matter what. No giving up. No turning back."

She set her palm on his cheek, overcome by the beauty of him. HE LOVED HER! "I love you, too."

His face settled into a grave expression that asked, *Are you sure?*

"I'm discovering that transparency's getting easier with practice." She wove her hands together behind his neck. "I love you. See?"

He looked shocked.

Genevieve laughed. "I love you."

How could God have been this good to her? She shouldn't have received the flowers, the cookie bouquets, the gift baskets. She certainly shouldn't have received Sam's love.

And yet . . .

And yet. God had lavished them on her anyway.

Her mind spun like a golden, dazzling pinwheel. Her body felt too insignificant to hold joy this large.

And then Sam's mouth claimed hers, sealing his words and hers with a kiss that caused the rest of the world to whisk away. Only she and Sam were left, ringed by blossoms and freedom and sunlight.

591

Genevieve

I grab Natasha's hand. I'm shaking, and I can feel her shaking.

The building is coming down around us, just like the last time. "God, God, God, God," I whisper.

The structure stops trembling. Quiet comes. Slowly, the dust begins to float away. Where the wall across from us used to be, there's now a huge opening. I can see the surrounding buildings and the sky — bright blue, without clouds.

From within the dust, I see movement, and the movement becomes figures. Three men and a woman, dressed in uniforms with hard hats that have lights on the front.

Behind them a helicopter soars into view, drawing closer, its big blades cutting the air.

The man in front is smiling. He's strong and confident and big.

We're going to live.

"Are all five of you okay?" he asks.

"Yes, sir," Ben answers.

"Excellent." He bends toward me, offering his hand. "Ready to get out of here?"

"The Word became flesh and made his dwelling among us. We have seen his glory, the glory of the one and only Son, who came from the Father, full of grace and truth."

John 1:14

DISCUSSION QUESTIONS

1. According to the Centers for Disease Control and Prevention (CDC), 130 Americans die from opioid overdoses every day. Did you learn anything new about opioid addiction while reading *Stay with Me*? Was there anything about Genevieve's recovery journey that surprised you?
2. Becky chose to tell the story of the earthquake in short accounts written in first-person point of view between each chapter. Why do you think she chose to reveal the Miracle Five's backstory in that particular way?
3. Genevieve, Natasha, Sebastian, and Ben have maintained their friendship since middle school. Have any of you walked through a life-altering event with a friend? If so, how did that impact your connection with that person?
4. Sam is an organic farmer who eats

extremely healthy. Why do you think that Becky gave him that profession and characteristic?

5. Sam delivered supplies to Genevieve when she was suffering through withdrawal, and later he cooked for her. He showed his love through his actions long before he could bring himself to admit his love to himself or to her. Do you find acts of love or words of love more powerful? Why?

6. What aspects of Genevieve's personality were used by God to alter Sam's life?

7. As the plot line surrounding the mysterious letters unfolded, did you form any theories about what had happened with Caroline and Judson in the past? If so, what were they? Do you think Alice's decision to extend grace to Judson was fair?

8. Genevieve was gifted and called by God. However, in trying to fulfill her calling, she sacrificed her physical health and mental well-being. Do you think the challenge of maintaining balance is harder now than it was in the past? In what ways?

9. *Stay with Me*'s theme is transparency. Did you feel that it was necessary for Genevieve to admit her failings publicly at the end of the novel? Why or why not?

10. Did you notice that Becky set up a love

triangle for her next novel, *Let It Be Me?* What do you think might happen with Ben, Sebastian, and Leah?

ABOUT THE AUTHOR

Becky Wade is the 2018 Christy Award Book of the Year winner for *True to You.* She's a native of California who attended Baylor University, met and married a Texan, and moved to Dallas. She published historical romances for the general market, then put her career on hold for several years to care for her three children. When God called her back to writing, Becky knew He meant for her to turn her attention to Christian fiction. Her humorous, heart-pounding contemporary romance novels have won three Christy Awards, the Carol Award, the INSPY Award, and the Inspirational Reader's Choice Award for Romance. To find out more about Becky and her books, visit www.beckywade.com.

The employees of Thorndike Press hope you have enjoyed this Large Print book. All our Thorndike, Wheeler, and Kennebec Large Print titles are designed for easy reading, and all our books are made to last. Other Thorndike Press Large Print books are available at your library, through selected bookstores, or directly from us.

For information about titles, please call:
(800) 223-1244

or visit our website at:
gale.com/thorndike

To share your comments, please write:

Publisher
Thorndike Press
10 Water St., Suite 310
Waterville, ME 04901